the Roots of Betrayal

JAMES FORRESTER

sourcebooks
landmark

Published by Sourcebooks Landmark, an imprint of Sourcebooks, Inc.
P.O. Box 4410, Naperville, Illinois 60567-4410
(630) 961-3900
Fax: (630) 961-2168
www.sourcebooks.com

Originally published in 2011 in the UK by Headline Review, an imprint of Headline Publishing Group

Library of Congress Cataloguing-in-Publication data is on file with the publisher.

Printed and bound in the United States of America.
VP 10 9 8 7 6 5 4 3 2 1

Also by James Forrester
Sacred Treason

In Memory of Bridget Barker (1959–2010)

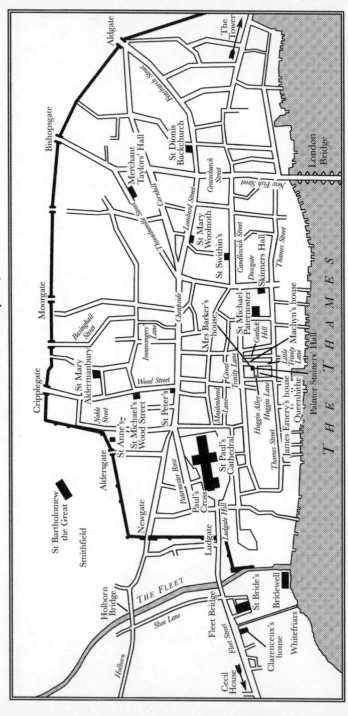

LONDON, c. 1564

The roots of betrayal lie in friendship;
those of treason lie in loyalty.

Prologue

Ascension Day, Thursday, May 11, 1564

Everybody knew at least one story about Raw Carew. There was the matter of his birth: the illegitimate son of an English captain who abandoned his mistress to die in a Calais whorehouse. There was his refusal to surrender when Calais fell to the French in 1558. Although only seventeen, he had commandeered a ship and fought his way out of the harbor. Then there were the stories of his courage. Some of these were true, such as his boarding a Spanish vessel by jumping on to the rigging from the main mast of his ship in a heaving storm. Others were only loosely based on events or were fictitious. But even the tallest stories carried a modicum of truth. They were all wrought around an extraordinary man—brave as well as capable, regardless of whether the tale told was one of courage, seduction, loyalty, or revenge.

If William Gray, the captain of the *Davy*, had known that Raw Carew was at that moment in a skiff just two hundred feet away from his ship, he would have paid less attention to the young girl in his cabin and more to his crew, who were laughing, playing dice, and drinking by the dim light of the candles and lanterns on the main deck.

Attack was the last thing on his mind. The ship was safe, anchored in Southampton Water, only four miles from the port itself. Gray knew that Sir Peter Carew was at that very moment patrolling the Channel with five ships and a royal warrant to hang pirates. The idea that Sir Peter's own illegitimate nephew might take a vessel from its overnight mooring was unthinkable. Besides, Gray's men had worked hard to sail so far that day. Leaving the Thames estuary five days earlier, they had been hit by a storm and had had to take shelter in Dover. It would not have been reasonable for Gray to insist that they stay on guard all night. The long hours in the rigging had been cold, and the wind coming up the Channel had delayed them. They deserved a rest.

Hugh Dean looked up at the black silhouette of the *Davy*. He had been the quartermaster on Raw Carew's last ship, the ill-fated *Nightingale*, and retained his position as second-in-command. The smell of seaweed filled his nostrils as he crouched in the prow of the skiff. It was a new moon; the thinnest silver starlight touched the taut anchor chain and furled sails. He waited, listening to the lapping of the water and the slapping of the rigging in the brisk south-westerly wind. As the skiff came up to the *Davy*, he reached forward and placed his hands against the wet caulking of the hull, softening the impact. He whispered a single word—"Go!"—and the two men behind him hurled grappling irons over the starboard gunwales. They made sure they had caught, then started climbing the side of the boat. Two more men followed them. Three others could not wait and, having gained a handhold on an aperture or grabbed a piece of trailing rigging, they too pulled themselves up the wooden wall of the ship. Hugh Dean himself was one of these, determined to be at the front of any fray—the quartermaster's proper station.

On the far side of the *Davy*, Raw Carew's skiff also touched the ship. Up went the grappling irons and Carew began to climb, followed by his men.

The silence was broken by a shout. "Who's there?"

Several men ran to the source of the noise, their feet thundering on the timber. A moment later, a throttled yell was heard as the sailor tried to call out again while a man cut his throat. A second guard, hearing the commotion, stamped hard, shouting, "Boarders! Boarders—on deck—" They were his last words. A sharp blade sliced through his gullet and sent a spurt of blood splashing onto the planking. A third guard did not even have the chance to cry out; a hand closed over his mouth and a dagger was forced through his back and into his lungs, once, twice, and then a third time. His killer felt the man's weight crumple onto the deck. He threw the body against the gunwale and tipped it over the edge. It fell with a huge splash.

Only a handful of the fifty men below in the stinking dimness of the main deck heard the first shout. But all of them heard the stamping, the running, and the splash. Many hurried toward the ladder and climbed, only to find the hatch above them shut fast—locked from the outside.

They listened in fear. There was a second splash of a body into the sea, then a third. They could hear men striding across the deck above their heads. Hands fastened on the hilts of knives. Those with swords and daggers seized them and prepared for a fight. A ship's lantern fastened to the base of the main mast flickered and went out, so that there was even less light. The boatswain of the *Davy* signaled for men to surround the ladder.

A full minute passed. Then they heard the creak as the heavy hatch was lifted.

Raw Carew stepped down slowly, into the candlelight. He was not tall. His only physically imposing feature was his upper body muscle, especially his powerful arms. He could climb a rope without having to touch it with his legs. His twenty-three years of hard living showed in his face, but they had not marred his good looks. His short blond hair stood on end, somewhat tousled. Smiling blue eyes darted between the men below deck, checking the shadows for possible lines of attack while preserving a confident expression. They were kind eyes: under their gaze each face unwittingly gave itself up for his examination. Four or five small golden earrings studded each ear. His velvet jerkin and linen shirt hung loose in an outlandish fashion. He wore a red scarf around his neck and several gold rings, including an enameled yellow one, with three black lions, on his middle finger.

The man nearest to the ladder challenged him with a blade, holding it up before his face. Carew raised an arm and gently pushed the blade to one side. The crew could see that he was carrying no weapon. His easy manner left them confused. A tall black man in his thirties, bald and bearded, with the furrowed brow of a general on the field of battle, followed him. His hand on a cutlass, with another blade in his belt, he looked around in the wick-lit darkness. The black-haired figure of the quartermaster Hugh Dean was next through the hatch, his leather jerkin and belt stuffed with three pistols. He also carried a pistol in each hand, and he pointed them at whatever caught his attention. His grinning eyes and the gun barrels flicked from man to man. His expression had all the relish of a huge bear that has just come across a pool of salmon.

The pirates came in a stream: the diminutive Stars Johnson,

dreamy eyed, pale skinned, and armed with a dagger; the fat, bald figure of John Devenish, in a huge white shirt, flouncy blue breeches, carrying a curved Moorish blade. Then the next man and the next.

As Carew's men assembled around him, he looked at the crew of the *Davy*. "Stay rested, all of you. We have no argument with you. But I will have words with—" There was a movement and a shout from a man nearby and a deafening explosion resounded through the vessel.

The noise subsided to a deep laugh. "Come on, more of you—come on!" Hugh Dean roared, shaking the still-smoking pistol in their faces. The smell of burnt gunpowder scorched the fug of the main deck. Only then did some of the crew see, in the dim light of the tallow candles, that the fallen sailor's head had been blown clean away, leaving a raggedy stump, and blood splashed all over the beams.

"As I was saying, I wish to have words with the captain," finished Carew, turning to the door beside him. More men came down through the hatch. He tried to unlatch the door; it was locked. "Hugh," he said, placing a hand on the quartermaster's shoulder. "If you please."

Hugh Dean turned, aimed, and fired a second pistol into the lock. He kicked the door. It held good. He muttered a curse, but the tall black man who had followed Carew through the hatch launched his whole body at the timber, hitting it with his shoulder. The lock and the door gave way, and he stumbled into the cabin beyond.

Carew nodded. "Thank you, Kahlu."

He turned to the stunned mariners, bowed to them curtly, then went into the cabin, followed by three other men: John Devenish, a ginger-haired man called William "Skinner" Simpkins, and Luke Treleaven, a black-haired Cornishman of about twenty-five years, with brilliant green eyes. The others—eight of them now—stood ready, guarding the door and the ladder to the hatch. Stars Johnson took Hugh Dean's first pistol and started to reload it, cleaning the inside of the barrel with a dampener and unfastening his powder flask. Dean took another out of his belt and swung it around, glaring at the crew in the shadows.

"I know what you're thinking," he began in a loud voice. "You're thinking that you outnumber us. Let's see, forty, forty-five…maybe there's even more of you. And just a dozen or so of us. Well, that doesn't include those still on deck." He paused, looking from face to face. "Besides, if you try anything and force me to shoot you, you'll miss Captain Carew's speech. I'm sure you want to know what he is going to say. You do realize who our esteemed captain is? Most of you will be drinking with us before the night is through."

In the captain's cabin, Carew looked around, taking in the dimensions, the hiding places. It was about ten feet by twelve, with a small window shuttered against the night. There were three candles: one in a lantern on a hook by the cupboard bed, the other two on candlesticks projecting from the wall. There was a wooden berth on the left-hand side, a table on the right. The ceiling was low, so Kahlu had to cock his head to one side when he stood up straight; he leaned back against the wooden wall and rested his crossed arms on his chest.

Carew fixed his attention on William Gray. The captain was about forty years old with gray in his hair, dressed in loose breeches gathered at the knee and a white shirt covered by a red doublet. There were gold rings on three of his fingers.

Carew took the chair and beckoned to the captain. Gray hesitated but then moved forward. As he did so, there was a movement behind him and Carew saw the girl.

"Who is she?" he demanded.

"My niece," replied Gray.

The girl's smock was stained, her hair uncombed. Carew saw the fear in her eyes and her youth. She could not have been much older than twelve. He took a deep breath and gestured for the captain to be seated.

Gray's eyes flicked to the door. "Sir, I have a commission from—"

"Be seated!"

Gray glanced between the pirates' faces and sat.

Carew stood behind him, looking down on his head. He noted the gray hairs, the wiry-thin fair ones in the candlelight. It had started to recede. It made Carew despise the man's possession of the girl even more. "Put your hands on the table. I want to see them. No tricks."

Gray tentatively placed his fingers on the edge of the table.

"Flat, on the wood."

Carew gave a signal to John Devenish and Luke Treleaven. They stepped around to Gray's side of the table. Each took one of his arms. "Let go! Leave me!" shouted Gray. He started to struggle. Kahlu uncrossed his arms. Gray looked up, terrified and angry. "This ship is protected by the laws of England." He tried to turn to face Carew as the men placed his hands on the table. There was a sudden movement, the thud of a knife entering timber, and Gray let out an agonized scream. Kahlu had brought the dagger down hard and driven it straight through the man's right hand, pinning it to the wood. Instinctively Gray had tried to pull his bleeding hand away but his movement did nothing but drag the edge of the blade through his flesh. He screamed more, the pitch of his anguish rising with the waves of pain. "Jesus Almighty! Christ curse you and kill you!" Then there came another scream—a high-pitched inarticulate one—from the girl, as she realized what had happened. Immediately she tried to stop herself and her body began shaking, her eyes distraught with the image. Captain Gray was gasping, crying, and swaying. "Damn your bleeding eyes! The devil spit on your godforsaken soul."

Carew turned around to look at the girl. Her face was dirty, her nails broken. "This man says you are his niece. Are you?"

"N-n-no, sir," she cried, shivering. The terror showed in her eyes. "No, no! This man…he said he would take me home. My mother took me to the market in Dover and…and I was lost and went to the quayside, and this man…he said…he told me…he said he knows my father."

Carew walked forward and touched her cheek. He held her face for a moment, looking into her eyes. Then he ran his hand down over her childish breasts, smoothing the cloth over each one with his thumb. "Did he touch you? Did he force himself on you?"

The girl looked at the captain, trying to speak. No words came out. She burst into tears.

Carew turned to the captain, whose cries had given way to grimaces and gasps of pain. He walked up close behind him and crouched down behind his right ear. "If I did not have an important question to ask you, you would be dead already. I would have thrown you overboard—in pieces. I would have had you tied between two planks and sawn up alive, starting with your feet. I have very few principles. In fact, just four. One: men should obey orders. Two: they should be honest. Three: they should throw their religion over the side of the first ship they sail in. And four: they should protect their companions, especially those who are vulnerable, like women and children." He looked at the man's neck, which was twitching. "But I did not come here for your moral instruction. You know what I want. The Catholic Treasure."

Gray shook his head, tears running down his face as he fought the pain in his hand. He said nothing.

"Put his other hand out," Carew said to Luke.

"No!" gasped Gray. "No." He saw the faces of the other men and searched them for a sign of compassion. All he saw were curled lips, toothless smiles, and mild amusement. "Please, in God's name, have mercy! Have a thought for your eternal souls, have pity!"

Skinner Simpkins pushed in front of Luke, grabbed the captain's fist and held it on the table. Gray fought to keep his fingers tight together but Skinner simply drew his cutlass and smashed the hilt into the captain's forehead, jolting his head back and causing a gash to open up just above his left eye. Then he brought the metal hilt down hard repeatedly on the captain's knuckles, causing him to yell out and wrench his right hand against the pinning blade. Having broken two or three of the captain's fingers, Skinner was able to splay the man's hand.

"There is no treasure on this boat," screamed Gray. "None. Look—look anywhere, everywhere! Look for yourselves!"

"Skinner, wait," said Carew. "No treasure, you say?"

Gray bit his lip, weeping. Skinner waited. He turned the dagger in his hand, ready to pin the flesh to the table.

Carew inspected the wainscoting, the shuttered window. A basket of bread and cold meat stood on a rimmed shelf. There was indeed no sign of wealth in here. Apart from the space under the berth, the only other place where treasure might be kept was the chest. He pointed. "Luke, open it."

Luke stepped around the table and lifted the lid. He tipped the chest forward: clothes and linen tumbled out, along with a Bible, a rosary, a small box, a cutlass, a pistol, a powder flask, some fine cotton kerchiefs, a comb, a purse, some documents, three pewter plates, two pewter cups, and a flagon. He then opened the small box and let the contents fall on to the floor: two rings, a few gaming pieces, dice, quills, and a small inkpot made of horn. The top came off the inkpot and the ink started to spread across the linen.

Carew turned back to Gray. "Where is the treasure?"

Gray remained motionless, in too much pain to react. His jaw started to move before any sound came out. "I…I do not know…I have not…heard of—"

"You must know! Why are you here? Who sent you?"

"I brought the woman—and the man."

"What woman? What man?"

"Rebecca Machyn was her name. The man was Robert—Robert Lowe, I think. I…I was paid…to bring them to Southampton."

"How much?"

"Two h-h-hundred…pounds," stuttered Gray, shivering. "One hundred and fifty…in advance. It is under the bed."

Carew looked at Kahlu and glanced through the door. Hugh Dean was still guarding the crew.

Kahlu went to the bed, reached beneath it, and pulled out a second small chest. He opened it, showing the contents to Carew. The bottom was covered with gold coins.

Carew grabbed the captain's hair and gestured to his broken left hand. "Skinner!"

A moment later, although the captain lifted his arm and tried to clench his broken hand, his fingers barely moved. Skinner Simpkins placed it flat on the table and drove his dagger through it with a thud, causing a trickle of blood to run quickly across the wood. Gray screamed again. Another scream lifted his body from the seat and tore his hands further. As the first screams subsided, more surged in him. Carew waited, still holding the man's hair. When Gray's cries had turned to sobbing and gasping, Carew started to pull the man's head back, drawing the knives' blades into the flesh of his hands.

"No one is running to your aid," he said, looking at the door. "None of your crew. Perhaps it is because you are a bad captain? Perhaps because you keep your door locked, like a coward, when intruders board your ship? Perhaps because you abduct defenseless girls? What were you going to do with her? Take her home so she could inform the authorities what you did—or throw her overboard in the middle of the Channel? I know your sort." He let go of the man's hair.

Gray, with his bloody hands splayed out in front of him, lurched forward. He put his head on the table, trembling with shock.

"Where is the treasure?" said Carew.

"I do not know," sobbed Gray. "I do not know what...you are talking about."

"What was your mission?"

"To deliver...the man and the woman."

"Who paid you?"

"A man called Percy—Percy Roy."

"When? Where?"

"In London."

"Who is Percy Roy?" When the captain hesitated, Carew grabbed his hair once more and pulled it back. Gray screamed as the blades cut his hands again. "Speak!"

"His real name...is Denisot. He did not tell me, but I know—from the old days. It is Nicholas Denisot."

Carew let go of the man's hair. For a long time he was quiet, staring at oblivion through the wainscoting of the cabin. Then his eyes focused on something inside his mind. "Where is Denisot?"

"London."

"Where in London?" he demanded, regaining his urgency, as if *he* was now the one feeling the pain. "*Where in London?*"

"I don't know, I don't know."

Carew drew the knife from his belt and held it before the man's eyes, then placed it against his throat. "Tell me. *Now!*"

"I cannot," cried Gray, with tears in his eyes. "I cannot say, for I do not know. All I know is that Denisot…he came to me in a tavern by London Port saying that he wanted me to take a man and a woman to Southampton, that same day, to be delivered as soon as possible. I asked who was employing me and for how much…He said, 'Percy Roy,' and an hour later he gave me one hundred and fifty pounds in gold—with a promise of another fifty on my return. But it was Denisot…That is all—all I can tell you."

"Where is he living?"

"For God's sake, I do not know. I do not know." The captain started sobbing uncontrollably.

Carew seemed hardened by the news. "Tell me! Tell me how you know the names of the man and the woman. Why were they going to Southampton? I need to know everything."

"I do not know them—only that they mentioned another man…"

"Who? Tell me!"

"The woman—I overheard her. She said that Mr. Clarenceux… that Mr. Clarenceux would never forgive them."

"Forgive them for what?" Carew struck the captain on the side of the face.

"I don't know! I have told you everything—I swear it."

"Who is Clarenceux?"

"I don't know, I don't know." The man collapsed in sobs, his head falling forward.

Carew noticed Kahlu gesticulating. The black man held his left arm out in front of his breast and with his right drew the outline of a shield.

"A herald," said Skinner. "They often have foreign names."

Kahlu pointed to Skinner and nodded.

"It looks as though we have found a treasure—albeit not the one we were looking for," Carew said. "I would value Denisot's head more than any amount of gold and silver." He glanced at the girl and bit his lip, thinking, before turning back to Gray.

"First, let's take this devil up on deck, cut his throat, and throw him overboard. Then we will escort this girl back to her mother—it is what our law requires. Is Alice here?"

Kahlu shook his head.

"She's ashore still," added John Devenish in a deep voice. "At the Swans."

"Bring her aboard. Bring everyone aboard. This is our new ship. Those out there we will deal with in the normal way—the usual terms. Then we will hold the election. If elected, I will go after Denisot, sailing to London. If I can't find him, I will find this Clarenceux and I will make him tell me where Denisot is—if I have to cut him open to get the information out of him."

1

Twelve days earlier
Saturday, April 29, 1564

William Harley, officially known by his heraldic title of Clarenceux King of Arms, was naked. He was lying in his bed in his house in the parish of St. Bride, just outside the city walls of London. Leaning up on one arm, he ran his fingers down the skin of his wife's back, golden in the candlelight. He drew them back again, slowly, up to her shoulders, moving her blond hair aside so he could see her more fully. *She is so precious, so beautiful*, he thought. *My Saxon Princess. My Aethelfritha, my Etheldreda, my Awdrey.*

He withdrew his hand as the candle in the alcove above him spluttered. He looked at the curve of the side of her breast, pressed into the bed. The feeling of their union was still with him. The ecstasy had not just been one thrill; it had been many simultaneous pleasures—all of which had merged into one euphoria that had overwhelmed him, leaving him aglow.

She turned her head and smiled up at him again, lovingly. She was twenty-five years of age now. He felt lucky and grateful. Not only for the pleasure but also for the knowledge of just how great his pleasure could be. He leaned over and kissed her.

The candle in the alcove above the bed went out.

He lay down and let his thoughts drift in the darkness. Six months ago he had almost destroyed his own happiness, disconcerted and attracted by another woman. Rebecca Machyn. He shuddered as he remembered how he and Rebecca had been pursued, terrified together. She had seen him at his lowest, and he her. They had supported each other and, in a way, he had fallen in love with her. But he had never had doubts about his loyalty to his wife. That was what troubled him. Two women and two forms of love. It was not something that most God-fearing men and women ever spoke about.

What did he feel for Rebecca now? In the darkness, he sought his true feelings. There was a part of him that still loved her. His feelings for his wife were an inward thing: a matter of the heart. He loved Awdrey because of what he knew about her and what they had built together, what they shared. His affection for Rebecca Machyn was the opposite: an outward thing. She showed him what he did not know, the doubts, the wonder, and the fear that he knew existed in the world.

That outward-looking, questioning part of his nature worried him. The reason he had spent so much time with Rebecca was his possession of a secret document, and that document was still here, in this house. Awdrey did not know. That in itself felt like a betrayal. The document was so dangerous that men had died because of it. When Rebecca's husband, Henry Machyn, had given it to him the previous year, the man had declared that the fate of two queens depended on its safekeeping. And when Clarenceux had discovered its true nature—a marriage agreement between Lord Percy and Anne

Boleyn, which proved that Queen Elizabeth was illegitimate and had no right to the throne—he had understood why it was so sensitive. Only when Sir William Cecil, the queen's Principal Secretary, had asked him to keep it safely did his life start to return to normal. But never did he feel safe. Not for one moment.

He knew, later that morning, he would go up to his study at the front of the house and check that the document was still where he had hidden it. It was a ritual. More than a ritual: it was an obsession. Sometimes he would check it three or four times in one day. The knowledge that he possessed the means to demonstrate that the Protestant queen was illegitimate and that the rightful queen should be one of her cousins—either the Protestant Lady Katherine Gray, sister of the beheaded Lady Jane Gray; or Mary, the Catholic queen of Scotland—was not something he could ever forget. His fear of what would happen if he should lose the marriage agreement beat in his heart like his love for Rebecca Machyn. Both were dark and dangerous. The ecstasy of his lovemaking with his wife was so blissful and so pure by comparison—and yet he could not ignore the dark side within himself.

He felt Awdrey turn over and cuddle up beside him, nestling under his arm. He was a tall man and she of average height, so his arm around her felt protective. She ran her hand over his side, where he had been scarred in a sword fight five months earlier.

"How is it now?"

"Fine."

"I don't want you to exert yourself too much."

"If it had torn just now, it would have been worth it."

He remembered the day when he had suffered the wound—at Summerhill, the house of his old friend Julius Fawcett, near

Chislehurst. He wondered how Julius was now. "What would you say to the idea of going down to Summerhill next week?"

"I promised I would take the girls to see Lady Cecil. She wants them to play with her little boy, Robert."

Clarenceux lay silent. Sir William Cecil's wife was godmother to their younger daughter, Mildred. The idea of Annie and Mildred playing with Robert was a little optimistic. Robert Cecil was three, their daughter Annie was six, and Mildred just one. It was Awdrey's polite way of saying that she would not refuse the invitation. Lady Cecil, being one of the cleverest women in England, was something of a heroine to her. Both women had been pregnant together and, although that child of Lady's Cecil's had died, she was expecting again, which made her call more frequently on Awdrey. The relationship was not without its benefits to him too. It was immensely valuable to have a family connection through Lady Cecil to Sir William, the queen's Principle Secretary and one of the two most powerful men in the country, the other being Robert Dudley, the queen's favorite.

Awdrey moved her hand over his chest, feeling the hair. "You could go by yourself."

He was meant to be planning his next visitation. Soon he would have to ride out and record all the genealogies in one of the counties, visiting all the great houses with his pursuivants, clerks, and official companions. The purpose was to check the veracity of all claims to coats of arms and heraldic insignia, and to make sure that those with dubious or nonexistent claims were exposed as false claimants. He had completed a visitation of Suffolk three years earlier and one of Norfolk the previous year. He had finished his notes on the visitation of Devon, and had discussed the gentry of that county at length with his friend and fellow antiquary John Hooker. But he could put off actually going to Devon until June, and so could delay the planning for another week and enjoy the late spring in Kent with his old friend.

"I may well do that," he replied.

Awdrey touched his face. He felt her hand move over his beard and cheek. Her finger traced his lips, then slipped down over his chest, to his midriff.

"How tired are you?" she asked.

2

Sunday, April 30

A piece of mud thrown up by the hooves of his partner's horse caught Philip France in the eye, and he took a hand off the reins to wipe it away. It had been raining for the last six miles now—indeed, it was the rain that had alerted them to the messenger. The man had been galloping through a heavy downpour when they had spotted him from where they were sheltering beneath some trees. No one would be out in this unless they had an important and urgent mission. The fading light was not a good enough reason by itself, not with the rain coming down so hard. Moreover, they had seen this man twice before, in the vicinity of Sheffield Manor, taking messages to or from Lady Percy, the dowager countess of Northumberland. And their instructions, as given to them by Francis Walsingham himself, were unambiguous. "Arrest ten innocent men rather than let one conspirator slip by."

France dug his spurs into his horse's flanks and drew up alongside his friend and companion, George Latham. "What if he doesn't stop in Melton?" he shouted.

"Then we press on," Latham yelled back, his hat in his hand and his black hair plastered wet across his forehead. "But he'll stop. His mount must be as tired as ours."

They rode into Melton Mowbray ten minutes later. The man they were following entered an inn: a stone-fronted building called the Mowbray Arms. France and Latham watched him pass beneath the central arch.

"I presume you have our warrant?" asked Latham.

"Aye. But need we arrest him in the inn?"

"Are you worried?"

"No, not unduly," replied France. "But if there are many people, and they know him…We are a hundred miles from London."

Latham smiled. "You *are* worried. Like when we slipped out of college."

France did not rise to the taunt. "What if we are wrong? What if he is riding hard in this weather because his mother is ill or his wife is in labor?"

"We have seen that man twice before, two weeks ago, on both occasions riding hard near Sheffield Manor. It would be something of a surprise if his wife lived so near to Lady Percy."

France allowed his horse to step forward and then sat there in the rain, watching the gate. "So, we take him in his chamber?"

"Yes, in his chamber." Latham began to ride forward too. He did not stop.

The inn was a proud structure, with a central arch giving way onto a puddle-streaked courtyard. There were stables on the far side, outbuildings built along each flank. France and Latham dismounted and led their horses through, passing the reins to a stable boy who ran forward to greet them, taking their names and making a polite little bow before taking their mounts away. The door to the hall was on the left, up a couple of steps. As they approached, one of the inn servants came out carrying an empty pitcher, and in the moment that the door was open, they heard the noise of the crowd within.

The hall was between thirty and forty feet long and darker than they expected. A second floor had been inserted, cutting in two the pair of high windows on the courtyard side. There was a candelabrum with half its candles alight above them. France counted how many people he could see—thirty-one. A young lawyer was sitting beside a haughty-looking well-dressed woman, a young boy playing with a kitten at her feet. A tall traveler with a wide hat was plucking a stringed instrument, clearly hoping to catch the woman's attention but she was not giving in to his musical entreaties. Standing at another table was a maid in an apron, offering a plate of food and a flagon of wine to a modest man and woman who were clearly traveling together. Two merchants stood to one side, one nodding gravely as he listened to his companion and ate a piece of cheese. A servant was clearing up some spilled oysters from a table at which four hearty yeomen were dining, striking out with his hand to keep a small dog from gnawing the food. Beside the near-dark window, a student was trying to read a book.

Latham caught France's arm and gestured toward the furthest corner. There in the shadows, sitting at a table, was the man they had been following. He was bearded, about thirty years of age, with a gaunt expression. His sopping wet jerkin hung heavily from his shoulders, and he wore no ruff. He was watching them, a piece of bread in both of his hands, which he had just broken but was not eating.

"I think we have just lost the chance of surprise," Latham murmured.

France looked around. "It doesn't matter. He's cornered. There are only two doors—and if he leaves by the one on the far side...It must lead back into the courtyard."

Latham caught the attention of the woman in the apron as she began to return to the kitchen. "My good woman, can you tell me where that far door leads? And are you familiar with the man at the table in the corner?"

"The door leads to the stairs, which go up to the best chambers. They are all taken. But there may be space in one of the second-best chambers, off the gallery. In this weather we have our hands full."

"And the man?"

She looked in his direction. "Can't say I've ever seen him before. He just came in and demanded something to eat. He said he did not mind what. I gave him a piece of bread and told him I'd send a maid with some pottage when it's done. Will you and your friend be joining him? I am sure there will be pottage enough, and it's both beans and bacon. Three pence a bowl, four with bread."

Latham put a friendly hand on her shoulder. "Thank you. Some pottage would be a fine thing. First, though, about that man over there. He is no friend of ours—nor of yours. We are carrying a warrant from Sir William Cecil, her majesty's Secretary, to arrest him on suspicion of sedition."

The woman looked blankly at Latham.

"He is a Catholic spy," France explained.

"There's not going to be any trouble, is there?" the woman asked anxiously. "I mean, there are many guests, some children too."

"Don't you worry," replied France. "All we need you to do is to close and secure the main gate until we have apprehended him. When he is locked up in the nearest magistrate's house, we will be back—looking forward to some of that pottage."

"I really ought to be asking my husband. When he returns, I'll do as you say. We do usually close the gate at this hour, at dusk."

"Where is your husband?"

"At the mill."

Latham glanced again at the man. He was eating the bread, still watching them. "Look, my good woman, trust me. Close it now, just for five minutes. We will arrest him quietly and lead him out through the upstairs passage if that would suit you better."

"George, he's getting up," said France. "He's leaving by the far door."

"Go after him. I'll head him off at the gate."

France stepped forward. The general chatter subsided as he pushed past the seat on which the well-dressed woman was sitting and knocked the lawyer into another man who stumbled backward, falling almost on top of the boy and the kitten. He did not listen to the complaints nor the calls for him to be careful, but kept on toward the doorway. When he reached it, he swung blindly around the jamb—and ran straight on to the poised knife of the man, who was waiting immediately around the corner.

Philip France's first reaction to the blade entering his chest was to look down. He saw the blood pouring out, as water pours from a drain in a storm. His second reaction was to look up at the face of the man who had stabbed him. No words passed between them but enough time elapsed for France to look questioningly at him. The man turned and fled up the stairs. France's last clear thought was that he ought to tell George to look out for himself. He took only one step more, then felt suddenly very weak and slumped in the doorway, barely aware of the shouts of alarm from the guests as his life ebbed away.

George Latham heaved the drawbar of the gate into place and stood ready. He heard the sound of a man running along an upstairs corridor, then he heard the shouts. There were rapid footsteps on a stone staircase and a shadowy figure suddenly emerged from a door nearby.

At that moment, the innkeeper's wife ran out of the hall and shouted, "Your friend has been wounded! He is bleeding." She saw the killer's dark shape on the other side of the archway, the knife still in his hand. "Look out! He's got a dagger!"

George Latham had only once before wielded a blade in anger. That had been during his time at Oxford, in a drunken brawl with some of the townsmen who had turned vicious. But he knew the rudiments. His lack of experience was the last thing on his mind. He had forgotten his orders from Walsingham. All that mattered now was that the bearded man before him had stabbed his most faithful friend—a companion since his schooldays.

"You want to get out?" he shouted at the shadow. "To leave?"

The man did not move.

"Well, go on then," snarled Latham, approaching him. "Go on— leave. All you have to do is open the gate and go."

The man looked across the yard to the stables.

"If you run, you are going to have to run on foot. If you reach your horse in the stable—which will have been unsaddled by now—you will be trapped."

"Don't go near him. Call for the constable," cried the woman, as the men who had been inside the hall came out. "Raise the hue and cry."

At the same time, there was a loud knocking on the gate, and a man from outside demanding: "Who has barred my house against me? Damn your eyes, open up!"

The innkeeper's wife ran across and started to pull back the drawbar. At that moment, sensing that the man might go to the gate, Latham reached for the knife at his own belt, drew it, and rushed forward. The man saw him coming and ran across the yard. Latham sprinted after him. Not far behind came the man he had seen eating cheese, closely followed by the lawyer. None of them had a lantern but all were grimly determined. The traveler with the hat joined them too. And then the boys from the stable appeared, one with a small lantern.

The killer swerved and ran down a dark alleyway between the stable and the perimeter wall of the inn. Latham knew the man was trapped. Inns that depend on the security of their guests' horses and possessions do not have easy access points behind stables. The Mowbray Arms was no exception. A moment later the man found himself in the near-darkness of a dead end, with four shadows blocking the only way out. And then the stable boy with the light joined them.

For a long moment, the man held out the knife in front of him, his hand shaking.

"Drop the knife," shouted the traveler in the hat. "Drop it now! You will only make your punishment more severe."

"He is going to hang whatever," said the lawyer. "The question is whether he repents first."

Latham stepped forward. "Who are you?"

"Go to hell," muttered the man. Then he said it again, louder. "Go to hell!"

Latham looked at the man's shape in the dimness and held out his left hand, palm upward for the knife, concealing his own blade. "Give the knife to me. There is nowhere else to run."

But at that moment the man lifted the knife above his head and, with a loud cry, ran straight toward them. As he came to Latham, he brought the blade down. Latham dropped to a crouch and threw himself at the man's legs, bringing him to the ground. He whirled around with his own knife and stabbed the man's thigh. Then he stabbed him in the groin as the others there also set about the felon with their day-to-day knives. It was hysterical, a frenzy of stabbing—men killing out of fear and revenge. Suddenly it was over. The killing moment was done.

"The beast is dead," said the lawyer, his voice betraying his excitement and relief. The stable boy with the lantern held it close to the corpse.

Latham looked down at the bloody torso. It had been bad butchery: he could see a rib and pink organs. He felt sick. The man was dead—and these fellows were smiling and congratulating themselves. But what were they doing here? What was he doing here? Who were all these people around him, talking, laughing, and shouting? Only when the innkeeper called for silence and demanded to know the identity of the dead man did Latham catch the one strand of purpose left to him.

"He is a spy," he gasped. "A Catholic conspirator." As he spoke he knelt down and felt the side pockets of the bloody jerkin. Finding nothing, he started to undo the jerkin itself. His hands became smeared with the man's warm blood, fumbling inside the gore-soaked linen of his shirt. And then he felt a folded paper. He took it out and slipped it into his own pocket. Standing up, he wiped his brow, leaving the others to drag the body away into the yard.

3

Wednesday, May 3

Clarenceux walked over Fleet Bridge and westward along Fleet Street, toward his house. It was late morning. The bright sun shone on the houses on the north side of the street. His house was on the south side. He looked up at it: a typical, three-story merchant's house. There was a shop at the front—which he did not let but used for storage, so the shutters were always closed—and two floors of accommodation above, with a large hall occupying most of the first floor. It was not much to show for a lifetime in royal service, first in the army at Boulogne, then in the various heraldic ranks at the College of Arms. It was very little, considering he had been born the son of a gentleman. But it was something. And it was more than most followers of the old religion possessed.

The old religion. Catholicism: loyalty to all things holy, as he understood it, including the offices of the Church and the pope. England turning against the old religion had been the tragedy of his life. He had been still young in 1534, barely sixteen, when the old king, Henry VIII, had passed the Act of Supremacy that made him Head of the Church. At the time Clarenceux had not understood the significance of this. It had only struck him when the first wave of monasteries were closed two years later. Three years after that, all the greater monasteries were shut and their possessions confiscated, even the great foundations of Glastonbury and Westminster. Many of the churches that he knew, and where he had studied the arms on the tombs as the dust drifted in the stained-glass light above him, had been pulled down. Some had been sold off—the land, stone, glass, and lead all going to the profit of one of the king's friends. Even the books had been sold off—those that were not destroyed by the abbey's new owners. These actions had set his heart against the tyranny of that king.

When Mary Tudor had succeeded to the throne, there had been no funds to repurchase and rebuild the hundreds of closed founda-tions. A few monks and abbots were restored, in a token gesture, but the queen had been too conciliatory. She had put her efforts into the persecution of heretics who preached against her and had ignored those heretics who now rebuilt the sacred abbeys as their halls and homes. That had just made the reformers more embittered. The first statute of Queen Elizabeth's first parliament had been wholly uncompromising, ushering in a new age of tyranny. If he was caught maintaining the spiritual authority of the pope, as he believed was right, he would have his house and all his goods, lands, and chattels confiscated. If he was found guilty of maintaining the preeminence of Rome three times, he would be sentenced to death. Heresy—not following the rites of the official Church—could lead to hanging too. Even declining to use the new *Book of Common Prayer*, or speaking of it in a derogatory manner, would lead to imprisonment.

He entered his house to see his manservant, Thomas Terry, who immediately welcomed him in and shut the door. Thomas had served him for many years and was practically a member of the family. He was a strong-minded character. Clarenceux compared him to a slowly rusting iron bar—still unyielding despite all the outward appearances of aging.

"Mr. Clarenceux, sir," said Thomas, "there was a message from Widow Machyn while you were out. She says she would like to see you, if you would do her the honor."

Clarenceux nodded and went up the stairs. "Did she say when?"

"No, sir," said Thomas, following him, "but she seemed very anxious. I presume what she has to say is important."

Clarenceux paused at the top, trying to think of what it might be. "Thank you, Thomas."

He turned into his hall, strode past the elm table in the front window to a door in the corner, and ascended the narrow staircase beyond. The age of the house showed most here: the wooden stairs creaked beneath his weight and, at the top, there were a couple holes in the door to his study, where gnarls in the wood had shrunk and fallen out. The room itself was untidy, as usual, with papers and books scattered across the floor where he deposited them in the course of research. There was an empty space above the fireplace where the portrait of his father used to hang. It had been smashed in the searching of his house six months earlier. His father's damaged sword had been straightened and now hung nearby, along with a new blade that Clarenceux had acquired for his own use. Some of the books had been repaired too, and were now stacked in the presses against the walls.

He went to the far side of the room, as he always did on entering, where a small instrument hung with its face against the wall. It was a *chitarra*: a lute-like instrument with a thin neck and five courses of strings. It had an intricately carved grille over the sound hole. He reached up, turned it face outward, and plucked the strings one by one. They were in a particularly unusual musical sequence—just as he had left them. But, even so, he lifted the instrument down and removed the grille. He pushed his fingers through and felt the edge of the document glued there, deep inside. Satisfied, he replaced the grille and put the *chitarra* back, face against the wall.

He wished that he could forget about the document. It was a constant worry. If anyone knew he had it, they might do something extreme. His daughters might be kidnapped and held to ransom. He might be tortured. The very fact that he knew of its existence was a risk. Catholic houses were regularly searched for seditious documents: if royal officers were to come and find it, then Sir William Cecil would not save him. As a Protestant and the queen's Secretary, Cecil would be heavily compromised if anyone found out that he even knew of its existence. No one would step in to save him, Clarenceux, from the gallows.

It was ironic. Here he was, in possession of the means to dethrone a queen—and, moreover, a queen who was an enemy of his faith— and yet he did nothing. His only weapon was one so powerful he dared not use it. It actually made him more vulnerable. He told himself, the moment to use it had not come. In his heart, however, he knew that that moment would never come. He was not reckless enough to start a revolution. Nor did he want a return to the old days, when men and women were burnt at the stake for their religious beliefs. He wanted a quiet life and mutual understanding. That in itself set him against all those who knew he had the document, who were ardent for him to proclaim the queen illegitimate in his role as a herald. The surviving friends of the late Henry Machyn—a secret Catholic fraternity organized to protect the document—expected him to do much more with it. They were collectively called the Knights of the Round Table. They would not wait forever.

He sighed heavily. And wondered why Rebecca had come to see him.

4

Late that evening, Francis Walsingham was riding through the city, looking up at the open windows of some nearby houses. He wondered who might be watching him. It made him think about spies, and how many there were hidden behind the opaque routines of everyday life. Men who watched their servants for signs of theft of goods or money. Those who watched their neighbors. Servants who listened through thin, plaster-covered partitions to their masters' words in the next room. Clergymen who observed their flocks for signs of sin. Later there would be the night watchmen patrolling the city for strangers out after curfew. The more one looked at a city, the more it seemed that everyone was on the alert. The business of mankind was increasingly that of watching itself, listening to its own sins, weaknesses, and betrayals.

And then there was him, Walsingham, the eyes and ears of her majesty's Principal Secretary. He was the one who felt the pulse of society for signs of rebellions and revolutions, dissent and disservice. His role was to gather all the knowledge that others heard and saw, and to advise accordingly. And when knowledge was not enough, he acted on instinct. That was perhaps the most important part. He had to use a measure of instinct to know when someone was withholding information. Or to know where a plot was likely to emerge, and to be there, listening, to preempt it. As Sir William so often reminded him, if they were to foil nineteen plots out of twenty against the queen, they would have failed.

He turned a corner near his house in the east of the city and saw the high walls of the Tower of London ahead of him. Shielded in that great fortification, he would hear nothing. The queen in her palace heard nothing. Sir William himself heard little. It was essential for him, Walsingham, to be the listener that the queen and Sir William so desperately needed. He had to be in the streets, amid the smells, in order to understand what people told him. But what they really needed was for all these people with their shutters open, listening, to be the queen's agents. A truly loyal people would report dissent and subversive conversations as a matter of course. Their love of their monarch and their spiritual duty to protect her majesty required it of them. Yes, that was what he should be planning: how to make the whole population his agents. How to make them betray one another. Each one could report to the constable of their ward or manor. And those constables could report to the hundredal officers or, better still, the lord lieutenant.

As he approached his house, he saw a horse tethered outside. He did not recognize it. That meant little; he was a poor judge of horses. But even he could see this one was exhausted and covered in sweat.

Walsingham rode through to his stable and dismounted. He shouted for a boy to attend to his mount and went through a passage-way to the main hall, a large room open to the roof beams. The walls were relatively plain, decorated only with a pair of rather unflattering family portraits and two faded tapestries. A man was talking to one of his servants. They turned toward him when they heard his footsteps approaching across the flagstones.

"Good day, Mr. Walsingham," said his servant with a small bow.

The other man said nothing. Walsingham looked at him. "George Latham, is it not? I sent you to Sheffield with your friend, Philip French—"

"*France*, sir," said Latham. "His name was Philip France."

"Was?"

Latham held out a piece of paper. It was covered in blood. "He gave his life in your service, sir. The blood you see is that of the man who killed him."

5

Thursday, May 4

Mrs. Barker, kneeling in a black silk and velvet dress, made the sign of the cross over her breast. She watched her priest, Father John Tucker, as he folded away the portable altarpiece that graced the table in the chamber that she used as a chapel. He was tall and thin, in his early forties, with a neat brown beard and sharp, concentrated features. He looked shrewd and serious.

She was much older—more than sixty years of age. She rose to her feet somewhat awkwardly. "Have you spoken to the others?"

"I have, my lady. They are all with us."

"And Widow Machyn herself—she is still willing to cooperate?"

Father Tucker hesitated. "Yes."

"You sound unsure. Do you think she will regret betraying Mr. Clarenceux?"

"The way she spoke, I think she truly believes in our cause. She knows that he should have acted by now. She too feels guilty. Her late husband died in the hope that that manuscript would be used, and that Parliament would act to set Elizabeth aside as illegitimate and proclaim Mary. Our patience and pressure over the last few months will pay off; she will do as we ask."

"Good. The arrangement to switch her to a French ship—is that settled?"

Father Tucker lifted the missal that he had been using and placed it in a concealed cupboard built into the paneling. "Everything is in order. Rebecca Machyn will soon be far away from London." He closed the panel door and turned to her. "And so will the Percy-Boleyn marriage agreement."

6

Friday, May 5

It was late morning. Sunlight poured in through the window of the study of Cecil House, on the north side of the Strand, and gleamed on the gilt frame of the portrait above the fireplace. *Sir Wyllyam Sessylle, aetatis suae xxxii* was painted in gold in the top right-hand corner. Francis Walsingham saw Cecil's judicious face staring down at him from a quite different time, twelve years earlier. He reflected that he was now the same age as Cecil had been when that picture had been painted: thirty-two. Would he be in Cecil's place in twelve years? Or still dependent on the sly political genius of his mentor and patron?

He turned away and walked slowly across the chamber. Dust shifted in the sunlight. He took a book from a shelf, turned it over in his hands, and opened it. His eyes focused on the words but he could not concentrate on their meaning. He replaced it and sat down at Cecil's empty writing table, facing the door.

After a minute or two he got up again. Words drifted up the grand staircase outside, too indistinct for him to understand. Something was happening downstairs. He adjusted the close-fitting black cap that covered his receding hair and made sure his ruff was fluffed out and smart. He pulled the sleeves of his black doublet down to their full length and waited. Finally, after another five minutes, he heard footsteps and voices on the stairs as several men ascended.

Sir William Cecil entered the study, carrying a large pile of folded papers, followed by six attendants. His bright eyes were his most distinctive feature, even more noticeable than his reddish-brown beard, which was rapidly turning gray. His hair was thinning a little. The deep-blue velvet of his doublet contrasted strikingly with the pristine white of his ruff. "And remember, for everybody's sake, don't allow the ambassador to see the docks too closely," he was saying to a clerk. "A glimpse is fine—it will reassure him that we are not hiding anything—but the rebuilding of five galleasses will have the opposite effect." He turned to another clerk. "I need further details on the nature of the dispute between the Merchant Adventurers and the Company of Hanse Merchants at Antwerp. This impasse is most unsatisfactory. If they need an ambassador, I will send them one." He saw Walsingham. "Ah, Francis, I was told you were here." Cecil gestured for the other men to leave. "Go, all of you. I will deal with any further matters at one of the bell, in the great hall."

Walsingham bowed. "Greetings, Sir William. I am glad of your return."

"The feeling is mutual. If I am to be hounded day and night by requests and complaints, let it at least be in the comfort of my own home. But even so, look." Cecil held up the pile of papers. He flicked among them, found one, and opened it, passing it to his protégé, setting the rest on the table. "Trade with the Low Countries is on the point of collapse. The Merchant Adventurers cannot access the ports because the Hanse has reimposed trade restrictions. It means Spanish intervention, of course; we all know it but we cannot say it. And that is the least of my worries. What am I to do about the earl of Hertford and Lady Katherine Gray, the queen's cousin? Hales's book has just made everything ten times worse."

"I am sorry, Sir William. Hales's book? You'll have to forgive me. Who is Hales?"

Cecil walked across to a table beside the window, where a pair of silver goblets was standing next to a lidded pewter wine flagon. He filled one and quaffed it. "When Lady Katherine Gray gave birth, she confessed to my wife's sister that the father was Lord Hertford and that Hertford had secretly married her in a Catholic ceremony."

"That was at least two years ago."

"Indeed. But do you recall the consequence—that trial, at which the marriage was declared void? Lord Hertford was found guilty of violating a virgin of the royal family."

"It's not the sort of thing one forgets," said Walsingham. "He was fined fifteen thousand pounds. For sleeping with his wife."

"Quite. His wife just happened to be the queen's cousin, and the queen…Well, you know what I think. My suspicion is that our queen would rather neither of her cousins have any children, so there are no potential heirs to rival whomsoever she eventually chooses. So when Lady Katherine takes matters into her own hands…" Cecil gestured to suggest his frustration. "But the queen's spite has no basis in law." He took a deep breath. "A man called John Hales has written a pamphlet pointing out that Lady Katherine's children should be recognized in the order of succession. Privately, I agree. I had Lord Hertford transferred to Hanworth last year, on the pretext of there being an outbreak of the plague, and placed him in the keeping of his stepfather, Francis Newdigate. I was trying to lessen the injustice of her majesty's ire. Now it turns out that Newdigate has involved himself in the composition of Hales's book. I have here letters from Newdigate, Lord Hertford, and John Hales all seeking clemency and intervention. Even that damned Robert Dudley has written one. The queen is isolated—and yet she wants me to bring charges of treason against them. It is a disaster. I am meant to arrange for Hales to be found guilty. Ultimately Hertford is guilty of nothing more than falling in love. Frankly, having seen Lady Katherine, I cannot blame him. She could easily make traitors of us all."

Cecil paused and took another gulp of wine. "Hales's only offense is to point out the legal situation that automatically follows on from them marrying—which no one can deny they have done, with witnesses, and willingly. That the queen does not like it does not render it unlawful: we do not follow Roman Law in this kingdom but our own Common Law. It is hardly surprising that there are plots against her. It's not made any easier by the fact that she won't marry. She has said categorically that she will not marry one of her own subjects. So what are we to do? We look overseas. I favor the house of Austria. Throckmorton, from whom I have just received yet another letter, says that he too favors Austria. Roger Strange favors Austria. Robert Dudley also favors Austria. And what does the queen say? 'No, Sir William, not Austria.' I despair."

"I am all the more sorry to be the one who bears you further reason to frown."

"Francis, you are *not* sorry. It is a constant delight to you, to bring me new challenges. But I trust you not to bother me with trifles. That is why I came back as soon as I could."

"Thank you. This concerns the dowager countess of Northumberland. You asked that I keep her ladyship under close watch. Several weeks ago I instructed two young men from Oxford to take up lodgings in the area and monitor the movements of those coming and going to her at Sheffield Manor. The day before yesterday, one of them, George Latham, came to me. He had ridden hard, changing horses, and was in a terrible state. Three days earlier, on the thirtieth, he and his companion noticed a messenger riding through the rain toward Sheffield—a man whom they had previously seen carrying messages to her ladyship. And so they moved to intercept him. They caught up with him at Melton Mowbray, in an inn. The messenger killed Latham's companion, and then was himself killed. When Latham searched the corpse, he found a message. The original was soiled in the man's blood, but here is a copy."

Walsingham reached inside his doublet and pulled out a neatly folded paper. He walked closer and handed it to Cecil, who opened it. In neat black pen was written the following:

CCCCX>CCDCCICCCIIIMMCII-<\CCCCCC-,
/IMMMD\C\ICCCCMMV/CMMMCCX+II-CCVI-CCCC-
<-XI-/C\ICCCCX, MMMDCCCCI<DX\, MMMLCCCC\
CCCMMMXCCCC+-CCCC<XIVMMV, /DCCIIX/\
IIXMMMIIXMMMMX,>D\/\IICCVDMMMCC->V,D\
CCCC-MMMD\CCCC-DCC-<VDCC\MMX<DCCCC-
VMMMICCCC-D\IMMMMMM\DCCVDC\IV, /II-D\>-
DCCCCCCCCCX>CCD-LL-<DXDMMMDCCCCIDCCMMMCC-
<DXDMMMDCCCCIDCCMMMCC-IIXMMMMIII-/-MMM+
VD<CC-/IIICMMMCCX+X, DCC-<\CCC+V, C\LCCCC\
III-CCCCDMM\IILCCCC\CCCMM\, /\, D\MMMV, /IIX<
CCV, /DCC-CCCC-<CCV, >-/D\VIMMMMMMMMMIII\I,/L\
CCCCMMM<\DMMV, /IICC-CCCC-I+\, MMMCC-IIXMMMM<

\, LXCCCCCCCCC-CCCCVCCCCCCCCXIVMMIIXDCCC
ICCCCCCCC-+CCCC-MMM-, DVDXI-MMMMMMCC-
IIXMMMMMM-VI-LCCCC\CCCMM\, ∧, VD/VII, \, DCC-
MMM-I-,DCCDCCVDII-CCCVCIII-MMMICCCC-C
IIIXMMMMMMM-, /C\ICCCCCCCC-+CCCC-MMM-,
DVDXI-MMMD\CC\MMCCCCC\\/II-III->C\IMMM-,
/II\CCCC/IIICDCCXMMMMMMVCCC-CCC-MMMMMM-,
>-CCCC>\/MMM+- - /C\ICCCCMMV/CMMMCCX+C
ICCCC/-I\D-/MMM-CCCCIV, DMMM+- CCCC<CCCCC\C

Cecil glanced at him. "Is it a cipher? Or a code?"

"I do not know yet. But whichever it is, it shows that Lady Percy is involved with Catholic plots again. She is communicating in secret with someone south of Melton Mowbray, probably here in London. And this new development must be serious. Normally her agents use cut-out templates that relate to commonly available books. To decipher those, all we need is the name of the book and the relevant page numbers, and often that can be determined by a search of the sender's and recipient's premises, coupled with some persuasive questioning. This is different. It is hard to decide whether it is a cipher or a code— because it is based partly on Roman numerals and partly on symbols. If it is a cipher, it is not a straightforward one."

Cecil studied the document. "There are repetitions nonetheless. I see a few instances of 'DCC-.' It should not be too difficult."

Walsingham stood beside Cecil, pointing with his finger. "But there are six consecutive appearances of the letter 'C'; here, seven; and here eight of the letter 'M.' No word has a treble letter in it, let alone six, seven, or eight. These are Roman numerals. And that is where the problem lies, for there is no easy way to determine whether

'CCCCC' is one word or one letter, or two letters, or two words or a single number representing a sentence. Likewise the appearance of 'IV'—is that one letter, one word, or two?"

"Someone must be able to decipher it, Francis. If it is meaningful, there has to be a way to extract that meaning." Cecil looked at the DCC and tried the usual first step of substituting the most common element in the message with the most common word in the language. But the most common four-letter words with a double letter in the middle used vowels—EE and OO—and those did not fit the other appearances of CC in the code. Even separating out the numerical equivalents—500, 200, and a dash—did not simplify things. If that was a common three-letter word like "and," for example, then 200 was an N and the first word had to begin with a double N. If 200 was "the," then the first word began with a double H.

"I see what you mean," Cecil acknowledged. "This is nothing like a straightforward Caesar cipher."

"There seems to be a pattern of variation on numbers. Two hundred appears regularly, in the form of 'CC.' But does 'IICCV' relate to two, three, or four numbers? It is difficult to know where the breaks are, where a word begins and ends."

"The messenger riding through the rain—do we know who he is? Where he comes from?"

Walsingham walked to the small table by the window and poured himself a goblet of wine. "No. I have asked for the body to be embalmed and brought to the city as quickly as possible. It will take some days. No one locally knows him. Latham says that he took fright immediately when accosted. Also, he was riding hard through very heavy rain when they noticed him. This message, whatever it means, was urgent. Given that fact and its originality, it must be important."

"How many men do you have working on it?"

"Two. I had three copies made last night. The original is safely stored in my house."

"Good." Cecil paused. "The more men, the greater the danger of information leaking out. Work your clerks around the clock. Offer them every incentive to keep going. Decipher it quickly, but don't make any more copies—and don't let the existing copies out of your house. Until we know what this means, treat it as dangerous."

7

Clarenceux closed the heavy volume of the Skinners' Company accounts. He had been checking them in his capacity as one of the Wardens but had not been able to concentrate. His mind had been elsewhere. Seven or eight times he had realized his additions had not tallied with the written entry, and almost every time a second check had revealed that he was at fault, the written entry was correct. Only one correction was marked—one correction to show for an hour sitting in blurred contemplation.

He got up and set the account book back in its place on a shelf and left the chamber. He waved good-bye to the porter and stepped out into the mild air of the street. It was a short walk to the Machyn house in Little Trinity Lane. Every so often a quarrel of glass in an upstairs window would catch the sun and reflect a brilliant ray of light into his eyes. The mud had dried and was firm to walk on—except at intervals where a cellar or drain had leaked and the ground was still wet, churned by cartwheels and hooves. He breathed deeply of the summer air, tinged with the familiar and not dislikable aroma of the clay, mud, and horse dung of the streets, and a slight whiff of seawater. It was a good day to be out of doors. It would be even better if he were already riding down to Chislehurst, to see his friend Julius.

Perhaps Rebecca would accompany him?

Immediately he put the thought out of his mind. Although she had gone to Summerhill with him last December, that had been when they were fleeing for their lives. The moral code that permitted them to be together then now stipulated that he, a married man, should keep a respectful distance from Widow Machyn. There was no doubt what people would say if he were to be seen riding out of the city with her. He had witnessed too many otherwise respectable people clothed in white at the church door repenting of their sins to have any doubt in the matter.

Outside Rebecca Machyn's home, he paused and looked up at Mrs. Barker's elegant house on the other side of Little Trinity Lane, with its high glazed windows and its carved jetties supporting the upper floor. He recalled the horror of last December, when he had killed a man in this street and fled through the backyards behind that house, desperate beyond belief. He made the cross over his chest and closed his eyes in prayer. *Oh Lord, may such fear and doubt never enter my heart and mind again.*

He knocked on the oak door of the Machyn house with the hilt of his eating knife and waited. After a short while he heard a woman's voice and footsteps. Rebecca opened the door.

Instantly his heart felt glad. He saw her long dark hair, her brown eyes, the large mole on the side of her face. He saw the tragic beauty of her countenance. He saw the woman with whom he had shared so many dangers. He felt purposeful. He smiled.

"Good day, Rebecca. Thomas told me you called."

She did not respond. Just as he had been instantly gladdened by the sight of her face, now he was just as swiftly alarmed by her lack of welcome.

"You *did* call at my house?"

"Yes, I did. It was…nothing." She looked at him, almost tearful.

"May I come in?"

She nodded, left the door open for him, and turned and walked along the corridor to the hall. Clarenceux shut the door behind him. It was dim and chilly inside, especially standing here alone. This was not the reception he had expected.

Henry Machyn's old workshop was at the front, on the right. This used to be filled with his rolls of black cloth and heraldic paintings; now it was almost empty. Looking through the open door Clarenceux could see four large chests in the center. The rest of the room was bare, the walls stripped of their decoration, the work table gone.

He walked down the corridor, past the staircase, and into the hall. Opposite was a large fireplace of stone with a bread oven built into its side. Tallow candles lit the room; there were no windows in here. Two chambers above, the storeroom at the rear and the workshop at the front blocked out any light. A series of cloths painted by Henry Machyn hung on the walls. In one or two places they had started to fray. The floor was covered in straw and there was a smell of stale ale and urine. Two chests were the only storage. A wooden table stood in the center.

"Oh, fie! What brings you here, Mr. Clarenshoo?" asked a red-faced man of about twenty-five. He was sitting on a small bench beside the table, with his legs splayed, wearing a loose, dirty linen shirt and a sleeveless mariner's leather jerkin. He was drunk. His blond hair was a mess. "No coats of arms here. None at all."

"Good day, John. I've come to talk with your stepmother."

"Talk? No, you want to do more than that. Lots of men like you want to do more with her. You're not the first…"

"John!" snapped Rebecca. "Enough."

"I have a right to speak. This was my father's house and now it is mine." John Machyn lifted an earthenware flagon to his lips. "And a man can say what he likes in his own home."

"Shall we talk in the other room?" asked Clarenceux, glancing at Rebecca.

She tried a weak smile and led the way out of the hall and through into the workshop. "He's impossible," she muttered when Clarenceux drew close. "All he does is drink, swear, and complain. He has no manners. He pisses in the corner of the hall at night rather than go outside. I wish he would go back to sea."

"You would be welcome to stay at my house."

"You know I cannot. Nor would I want to." She still did not look at him.

"What is the matter, Rebecca? You are out of keeping with yourself. Tell me."

She sat down on one of the chests. "I am going away."

"Forever?"

"Probably. I don't expect we shall meet again. In fact, I hope we do not."

Clarenceux felt as if he had been punched in the stomach. "Why? What have I said or done? Have I neglected you? Is that the reason?"

Her eyes were sad. "It is nothing you have said or done. I can hardly say you have neglected me. I have no claim on a married gentleman like you. No, I have been glad of your attention. But we are both laboring under a great weight. You seem to be able to deal with it better than I."

"I do not understand. Do you mean we are under scrutiny in our personal lives? Or because of the document—the marriage agreement?"

Rebecca sighed. "Both. The document mostly. Other people know about it. The surviving Knights of the Round Table know, including my brother Robert. They all expect you to do something, Mr. Clarenceux. And in some ways, so do I. I am too vulnerable to continue living like this."

"I am the one who guards the document. I am far more vulnerable than you."

"But you are an important and well-connected man. There are people to whom you can turn for protection. I have no one. And when powerful people come into my house and ask me when you are going to proclaim the queen illegitimate, I have no answer. I wish I did. They talk to me so much; they tell me that allowing you to keep the document was a mistake. They talk of stealing it."

"What are you trying to say? That I should start some sort of rebellion, with no coherent plan or support, just to please a few disaffected supporters of the old religion? If they are so keen to foment change, let them say so openly. Let them risk their lives, and the lives of their families. I have too much to lose. And so have you."

"Oh, for the Lord's sake, keep your peace, Mr. Clarenceux. I do not want to hear another word. You are condemning me for the way I feel, for being weak as well as poor and useless."

He shook his head, unmoved. "You told me once you did not want to start a revolution; you just wanted to be safe in your own home. But now, that is not enough. You want a revolution and you want to be safe—you cannot have it both ways."

"Oh, Jesus Christ!" she yelled. "Go on, stab me some more. It seems you find it quite to your liking. And I, who took so many blows for you just six months ago, who went through all that in the hope that we would be safe…"

She started crying. Clarenceux instinctively wanted to comfort her but in her present mood he dared not touch her. He looked at her sitting on the chest, sobbing, and felt at a loss. He so wanted to make her smile again.

"Go. Go away—out of my house," said Rebecca. She glared at him through her tears. "Please, leave now."

Clarenceux looked at her and she held his gaze. He could see that she still held a love for him, but he could also see the strength of her conviction. She was doing this in spite of her feelings.

"Please, Mr. Clarenceux. Go."

Clarenceux moved toward the door. He paused beside her and put his hand on her shoulder. She did not say anything. Nor did she move. He then walked out of the room into the corridor, opened the door to the house, and closed it behind him as he emerged into the street.

Two boys were playing in the shadow of Mrs. Barker's house. It felt as if he had walked between two distant cities in an instant. Here he was looking on new faces and a brighter future. He had come with affection in his heart and he was leaving with a pain-filled hollow.

8

~

William Gray sat at a table in a tavern on Thames Street, a little to the east of the Tower of London. It was an inexpensive but respectable establishment, with cloths on the tables and good wine on display in marked barrels. The bread was good, and he ate it hungrily. Freshly baked white bread was something he missed at sea.

It was still before noon. Men were eating and drinking at the tables, talking in low voices. They were almost all gentlemen mariners: men who dressed well and looked at the sea as one vast opportunity. They transported their chests aboard, full of their most treasured belongings, and slept on mattresses in their own cabins. They had little to do with the penniless urchins who slept where they could in the shadows of the lower decks, before the mast. These men tended to be ruthless, selfish, and lustful. William Gray felt at home among them.

The tavern door opened and Gray found himself looking at the face of a man he had not seen for six years. He had lank black hair and a narrow face. His hose were of the loose, flouncy style and he was wearing a doublet and cape. Without invitation he sat down opposite Gray, looking at him.

"Nicholas Denisot," said Gray, chewing his bread. "What do you want, after all this time?"

"I've come to thank you for rescuing me from Calais."

"A little late," he said, still chewing.

"Even so. I did say that one day I would repay my debt. I have a task for you, one that will prove lucrative."

"Go on."

"My employer has an urgent need for two people to be transported to Southampton, a man and a woman. They are inconspicuous and socially unimportant, but they bear something of great value—inestimable value. I cannot tell you what it is. Suffice to say, my employer refers to it as 'the Catholic Treasure.'"

"And after I have taken them to Southampton?"

"That is all you have to do. Take them, as quickly as possible. If you set sail this afternoon you should arrive in four days."

"Five, with the wind coming up the Channel. How much?"

"Two hundred pounds. In gold. As long as you get them there within four days. Five at the most."

Gray stopped chewing. He stared at Denisot. "Why such a sum?"

"Two hundred is the maximum I am authorized to offer, no more. I could bargain with you but that would be a waste of time. The Catholic Treasure is a precious cargo. And you are to ask no questions of either the man or the woman. Nor are any of your men."

Gray was still unsure. "Who is my employer?"

"If anyone asks you, you are to say 'Percy Roy.' That is all you need to know."

Gray lifted his mazer of wine and took a draught. He turned the silver-mounted wooden cup between his fingers. "I cannot guarantee the weather. And as this is not ordinary business, I will want more than half in advance."

Denisot looked around and caught the taverner's attention. "More wine and another cup." He turned back to face Gray. "You are quite right. This is *not* ordinary business. If you guarantee you can set sail today, I will arrange delivery of one hundred and fifty in advance. A message has already gone ahead to Southampton for a local agent called James Parkinson, the captain of Calshot Fort, to look out for the Catholic Treasure on the tenth. You should fly three St. George's flags from the main mast as you come into the harbor and send the passengers ashore in a rowing boat. Captain Parkinson will confirm their safe arrival by a letter, and he will direct you to where in London you are to go to pick up the last fifty pounds. One word of warning, though: if you disappear with the passengers, it will not be in a court that my employer seeks redress."

The taverner placed the wine and cup in front of Denisot. Gray set his own cup firmly on the table and looked up. "Why me?"

Denisot shrugged and poured his wine. "Because I value what you did for me all those years ago. I am glad I can put this business your way. Also, I need a captain I can trust."

"Does your employer know who you really are?"

"I need a decision from you. Two hundred pounds—or would you like me to make inquiries elsewhere?"

"One hundred and fifty pounds in one hour. And another fifty on my return."

Denisot lifted his cup. "Let's drink to the wind being in your favor."

9

Clarenceux hung his hat and cloak on a hook and walked wearily up the stairs from his front door to his hall. Awdrey was there to greet him.

"How does the idea of becoming her majesty's ambassador to the Low Countries appeal to you?" she asked with a smile. "To take up a post in Antwerp in six weeks, to be exact?"

"Ambassador?" Clarenceux was astonished. Heralds were gentlemen but few gentlemen were of sufficient social rank to aspire to be diplomatic representatives. The nearest he had ever come to such a position was declaring war against France in Rheims, on behalf of Queen Mary. That was different. That was a matter of arms and war; it was natural it should fall to a herald. Negotiating with the Catholic Spanish rulers of the Protestant Low Countries was quite another thing.

Awdrey pushed her long golden hair back behind her ear. "I spoke with Lady Cecil today, at Cecil House. She told me that Sir William needs someone to sort out a dispute between the English Merchant Adventurers and the Company of Antwerp. The Spanish are preventing the English from trading, and the Dutch are similarly frustrated because they cannot get hold of the raw materials they need from England. Sir William needs someone who is experienced in international protocol, of a logical mind, loyal, and of sufficient rank to tell the merchants what they must do. Lady Cecil suggested you. Sir William thinks you would be ideal. He told me himself."

Clarenceux walked into the hall and called for Thomas to bring him some wine. Awdrey's excitement indicated that she expected to travel to Antwerp too. That was understandable: the commodities passing through the Low Countries these days made it a center of fashionable interest and conversation. But it would entail their elder daughter Annie having to have a personal tutor. Clarenceux himself would have to give up being a herald. He had only recently agreed with Garter King of Arms that Devon would be the subject of his next visitation. He would lose his position, and thus he would lose much of his income. No longer would he be able to ride off down to Chislehurst to see a friend when he chose to; nor would he be able to return to England at all until recalled by Sir William. If he was successful, who knows where he might be sent next. However, if he was not reappointed, he would lose his principal income. He were not like most ambassadors—able to retire to a country estate if all went wrong.

Clarenceux took a goblet from Thomas and sat on a form, leaning forward. He scratched his beard. The truth was he did not want to be a diplomatic representative—not if it came at the cost of everything he had achieved and enjoyed. But how could he refuse and not incur Cecil's displeasure? He sat there mulling over the problem in silence for some minutes.

"I know you will curse me for this, but the answer is no."

Awdrey looked at him through disbelieving eyes. "How can you be so dismissive? This is a wonderful opportunity!"

"To do what? Disrupt our family and way of life? To put an end to my work?"

"Your work as a herald is…Well, it is less important. Someone else can do it. This is national and prestigious; it benefits the whole commonwealth."

"My work as a herald is both national *and* prestigious," he replied firmly. "And not just anyone can do it. I do it well, better than anyone else. Just because you can't even describe our own coat of arms does not mean such things have no value."

"Your heraldry pays little, William. And it is demeaning to both of us. You could be so much more. You are fit, you are clever, and you are brave. You could be properly influential—not having to scrape around for whatever operations Sir William deigns to give you, or Robert Dudley, not that *he* gives you anything."

"Is that what this is about? You want me to be more influential and rich and unhappy because it would boost your pride and help you win the respect of well-connected friends like Lady Cecil? Well then, I have all the more reason to refuse."

Awdrey turned and faced the fireplace. "So, is that it? We are not going to Antwerp because you take more enjoyment and pride in drawing shields?"

Clarenceux got up. "I am going up to my study. To work."

He opened the door in the corner and walked briskly up the stairs. He opened his study door equally abruptly and cursed as he sat down at his writing table. How had it happened? One moment, not so long ago, he had been very happy. Now it seemed that, without having done anything wrong, he was balanced on the blade of a knife, feeling the pain.

He sat back, growing calmer, and made himself think about the situation from Awdrey's position. It was true; he did hold back from high office—for the same reason that he did not want to do anything with the Percy-Boleyn marriage agreement: he wanted those around him to be safe and secure. His very possession of the document worked at his mind in such a way as to make him a little on edge, all the time, and Awdrey had to bear the brunt of his bad moods.

But would he be any happier if he did seek a position of influence? Would he actually get one suited to his abilities? Would he be any happier if he had more money and more responsibilities—would Awdrey? Perhaps he would take the position in Antwerp only to find that Awdrey hated being there. Few people would speak English and she knew no foreign languages. Perhaps her youthful enthusiasm for being elsewhere would diminish all too soon. But there would be nothing left in England for them to return to.

Then there was that other problem. Clarenceux's faith in the Holy Catholic Church of Rome had become impossible for him to profess publicly. Perhaps that was what Sir William wanted? The proposal was a test of his religion. In sending him to Antwerp, the Cecils had a hidden agenda: to force him and Awdrey to accept the Protestant way.

Clarenceux left his study and went down into the hall. He called for Awdrey: no answer came. He walked to the other staircase and out onto the landing. One flight led down to the service rooms at the back of the house: the buttery, kitchens, and stores. The other led up to the sleeping chambers. He went up.

Awdrey was lying on their bed, facedown.

"That offer is not what it seems," he said.

Awdrey did not reply. Mildred started crying in the next room. They both listened as Joan, Awdrey's maid, comforted the infant.

"If I accept Sir William's offer, our religion will be under examination. Men will watch us in church, to see if we abide by the Protestant rites or those of the old religion."

"But Catholics and Protestants live side by side in Antwerp."

"We will not be able to. As her majesty's representatives, we will be expected to observe the rites authorized by her government. Exclusively."

Awdrey remained quiet.

"Few people speak English in Antwerp," he added. "Very few."

"I was happy for you," she replied, looking up. "Did that deserve such a flat rebuttal? To want you to be more important than you are? To be recognized as a leader?"

"No, it did not. I am sorry. I did not mean to upset you."

She smiled weakly, tears in her eyes. "You never do. But you are so forceful when you are passionate about something. It does not take much for you to frighten me." She moved across the bed, allowing him to sit beside her. "I can see the religious problem. But I still wish we could go there."

"Perhaps we will, one day."

10

Rogation Sunday, May 7

Clarenceux was awake early with the sound of wind and rain. He slipped out of the bed and opened the shutters on his side of the chamber. There was no glass here; only the front windows of the house were glazed. The wind spat rain in his face. Dark clouds above the heavy downpour were moving rapidly across the sky. He left the shutters part closed to stop the rain entering.

Awdrey blinked, sat up, and rubbed her eyes. She let her arms fall across the linen counterpane and watched as he poured water from the ewer into the basin to wash his face and hands.

"Good morning," she said.

"Good morning." He heard a child laughing in the next chamber. "That was a good night's sleep."

"We needed it," she replied. "You are often grumpy when you are tired."

"Thankfully I am married to the most understanding woman in the world."

He took off his shirt and threw it to one side. Lifting a fresh one from his clothes chest, he pulled it over his head, and took a pair of clean hosen. His velvet doublet was laid over a pole nearby. He buckled his shoes, tied his lace ruff, and went through to check on their daughters—just as a crack of thunder split the distant sky.

Mildred was awake and sitting up in her cot, trying to climb out. Annie was out of bed, playing with two wooden dolls on the floor.

"Good morning, sir," Annie said when she saw him. "Was that thunder?"

"Yes, Annie. It looks as though the Lord wishes that we get wet on our way to church. But go and see your mother." He lifted Mildred from her cot and let her walk unsteadily through to the next chamber, holding his finger. He saw Annie climbing onto the bed, cuddling her mother as she lay there, listening to the rain. "Good girl, Millie, walk to your mother. That's good." A flash of lightning lit up the chamber for a moment. He counted to twelve before he heard the thunder. "Annie, come now, it is time we should be getting ready for church."

"Do we have to go?" Annie whined. "It is raining."

"Yes, we most certainly do have to go. It's Rogation Sunday. And it is the Lord's will that it rain today."

"What is Rog…Rogazing—that day you said?"

"It is the day when we ask for God's mercy and for Him to bless the corn in the fields and the animals in the pastures. And people who properly obey God's laws do not eat but follow solemn processions led by priests in purple clothes. We ask that the good Lord sends rain, so our crops will grow well."

She looked up at him. "Will you wear purple clothes?"

Clarenceux smiled. "No, Annie, I am not a priest."

Joan, the maidservant, came up the stairs from where she had been preparing the kitchen fire ready for the cook later. She made a small bow. "Godspeed, sir. How is it with you?"

"Good day, Joan. All is well," answered Clarenceux. "We are just getting ready."

A shutter banged in the wind on a house nearby. "Can we wear purple clothes?" Annie asked Awdrey.

An hour later Clarenceux led his wife, two children, and maidservant in their traveling copes through the hard rain and wind to the nearby church of St. Bride, just off Fleet Street. As a parish church it was Protestant, but as it was their parish church, Clarenceux felt his family needed to make an appearance. He knew that those who did not—"recusants" as they were called—only drew attention to themselves. They were all dressed in their best clothes, even little Mildred. Thomas, the cook, and the stable boys stayed at the house. Someone had to. Thieves thanked God for church services.

11

In London the rain was a mere inconvenience. It meant that there would be mud in the streets tomorrow. Women who had hoped that they could have dried their laundry would be disappointed. Messengers knew they would have to ride a little slower. In the Channel, however, the weather meant hardship and death. As it was a Sunday, most fishing vessels were neither at sea nor about to set out. But for a few ships, including the *Davy*, the weather spelled danger. The sea heaved in great waves that left boats bobbing like corks on the surface. The rain prevented sailors from seeing the rigging clearly—and if they fell from a height onto the deck, they could expect to break their backs or necks. If they fell into the sea, the chances of them ever grabbing hold of a rope were very slim. Most men and boys who fell overboard in a storm were not missed until after the danger had abated.

Off the Kent coast, William Gray knew it was going to be tight. The timbers of the *Davy* groaned as he wiped the spray of a wave from his face and yelled at the boys and men in the rigging. But moment by moment, as he swayed with the deck and cursed the clouds, he saw that his change of direction was slowly bringing him nearer to safe harbor. The people he had to deliver to Southampton would be very sick, but that would be the limit of their problems. As soon as the storm abated, he would press on, hoping to reach Southampton on the tenth.

One hundred and fifty miles southwest, things were very different for the *Nightingale*. A galleass built thirty years earlier, she was nearing the end of her useful life. She had been built in England, captured by the Scots, recaptured by the English in 1544 and converted into a galleon, then captured by the French in 1552, and finally seized by Raw Carew in the Bay of Biscay two years ago. Now her deck leaked, her hull was so patched as to render her barely seaworthy, and her hold was waist-deep in water. The eight cannon she carried were worth more than the rest of the boat. That was why Carew particularly wanted to bring her ashore in Southampton. It was one of the few ports where he could dock her and disembark the cannon without her majesty's officers arresting him. The only problem was Captain James Parkinson, the constable of Southampton Castle and captain of Calshot Fort. He exercised a loose extortion business on the town, charging merchants' ships a toll for passing Calshot into Southampton Water. That was the way of things in these parts. For Carew it was both a good thing and a bad one. It meant a vicious rule from an unpredictable brigand with royal protection, but this was the safest port for miles around. The next one he could call home was near-lawless Dartmouth. Only in these two places could he offload ordnance and find a purchaser who would ask no questions.

Now, as the thunder rolled above them, the main mast snapped, crashing down on the deck, and Carew knew that the *Nightingale* would never see land again. Loosening the rope binding him to the sterncastle, he let go of the whipstaff and tried to get to the hatch. Suddenly the vessel heeled to one side; he slipped and was almost washed overboard as a great wave crashed down on the deck. Grabbing hold of a rope that had fallen with the main mast, he held on until the ship righted itself, and scrambled back to the hatch. Crawling inside, into the darkness of the main deck, with the wind still howling above his head, he stumbled toward the center of the boat, feeling his way past frightened people to where the main mast traveled down through the main deck to the orlop deck below.

"Are there any lights left?" he shouted, holding on to the metal ring around the base of the main mast, where lanterns were normally fastened.

"They went out the first time we heeled over."

There was a flash of lightning from above. "Is there anyone on the deck below?"

No one answered. All around were cries and groans. "Is the ship sinking?" called a woman's voice. "What are we going to do?"

Carew could hear the note of panic. "I'm going down to make sure there's no one below," he said calmly. In reality his mind was filled with two words: the name of a ship that had haunted him all his life, the name of the ship on which his father had drowned. *Mary Rose*. But now was not the moment to let his fear overcome him.

He felt his way beyond the stem of the main mast and started crawling toward the opening down to the orlop deck when another mighty wave smashed against the side of the vessel. She heeled over perilously, sending people, belongings, flagons, swords, platters, stools, lanterns, musical instruments, chests, and everything else on the main deck crashing to the port side. A demi-culverin broke away from its fastening and slid back, crushing a man against the side, breaking his pelvis and leg so that he started screaming in agony and fear. This time the ship did not right herself. She was listing, at about twenty degrees to port.

Carew cursed and pressed on to find the hatch down to the orlop deck. Pulling it open, he shouted down into the darkness. "Anyone down here?" No one answered. He could still hear the wind from above but there was another, more ominous sound—oak timbers grinding against one another and the rushing and splashing of the sea. Reaching out and feeling the ladder, and gripping it to make sure it was still firm, he started to descend. Five steps down his foot plunged into cold water.

The ship took another battering, sending her further over so that she was now listing at about thirty degrees. Nothing could save her now. "Is anyone down here?" yelled Carew. "If there is, call out." Another wave shook the ship. Carew wiped his soaked face and started to climb back up into the main deck. "Gather above," he called to everyone there. "We are abandoning this ship. Take nothing with you that you are not already holding. The ship is sinking. Gather on"—a wave crashed through the hatch, soaking him and filling his mouth with salt water—"on deck."

"Captain, I can't move," yelled the man whose leg had been smashed by the cannon. "Don't let me drown, please don't let me drown, for the love of God, please, Mr. Carew! Don't leave me here!"

Supporting himself by holding on to the side of the ship, Carew shouted back, "I have no love for God, Stephen, but I do for you, as I do for all my men." He hoped the man would not see him draw the knife in the dim light. He bent forward and, holding the man's cheek close to his own, he kissed him—then cut his throat.

Another wave broke over the ship and Carew was flung across the man's dying body and the frame of the demi-culverin. He pushed himself back and got to his feet, still holding the knife. He sheathed it and steadied himself against the wall of the ship as he watched men climb the ladder up onto the deck for what they knew would be the last time. He waited for the last to go. And waited too long.

The fear crept up on him faster than the water as he leaned against the mast. The dark sea swamped his eyes and sank through his mouth and nostrils, filling every crevice of his body and stopping him breathing: a sea of pure fear. The next moment he was drowning in that same fear, his body neither at the surface nor at the depths of the sea, lashing out, struggling against his father's fate, which had washed over him ever since he was four years of age.

Another wave broke through and struck his face, bringing him to his senses. It washed around his feet—but then he realized it was not the wave. The water had risen through the orlop deck and was sucking the ship down. "Are all gone, all from down here?" He waited a moment longer and then jumped for the ladder as the eddies of water swept around the mast, sending the chests and wooden things floating up behind him.

The ship lurched suddenly as another wave broke over the deck. It was listing now at sixty degrees. Carew could see men in the water. Hugh Dean had taken one of the skiffs and was hauling them aboard. But each skiff held only ten men—twelve at the most. And the ship was fast disappearing beneath the waves. Carew looked across the deck and saw the main mast floating now, with half the ship submerged. Men were clinging on to it, waves crashing over them.

Carew could swim. Most seamen regarded it as bad luck to learn, and few non-mariners even thought about it, but Carew was different. He loved the water and had learned as a boy, delighting in showing off his swimming skills. Now he plunged toward the main mast and, reaching below the water, he unsheathed his knife and cut the stays and ropes that fastened it, allowing it to float free. Then he swam further and reached the foremast, where the ship's ax was fastened. Carew yanked it free and, sitting astride the mast, started to chop at the wood. Being Norwegian pine, the wood chipped easily, but the high waves crashing down threatened to sweep him away. The half-submerged vessel rose and wallowed ten or fifteen feet every time. Still Carew chopped and cut, reaching a frenzy of cutting and hacking as he watched the *Nightingale* descend further beneath the water. Lower she went, sinking and then higher on a wave—only to plummet down with groans of timbers as the futtocks splintered. Several planks had already come away from the half deck of the sterncastle. Still Carew chopped, hearing the cries of his men around him in the water, clinging to the rigging, in constant danger of being washed away.

The ship was almost gone; most of the deck was below the waterline, the foremast lifting out of the sea and the hull breaking up with every wave. Carew continued to chop at the deep scar in the mast. As he did so he saw a shape move to his left: Kahlu was swimming back to him. "Grab the rope!" Carew yelled, pointing to the trailing rope of the foremast topsail. Another wave surged and crashed over them but still Carew brought down the ax as hard as he could. The forecastle disappeared beneath the next wave. Carew tumbled forward into the water as more planks split from the sinking ship. He swam as hard as he could away from it, fearful of being dragged down. As he swam he thought of Kahlu still holding the rope—Kahlu, who came from another continent, who could not speak but had so much to say. He knew that Kahlu would keep on holding that rope even if it dragged him down to the seabed. At that moment his hand struck flesh and his head broke the surface. Kahlu was indeed still holding the rope. The mast had cracked under his weight at the last instant, as the ship had heaved and gone down.

Treading water, Carew put his arm around Kahlu and shouted in his ear, "Thank you, my friend." They looked at the place of the sinking. The heavy guns, the ballast, and the brick ovens in the galley had dragged down the water-filled hull, but much wood remained afloat. Planks were everywhere. A stool bobbed to the surface as a wave crashed over them. Then a small pipe appeared. Carew grabbed it and stuck it in his mouth, clenching it between his teeth as he swam to the nearest skiff, which was already heavily overloaded. Reaching it, he looked around again.

The amount of wood and the number of corpses that floated before his eyes was shocking and saddening. It seemed that twenty dead men and women were rising and falling with the waves. Already the sea had scattered the bodies of those who had been so close to him in life. Time and the sea were washing them all to their separate oblivions. Another huge wave swept down. But as it descended he caught sight of the other skiff, with just six or seven men aboard. And the main mast about fifty yards to his right.

Another great wave splashed over them. Carew knew that if he did not bring them all together now, they would be washed away. He took the pipe from his teeth and blew it. Water poured out and just a squeak of sound. He shouted instead. "Hugh! Take this boat and lash the foremast to it. I'm going to the other boat to gather in the main mast. We must build from whatever is left floating." As Dean nodded to show he had understood, Carew started to swim through the cold waves toward the other skiff, which was drifting farther and farther away.

12

Thomas opened the front door and Clarenceux let Annie step in first. She took her muddy shoes off as instructed, and ran up the stairs. Joan, who had been carrying Mildred, put her down on the bottom-most stair and let her start climbing. Clarenceux followed behind Mildred, patiently. When she reached the top, he clapped at her achievement, smiled at Awdrey, and then went up to his study.

He looked at the manuscript on his desk, to remind him of where he was in his heraldic work, and crossed the chamber. He lifted the *chitarra* in one hand and strummed the strings with the other. A discordant series of low notes rang out.

All his thinking froze. It cracked, like a mirror, into jagged edges.

He struck the strings again, only to hear the same discordant noise. Lifting down the instrument, not caring for its delicacy, he pulled off the grille that covered the sound hole and felt for the document. It had gone.

He trembled, uncertain what to do. Then he threw the instrument to the floor and stamped on the rounded wooden back. Sinking to his knees, he turned the pieces over. *Oh Lord! Have mercy upon me! Jesus Christ, Lord, restore to me this thing, I implore Thee. If I have ever sinned against Thee in any way that deserves punishment, please let it be in some other manner.*

He crossed himself. All the people who knew he owned the document were Catholics. That included all the Knights of the Round Table—all the men whom Henry Machyn had given a knightly identity and enlisted to help guard it. Two of their companions had died for the cause: Daniel Gyttens and Henry Machyn himself. Five of them had been imprisoned for protecting it. Several had demanded that he hand it over to them. Nicholas Hill had been one of these, or "Sir Reynold" as he had been known. James Emery, "Sir Yvain," had been another. Rebecca Machyn's brother, Robert Lowe, "Sir Owain," had similarly been unhappy at the prospect of Clarenceux holding on to the document.

Then he remembered Rebecca Machyn. Upset and dismissive. Running away. He crossed himself again. *No, no, let it not be.* But even as he whispered, he knew he was deceiving himself with prayer. Of all the people who knew he owned the document, she was the most vulnerable—she had said so herself. The Knights of the Round Table all knew she was very close to Clarenceux. They knew that he would confide in her. She knew the layout of his house—the whole idea of hiding the document in a stringed instrument had been hers. And she had mentioned that people had suggested to her that the document be stolen.

Clarenceux clenched his fist and hit the floor. She had not just taken something and given it away; she had destroyed their mutual trust. She had set aside the decision that they had reached together—that this document was too dangerous to fall into the hands of Catholic plotters. It would result in civil war, in the burning of men and women for heresy. But she had given in to the pressure of others. She had put them above him. The protection he had offered her—that was nothing. No wonder she had said she did not want to see him again.

He shook his head in disbelief. The Knights of the Round Table would expect him publicly to endorse this document and declare it authentic in his capacity as a herald. Even if they failed in their plot to remove Elizabeth from the throne, they would implicate him. They would name him in their confessions. He could see his house being searched again, his possessions destroyed. He could see Walsingham demanding that he be tried for treason. He could see his wife forced to go into hiding with their daughters.

I cannot do it. Not again. I am not strong enough. Not now. Tears began to form in his eyes. He hated this weakness in himself but it was undeniable. He was crying. He struck the floor again, nausea growing in his stomach.

But how could she have broken into this house? She must have had help. Where was Thomas?

Clarenceux got to his feet. He breathed deeply, wiped his eyes on his sleeve, and walked to the staircase. He descended rapidly. At the foot he pushed the door open and stepped into the hall.

"Thomas!"

A few seconds later he heard the old man's footsteps. Thomas entered. "Yes, Mr. Clarenceux?"

"Who came here this morning? While I was at church?"

"No one. I can assure you."

Clarenceux struck the wall with his fist, fury rising within him. "No, someone did!" Then he recalled that he had not checked the manuscript the previous night because of his argument with Awdrey. "Who came here yesterday, while I was out?"

Thomas frowned. "Sir, after you left in the morning, no one came here. Mistress Harley went with the children and Joan to call on Lady Cecil. When they had gone, I went with the stable boys to order a delivery of new hay."

"No one called?"

"I was not here, sir. But as far as I know—"

"How long was this house unattended?"

Thomas considered his answer carefully. "An hour at most."

"Could somebody have entered during that time?"

Thomas did not answer. His face was growing whiter. "Sir, I made sure everything was locked, as per your instructions. The front door and the back."

"I am asking, could somebody have broken in?"

"Sir, if someone wanted to break in, they could have picked the lock. A good locksmith has no great difficulty opening a warded lock."

"I know that, Thomas—I know about skeleton keys. But something has been stolen from this house. Something very precious."

"Is it one of your books, sir?"

"No! It is not one of my books. I was keeping a…a document." He put his hands to his head. "All our lives are at risk, Thomas. We must disappear again, all of us—like last December. I thought all that was over. But I…I am going to be involved in a treasonable plot. If I am alive in another week's time, it will only be by the grace of God."

Clarenceux glanced at the end of the hall. Awdrey was standing there. "Does that mean we are not going to Antwerp?" she asked.

"Damn it, woman, no, we are *not* going to Antwerp. We are going to run for our lives."

13

In a chamber of his house near the Tower, Francis Walsingham sat studying the code. Being a man who felt the cold, there was a fire in the hearth beside him.

He had begun systematically, noting the number of times each letter appeared. But then he had realized something. The letter C appeared by itself, and in twos, threes, fours, fives, sixes, sevens and eights. Four C's might be a single letter or they might be a combination of two double C's. But eight C's could not be four CC's. These eight combinations represented four separate letters or words at most. And given that DCC- appeared so often, CC was probably a letter. But he had written down a list of all the three-letter and four-letter words he could think of, and none of them fitted in a way that allowed him to make sense of any other part of the message.

He started to see more problems. Had this been written by someone who spelled more phonetically than he? Was it even in English? This was a Catholic plot, after all: Latin was more likely, or French. Castilian was possible too. The commas did not seem to make sense either, being too close together in places. Indeed, that suggested the letters were words, which rendered his theory about the various combinations of C void.

Frustrated, he screwed up the piece of paper he was working on and threw it into the fire. He closed his eyes and tried to remain calm. After a minute he reopened them, took another piece of paper, and started again. This time he wrote a list of all the short Latin words he knew.

14

Clarenceux walked to the window. "It is not all over," he exclaimed. He looked out at the other people in the puddle-filled street: a milk girl with pails on a yoke across her shoulders coming into the city. A water carrier followed her, leading his tired pony, mud being flung from the wheels. A man with a cart full of dung was heading in the opposite direction. There was no sign of anyone watching the house.

He turned back to face Awdrey. "I did not want to alarm you or worry you unnecessarily, but a document was left in my possession. A valuable document—one that proves that our current queen is illegitimate and an unsuitable woman to be on the throne. Needless to say, there are those who would very much like to take possession of it. Someone now has."

"But who? Who would dare to come into this house and steal it? Who knew you had it? And how did they get in?"

"I am asking myself the same questions. And I have only one answer: Widow Machyn. She knew I had the document; she even knew where I kept it—in that Italian *chitarra* in my study. Her late husband gave it to me. I am sure that it is his surviving friends who are behind this, not Rebecca herself. They call themselves the Knights of the Round Table. They have not forgiven me for not using the document to start a revolution against Queen Elizabeth."

"Why did you not tell me these things?"

"Because I did not want you to be in danger, or even to know we had such a dangerous thing in our possession."

Awdrey shuddered. "I can't go through all that again. Not again. Our house wrecked, our possessions…" She turned to the old stern-faced servant. "Thomas, did you see anything? Were you not here?"

The man shook his head. "Mistress Harley, if I had been here, they would not have entered. At least, they would have had to kill me first. I took the boys to Snow's tenement to buy hay for the stables. I had no idea that anyone would even think of entering, still less steal from Mr. Clarenceux. But locks are easy to pick. If the thief came in by the back door, if he knew what he was after, he could have been out within a few minutes."

"Not 'he'—'she,'" Clarenceux frowned. "I saw Rebecca Machyn yesterday, and she was not at all normal. She told me she was going away—even said that people had been encouraging her to steal the document."

"Sir, with respect, she might simply have told those same people where to look. She did not necessarily steal it herself or even sanction the theft."

Clarenceux nodded. He glanced at Awdrey and knew what she was thinking. *You should not have trusted Rebecca so much.* He knew because she had been proved right.

"What now?" she asked.

"Well, I am now a traitor in the eyes of those who would have Mary Stuart proclaimed queen, and a traitor in the eyes of Elizabeth's Protestant supporters. It is likely this house will be searched as soon as the authorities realize where I stand. Most searches take place after dusk, when people are at home and alone. We need to be prepared."

"I cannot believe this is happening," muttered Awdrey.

"Awdrey, it *is* happening. I am going to be arrested and tried. Our possessions, goods, and chattels will be forfeit. If the searchers come this evening…" Clarenceux paused. "The Lord preserve us. Thomas, I want you to leave now. Go to your nephew's house. You cannot stay here."

"Mr. Clarenceux, I intend to stand by you."

"Thomas, the best outcome to this situation I can imagine is that you and I are alive in a month's time. I can ensure that that will be at least partly the case by sending you away now. There is nothing you can do for me here."

"Sir, I am disappointed to hear you say that."

"Thomas, old friend. I want you to live. The theft of that document may well cost me my life." Clarenceux looked him in the eye. "One day you may serve me again. But not now."

"I am not going, Mr. Clarenceux," Thomas told him obstinately. "I will always serve you."

"If you are so determined, then look after my wife and daughters." He glanced at Awdrey. "I want you to go to your sister's house in Devon."

She looked at him steadily. "So far? I would rather stay with Lady Cecil. Or even your friend Julius."

"You do not understand how serious this is. People will use you and the girls to get to me. Walsingham knows about Summerhill— he has sent men to search Julius's house in the past. And what reason are you going to give Lady Cecil for seeking Sir William's protection? That I have lost a politically valuable document? Sir

William himself charged me with guarding it with my life. You must go further."

"I am not going further than one day's ride," Awdrey declared.

Clarenceux stared at her. He thought of all the dangers in the city and how he needed to confront certain people and how they might retaliate against his family. Julius was at least wholly trustworthy. "Very well. Thomas will escort you down to Chislehurst tomorrow morning. Take Joan with you. Take all the horses too. If I need a mount, I will hire one. Pack in readiness now. I will write to Julius and explain. I'll tell him I will join you when I can."

15

That afternoon, Clarenceux took down his sword from above the fireplace in his study. He often said that guns were of little use: fire them once and you have to spend the next five minutes reloading them, during which time your assailant might run you through with the meanest weapon. It was easy to say that in a tavern conversation. Now, considering the danger, he wished he had the equal of the armaments that people might use against him. If someone drew a loaded pistol on him, he would have no defense but to hope the wheel did not ignite the gunpowder or that the person aiming it missed.

He put the sword back regretfully. He had to walk across London. Carrying a sword would be foolish, enough to get himself arrested by a constable. Instead he fastened a sheathed dagger with a foot-long blade onto the left-hand side of his belt, and a shorter-bladed knife to his right. They would be concealed by his cloak. He took a deep breath and mentally braced himself for what he had to do, then went downstairs and out of the house.

He walked quickly across the Fleet, stepping between the puddles, toward Ludgate. Normally the center of the street was a packed line of horse dung, trodden into the mud; now, after the heavy rain, it combined with the clay soil to give the street a rich, earthy smell.

Cartwheels had churned up the surface. In such conditions anyone of quality would normally insist on riding or being carried in a chair, to preserve their clean clothes. Clarenceux was too anxious for such niceties. When a cart passed, flicking up mud, he simply walked faster.

Passing under the old stone arch of Ludgate, he wanted to run to his destination. But he knew that would draw attention to himself. He threaded his way between the people, walking through the lanes and alleys, beneath rows and rows of houses, all darkened with the upper stories projecting out over the lower ones. The barrels that were meant to be full of water in case of fire were mostly full of refuse, empty, or leaking out into trampled muddy patches of ground. Some alleyways were littered with detritus where people passing along had dropped parts of pies or bones, and the local householder had not cleared up outside his front door. In places people had strewn old rushes from their halls across the street. Clarenceux carried on through the noisome foulness toward Little Trinity Lane, mainly along the back streets, always avoiding the eyes of people walking toward him.

At the door to Rebecca Machyn's house, he drew his day-to-day knife and banged hard with the hilt three times on the oak. He waited barely twenty seconds and then knocked again. And again. There was no sound from within. He stepped back into the street and looked up, to see if anyone was watching from upstairs. But if so, they avoided him. He knocked on the door again.

He knew that, when watchmen had gone looking for Rebecca in the past, she had taken refuge on the other side of the road, at Mrs. Barker's house. He glanced at that proud building, wondering if she was over there now—perhaps even observing him.

Still no answer.

After another minute he walked to the end of Little Trinity Lane. Then, counting his steps—one hundred and fifty—he turned right at the end and then right again, counting the same number of paces down Garlick Hill. When he reached the correct spot, he found the nearest passageway through to a backyard tenement. Many of the old merchants' properties here were subdivided, due to the heavy overcrowding, with ramshackle houses built in adjoining yards, each containing one or two rooms. He went down an untidy alley, with an overflowing trough of water and puddles beneath the eaves of the shingle-covered roofs. An old woman was sitting spinning in the doorway of a single-story lean-to. He nodded to her politely.

"My good woman, is that the back of the Machyn house?"

She looked at him suspiciously. "What do you want to know for?"

"My name is William Harley, Clarenceux King of Arms. I am a friend of Rebecca Machyn. She is sick, taken to her bed, and no one is looking after her. Her stepson is a wastrel, so I am worried that the front door is being left unanswered."

"'Tis indeed Goodwife Machyn's. And I know the young man. Drunkard, he is. It sounds as if it is a good deed that you do—and I can see you're no thief, sir."

Clarenceux thanked the woman, then shifted a barrel to enable him to climb over the wall and up on to the roof of the outhouse, making sure the weapons underneath his cloak remained concealed. After jumping down into Rebecca's yard, where he was greeted by the stench of the privy, he unlatched the rear door and entered the house.

It was silent. The storeroom at the back was where the food was kept: a sack of oats, another smaller one of flour. There were turnips and apples, leeks and onions. Hanging up on a hook were the thin remains of a flitch of bacon, most of which had been consumed.

"Hello? Rebecca? John? Are you here?"

He went into the hall. The ash on the hearth was not even warm. An empty wooden tankard and bowl stood on the table, with crumbs of bread strewn across the surface. There were two old candle pricks there too, and a rushlight holder. A pottery wine flask, covered in wicker, lay on its side on the floor. The rushes needed changing.

Clarenceux started to look around the hall systematically. There was no proper paneling, only a section in one corner that had remained when most of the original wainscoting had been removed. The walls had been whitewashed and were bare, except for Henry's painted cloths and a crucifix. There was a lidless chest of cookware by the fireplace, full of old chafing dishes and skillets, brass pans, and bashed pewterware. Apart from that there was only one other chest. He lifted the lid and looked through the contents: a rolled-up old shirt, a blanket, several towels and tablecloths, and two old books in which Henry Machyn had written some heraldic notes. In addition, there were some old wooden toys, a linen sheet painted as a St. George's flag, some dice, a couple of wooden board games, and a pipe. A cursory inspection was enough for Clarenceux to be sure that the document was not in this chest. Nowhere else in the hall looked likely.

He went through to Henry Machyn's old workshop at the front of the house. Nothing had changed since his visit the previous day. The four large chests were still there, in the dim light. Clarenceux pulled back the shutters and lifted the lid of one. He had presumed they were Rebecca's possessions, ready for her departure; but inside were the old tools of Henry Machyn's trade as a merchant tailor. There were scissors and knives, rulers and various scraps of cloth. The next chest he opened contained rolls of black cloth and tenterhooks for hanging the same. There were also a couple of books showing the heraldic designs used by members of the nobility and gentry, whose arms Henry had been paid to depict at their funerals. A third chest was full of candles, many of wax and good quality. The last held rolled-up lengths of linen.

Clarenceux climbed the stairs and went into the front chamber, above the workshop. It was almost empty, except only for a large old featherbed, unmade, with sheets that were so creased and soiled they were disgusting. There was also a sea chest in the corner, which obviously belonged to John Machyn. Clarenceux ignored it and went into the back chamber, directly above the hall. Here there was a small fireplace with firedogs and some skillets and other cooking apparatus. A small bed was set against the whitewashed wall opposite the fire; a table and a chair stood next to the rear window, which was unglazed. Candlesticks and pewterware adorned the table, and bellows, tongs, two low stools, and andirons were neatly arranged in front of the fire. The shutters were ajar, and Clarenceux could see out over the yard. A chest in the corner was full of neatly folded, clean bed linen. Another chest held Rebecca's personal linen and dresses. On the topmost sheet in the clothes chest was a book—a copy of the New Testament in English. He recalled that her late husband had taught her to read. In a small wall cupboard was a box containing needles and thread.

Clarenceux was perplexed. The house was not well kept but nor was it falling down. Many families were crammed into single rooms in and around this part of the city. Here, Rebecca and John Machyn both had space. Her living quarters seemed to have shrunk to this single room: she cooked and ate, read and slept in here. Downstairs had been largely abandoned to John Machyn and the chest full of memories of another era. But there were signs of a modest wealth, such as the books and pewterware—all of which were worth money. There were candles and a great deal of linen: these too could have been sold. It gave Clarenceux the impression that Rebecca had not been entirely honest with him, for she was not as short of money as she claimed.

He felt the mattress of the bed for any sign of the document but found none. He then embarked on a thorough search of her chamber; it was not there. Eventually he gave up and went up to the top floor. This was dim and did not contain much. There was an old cradle, an old broken bedstead, a loom, some worn-out curtains for a bed, a broken chair, and a cot. A chest in a corner turned out to have nothing but old coverlets and blankets in it: a spider crawled across the topmost one as Clarenceux opened the lid.

There was nothing here. She had abandoned the house. She had abandoned everything.

She had abandoned him.

16

Clarenceux did not go to bed until very late. He waited up long after Awdrey had gone to sleep, fearful that Walsingham's men would come to search the house. When he finally did retire, he did not sleep soundly. His mind shifted between horrible illusions and terrible realizations. In the early hours, long after the candle above had spluttered out, he rose and felt his way downstairs. He had no wish to wake Thomas, who was sleeping in the hall. He sat in the kitchen, by the small light of the glowing coals of the fire.

Lady Percy, the dowager countess of Northumberland, was the person most on his mind. Of all the people who knew he had the document, and how powerful it was, she was the most likely person to have ordered it to be stolen. He and Rebecca had visited her at Sheffield Manor just before Christmas. She had exhorted him to use the document—and had given him money in the belief that he would do so. She was so bitter about her treatment at the hands of Henry VIII, and so coldheartedly jealous over Lord Percy's affections for Anne Boleyn, that Clarenceux knew she would have been angry to learn that he had done nothing. And she was not a woman to be left angry.

Lady Percy had shown a fondness for Rebecca too. She liked

strong-minded women. Perhaps Rebecca had gone to Sheffield Manor with the document? Maybe at Lady Percy's direction?

Now, as he gazed at the embers of the fire, Clarenceux acknowledged that he had overlooked Lady Percy. She knew what was going on, surely; she certainly knew about the document and the Knights of the Round Table. She had spies and contacts with Queen Mary in Scotland. Most of all, she knew the identity of Sir Percival—the one so-called Knight who was the linchpin of the secret organization. Not even he, Clarenceux, knew that. He suspected that she could activate and instruct the remaining Knights whenever she felt like doing so. The distance from London to Sheffield had meant that Clarenceux had not taken her into account. Now he saw that she was like a poisonous snake lying hidden, waiting for its prey.

Getting up from beside the fire, he poured himself a large draught of wine then gulped it down, hoping it would help him sleep. He would go and see all the surviving Knights, he decided, starting the following day.

17

Monday, May 8

James Emery's house was in Huggin Alley, which ran between Little Trinity Lane and Huggin Lane, almost directly opposite Painter Stainers' Hall. It was a modest merchant's house, not as prestigious a building as Mrs. Barker's nearby, having none of the carvings on the projecting first-floor beams and much less glazing. Nevertheless, it was well kept. It had not been divided into tenements and had been maintained by its occupier with its old stained glass, carved stone fireplace, polished iron chandeliers, and painted wainscoting.

It was late morning. Bright sunlight was drying out the mud of the previous day's downpour. Clarenceux was wearing his longest cloak, which reached almost to the ground. He had strapped his sword beneath. When he knocked, an elderly manservant came to the door.

"Good day to you," Clarenceux said. "I wish to speak to Mr. Emery."

The man frowned. "You are not welcome here, Mr. Clarenceux. I would have thought you would have known better than to come."

"As I said, I wish to speak to Mr. Emery. Unless he would prefer that I shout out what I have to say from down here in the street, you had better admit me."

"Mr. Clarenceux, I really—" But he got no further than that. Clarenceux pushed past him and stepped into the house. The elderly man tried to block his way, but to no avail.

"Is he upstairs, in the hall?" Clarenceux looked at the man and judged from the lack of response that he was. He turned and headed up the stairs, climbing two at a time.

James Emery was gray haired, about ten years older and five inches shorter than Clarenceux. He was seated at a table, eating alone, with a book open beside him. Hearing the heavy footsteps, he threw his napkin onto the table and rose to his feet.

"What are you doing here?" he asked, seeing Clarenceux. "I will not have you in—"

"Where is Rebecca Machyn and where is the Percy-Boleyn marriage agreement?" demanded Clarenceux, striding forward.

"You should not have come here."

"Damn what I should and shouldn't do. The very fact you say I should not have come here makes me certain that this is exactly the place to be. Now, where is she and where is the document?"

"I know neither of those things, and that is the truth."

"But you know who is behind this. You know why she has gone and who is advising her."

Emery remained silent.

"I thought as much." Clarenceux walked over to the table and glanced at the bright plate and the meat on it, the wine flask and the bowl of last season's apples and pears beside it. The elderly man-servant entered. Ignoring him, Clarenceux turned back to the table, lifted the flask, and took a swig. "Sit down," he said. Emery was hesitant but Clarenceux pulled the chair out for him and took a step away, giving him space. Emery sat.

"You, in the doorway," said Clarenceux, "you can go. I am having a private conversation with Mr. Emery."

The manservant looked at Emery, who nodded. "Yes—go, Adam. Mr. Clarenceux is unwelcome but he seems determined to have his say. I am not afraid of him. Go and tell Simon and Robert to be prepared, in case of trouble."

Clarenceux watched the servant depart, then turned back to the seated man. "I need to know where she is. And unless you tell me, I will make you pay. Not here—not in a sordid manner—but I will."

"I told you, I do not know."

"She is not as poor as she feared she would be. Someone has been giving her money. Someone has encouraged her to betray me—either for money or for reasons of religion. You are one of the very few men who know that I had possession of what she stole from me. In fact, the only people who saw the document at my house were Rebecca Machyn herself; her brother, Robert Lowe; Nicholas Hill and his late father, Michael Hill; and you. That makes a total of five, Goodwife Machyn and four Knights of the Round Table, one of whom is now dead. Either Lowe, Hill, or you have persuaded Goodwife Machyn to do this, or bribed her, or informed someone who has persuaded her."

Emery turned and stared at the wall.

"I will not accept your silence. You do not know this but a sixth person knew I had that document. Sir William Cecil, her majesty's Secretary, charged me to guard it with my life. Now it has been stolen. Do you see my predicament? And how impossible it is for me to rest until I have found it?"

Still Emery stared at the wall.

Clarenceux took a step nearer and bent down, speaking right in his ear. "I am going to tell Sir William Cecil what happened. I will say that you paid Rebecca Machyn to steal that document. He in turn will instruct Francis Walsingham to recover it—and I am sure you know *his* methods. He will torture you first and then make inquiries. He will hang you by your hands, break your legs with an iron bar, and then cut you down."

Emery turned and looked at Clarenceux. "It was not me," he said slowly. "You may talk to your friends Cecil and Walsingham, if you wish. But it was not me. I know nothing about where the woman has gone. And you, you are no better than Cecil. Call yourself a religious man? Dutiful? Curse you and the Devil, who rides with you. The Knights only took action because you failed to do so. Henry Machyn gave you that document not so you would hide it in a fearful way but so you would use it. We all suffered imprisonment and torture because of you." Emery was silent for an instant, looking for some sign of recognition in Clarenceux. "Have you forgotten so soon? We were all tortured. I still have the scars on my back where they whipped me—with a leather lash that ripped my skin away. Others fared worse. Daniel Gyttens was beaten to death; Henry Machyn was killed. You betrayed him—you betrayed all of us. I am glad Widow Machyn has taken back that document, and I am glad it is out of your keeping. Maybe she will put it to good use, like a good Catholic, and destroy that interloper queen, Elizabeth."

"At last we're getting somewhere. Tell me exactly what happened. Who put her up to it?"

Emery shook his head.

"Who did it? Who paid her, damn you?" Clarenceux shouted. He slammed his fist down hard on the table. "Who in God's name endangered all our lives by making her steal it?"

Emery said nothing.

"*Answer me!*" yelled Clarenceux. The next moment he lifted the edge of the table and tipped it over, sending plates, bowls, cloth, napkin, goblet, apples, and pears tumbling to the floor. Turning the table onto its end, he hurled it out of the way. He stepped forward and seized Emery by the collar of his doublet. "Tell me now who put her up to this! If not you, I need to know who it was, because I do not want to kill an innocent man!"

Emery struggled to shake off Clarenceux's grip but the latter swung his fist and connected with his jaw. Emery was sent sprawling on the floor. Clarenceux moved to one side, aware that Emery's companions would soon arrive through the door behind him. "I am going to give you one chance."

Emery tasted blood on his lip and wiped his mouth on his sleeve. "She has betrayed you, Clarenceux. You betrayed us and she has got revenge. She said you were soft on her, and that you would give her what she wanted. I think you can consider yourself beaten by a woman."

There was movement at the doorway, and two young men appeared: a burly red-haired one with freckles and a leather jerkin, the other a dark-haired robust-looking fellow from the stables. They saw their master on the floor, and Clarenceux standing by.

"Help him up," ordered Clarenceux. Until this moment he had not quite believed that Rebecca Machyn had really betrayed him. He knew it with his mind but not with his heart. One moment he felt bitter, the next close to tears. "Help him. He was about to tell me something that might save all our lives."

They raised their master to his feet. Emery mopped his cut lip, saying, "This man assaulted me. Take him to the constables."

Clarenceux swept back the long cloak over his shoulder, to reveal his sword and long-bladed dagger. He placed his hand on the sword hilt and suddenly drew it. "I strongly suggest that you two good men both find yourselves seats." Clarenceux pointed with the blade. "There is one over there—and you, there is another there, in the corner."

After a nod from their master, the two young men righted the seats and sat. Emery stood against the wall.

"The situation is as follows," continued Clarenceux, looking from one man to the other. "I am a herald, an officer in her majesty's household. Your master and two or three of his friends persuaded a woman to steal a document from me. I had been charged by her majesty's Secretary to guard that document with my life. The last time it went missing, Francis Walsingham sent a man to find out what had happened to it. He hanged one of my servants. If I do not find that document, I suspect that eventually Mr. Walsingham will hang one of this household's servants too, as well as Mr. Emery himself. I wish no harm to come to any of you—but I must find Rebecca Machyn and that document. If anyone tries to use it to promote the Queen of Scots, there will be a bloodbath. I believe it would lead to the mass extermination of all Catholics in this kingdom. I am not prepared to see that happen."

"We understand the situation as we ourselves see it," replied Emery. "Not as you would have us believe."

"Where is Rebecca Machyn and where is the document?"

"I have told you, Mr. Clarenceux, I do not know. None of us do. The remaining four knights agreed in March that something should be done. It was agreed that if you had not acted by Easter, then we would take the document."

"And the money—were you paying her?"

"No."

"Who was?"

"I do not know. Perhaps her brother, Robert Lowe."

"Do you know where she is hiding?"

"No."

"Would you tell me if you did know?"

"I would not betray a friend."

Clarenceux sheathed his sword. "I am sorry I struck you," he said to Emery. "And that I interrupted your meal. I understand why you agreed to act with the Knights, even though I think it deeply unwise and dangerous. I hope you can understand why I must stop what you have set in motion. The thought of men and women being burnt alive for their faith is something I cannot bear. It is not a price worth paying for a return to the old religion. Nor do I want to take part of the blame for allowing it to happen."

With that he bowed to the men, turned to the door, and left.

18

Clarenceux looked around his house. Ten minutes ago he had been helping Thomas load up the cart with Awdrey's traveling chest and the children's bags. Then, all too soon, they were gone—to Chislehurst, eleven miles to the south. Watching them come down the stairs he had been sorely tempted to go with them and to turn his back on the loss of the document; but he knew that it was impossible. Instead, he had experienced a sinking feeling, as if all the blood and love were being drained out of him.

Saying good-bye had been the hardest part. It was the memory of last time. Holding each of his daughters and kissing them good-bye, knowing he could not be sure he would ever see them again, pulled at his heart and drew tears to his eyes. But when he embraced Awdrey in a farewell, he had looked through his tear-filled eyes into hers and could not believe they were being separated again. The sadness was there, inside them and all around them, and it was overwhelming him. It was like a form of lovemaking, it embraced them both so much, but instead of joy they were combined in grief.

"Go, go now," he had said. "Go with all my love. Go and be safe." She had drawn away from him slowly, holding on to his fingers, finally letting go to wipe her eyes, and climb onto the cart.

Now he was coming to terms with the silence in his house.

In the hall, he filled a mazer of wine and sat down at his elm table. He had arranged all his weapons there: two good swords, one old one, two daggers, three other assorted knives, and two small axes. He looked at them and drank the wine.

Something was preying on his mind—something to do with the Knights of the Round Table. Emery had revealed that they had been speaking to Rebecca Machyn and that they had agreed to persuade her to steal the document from him. At least, four of them had. There was no doubt who three of them were: Emery, Robert Lowe, and Nicholas Hill. The fourth man had to be either Hill's late father, Michael Hill, or the last Knight, Lancelot Heath, who had fled last December. But which of them had persuaded Rebecca to betray him?

It was almost dusk. He went back down to the kitchen with his wine, a sword, and a dagger, and placed a few pieces of wood on the fire there. He sat on a small stool beside the hearth within the great fireplace. The only windows in here were relatively small and high up, so it was barely possible to see across the room. Clarenceux used the point of the dagger to push around the burning sticks, watching the flames lick the edges and sip momentarily at the air.

He took another draught of wine. Gradually the light diminished. He put more wood on the hearth and returned to thinking about Emery. The man had not been fearful or in hiding. He had not been aware that something had just happened, even though he had agreed it with the other three surviving Knights. One of the others was probably coordinating Rebecca Machyn's actions. Robert Lowe was the most likely, being her brother. But he and she were not close. As for Lancelot Heath, he was a reluctant foot soldier of the old religion. That left Nicholas Hill. He was certainly the most ardent of the Knights whom Clarenceux had met and the keenest to have custody of the document. He had been persuaded to give it back to Clarenceux by his father, Michael. But Michael was now dead. That might have changed everything.

Clarenceux looked up from the flames and realized he was sitting in darkness. He fumbled around the kitchen for a lantern, found one, and lit the candle inside from the fire. Taking his mazer, he went through to the buttery to refill it from the barrel and then resumed his seat.

There had been eight Knights originally, besides Henry Machyn and, later, himself. Of those, six yet lived: Emery, Hill, Lowe, Heath, and two others. William Draper had been one, a rich merchant who had betrayed them all and was lucky to be alive. The other had been…

At first Clarenceux could not think of the name. Then he remembered: he had never known it. The man's knightly name was Sir Percival. It had been his role to inform Lady Percy, the dowager countess of Northumberland, whenever the document changed hands.

Clarenceux clenched his mazer tight. He might have been wrong to assume that the fourth Knight was old Michael Hill or Lancelot Heath. It could have been "Sir Percival," whoever he was. Another thing occurred to him. Emery had referred to the *remaining* knights. They had not replaced the fallen. That was the detail tantalizing his mind. The Knights were the same ones as before. Apart from Sir Percival, they were all known to him.

19

James Emery sat hunched in the wherry, listening to the ripples of the Thames. He drew his cloak close around him—partly because of the cold but more because he did not want to be seen. It was illegal to use the river after curfew. Although there was no moon, the sky was clear and filled with stars. The waterman spoke low. "We are nearly at Queenhithe."

They moved closer and closer to the bank. The waterman drew in the oars and let the wherry drift toward the quay. Fortunately the tide was not yet full; as they came closer to the quay, they slowly disappeared beneath its shadow. The waterman carefully brought the small boat up to the steps.

"Good luck to you, Mr. Emery," he said in a low voice.

Emery crept up the steps. He checked that there were no watchmen and made his way across the quay to the shadow of the warehouses. Walking briskly, he went north to Thames Street and then over, into Little Trinity Lane. Here, with the overhanging stories of the houses darkening the whole street, he was relatively safe. At Mrs. Barker's house he knocked at the door, just loud enough for his signal to be heard. The door opened; a small lantern light shone from within.

"My name is Sir Yvain. I have an urgent message for her ladyship."

"Come in," replied Father Tucker, who had opened the door. He closed it quickly, then raised the lantern to see Emery's face. "There is bad news. I will leave Mrs. Barker to tell you."

James Emery was led to a chamber on the first floor of the house. Three candles on a stand illuminated the paneled room. Otherwise it was empty but for two short benches along one wall. Mrs. Barker entered in a long black dress with an upright collar, wide stiff skirt, and long hanging cuffs that revealed an orange silk lining. Her hair was tightly tied back. She sat at one bench. Father Tucker stood beside her.

"Mr. Emery, you may speak."

"Thank you," said Emery. "Mr. Clarenceux came to see me at my house this morning. He was most aggressive. He wanted to know where Widow Machyn has been taken."

"What did you tell him?" Mrs. Barker asked in a curt voice.

"Nothing—nothing that he had not already worked out for himself."

"What had he already worked out for himself?"

Emery glanced at Father Tucker, and then back at Mrs. Barker. "He forced me to admit that we had agreed to ask Widow Machyn to acquire the Percy-Boleyn marriage agreement."

"That is regrettable but perhaps inevitable. However, your coming here is timely. Mr. Clarenceux is only one of our worries. Widow Machyn and the document have gone missing. She was meant to sail with Robert Lowe from Queenhithe yesterday morning, to change ships at Sandwich. Neither she nor her brother was there. The shipmaster waited three hours, then he sent word. No one knows where they are."

Emery's eyes widened. "For whom has she betrayed us?" he eventually asked, turning from Mrs. Barker to Father Tucker, then back again.

"I would very much like to know that myself," answered Mrs. Barker. "You don't think it was Clarenceux?"

Emery shook his head. "No, no. When he came to my house, he seemed quite upset by the thought of her betraying him. He was violent, forcing his way in, drawing a sword, overturning my table. Robert Lowe was no friend of his—it doesn't make sense."

"His violence may have been pretense," suggested Father Tucker. "If I wanted to give the impression of being upset, overturning a table and drawing a sword would be the way to do it. He did not actually use the sword, I assume?"

"No," admitted Emery. "But he was earnest."

"What else did he say?" inquired Mrs. Barker.

"He knows that someone was giving her money," said Emery. "He wanted to know where she had gone and where his document was."

"It is not *his* document!" shouted Mrs. Barker suddenly, getting to her feet and starting to walk up and down the room. "He knows she has taken it. He knows she has betrayed him. He knows that she has received money and that you and the other Knights agreed that this should happen. But does he know she has betrayed us too? If he does, maybe he also knows for whom."

"I said nothing about your house."

"It doesn't matter," replied Mrs. Barker. "He knows too much already." She paused and looked at Father Tucker. "But precisely because he knows so much, we can predict what he will do. He will come here. Or, having failed to find out where Widow Machyn is from you, he will try Nicholas Hill. Whatever Hill says, eventually Clarenceux will come here."

Father Tucker spoke. "My lady, we could ask Hill to supply him with misleading information."

"No. Clarenceux would see through him straight away. But we

do have the element of surprise. You realize what we have to do, don't you?"

Father Tucker nodded. "We must put some questions to Mr. Clarenceux, some very searching questions—and something to loosen his tongue."

"Might we accomplish such a deed without drawing attention to ourselves?" she asked.

"Yes, as you said, he will come here. He is bound to. When he does, we will be able to trap him easily."

"How?" asked Emery.

Father Tucker looked at him. "We will take advantage of his faith."

20

Tuesday, May 9

Clarenceux jolted awake. It was dark. He had fallen asleep in the kitchen and the wine had slipped out of his hand, wetting his knee. He stood up in the fireplace and felt his way around the corner to the kitchen door, then up the two flights of stairs to his bedchamber. It felt cold and unwelcoming without his wife. Normally when he retired for the night, there was a golden glow in the alcove above their bed. Now even the sheets were cold. He let himself fall onto the mattress, still clothed, and waited to sleep in the darkness.

He did not fall asleep. In the course of walking up the stairs his mind had fastened on to the realization that, although he did not know who Sir Percival was, the three other Knights did. Nicholas Hill would definitely be the hardest man to make talk. He was physically tough, strong-minded, and younger than Clarenceux. Most of all he believed in the Catholic cause and the idea of using the Percy-Boleyn document, having it proclaimed immediately. Robert Lowe was different. A blacksmith in his thirties, he was probably as tough as Hill physically, but he was not so fervent. At least, he had not been so ardent in December. James Emery was the easiest of the three. But he had been forewarned.

Clarenceux sat up in the darkness. Feeling cold, he got off the bed and went to the window. The shutters were still open. Looking out, he could just make out the faint start of the dawn, a lightening of the darkness. The stars were beginning to fade.

He went to his clothes chest and rummaged, feeling for an extra garment. He found another doublet and put it over his shoulders. Rather than go back to bed, however, he leaned over the window ledge, watching the dawn seep into the landscape. From here he could see across the roofs of neighbors' houses, all dim in this early dawn light. He breathed in the cold morning air and heard a seagull call, disturbed from its rest.

Eleven miles to the south, Awdrey and his daughters were asleep. Did thoughts and prayers pass through the night? Perhaps if he thought of her, and Annie and Mildred, he might enter their dreams. Who could ever know? Only God, he reflected. Unto Whom all desires were known and from Whom no secrets were hidden. And Rebecca—did God see *her* heart? Of course. Then why did He not return her here? Clarenceux shook his head; it was more than he could understand.

A cat screeched in a fight in a yard not far away. He could see the Thames and the outline of the houses on the great bridge. Here and there were the masts of stationary boats moored on both banks. In the still-dim light, he thought he saw one move. That would have been against the ordinances and laws of the city. There were more than two thousand boats on the river; it was the easiest way of crossing the city quickly. Perhaps, if it was a boat moving, it was James Emery fleeing from the city? *Tiredness is leading you to speculate wildly. Get some sleep while you still can.*

But still he did not move. The whole world seemed beautifully at peace. So quiet, and yet all nature was living and breathing. Cats were prowling the night, birds stirring from their rest. Men and women snoring. And every night it was like this: a perfect peace upon the whole world, with no light but the flickering of a candle before the dawn. *That peace is like God. No one sees Him, no one notices. He is like a nighttime to us, coming among us when our eyes are closed, calming us, soothing us. In His world of night we need no food; we barely stir. We see nothing of Him and yet He is unholy real.*

Clarenceux remained standing at his window until he could see the whole landscape of boats and houses. Later, he heard the shouts of fathers to their sons to be up and ready for school. He heard a woman scold a girl and people shouting orders at their servants as the first glimmer of sunlight neared in the east.

He would call on Emery again.

21

I t was dawn. Harry Gurney looked up and stopped playing the pipe that Raw Carew had plucked from the sea a day and a half earlier. "Now God be praised for sending an angel to bugger the Devil and all his plans," he declared in an excited voice.

"At last," said Carew quietly, pausing in his oar stroke to look across the water. It was calm now. He looked at the raft they had made, hardly able to believe it had held together. They had taken the masts, with the ropes still attached to them, and lashed them across the two skiffs. They had tied as many planks as they could on top of the masts. About half of the fifty-seven survivors were crammed into the skiffs; the remainder were lying on the planks. The ropes gave a little and the whole raft creaked with every wave. Several times in the night Carew had feared it would break up, but it had proved strong enough.

"You're a bloody angel, Raw," said Alice. She was a corpulent, plain woman with a determined jaw, thick fleshy arms, dirty brown hair, and a strong West Country accent. Her eyes were her only beautiful feature, but they were buried deep in a face that was so much jowl that few people actually saw them.

Hugh Dean rose to his feet. He pulled out a pistol, which he tried to discharge into the dawn sky. It did not fire, but his enthusiasm was undiminished. "Let's hear some cheers for Captain Carew," he roared across the masts and planks. "Let us applaud him—a man who can navigate for two nights and a day without stars, without a map, without a compass, and without a ship!"

Fifty-one men and four women responded with shouts of approval, despite their exhaustion and the cold. A young woman called Charity Pool was sitting with her arms wrapped around herself. "I never want to come to sea again," she said. "There are too many ghosts out here."

"There always were," replied Raw Carew.

"It is different now. I know their names."

Everyone was chilled to the bone and worn out. They knew that the men and women whom they could not see they would never see again. They had either gone down with the ship or fallen off the raft and drifted away in the night.

"The *Nightingale* was an ugly ship," said Carew, trying to stop himself shivering. "We are better off without her."

"No more water dripping all night from the deck," said Luke.

"No more deck," agreed John Devenish, pulling on an oar. "All that's left are the masts."

"I've seen a ship without masts many a time but never masts without a ship," said Skinner.

Carew was pleased to see that Devenish still had his Moorish blade strapped to his side. "We will not be long without a ship," he said. "Alice, tell us: in what sort of vessel shall we sail out of Southampton? One with a big, fat hold? Or something sleeker, with all her firepower up top?"

"We'll have plenty of time to take our pick," she replied. "One thing I know: we won't be leaving Southampton until every sailor here has ridden every whore in the town, both those with big holds and all the muzzle you could fancy!"

Three or four cheers followed this exclamation.

"What about you, Raw?" Alice continued. "Can you see that Amy yet? Is she waving to you?"

Skinner looked up. "Truth is, as soon as we are home, we'll be asleep. We won't be able to lift a leg to put one foot in front of another, let alone get a leg over."

"Hark at you," replied Alice. "Show me a strong young lad, stiff as a cannon, and you'll see if I sleep or not."

"You'll be snoring along with the rest of us."

"Won't stop him though, will it? I can sleep and fuck at the same time. Good thing for some of you that I can."

A wave slapped against the side of the boat and a little spray hit those sitting there. "Alice is right," said Carew, putting his arm around Kahlu's shoulder. "No matter how tired you are, you will want to eat and sing and dance and revel in being alive."

He looked at the shape of the land. It was growing clearer. That was indeed the Isle of Wight and the opening to Southampton Water. There were two large ships visible. Was one a naval vessel? Perhaps he had rescued his crew only for them to be arrested and hanged. And supposing they made it to Calshot, how would James Parkinson, the captain of Calshot Fort, treat him this time? Carew had once fought a duel with him over his right to sail unimpeded up and down Southampton Water. On another occasion Parkinson had wounded him in the hand. But it would be worth fighting him again—to eat beef and spend a night in a dry bed with a sweet woman and a flagon of wine.

Soon color started to fill the outline of the horizon. Carew shouted to Hugh Dean, "We'll land to the west of the fort and cut the masts loose there. We'll take the skiffs past Calshot—and damn Parkinson. He's probably still asleep anyway. Those we set ashore will walk to town, but we'll all dine at the Swans this evening."

22

Clarenceux hammered on the door of James Emery's house for the third time. It was still early. If Emery had left already, with servants too, that was indeed unusual. He knocked again and looked up at the gathering clouds.

The door opened. A boy looked out, holding it only just ajar.

"Good day to you," said Clarenceux. "I presume that your master is away?"

The boy looked nervous. "Sir, he has not been home since late last night."

"And his servant, Adam? The man who normally attends to callers?"

"He is also absent, sir. He traveled yesterday. I do not know where he was going."

"He told you to tell me that?"

The boy hesitated. He did not know what to say. Clarenceux just waited until eventually he received the answer. "Yes, sir."

He nodded. "Thank you. You have been most helpful. Good day."

He walked slowly along the uneven mud of the street into Huggin Lane. There he stopped and looked back, not at Emery's house but at Mrs. Barker's, on the corner where Huggin Alley met Little Trinity Lane. He wondered whether he should call. He did not know the woman; he had never met her or any of her servants. He pondered further, tapping one of his boots against the other. It would be a last resort—if everything else failed—to seek her help finding Rebecca. *The chances are that Mrs. Barker has never heard of me. She might see it as her role to protect Rebecca from everyone she does not know.*

He began to walk north, deciding he would next go to Robert Lowe's house, adjacent to the wall near Cripplegate. He crossed Old Fish Street, turned into Bread Street, and marched past Gerrard's Hall into the parish of St. Mary le Bow. Lines of tiled roofs greeted him: two-story houses, three-story houses, with shops at ground floor and leaning upper structures. Old houses and new, glazed houses and those just with shutters. At Cheapside there were crowds dawdling around the market stalls and looking in the unshuttered shop fronts along the street. Some people were queuing at the conduit; others had stopped to watch a street juggler. Clarenceux crossed straight into Wood Street, his mind fixed on Robert Lowe.

When he arrived at the blacksmith's house, he glanced up at the windows. They were all closed. It was not a good sign. Still, he knocked and waited for a full minute before walking down the side of the house to try the gate through to the backyard and the forge, where Lowe worked. This too was locked.

He looked back along the street. He knew he could climb over and into the yard, but that would not necessarily give him the information he needed. It was suspicious that Lowe was not at home on the same day that Emery had stayed away overnight. Had Emery spoken to Lowe?

It did not matter. There was one person left who might be able to answer his questions: Nicholas Hill, in St. Dionis Backchurch.

23

In the parlor of his house, Walsingham rubbed his hands to warm them and sat down again at the table. It was covered in papers. These in turn were covered in black ink: symbols, lists, and calculations. It now seemed certain that the cipher was alphabetic, not numeric, so that it was the shapes that represented the actual letters, not their numerical value.

A knock came at the door.

"Go away," shouted Walsingham, loath to look up from his notes. The door opened. He glanced up to see who it was.

A well-dressed man in his early twenties entered and bowed. "Mr. Walsingham, if you will permit me, I have some suggestions."

"Master Richards. You have discovered something?"

"I think so, sir. The message is a cipher, written in English. May I show you?"

Walsingham beckoned him forward. The young man placed a sheaf of papers on the table. He shuffled one to the top.

"This is the message as received. You remarked on the recurrence of the sequence DCC-. As you know, it is not at first clear whether this is a code or a cipher. Also, if it is a cipher, then we need to know if DCC- represents one, two, three, or four letters. I tried all the common three-letter words and none of them worked, so I set about trying all the common four-letter words with a double letter. That proved false too. The French solution did not work either. There are very few double letters in Latin. That set me thinking. Why did we think the three-letter solution false? It was because of the commas. If you recall, we found instances of a pause or a comma followed by two letters and then another comma, and so we concluded that the two letters had to represent a single letter—A or I—but that did not work elsewhere in the message. But what if the commas themselves were part of the cipher? That way of thinking is more productive. In fact, the message starts to work."

"Show me."

John Richards placed a second piece of paper in front of Walsingham. "I went back to our first theory—that DCC- stands for a common three-letter word, such as 'and' or 'the.' Taking the latter possibility, the D would be a cipher for *t*, CC for *h* and - for *e*. Identifying the *th* is important because it shows where the word *that* is most likely to occur, and that reveals the important cipher for a second vowel, A, which turns out to be a V. If you look at the message, you find a comma followed by the letters *ththat*. For this reason we initially ruled out the possibility that DCC- could mean 'the.' But if the comma is part of the cipher, then it makes sense. The section in question reads 'the MMMeIe, ththat' or, spaced properly, with the deciphered letters underlined, '<u>the</u>MMMe<u>Ie</u>,<u>th</u> that.' Obviously a triple letter MMM is impossible, so that must be a cipher either for a single letter or a diphthong. But, look at the comma in that passage: there are very few words that end with the four letters e–something–th. Even allowing for phonetic spellings, that pause can only represent a *d*, an *n*, or an *r*.

"Now, there is a long sequence repeated toward the end. I've underlined the letters already hypothesized from the words 'the' and 'that.'" He placed a third sheet over the top of the second. It had just a section of the text:

TCCC\ICCCCCCCCE+CCCCEMMME,
TATXIEMMMMMMCCEIIXMMMMMMEAIELCCCC
CCCMM\, /\, AT/AII,\, THEMMMEIE,
THTHATIIECCCACIIIEMMMICCCCEC\IIIXMMMMMMME,
/C\ICCCCCCCCE+CCCCEMMME, TATXIEMMMT\H

"What jumps out is the deciphered sequence of letters 'tat.' It appears twice—and both times they are preceded by the letters 'CICCCCCCCCE+CCCCEMMME,' and followed by 'XIEMMM.' But the interesting thing is that the first time they are followed by two 'MMM's and the second by only one. As one cannot have a triple letter, 'MMM' is probably a single letter. Now, going back to the section we identified earlier"—Richards pointed back at the second sheet—"the 'MMM' in 'MMMEIE,TH' must also be a single letter. There is only one seven-letter word that fits that pattern: 'seventh.' And finally"—he placed his last sheet of paper on the table—"if you test this hypothesis, the message does start to read more coherently, because that repeated long word that I mentioned becomes decipherable: '\VCCCCCCCCE+CCCCESENTATXVEST.' You can see the word 'representatives' so 'CCCC' must be an R and X is the cipher for I."

Walsingham looked at the last page, which Richards now placed before him. It read:

RI>HTHICCCIIIMMCIIE<\CCCCCCCEN/VST\C\VRMMA/
CSHIPIIEHAVERE<EIVE/C\VRINSTRV<TI\NSLR

CCCSIRPER<IIAMMAN/THEIII/\IIISIIIMMMMIN>TV
IIHATSCCE<ANT\REST\RETHE<ATH\MMI<TREASVRET
VSS\THATC\VAN/IIET\>ETHERCCCI>HTELLE<
TITSTRVTHSHEIIIMMMMMIIIE/ESPAT<HE/IIICSHIPINTHE<
CCCPANC\LR\IIIERTMM\IIELR\CCCMM\N/\NT\SAN/
III<HAN/THERE< HAN>E/T\AVESSEMMIII\VN/L
RS<\TMMAN/IIHEREVP\NSHEIIIMMMM<
NLICCCCCCCHERARRIVAMMIIITCCC
VRREPRESENTATIVESSHEIIIMMMMMMEAVELR
CCCMM\N/\NAT/AIIN
NTHESEVENTHTHATIIECCCACIIIESVREC
IIIIMMMMSEN/C\VRREPRESENTATIVEST\H\MMCCCCC\V
IIEIIIE>C\VSEN/II\R/IIICTHISSACCCECCCESSEN>ER>\/
SPEE/C\VRMMA/CSHIPC\VR/EV\TE/SERVANTSPER<CR\C

"I can see the word 'treasure,'" said Walsingham. "I can also see 'servants'…yes, and I can see the word 'instructions'—look, that diagonal line must be an O."

"And the first word is 'right,'" declared Richards, reading over his shoulder.

"Which means that 'essenger' appears near the end, so 'CCC' is an 'm.' This is excellent, Richards." Walsingham nodded at his protégé approvingly. "Sir William will be very pleased."

24

Clarenceux's stride grew faster as he walked along Lombard Street. He was angry. He looked up at the tower of St. Mary Woolnoth and frowned, despite the pleasant blue sky, patched with white clouds. Hours were passing and he had nothing to show for the day. His enemies had betrayed him and now they were stealing his time as well. Minute by minute he was losing the chance to trace Rebecca.

He walked across wide Gracechurch Street and stepped over a pile of dung. Refusing to wait for a stream of carts to pass, he dodged between two of them and walked on swiftly past St. Benet's until he could see St. Dionis Backchurch on his left. Here the city shrank in scale. There were tiny alleys barely wide enough to walk along two abreast and places where houses' first-floor jetties were so low you could bash your head if you were not careful. There were paths so intertwined and twisting that you could easily get lost, especially when the London fog descended. Old sites had been divided at every rebuilding, each old messuage turned into three or four merchants' houses. Half of those had been turned into single-room tenements, so that a merchants' house of six chambers might now be home to twenty people. The other half had been pulled down and were ugly one- and two-story cheap wooden tenements put up by unscrupulous merchant landlords, who did not care that their tenants lived in close proximity to a communal cesspit and had to walk all the way to the conduit at the corner of Gracechurch Street and Cheapside to fetch a bucket of water.

In these gloomy alleys—more like paths through a forest than streets in a city—the wardens and parish officers did not walk alone but only in twos and threes. The fetid mud stank of feces and urine, and the water dripping from the overhanging eaves gave the whole area a dismal feeling. The smoke from the wood of the cooking fires was a blessing; it was the only wholesome thing about the place. Clarenceux worked his way through the maze of houses by the occasional patch of sunlight on the lanes and the church towers and spires. He knew if he continued walking north from the parish church he would come to a narrow alley on his left that split into two, one side wider than the other. The wider one had a two-story building on the right with scallop shells above the door.

Five minutes later, there it was. The piece of carved wood covering the lintel was coming away and hanging down slightly, and there was no doorframe. But the four irregularly spaced scallop shells, nailed above the door and green with age, were clear enough.

Clarenceux drew his knife and hammered on the door. It opened: a woman in her late twenties with her hair tied up in a dirty white scarf answered. She looked shocked to see Clarenceux. The door swung open into a dimly lit living space with a stone fireplace and old baskets hanging from the ceiling. A small cooking fire was on the hearth, with a chafing dish set into the ashes on one side and a small cauldron suspended above the flames. Nicholas Hill was standing beside the stairs, unshaven, his belly proud before him, his jerkin loose over his shirt. He was dressed in the same fawn doublet he had been wearing when Clarenceux had first met him last December.

Clarenceux walked straight in. "Did you think the Knights of the Round Table could just take that document and that I would do nothing about it?" he demanded. "Well—did you?" Without thinking or pausing to check his rage, Clarenceux found himself aiming a fist straight at Hill's jaw. Hill, however, saw the punch coming, and stepped to one side, leaving Clarenceux to lurch off-balance.

"You should not have come here, Clarenceux. You should have proclaimed that marriage agreement while you had the chance."

"I was charged to look after that document with my life."

"Then you value your life more highly than the True Faith," said Hill. "And that is bad. But not as bad as the fact that you betrayed us."

"I did not betray you. I saved you from Walsingham. You would still be in his prison if—"

"You led Walsingham's men to our doors! You stood by and waited for us all to be arrested. For what? So you could keep that document as if it's an heirloom, a grant of arms or some historical treasure. Shame on you, Clarenceux, shame on you! You did not act as Henry Machyn told you to. You withheld us from our purpose."

Clarenceux glared at Hill. "Where is Rebecca Machyn? Where is the marriage agreement?"

Hill leaned forward, as if taunting Clarenceux. "My...lips... are...sealed."

Clarenceux lashed out again. This time he was faster than Hill and his fist connected with the man's nose. Hill staggered backward, turned, and reached for a sword that hung on the wall. He swept around with it, drawing it from its scabbard, and moved to stab Clarenceux, but as he came forward, Clarenceux leaped aside and drew his own blade.

Hill's terrified wife let out a scream.

Clarenceux shouted, "How is it that your father has died and you are still here in this slum? Did he write you out of his will—for being a fool?"

"How dare you speak of my father!"

"He had more sense than you. He advised you to give up the document." As he spoke, Hill thrust. Clarenceux easily parried the blow. "To whom did he leave his house in St. Mary Woolnoth? Not to you, clearly. Is that what disturbs you?"

Hill's wife moved to the stairs. "Stop it, Nicholas," she cried. "You can't kill him. He's a gentleman. They'll hang you if they catch you."

"They won't. No one knows he is here. No one is waiting for him—he acts alone. At least he does now, since Rebecca Machyn chose to side with us."

Clarenceux knew how to use a weapon better than Hill. He had been trained. He could play with the man. He swept the blade across Hill's line of vision, then darted forward and cut him in the shoulder, drawing blood. He then drew the point back across Hill's face as the latter winced with the pain, moving forward and catching the wrist of the man's sword hand. "Drop it!" he commanded, holding the point of his sword at Hill's throat. "Drop it or I'll fight you in earnest."

Hill stopped. But he did not drop the sword.

"When did your father die?" Clarenceux demanded. "Was it in February?"

"He did not leave me his house because it was not his," Hill said. "He rented it. It was his way out of these alleys. I always hoped that religious change would be mine."

Clarenceux reached forward and took the sword from Hill's hand. He gave it to the man's wife, not taking his eyes off him. "Put it away somewhere safe until I have gone. I do not want to harm your husband but he is dangerous. I would sooner run him through than have him do the same to me."

Hill's wife took the blade and ran upstairs, the wooden soles of her shoes sounding loud on the steps.

"Does she know what this is about?" Clarenceux asked.

Hill nodded.

"And your children?"

"What children?"

Clarenceux paused. "None of you have children. You do not, nor does James Emery, nor Rebecca Machyn—all three of hers died. Henry Machyn's only son has turned into a drunkard and Robert Lowe has no children. Maybe if you had children you would be more mindful of the future and the necessity of protecting your offspring, not feeding them to religious fires."

Hill looked like an animal about to pounce. Clarenceux kept his distance, taking no chances. "Now tell me—when did your father die?" he repeated.

"February the sixteenth."

"So who is Sir Percival?"

"I do not know."

"Yes, you do. Mr. Emery told me four of you are left. None of you would trust William Draper. Lancelot Heath's whereabouts are unknown. Daniel Gyttens and your father are both dead. That leaves Lowe, Emery, yourself, and Sir Percival. Who is he?" Clarenceux looked Hill in the eye and lifted his sword to his throat, holding the point about two inches away. "I know Sir Percival brings and sends messages to and from Lady Percy. But who is he?"

"I will not tell."

Clarenceux darted upward with the blade and slashed Hill's cheek, surprised at how easily the sharp point sliced into his skin. Blood rushed to the surface and ran down his chin.

"I asked: who is he?"

Hill felt the blood with his fingers. "He is a holier man than you."

"Who is he?" Clarenceux insisted. "Where can I find him?"

"You will never find him. None of us knows his name, do you not remember?"

"But you have met him. And he knows who you are. How can I find him?"

"So you can chase after Goodwife Machyn?" the man sneered. "She has gone, Clarenceux, gone. And so too has the marriage agreement."

There was a single knock at the door. Hill stepped back and opened it: two men stood outside, in rough working clothes, both as muscular and grim looking as Hill himself. Both were openly wearing side-swords.

Hill looked back at Clarenceux. "Go, herald. Either go now, peacefully, or fight us three. I may not be able to match your swordsmanship alone, but I have more friends than you, and together we are stronger."

Hill's wife slowly descended the stairs. He continued, "When you live this close to so many, you can just knock on a wall to summon help. The rich and the poor all have their friends. Only those in the middle are alone. Which is where you are, Mr. Clarenceux."

Clarenceux stayed calm. "Stand away from the door. I will leave in peace if you give me space."

Hill gestured to his friends. Clarenceux slowly walked toward the door, his sword still at the ready, his left hand on the hilt of his dagger.

The two men drew away, backing into the street. Clarenceux looked at Hill once more, then turned and marched back the way he had come, listening carefully in case he was followed.

25

Pieter Gervys, landlord of the Two Swans at Southampton, was
half Flemish. Like many proprietors of houses of ill repute, he
and his Flemish wife Marie lived on the fringes of society. In the old
days, many stews and bordellos had been run by Flemish women, but
then the great pox had come to England. One by one the stews were
closed and the whores driven out of the cities. Those who had worked
in Southwark had almost all left by the end of Henry VIII's reign. The
city officials never gave a thought to where they went. Many citizens
saw the pox as a purifying thing, for they presumed the women had all
turned to more honest occupations. In reality they had either turned
to crime—organized theft—or removed themselves from the city to
carry on their trade elsewhere, in less rigidly controlled towns. Thus
Pieter and Marie had come to Southampton in 1555.

The inn they ran, the Two Swans, was on the quay. Behind its
respectable-looking front building was a second hall, the "long hall"
as it was affectionately known. In fact it was a barn that Peter and
Marie used when the occasion demanded. The return of Raw Carew
was just the sort of occasion. By eleven o'clock, they had been told
he was in town. By twelve, two casks of ale had been opened in the
long hall and a pig set to roast in the kitchen. By four o'clock, the

real festivities were beginning. There were bagpipes playing, and Luke Treleaven was playing a fiddle, his green eyes dancing between his fellow survivors as they sat on long benches and guzzled their way through the feast of pork and ale. Hugh Dean was plucking a lute in time to the bagpipes and Francis Bidder was lying on the floor, half wishing he was asleep and half wishing he could get up and dance some more. Harry Gurney was in a corner, laughing, with his hand up the skirts of a fat young woman, and Stars Johnson and Skinner Simpkins were dancing with another woman, who darted her kisses between the two of them, teasing them. George Thompson—a young man known as Swift or Swift George to his fellow mariners—had his arms around a woman in a corner, as she helped herself to ale from his flagon. John Devenish was leading a dozen others and their newly found womenfolk in a drunken line of dancers. Charity Pool had tied her hair up in an extravagant style, complete with ribbons and flowers, and was dancing with a dark-haired lad from the ship, Nick Laver, who had a soft spot for her. Alice had in her clutches two young men: one was an apprentice shipwright whom she had taken a liking to on the quay, and the other had heard the dancing and come in from the street. A third woman from the ship, dark-eyed Juanita, known for her fierce temper, was dancing alone in her native Spanish style, four or five men clapping and cheering around her as she lifted her skirts, jumped, and swirled in time to the music. With a hundred people laughing, singing, and dancing, with meat in their stomachs and ale in their flagons, it was a heart-warming sight.

Raw Carew was sitting on a table with a half-full ceramic flagon of ale. He was keeping one eye on the door. His attention was mostly on Ursula. Tall and blond—but sadly now afflicted with a long scar across her face—she was the elder sister of Amy, the woman with whom Carew had spent two whole days and nights in this inn, nine weeks earlier. Ursula was dancing with Hugh Dean, who grinned at her from under his mop of black hair as if she had wholly bewitched him. He put down the lute, stood behind her, and cupped her breasts in his hands; she wiggled her hips provocatively, pressing herself into his hose. Hugh was beginning to feel the effects of the ale on top of the two days without sleep, and she slipped away from him, holding her skirts.

"Amy not here?" Carew shouted at her as she spun around and another bearded sailor, Cleofas Harvy, a Breton, seized her and ran his hands appreciatively over her hips.

"She has a customer. One who pays good money," she shouted back, succumbing to Cleofas's groping hands and moving her neck as he almost slobbered over her with his ardent kisses.

"Who is he?"

"A watchman. From the fort."

Carew nodded and said nothing more. It was a wise thing to do, to keep Captain Parkinson's men happy. He turned back to the dancing. He had lost a ship, a number of friends, and a large amount of money—but with the help of Stars Johnson's knowledge of the skies, he had saved many and steered them back to safety. The end of the evening would be as usual—a lot of drunken men and women, a lot of mess to clear up, and an argument about the bill. Pieter Gervys was generally tolerant but he could prove a stickler for money, and even if he was content to let the bill mount up, it made him grumpy. Gervys would add sums here and there because he knew that Carew had nowhere else to go. Here a debt on the shop book would never be written off, and it would never be cheap; but it would not lead to a covert attempt to bring the constables to him in the night. For his part, Gervys knew that when Carew had money he did not stint but spent it generously.

The dancing stopped and the bagpipes and fiddle began a merry jig, accompanied by a horn blown by a drunken woman from the ship and a tabor played skillfully by Kahlu. Carew laughed as John Devenish tried to lift Harry Gurney and then both men fell headlong, crashing into a trestle table that promptly collapsed, sending flagons flying and two men and their women sprawling on the floor. Recovering, Devenish lifted one of the women and turned her upside down, and danced with her that way until her would-be bedmate raised a fist at him. At that he put the woman down and started dancing with her lover instead.

Ursula broke away from Cleofas and came over to Carew. "Are you not going to dance?"

Apart from the scar, of which she was very conscious, Ursula was still pretty. She had pale skin and freckles like her sister but she was taller and less given to laughing. She also lacked the vivacious spark and sexual beauty of her younger sister. But she was shrewd, imaginative, and caring. Carew liked her.

"Is that an invitation?" he inquired.

"I'll dance with you," she said. "Or are you asking for a business deal?"

"You mean, you won't take me for love."

"Love I get every day. It's money we need."

Carew lifted a hand to her cheek and ran a finger over her skin, down her neck, and over her breast. The same finger drew an imaginary circle on her dress and then followed the curve of her hips. "It does a man good to see you, Ursula. But something is not right."

Ursula leaned forward and kissed his lips. "It is good to see you too—and not just because we need the money."

"Tell me."

"Ralph is sick. Amy's already lost one child—losing another would be hard, cruel hard."

Carew remembered the bodies in the sea. He thought back to earlier times, worse hardships, terrible fears. The great sea of darkness. The truth was that he was proud to confront journeys and challenges that other men would not even dare to think about; yet the reward for such courage might be nothing more than oblivion and a watery grave. At that moment he understood that these women did something similar. They were proud to have men love their smiles and try to please them; it was part of who they were— desirable and beyond possession, only temporarily attainable. But then, in childbed, the reward for their loving might be nothing more than a feverish death, if not their own then that of a loved one. The death of a child might be tragic or it might be a blessing. In Amy's case she had loved her dead daughter, and no doubt she still did.

Ursula kissed him again, snapping him out of his reverie. "So? Will you dance?"

A moment later she was dragging Carew forward from the table and he was dancing with her—to and fro, then in each other's arms—as the crowd watched them and clapped or danced alongside them. As one dance gave way to another they grew bolder: Carew throwing Ursula up in the air and catching her. At the end of one dance he called for silence and then, after a long pause, held everyone spellbound as he sang a mournful ballad of companions who sailed no more; following this, he sang a fast song with which the bagpipes, pipe, and fiddle joined in, everyone stamping and thumping on the table. Then the dancing began again and he lifted Ursula and raised her skirts to show off her legs, while she playfully tried to fight him off and he carried her around the hall.

The drinking went on through the afternoon. Every so often Carew would stop trying not to remember, weighing the joy of life against the sadness of his memories. Every time he caught Ursula's eye the message passed between them, about Amy and her sick son. Every time he felt the sea swallowing him again, as it had almost done in the wreck, he would crack a joke to make Ursula laugh. The anticipation of having her later dabbed at the great tear welling within him. He did not know exactly what caused it: it seemed to be connected to so many things. The loss of the ship and the cannon. The loss of so many friends. But then he reflected that it was none of those things. It was the more distant past.

"Are you all right, Mr. Carew?" Ursula looked genuinely worried.

"I am, thank you." Then he shook his head. "Sometimes I think I ought to be different from what I am. I should have—I don't know—done other things."

"Like what, Mr. Carew?"

"Like…learning to write." It pained him to say the words. "Or marrying an honest woman."

"Mr. Caroooby—you're drunk!" giggled Ursula, and as she said the words, she sounded just like her sister, and she had the same sparkle in her eye. "You'll never marry anyone—you could not remain faithful for more than an hour. And I bet you've not been in a church since you was baptized."

Carew cleared his throat. "It would give me great pleasure if you and I were to retire now with this flagon of ale, go to your quarters, and stay there until dawn."

"Is this for cash or credit?"

"Don't worry. I won't charge you." He kissed her. Then kissed her again, more passionately, running his hands over her back. "Truth is, you could ask for whatever you wanted right now and I'd promise it."

26

Clarenceux walked down Little Trinity Lane in the early evening sunlight and knocked at the iron-studded oak door of Mrs. Barker's house. A dark-haired man answered, barely as tall as Clarenceux's shoulder.

"Good day. I need to speak with your mistress. Is she within?"

"Who seeks an audience?"

"William Harley, Clarenceux King of Arms—a friend of Rebecca Machyn."

"Sir, if you would wait inside, I will speak to her ladyship straightaway."

The front of the house was not quite as Clarenceux had expected. The door opened into a long, narrow reception chamber lit by glazed windows facing the street, with a fireplace at both ends and an elaborate plastered ceiling. There was a table large enough for about twenty servants, with benches on both sides and brass candlesticks and wooden and pewter drinking vessels in the center. About halfway down the long chamber was a staircase with elaborately carved newel posts. Although Clarenceux had been inside this house once before, he had only seen the rear corridor and a wine vault. This wide entrance and servants' dining hall was a surprise. Nor was the layout the only unexpected thing.

His eyes were drawn to the shields carved above the fireplaces: they were plain red and blue—no coats of arms were depicted at all. And now he saw that the arms carved on the newel posts similarly were plain silver. Whatever had been painted there before had been obliterated.

The short man was gone a considerable time. When he reappeared, he bowed respectfully. "I do apologize for the delay, Mr. Clarenceux. Mrs. Barker says she would be very pleased to receive you in her audience chamber upstairs. If you would follow me."

Clarenceux followed the servant up the wooden staircase. It was perfectly made; the oak steps were solid, like stone. The servant led him along a short corridor to a large room, with another decorated plaster ceiling and linen-fold paneling. One wall was covered with a bright tapestry showing Dido and Aeneas hand in hand at the mouth of a cave, with nymphs and satyrs watching them. Another wall was almost entirely glass: a myriad of small diamond-shaped quarrels, allowing in some of the evening sunlight. A log fire was burning in the fireplace; a table and chair in front of this were arranged for Mrs. Barker to write, not far from a candelabrum. She was seated there now, with various papers before her. A thin man in his early forties was attending her, standing quietly to one side.

Clarenceux bowed and studied her. Her face was narrow and elegant although her skin was wrinkled with age. Sharp blue eyes followed his movements. Her gray hair was pinned back in a neat coiffure, and her deep-blue velvet dress, cut at the front to expose a white silk lining, was pristine; its silk sleeves bound in gold brocade. She had an elegant poise, as if her body was balanced on a pivot and she was in total control of every movement, every nuance of expression and manner.

"Good day to you, Mr. Clarenceux," she said. "I am pleased to meet you."

"Good day, my lady. You have heard of me then?"

She smiled. "Of course. Rebecca Machyn often spoke of you. You were the herald in whom she placed all her trust, in whom she could confide. She made you sound very attractive."

Clarenceux paused. "I rather thought that *you* were her confidante. I confess, of late she has shown no trust in me."

"Oh? What makes you say that?"

"She has gone."

Mrs. Barker looked at him with a concerned expression. "Gone? Where? Do you know if she has other protectors?"

"No, I do not know. That is exactly what worries me."

Mrs. Barker looked up at her companion. "Leave us, Father. I wish to speak to Mr. Clarenceux alone."

Father Tucker caught Clarenceux's eye, then turned and bowed to Mrs. Barker. "Godspeed, my lady," he said and departed. The candles guttered at the closing of the door.

Mrs. Barker moved a loose strand of gray hair that had fallen across her cheek. "I know you and Rebecca were close."

"And I know that she used to find shelter with you, here."

"But you do not know where she has gone?"

"No. Do you?"

"I did not even know that she had departed. I get out very little. Most people who need to see me come to this house. If they do not come here, then I do not hear news of them, it is as simple as that. My limbs do not permit me to walk very far and, for reasons of religion, few people in this city invite me to visit."

Clarenceux walked closer. "Rebecca Machyn—has she stayed here or sought refuge with you since Christmas?"

"No, not at all. What makes you ask?"

"Her disappearance."

Suddenly a silence grew between them, as if neither knew how to continue the conversation.

"Why are the coats of arms in this house painted over?" asked Clarenceux.

Mrs. Barker coughed slightly. "I had the old arms covered up when I moved in and I never had my own painted. It is always hard to find good workmen."

Clarenceux frowned. "But you live next door to Painter Stainers' Hall."

She looked down. The silence continued. It became awkward.

"Is there something you are not telling me?" he asked.

"That man who has just left us, Father Tucker, is a priest of the old religion. He has a price on his head. Does that concern you?"

"If Mr. Walsingham were to catch him, there would be little chance of him keeping his head, whether or not there is a price on it. But his losing it would be none of my will. You know that."

"Rebecca attended Masses here several times over the past three or four months. In my chapel." She nodded in the direction of the tapestry.

"Do you have any idea why she might have fled?"

"No."

"Do you know about the document that her husband used to guard?" he said.

She said nothing.

"Do you, Mistress Barker?"

She started to get to her feet, holding the edge of the table. He watched her walk toward the fire. The roundedness of her shoulders and back struck him as more revealing of her age and frailty than her eyes and face. Except that her frailty was only physical. In spirit she was as lithe as a young killing beast.

"You know what I am talking about," he said to her back. "Did she tell you? Or did her husband?"

"A mutual friend told me. Years ago."

"Did you know that Rebecca was planning to steal it from me?"

She turned to face him. "I protected her, Mr. Clarenceux. When there were soldiers in the street, searching her house, I looked after her. When you killed a royal guard outside, I protected you too, in a manner of speaking. I know what happened that day I sent her to you in the street as you lay beside the corpse. I told her to arrange your escape."

"But why did you protect her? And why me? Was it for our benefit or yours?" The question hung in the air, turning it sour. "Did you intend to steal the document from me? Are you in league with the Knights of the Round Table?"

There was a coldness in her eyes now. Her poise was no longer delicately held; it was defiant—as the thinnest blade is not just the most delicate but also the sharpest. "You never showed any sign of using it—or even proclaiming its existence."

"You are one of them," he said, his mouth dry.

"No, Mr. Clarenceux, but I know what the Knights are planning to do. You would not act, so they had to. You had a choice; you had a chance. They felt frustrated and envious—angry too. If Widow Machyn hadn't been persuaded to take the document, I suspect the Knights would have taken your children. They might even have threatened to kill them."

"And Sir Percival? Are *you* Sir Percival?"

"No, Mr. Clarenceux. I am not one of the Knights. I am a woman."

"But…they meet here, don't they? In your chapel."

She paused for a moment and almost smiled. "Would you consider joining them?"

"I do not approve of the use of that document to foment revolution."

She shook her head. "You are not so far apart. You are a Catholic, no? At least, you believe the old ways are best. If you joined them, you could make your protest directly to them, in person."

Clarenceux looked at her. "After they have betrayed me like this?"

"There has been a misunderstanding, that is all. I suggest that you join us for Mass in my chapel on Thursday, Ascension Day, at dawn. My servants will prepare a chamber for you if you wish to stay tomorrow night. Or, simply come here before four of the clock."

Clarenceux walked slowly to the tapestry and lifted the corner, seeing the door concealed in the wainscoting. He glanced back at Mrs. Barker. The Knights had arranged the theft. They had organized Rebecca's departure. He had to put himself in their hands to find out where she had taken the document. "Very well. I will come for Mass on Ascension Day."

27

Raw Carew stumbled on the stairs in the near darkness. For a moment he felt dizzy, and placed a hand on the wall. He breathed deeply, felt Ursula's arm around him, and heard the fiddle and singing in the hall. With a candle in her other hand, she proceeded to help him up the stairs. "I need a bed," he sang. "A bed. A bed. A place for my head."

"And I thought you were the one man I could count on for a night of passion," she sighed. She took her arm off Carew to steady the candle she was carrying and then clasped his hand, pulling him up the stairs. He came along willingly, reaching down and tugging at her skirt. She knocked his hand away. "Not now, not here. Later."

Carew straightened himself and walked boldly and determinedly into her chamber. It was a small attic room, with a sloping ceiling, next door to her sister's. It had a ewer in one corner, a chest, and a bed—and nothing else. The bed was plain and, when he sat on it, did not give. It was not slung with ropes but had a base of planks beneath the mattress. He lay back, with his head on the pillow, and started to lose consciousness—until Ursula brought him wide awake by slapping his face, lifting her skirts, straddling him, and kissing him on the lips. "If all you want to do is sleep, you can sleep downstairs. I need a man who is going to do his loving and paying. You just seem to want to drift off."

At those words, still with his eyes shut, Carew put his arms out and hugged her to him. "Take your clothes off," he growled in her ear. "If you're going to preach at me, you can preach at me naked."

She smiled and promptly began to undress.

The bed in the next room started knocking rhythmically against the wall. "Amy?" he asked, unlacing his soft leather shoes as he lay on the bed and throwing them across the room one by one.

"That's my sister," replied Ursula. "Why? Would you rather be in there than in here?"

Carew opened his eyes. "No, not at all. I have no desire to spend a night with one of Captain Parkinson's men." He took off his hosen, breeches, jerkin, and shirt and lay watching her in the candlelight, taking in her lovely nakedness. He was wearing nothing but his red scarf. She clambered over him, naked on all fours, and kissed him. He ran his hands over her hips and then moved them to caress her scarred cheek.

"Six days ago I was fighting below decks with Barbary pirates in the mouth of the Channel," he said. "Two days ago I was fighting waves thirty or forty feet high and seeing the drowned bodies of friends float away. Moments like this are good. Touching you is all I want. You are every woman in the world to me now, every kindness, and every gesture of love. You are everything that is not the green sea of darkness."

28

Wednesday, May 10

Carew awoke at the sound of voices in the next room. By the bright light creeping in between the shutters he could see that the sun was already up. Ursula lay naked beside him, still asleep. Blinking, he raised himself onto an elbow and looked around at the shadowy shapes.

The door to the next chamber closed. A moment later he heard a man's footsteps going down the staircase. He thought about getting up, but was unwilling to break the spell of the night. Normally a night on land made him nervous and distrusting of his comfort; but this deep sleep had been different. He had come ashore without a boat and so none of the authorities even knew he was here. They would do soon, as rumors shifted from careful whispers to careless remarks. But not yet.

He pulled the sheet back slightly to look at Ursula as she slept. She stirred but her eyes remained closed. Her breasts were still rounded and young, her nipples pink and small. Her belly was not too thin, unlike so many whores in seafaring towns, whose lives were a struggle to make enough money to eat, nor did it show any sign of stretch marks from childbearing. But she had two scars on her arms as well as the one on her face. In her own way she had fought to survive in a world that was as dangerous and unpredictable for her as it was for him.

She opened her eyes and smiled at him. Then she reached forward and pulled him closer, to kiss him. "Would Mr. Carew like some more?" she whispered.

The door latch rattled. A voice called, "Is Raw with you?"

It was Amy. Ursula slipped out of bed, naked, and unlocked the chamber door. She immediately turned and nipped back into the bed.

Amy entered, dressed in a linen night-shift. Her long red hair swirled around her head and she turned to the door and locked it. Then, with a skip, she ran over to Carew's side of the bed and, in a single swift movement, bent down and lifted the night-shift straight over her head.

"This is what I call a proper greeting," said Carew, as he moved over on the bed to make room for her.

"Don't do him for free, Amy," said Ursula, putting her arm around Carew's waist. "He hasn't come back with a treasure-laden ship yet. In fact, he hasn't come back with a ship at all."

"It doesn't matter," said Amy. She kissed Carew. He liked the softness of her lips and her skin, which smelt of apples. She drew away and looked him in the eye. "Pillow talk—that is our rich ship," she said. Lying down beside Carew, she went on, "John Prouze spent all afternoon and all night with me. He's gone now because he has to watch the quay. The truth is, he is expecting a consignment of treasure to be offloaded here, in Southampton."

"What sort of treasure?" asked Carew, seeing the excitement in her eyes.

"Who cares what sort of treasure? Gold, jewels—I don't know." She kissed him again, more passionately.

"Tell us more," said Ursula, putting her hand between their faces. Amy giggled. "No, tell us, truly." Ursula put her arm around Carew. "No more kissing until you do."

Amy propped herself on an elbow. "We were eating in my chamber yester evening, Prouze and me, and I asked him if he wanted an early night, in a joking way. And he said, 'Yes, indeed, for I must be off early to watch the quay.' So I replied, 'Watch duty, is it? Extorting bribes for Captain Cutthroat?' And he told me, 'No, Captain Cutthroat is away, but an order has arrived from London to watch the quay for a ship with three St. George's flags on its main mast. It will anchor out in Southampton Water.' Prouze said that the ship's captain will send a rowboat to shore with the treasure—he called it 'the Catholic Treasure.'"

Carew felt Ursula kissing his shoulder. Her hand was moving down his body, stroking his midriff. He stayed her hand with his own. "When is this ship arriving? Today?"

"Maybe. Prouze said that he'd probably have to wait ages for it to come in and he'd rather be in bed with me."

Carew pushed Ursula's hand away. "What does Prouze look like? Do I know him?"

"Short tapering beard, young, a bit bad tempered. Nothing unusual. He has a high opinion of himself but actually is as frightened of Captain Parkinson as everyone else is."

Carew clambered over Amy. He stepped across the bare boards of the chamber to the window and opened the shutters. There was early-morning sunshine across the roofs outside, seagulls were calling across the town. The roofs were all at uneven angles, as if they had been strewn there, and then the gaps in-filled with more roofs: most covered with wooden shingles, a few with slates, and some with tiles. Beyond, between two steeply inclined roofs, he could see a small section of the quay, where already the workmen and laborers were beginning to prepare for the day's lading. A wooden crane was in position above a barge and two men were rolling a huge cask, avoiding a procession of men approaching another boat with sacks on their backs. Carew could see the tops of the masts of the larger ships moored there, but the angle of the window prevented him from looking across Southampton Water itself.

He spotted a gully between two adjoining roofs overlooking the quay. Sticks and debris lay there with the seagulls' guano. "Can one get down there, to that gap between the two houses?" he asked.

Amy slipped out of the bed and came and stood beside him. "Only with a ladder, from the gallery." She pointed to a corner of the inn's external staircase.

Carew leaned out further, estimating the drop and the size of the ladder needed. Then he came back in and looked at Amy standing there naked beside him. He saw the freckles across her shoulders and her blue-eyed smile. Then he glanced at Ursula watching him from the bed. Putting his arm around Amy, he kissed her neck and felt his desire stir. He pushed her back toward the bed and slapped her rump as she turned. "If that ship truly has gold aboard it, you women are in for one hell of a payday."

29

Clarenceux opened his eyes. He was lying on his bed, fully clothed. A moment later the hell of his situation cascaded down on him, as if each individual worry had been a heavy volume and someone had tipped a whole press of books on top of him. The document…his wife in Chislehurst. Ascension Day morning. Mrs. Barker in league with the Knights of the Round Table. They had turned Rebecca against him. He was going to enter the lions' den.

Crossing himself, he said a prayer, got off the bed, and opened the shutters. He then bent down to the basin where yesterday's water still remained and splashed that over his face, rinsing his hands thoroughly and wiping them on a dirty linen towel nearby. There he paused, listening. He could hear nothing unusual. After reaching for the dagger under his pillow and the sword hanging from one of the bedposts, he went down to the kitchen at the back of his house.

The fire was cold. The bread on the worktable was old and hard. He forgot the basics of managing a household when he was by himself. Finding a piece of cheese, he started to eat.

Sir Percival had to be the fourth Knight, still coordinating the other three. He reckoned that they had been instructed by Lady Percy, through messages carried by Sir Percival, to force Rebecca

Machyn to steal the document. She had agreed and taken it, probably with their help in picking the locks when he was away. They must know where she had gone. Collectively they would meet on the following morning, at Mrs. Barker's house.

It was a trap—it had to be. Had he not met Mrs. Barker, he would have assumed she might simply be a kindhearted old woman who had sheltered Rebecca and now was prepared to offer him, as Rebecca's friend, the same courtesy. But the woman was scheming and devious. She was luring him. She could be blatant because she was aware he had no choice. No one else could tell him what had happened to the document or Rebecca Machyn.

Finishing the cheese, Clarenceux looked up at the light coming in through the high windows of the kitchen, above the great fireplace. He was wrong; he did have a choice. He could simply forget that he had ever had the document. But how would it feel, never to know where it was? He could not afford to wait until Sir William called for it. Worse, if these Catholic revolutionaries or their superiors tried to declare the truth of the document, then there would be a bloody war. Thousands would die. There would be an attempt to stamp out Catholicism altogether. Queen Elizabeth might well respond by burning Catholics in the same way her sister had burnt Protestants.

That decided him. Going through to the cool dark of the buttery, he poured a jug of three-day-old ale from a barrel and drank straight from the jug. He would assemble his weapons. He would check three or four hiding places he knew around the city. And then he would go in search of one thing he had never actually possessed. A gun.

30

~

Walsingham and John Richards rode at a gallop westward up Fleet Street and into the Strand. Coming to Cecil House, they swerved in through the gate, their horses' hooves clattering on the cobbles. They kicked off their stirrups and dismounted at speed. "Take the horses!" shouted Walsingham at a lad who ran out to greet them. Richards followed Walsingham as he strode to the main entrance.

"Where is Sir William?" he barked at a servant in the hall.

"Sir, he is in consultation with an emissary from the merchants at Antwerp."

"Go and tell him I have broken the cipher. *Now.* Do not delay a moment."

The servant bowed and departed. Walsingham started pacing up and down across the width of the hall. John Richards stood nearby, excited at the prospect of meeting Sir William Cecil but anxious at the same time. Ten minutes passed before another servant appeared and asked them to come up and see Cecil in one of his private chambers.

"Good day to you, gentlemen. You have a deciphered version with you, I presume?" asked Sir William. He was standing beside a circular marble-topped table, dressed in a black robe, slashed to show its scarlet lining, with an elegant gold chain, a narrow white ruff, and a black cap of velvet ringed with jewels. He gestured for them to be seated.

Walsingham and Richards both bowed. "This young man, John Richards, is the one we have to thank," Walsingham said. "I applaud his efforts."

"As do we all, I am sure. Tell me."

Walsingham glanced at Richards and pulled out a neat copy of the message on folded paper from his doublet and read it aloud.

RIGHT HUMBLY WE COMMEND US TO YOUR LADYSHIP WE HAVE RECEIVED YOUR INSTRUCTIONS FROM SIR PERCIVAL AND THE WIDOW IS WILLING TO DO WHAT SHE CAN TO RESTORE THE CATHOLIC TREASURE TO US SO THAT YOU AND WE TOGETHER MIGHT EFFECT ITS TRUTH SHE WILL BE DESPATCHED BY SHIP IN THE COMPANY OF ROBERT LOWE FROM LONDON TO SANDWICH AND THERE CHANGED TO A VESSEL BOUND FOR SCOTLAND WHEREUPON SHE WILL CONFIRM HER ARRIVAL WITH YOUR REPRESENTATIVES SHE WILL LEAVE FROM LONDON AT DAWN ON THE SEVENTH THAT WE MAY BE SURE YOU WILL SEND YOUR REPRESENTATIVES TO HOLYROOD WE BEG YOU SEND WORD BY THIS SAME MESSENGER GODSPEED YOUR LADYSHIP YOUR DEVOTED SERVANTS PERCY ROY

Cecil nodded and looked at John Richards. "Well done, Master Richards. I am impressed. I see you are following in Francis's footsteps. God knows that the government could do with a few more good minds."

Richards bowed. "Your words of courtesy overpraise my

achievement; but you do me great honor, and I am most grateful, Sir William."

Cecil nodded. "Yes, well. Shall we be seated?" He gestured to the awkward-looking wooden seats around the marble table. "My apologies for the chairs. Her majesty does not like them either and offered them to me. I could hardly refuse."

Walsingham was impatient. "Two things particularly interest me. The first is the people mentioned—'the widow' and Robert Lowe—and the second is the signature. 'Your devoted servants' is in the plural and yet the name given is that of just one man, Percy Roy."

Richards saw an opportunity to show off his knowledge. "The name Percy Roy could be a reference to the Battle of Shrewsbury in 1403, when the supporters of Henry Percy, the eldest son of the earl of Northumberland, took arms against King Henry IV. His men shouted for Percy to be king at that battle—Percy Roy."

Cecil raised an eyebrow. "Or it might be a code name."

"There is no doubt whom the Percy refers to," said Walsingham. "The dowager countess of Northumberl—"

"I know," Richards interrupted enthusiastically. "George Latham was watching Sheffield Manor when he saw the messenger."

Walsingham did not like to be interrupted, especially not by an underling. He looked at Richards, who realized he had overstepped his mark.

Cecil smiled. "You are right again, young Richards. Only you are jumping to conclusions. Just because the name *could* reflect that ancient war cry does not mean that it does. Francis—you were going to remind us about Robert Lowe, I presume?"

"He is the brother of Rebecca Machyn. I have no doubt that she is the widow in this document."

Sir William nodded. "Yes. The Machyn problem…"

Walsingham was sitting forward, leaning over the table. "You let them go—her and Clarenceux."

Cecil glanced at Richards before turning to Walsingham. "You made up a false story to try to convict her and Clarenceux and the so-called Knights of the Round Table. I had no alternative."

Walsingham shook his head. "I was close. You know I was." He held up the paper with the message. "This is proof of their plotting. And it clearly says that the widow has agreed with a plan to restore 'the Catholic Treasure' to Catholic hands. What more sign of her guilt do you need? If she is guilty, so is Clarenceux."

Cecil narrowed his eyes. "You have no idea what Clarenceux knows and doesn't know. While on the whole I applaud your testing every hypothesis that suggests itself, and being thorough in examining every possibility, I will not have you denigrating and humiliating important men on a whim. It brings disgrace upon the government and it alienates those who would otherwise support us in our attempts to maintain the rule of law and the state of religion."

Richards could see the resolution in Cecil's eyes. He expected Walsingham to back away from such a stand. But Walsingham rose slowly to his feet. "Sir William, you are committing a grave error if you think that that message is not treasonable. It would be folly not to arrest the protagonists immediately. Robert Dudley will tear your reputation apart in front of the court, if he discovered you failed to act."

Cecil gestured to Walsingham to sit down. Walsingham did not take his seat, however. Cecil spoke in sharp tones. "Francis, I am not suggesting for one moment that you should do nothing. But I know there is great enmity between you and Mr. Clarenceux and I want you to put that out of your mind. I will not let you use a situation like this to abuse his good name. Last time you wrecked—"

"Last time you let him go," interrupted Walsingham. "Last time you said he was innocent and the Machyn woman too. That is why we have this problem now." With that he turned his back on Cecil and walked across to the window.

"I am glad you have brought this to me without delay," Cecil told him. "I am glad you have translated the message. But there is nothing here that incriminates Clarenceux. What we need to focus on is what this message really *does* say, not what you would like it to. What it shows us is that there is a Catholic plot afoot and that it answers to Lady Percy. It shows us there are at least two go-betweens—or there *were* two. One is dead—the bearer of this message. The other is here named as Sir Percival. Whoever Percy Roy is, or whatever it refers to, it seems that Rebecca Machyn has something of value to these Catholics and is being escorted by her brother into Scotland on a boat sailing from Sandwich."

Walsingham turned. "It also shows us that the Knights of the Round Table are still functioning. Whatever they may have been plotting last year, we did not stop them. And you know as well as I do that they had some hidden means of threatening her majesty—using Machyn's chronicle…"

"Enough!" said Cecil, holding up a hand. "You have seen Machyn's chronicle. Do you honestly think that *that* is the Catholic Treasure?"

Walsingham remained silent.

"No, it is not," Cecil went on. "But something is. And whatever it is has sailed from Sandwich with Robert Lowe. Do you not feel that you are wasting time here, arguing with me?"

"I have already closed the port of Sandwich. I have men looking for Robert Lowe and Widow Machyn."

"And the identity of the messenger?"

"Twenty-six men, all from different wards of the city, went to view the body at Hertford yesterday. Four knew him by sight—none knew his name. Two of those who recognized him lived on the river, in adjacent wards—Queenhithe and Bread Street. When the body comes tomorrow, we will start exhibiting it in those places."

"Good. Excellent. Have you contacted Admiral Clinton yet?"

"Yes. Lord Clinton is in the North Sea now. I have sent a messenger to tell him to intercept any ship heading north that might be carrying Robert Lowe and Widow Machyn."

"Even better." Cecil stood and Richards did likewise. "Master Richards, I am pleased to meet you, and I thank you for your attention to duty and your assiduous work. No doubt we will meet again. Francis, I expect we will meet on the morrow, when I hope you will have established the dead messenger's identity."

31

John Prouze was uneasy. It was now early afternoon and all day he had had the feeling that someone was watching him as he waited on the quay. He had been into a tavern at one point, and later he had stood under the eaves of a baker's stall. He had seen no sign of the ship—but he was beginning to suspect that he was not the only man expecting it.

There was the black-haired man with green eyes sitting on the old steps to the western wharf. He had been there since midmorning, just sitting there, only moving when someone needed to use the steps. He had a straw in his teeth and he seemed to have been chewing it for ages. He was waiting for someone or something. Every time Prouze approached, the green-eyed man looked at him. Prouze confronted him at one point and demanded to know his business. "Waiting," the man had replied. When asked what he was waiting for, he had replied, "For whatever comes along."

Halfway down the quay there was a fat man who wore a scarf around his head in the morning and around his neck in the afternoon. He was almost chinless and bald. His white shirt was newly clean, unlike his blue breeches, which looked as though he had been living in them, sleeping in them, and swimming in them for several months. His ears were pierced with earrings and his boots decrepit. On the few occasions when he moved from his post, he shuffled, dragging his feet. He too caught Prouze's eye on more than one occasion.

At the southern end of the promontory, sitting at the end of the quay, was a huge black man. Prouze presumed he must be the servant of a lord or a runaway slave who worked as a servant. There were several Negro men and women in the ports; most of the women were the parents of illegitimate half-colored babies, the results of their masters' adventures in fornication with women of another race. But this man's stillness was ominous. Negros always did other people's bidding, so if he was waiting there for hours, it was on behalf of someone else.

Prouze looked at the horizon, in the direction that the black man was looking. Gulls called overhead. Waves lapped at the quay. But no ships flying three St. George's flags were to be seen. He walked back along the quay past the workers lading the ships. A dozen laborers were off-loading woolsacks one by one from a cart and onto a wooden platform to be craned over the side of a boat bound for Bordeaux. He passed the captain and boatswain, who were looking up at the rigging that had seen damage in the recent gales. He ducked in through the door of the Two Swans and gestured to the landlord. The next twenty minutes were spent supping a large mug of wine, sitting at a table, glancing at the door.

When the mug was drained he paid the landlord, got up, and left. Gray clouds were gathering again, blocking out the sun. The birds screeched as they passed over, looking for fish. And coming up Southampton Water was a large vessel.

Prouze could not be sure that it carried three flags on its main mast, let alone that they were all St. George's flags. The vessel seemed to take ages, tacking this way and that, and half an hour had passed before he realized with disappointment that it was not the ship he was waiting for. It bore only one flag. When he looked again at the men who had been watching, all of them had gone. The place where the green-eyed man had been sitting was now occupied by a thin, ginger-haired mariner. The bald fat man's place was now occupied by a large black-bearded man who looked more like a bear with a haircut than a man. The Negro too had gone; his place was now occupied by a gray-haired man, who was staring out across Southampton Water.

Walking back along the quay, Prouze was no less aware of being watched. He looked up—and for an instant thought there was some-one in the valley of the roofs between the Two Swans and the ware-house built next door. He saw a head there, momentarily. When he looked back, it had gone.

32

In the fields north of the city, Clarenceux looked up at the sky. It was growing dark, not only on account of the gray clouds but also the dying of the light. It would not be long before the city gates closed, and he wanted to make sure he was inside the walls when that happened. He would stay in one of his hiding places that evening—a stable loft where he had hidden his swords under some hay. He would head to Mrs. Barker's house at four.

He looked down at the ground. On a small cloth on the grass and buttercups lay two German-made wheel-lock pistols, with large, rounded pommels, ivory handles, and sleek long barrels. A matching carved, ivory-covered powder flask lay there too, and a small wooden box containing pouches of gunpowder and the tools for maintaining the guns. Having spent two hours practicing that afternoon, ratcheting the firing mechanism with a spanner, he was confident that the guns would fire. He had had only one single misfire in fourteen shots. He also knew he could hit a target as small as a cabbage at a range of thirty feet. The only problem was reloading. It had taken him nearly seven minutes to reload the two pistols with bullets, damping, wadding, and gunpowder. The gun merchant had assured him that after some practice, he would be able to do each pistol in under a minute. Clarenceux had believed him at the time.

He knelt and packed up the guns. Before getting up, he looked at the nearby stone wall of the field, and the bluebells and buttercups. He crossed himself. When he arose and started walking back to the city, it would be with a murderous intent. He was nervous already; he would need God to steady his hand in the morning. He prayed, screwing his eyes tight. When he opened them, he saw the colors of the buttercups and bluebells. *Blue and gold*, he thought. *The colors of King Arthur's coat of arms.*

33

Carew walked along the quay with Kahlu beside him. It was almost dark and hardly anyone was working now. The tall wooden cranes were stationary, silhouetted against the sky. Most of the seagulls had left, to settle in some corner of the night to sleep. Only the occasional bird swooped over the water.

Carew had checked all the lines of approach. Skinner was still on the southernmost tip of the promontory. Carew raised an arm and signaled to him to return to the inn. He looked up at the last vestiges of the sunset and sat on the edge of the quay. Kahlu sat down beside him. Together they gazed at the sky.

"Do you think we should go back?" Carew asked. "Prouze is with her again tonight."

"Uh-uh," replied Kahlu, shaking his head.

"She has betrayed him though. He must have realized today—seeing the crew taking their turns on the quay, waiting. If he suspects, he will take it out on her."

Kahlu shrugged and made a sort of whining noise to suggest "Maybe." And then a series of low grunts to suggest male enjoyment.

"I know. He did not complain while she was giving him her breasts to lie on. But some men blame women for their own faults."

Kahlu stared at the deep-blue sky streaked with two lines of pink-ish gold above the western horizon.

Carew stared at it also. For a moment he recalled sailing off the coast of Guinea. The metal belt that fastened the upper and lower masts had grown so hot that when you spat on it, the spittle instantly sizzled and evaporated. The skies had been beautiful, and the sunsets unforgettable.

Kahlu suddenly nudged him, pointing at two men in the shadows behind them. He and Carew edged to one side to hide behind a pile of broken crates. The town gates would have been closed some time ago, at dusk. There were bylaws forbidding boats to come and go at this time. Respected burghers with a lantern were permitted to pass, but there was a chance that Carew's men could be accused of being nightwalkers. That in turn would lead to accusations of theft or attempted theft. Although in Southampton the authorities were lax about clamping down on those who brought illicit goods into the port, they would not turn a blind eye to thieves. If the watchmen saw Carew and Kahlu they would either arrest them or demand a bribe.

The watchmen walked around a corner, out of sight. "Time to go," said Carew. "We'll start again at dawn."

34

Ascension Day, Thursday, May 11

Clarenceux could not sleep. He lay on a pile of hay in that fitful state between sleep and wakefulness, too awake to let himself drift into unconsciousness and too far from consciousness to control and dispel his fears. His plan, which had been so well worked out earlier, now seemed makeshift, overoptimistic, and unreliable. The unreason of half-sleep was sickening him as if it were poison in his mind.

He listened in the darkness to the sounds of the horses in the stable below and the rats in the walls. The distant clamor of cats fighting reached him. Not much later there was the barking of a dog, roused from its sleep by someone walking in the night along the lanes. Then a minute's quiet. No cats, dogs, rats, owls, or nightingales. No voices.

He opened his eyes. It was dark in the stable loft. Neither was there any sign of light seeping in from outside. Nevertheless, he stirred himself as anxiety churned inside him. It was better to be fully awake than off-guard.

He got up and felt around in the darkness, placing his hand where he had laid out his weapons the previous evening. He felt a dagger and strapped it in its sheath to his left thigh. A knife he attached to his calf, inside his boot. A sword—which he would have to conceal as he walked through the city—he buckled to his belt. He used the spanner to cock the two pistols and tucked them into his clothes: one inside his doublet, which was fastened over the top; the other behind his back, in his belt. The spanner for loading the guns and the gunpowder flask he put in a pouch hanging at his side. The box containing the other tools and the remaining gunpowder, together with the key to the backdoor to his house, he hid under the hay.

Before he left the stable, he knelt and prayed. He looked in his heart for hope and thought of his wife and family. He remembered Annie singing in her chamber and little Mildred climbing the stairs at home, her curly hair framing her smiling face. He thought of Tom: his servant's deeply lined, careworn forehead, and the resolution in his eyes that left you in no doubt he would face an army singlehanded if ordered to do so. He thought of Julius. And his thoughts flickered around Rebecca. He had lain in this very stable loft with her once before. She was still a presence. He saw her long brown hair, her glad and sad brown eyes, the mole on the side of her face. He prayed for her too.

He stood up and felt for the great cape he had been lying on. He put it on and made his way to the ladder. The horses shifted in their stalls but did not whinny or cause alarm. Shutting the stable door, he was out in the cold of the morning. He looked up: the stars were clear but the faintest lightening was now in the sky, the black of night becoming the deepest blue.

The dark houses and the silhouettes of their roofs against the stars clearly revealed the pattern of the lanes and alleys in this part of the city. Every so often he caught a glimpse of a dark figure moving between the shadows: thieves, nightwalkers, and men of base intentions and ill repute. Maybe a few were like him, conducting their business under cover of the night. But those with honorable intentions would have been carrying a lantern; he did not. He had been too concerned to assemble his weapons and test his guns. On reflection, he was glad. Lantern candles, tinderboxes, and gunpowder in a hay-filled stable loft would have been a dangerous combination.

The smells of the city assaulted his senses even more at night. The burial grounds of the churches were full to overflowing but they did not stink like Cheapside, where any fallen market produce that was not swept up moldered away. However, the worst smells were to be found in the smallest alleys. Turning down one, he passed a line of tenanted houses with brimming cesspits in their backyards and basements. In places, the night heightened the stench of the horse dung trodden into the mud, or the ordure from where flocks of sheep had been driven along to market. Clarenceux put a hand over his mouth and nose, and looked up at the church towers and spires, like so many stone plants growing strongly out of this fetid, highly fertilized square mile of God's earth.

In Bread Street, a wave of nervousness flowed over him. He had two cocked pistols on him—and yet he felt weak, trembling. He strode more purposefully, reminding himself of what he was doing, bringing to mind all the anger he felt. Rebecca Machyn had betrayed him. She had stolen the document. That she had done so could only be due to these people whom he was going to confront. And they would betray her too. She was not safe in their hands—wherever they had taken her. All they wanted was the document and someone in a position of responsibility and authority to pronounce it true and legal. When that happened, they would not care for her. They would not protect her; she would have nothing more to offer them. That was the corruption of power—a series of betrayals, a sequence of disappointments and vendettas, a world of fear.

He came to Little Trinity Lane, his pulse racing. Looking at the low jetty of the Machyn house ahead, he saw Mrs. Barker's house on the opposite side of the street, with its shuttered windows. There was no sign of any light within.

He stood in front of her door, breathed deeply, and rapped on it with his knuckles. He waited. Ninety seconds passed before the door opened a fraction.

"Your name and business?" asked a voice from the shadows.

"My name is King Clariance. My business is that of the Round Table," declared Clarenceux.

The door opened more fully, allowing him in, and then shut behind him. For a moment there was darkness, then the servant opened the aperture of a lantern he was carrying. Clarenceux blinked, unable to see the servant.

"We have been waiting for you, Mr. Clarenceux."

The lantern moved off in the direction of the stairs. Clarenceux followed, feeling the round pommel of the pistol in his doublet. He crossed himself. But as he did so, the lantern flashed across the figures of two men waiting silently at the foot of the stairs. One was a man whom Clarenceux did not recognize. The other was James Emery.

"Good evening," said Clarenceux.

"We will talk upstairs," said the unknown man. The servant with the lantern turned to shine some light on the speaker. "Go up."

"Don't do anything hasty, Mr. Clarenceux," added James Emery. "If you do, you will regret it."

It was not just a warning. It was a slip, made by a man as nervous as he was. Clarenceux felt the pistol through his doublet and turned to follow the servant up the stairs. Emery and the other man came behind him. As the servant's lantern illuminated the landing above, Clarenceux saw the legs of another man standing there. Nicholas Hill.

"If you are carrying a weapon, Clarenceux, hand it over now," said Hill, looking down at him.

Clarenceux bit his lip, cold with nerves, seeing the flickering of the lantern and the long shadows it cast on the walls. He arrived at the top step. The servant moved his light to shine directly on him. Slowly Clarenceux moved his cape to one side and made to unfasten his sword belt. The servant trained the lantern on the weapon as it fell. Clarenceux felt behind his back for the pistol there, tucked in his loosened belt.

He took a deep breath. The next moment he threw himself sideways against Hill, striking the man's chest with his shoulder and driving him back against the paneled wall. He pulled out the pistol and pressed it upward into the top of Hill's neck. "Keep still! This will blow your head clean off. You have one chance to tell me where you have taken Rebecca Machyn and the document. Now!"

"A Godly creature you are not," gasped Hill, trying to free his arm, which was trapped beneath Clarenceux's weight. "If that is why you came here, you can hang yourself."

The door to the chamber in which he had met Mrs. Barker opened. The room was lit by a chandelier. Keeping the pistol on Hill's neck, Clarenceux turned and looked in. At first all he saw was the light. Then he realized his mistake.

There were many people in the room, including women. Two or three men were already in the doorway. Clarenceux pushed the pistol harder into Hill's cheek. "Damn you! Tell me!"

The men in the doorway faltered.

"Tell me!" shouted Clarenceux at Hill. Suddenly he jammed the pistol against the man's temple. "Put your hands up. Walk into the room."

Hesitantly, Hill did as he was told.

Clarenceux swapped the pistol to his left hand and held it against the back of Hill's head. He pushed his right hand into his doublet and pulled out the second pistol. He waved it at the men still on the stairs and landing, gesturing them to follow.

"Put the gun down," said one of the men in the doorway. "There are many of us. You have only two shots. We will take you even if you kill two of us."

"Stand back and keep silent, unless you want this man to lose his head."

The men withdrew cautiously, allowing Hill and Clarenceux into the brightly lit chamber. Emery, the servant, and the other man held back at the door. "You three too," snapped Clarenceux, gesturing to them with the pistol in his right hand.

Now he could see everyone. Not one but two chandeliers were burning, the large metal rings of candles providing light. More light came from the candles on a makeshift altar set up in front of the shuttered windows. There were about twenty men and women staring at him. He backed against a wall.

Mrs. Barker stepped forward, wearing a black and gold gown with lace at her wide cuffs and neck. "Mr. Clarenceux, you come here in war. You threaten these Knights and soldiers of the Faith. If you harm one of us, there can be no forgiveness."

Clarenceux looked from face to face, seeing cold judgment there. "Where is she? Where is the document? That is what I need to know."

He kept his left-hand pistol on Hill; the right-hand one he leveled at Mrs. Barker.

"We do not know where Widow Machyn has gone. She has betrayed us too."

"What do you mean? You are the ones responsible."

Mrs. Barker looked at him with a steady gaze. "Shoot me—if that is your intention. But I do not know where she has gone. None of us do."

Clarenceux sensed a shifting among those present, an uneasiness with what she had said. "The Percy-Boleyn marriage agreement was taken from my house. My life depends on its safekeeping. Even being here now will be enough in the eyes of her majesty's Secretary, Sir William Cecil, to warrant my execution for treason. I am not going to take any chances."

"You are taking a very great chance right now," said one man.

Clarenceux jerked the pistol against the back of Nicholas Hill's head. "Walk forward, away from me. Slowly. Join the others."

Hill did as he was told, taking four slow steps. "I will not forgive you for this," he said.

Clarenceux waited until Hill had stopped and turned, still keeping the gun in his right hand on Mrs. Barker. "Why are there so many of you here? I came here to celebrate Mass in a private chapel with the Knights of the Round Table, not a crowd of onlookers."

"These people are all supporters of the Knights' cause," said Mrs. Barker. "We call them Gentlemen and Ladies of the Round Table. The status of the Knights is undiminished. It is a calling. You too were called to be one of us, by Henry Machyn himself. You said you wished to join us again. But if you truly wish to take communion alongside us, you have set about it in an unfriendly way."

"You arranged for her to steal the document. *That* was an unfriendly introduction."

"That is another matter. It is growing light already—we are losing time. And we have all been betrayed. We will act together, but first we must pray. Will you hear Mass with us? Or are you determined to shoot one of us before the survivors cut you down?"

Clarenceux lowered the pistol in his right hand so that it was no longer pointing at Mrs. Barker. The one in his left he still held ready. "If she has betrayed you too, where does that leave us?" he asked, looking at the assembled faces. One man's was full of defiance. Behind him, he saw a woman of about thirty; she was trembling. Beside her was a young man who looked unmoved, cold. Clarenceux had seen that sort twenty years before, in the army. The sort of man who gives the order to shoot and is able to pretend that it does not mean he has broken the Commandment: *Thou shalt not kill.* Another woman looked tired, drawn, as if she had not slept. With one or two exceptions, these people were not revolutionaries.

He lowered the other pistol. In full view of everyone, he pushed both guns back inside his doublet. "Let us hear Mass," he said. "In the chapel. Just the Knights—and Mistress Barker."

He watched as Mrs. Barker turned and strode toward the tapestry on the far wall. The altar had been set up directly opposite, so everyone present could hear the service. Two men now lifted off the portable altarpiece and two others removed the altar cloth, lifted the table, and started to carry it back toward the chapel. No one spoke except in a whisper. People kept their eyes on Clarenceux as if he might start shooting. James Emery scowled at him as he walked past.

A priest, dressed in purple, appeared from behind the crowd. Clarenceux recognized him as Father Tucker. He followed him through into the room that was to serve as a chapel. The room was paneled, about twelve feet square. There was a large window, covered by internal shutters. The altar was in place; Father Tucker opened a wall cupboard and started setting out the chalice and paten in front of the altarpiece. Hill and Emery were standing side by side, Hill's comparative youth and obvious physical power making him a strange companion for the gray-haired Emery.

"I expected there to be more Knights," Clarenceux said.

"You know where they are," Mrs. Barker replied. "Daniel Gyttens was killed in prison. Lancelot Heath has not been seen for six months. Michael Hill died not long ago. Robert Lowe is with his sister. William Draper we will not speak about—he is no longer worthy of our acquaintance. That leaves just four men. How many more did you expect?"

"Henry Machyn used to appoint successors to take the places of the dead."

"Henry Machyn is no longer with us. He appointed you to take his place. You are in the position of leadership, should you wish to assume it."

Clarenceux looked at Father Tucker. He looked at Hill and Emery, then returned his attention to Mrs. Barker. "Let us pray."

Clarenceux knelt on the window-side of the chapel, Mrs. Barker in the center, and the two Knights nearest the door. Father Tucker's voice was melodious; he had obviously been trained in one of the singing schools. In his early forties, he was old enough to have learned before the old king closed the monasteries.

As Father Tucker sang and the minutes passed by, Clarenceux realized that he had been a fool. He had come here with the intention of threatening the Knights and Mrs. Barker. Had there been just the four of them, he could have got away. Now he was trapped. He had foreseen that it was a trap—he had even guarded against it—and yet he had walked straight into it.

Where was Rebecca? As he thought about the document, he realized that, if she had betrayed the Knights and him, then someone else must have gained some sort of influence over her. Lady Percy? It hardly mattered. Whatever he did in this house—even if he unloaded his guns into one of them—it would not stop the revolution. The pyres on which Queen Mary had burned hundreds of Protestants in the 1550s would be relit for Catholics. Heresy and treason would once more go hand in hand: the most frightening combination of human forces he could imagine. But a heavy dose of revenge would be added. No doubt Sir William Cecil and Francis Walsingham would arrange the trials and executions of the leading Catholics, dragging them through the city and then burning them in public. He himself would be one of the first.

As the singing continued, Clarenceux forced himself to examine every inch of the room for a way out. He saw the oil painting of the altarpiece and the highlighting of the linenfold paneling on the door and walls. He saw the wooden shutters of the window—too solid and close together to break through easily—and the oak floorboards. He looked up at the ceiling: elaborate molded plasterwork.

Father Tucker had stopped singing. Clarenceux was aware that the others were all surreptitiously watching him. The priest turned to face him. He was carrying the paten with the holy bread, the body of Christ. The paten was enameled silver of a sort much favored in the past by aristocratic families when traveling around the country. He looked at Father Tucker's purple robe and his hands on the paten. He glanced at the altar. There the chalice stood. It was similarly enameled, holding the wine that was the blood of Christ. Father Tucker spoke a Latin blessing over the paten and Clarenceux allowed him to place the bread on his tongue. Everyone was watching him. Clarenceux swallowed the bread, crossed himself, and said, "Amen."

Father Tucker resumed singing. "*Agnus dei, qui tollis peccatur mundi…*" Later there were prayers. As Father Tucker expressed his hopes of a restoration of England to the fold of Rome, Clarenceux's eyes were drawn to the design on the chalice. It was a coat of arms— the only coat of arms he had seen in the whole building. He remembered that he had seen shields on the woodwork downstairs but the designs had been painted out. Now he was looking at the arms of the Talbot family on the side of the chalice.

The Talbot family. The family into which Lady Percy, dowager countess of Northumberland, had been born.

Clarenceux looked up at Father Tucker, who nervously made the sign of the cross. *He either brought this chalice and paten from Lady Percy, at Sheffield Manor, or…*He looked at the floorboards, struggling to understand his own thoughts. *Or…Mrs. Barker is of the same family.*

He remembered the conversation at Nicholas Hill's house. *Who is Sir Percival? A holier man than you.* The floorboards seemed to move, he felt dizzy. Father Tucker was backing away.

"*You* are Sir Percival," Clarenceux said. "And you are…are…" His heart was beating frantically. This was not normal. His hands were shaking and he could barely control his movements. But as his throat and heart started to burn, he remembered the bread. The priest had given him poison under the guise of Holy Communion.

Rage burst through Clarenceux. He put his fingers to the back of his throat and retched. Out of the corner of his eye he saw Nicholas

Hill getting to his feet. He started to stand as well, but Hill was faster. Hill pushed him down and tried to grab the pistols from inside Clarenceux's doublet. Clarenceux twisted away from him and drew a pistol himself. Panicking, blind to everything but his own survival, he pulled the trigger as he staggered to his feet. A sharp recoil made him drop the weapon and he stumbled, retching again, as light and darkness flashed alternately across his eyes. He pulled the other gun from his doublet. There was a blurred shape in purple in front of him; he shot at it as he fell.

It felt as if he was on the head of a pin. A sharp pain seemed to be penetrating him through the belly. *God's needle.* But whether it was really a knife or the poison, or divine judgment, he could not tell. His mind was shifting like a cloud that one moment has one form and the next has quite another, through no will of its own.

"Lock him in the room at the top of the back stairs," said Mrs. Barker. "Fasten him down and give him another dose. We need to find out what he knows about us, and what he has told Cecil, before he dies."

35

Walsingham ascended the grand stairs of Cecil House. At the top, he saw Sir William himself, anxiously pacing from one end of the paneled landing to the other. He was only half dressed, wearing nothing over his linen shirt, which was most unusual for the queen's Secretary. Walsingham could not remember ever having seen him so incomplete in his attire.

"My heartiest greetings, Sir William," hailed Walsingham. "You look troubled."

"What do you expect if you send me such a message?"

"I am sorry, Sir William, but you did say—"

"Yes, yes. You did the right thing. I would be far more vexed if you had not told me." He stopped pacing. "I presume the identity of the messenger has been confirmed?"

Walsingham stood on the top step, his hand on the newel post. "The body is in the church of St. James, in Garlickhithe. Two neighbors agree. His name was Stephen Langhill and he was a servant in a house in Little Trinity Lane, directly opposite the Machyn residence."

"And the proprietor?"

"A woman who goes by the name of Mrs. Barker. Catholicism is suspected. The churchwardens have said that she is a recusant—she does not attend parochial services. The same goes for her servants. You see what this means? The Machyn plot did not come to an end. It never came to an end. Clarenceux is still plotting."

Cecil looked over the balcony. "Come into my study, Francis. We don't want to go speculating wildly out here, where servants, visitors, and all sorts of people can hear us." He walked to the door, opened it, and went through, leaving Walsingham to come in and close it behind him.

"Francis, if you are right, then we have a whole locality of Catholic sympathizers, a nest of vipers. But you need to be careful regarding what you say about Clarenceux's involvement. You may be right— but you must not let your distrust of the man cloud your judgment."

"Your *trust* of the man has allowed him to continue his activities. Did he take you up on the offer to go to Antwerp?"

"He has not yet responded, no. But there are many possible reasons why. It is a major decision for a man with a family."

"Forget the other reasons. He is reluctant to go because he wishes to concentrate on Lady Percy's conspiracy. Why else would a man like that not go?" Walsingham held Cecil's gaze. "I'll tell you why. Because he would be exposed as a Catholic sympathizer. He is afraid—for good reason."

Walsingham walked to the wine table and took a goblet but found that the servants had not yet refilled the flask. He set the goblet down again. "I have taken the liberty of having men search for him. They entered his house; no one was at home, not even his servants. With this in mind, I will have his house searched once again. I am also intending to search Mrs. Barker's house and the Machyn house. They are all being watched."

Cecil shrugged. "What can I say? It seems you have decided on your strategy."

"That coded letter said Widow Machyn is *willing* to restore the Catholic Treasure to someone. She has already set sail. And I believe Clarenceux knows where she is going."

Cecil listened and started walking slowly beneath the portrait of himself. "Francis, let me ask you this. What do you think the Catholic Treasure is? For that is the root of this plot. The people involved are just the branches and leaves. We need to concentrate on the root. Cut that, and we kill the whole tree. Do you have any idea?"

Walsingham shook his head. "I doubt it is a casket of jewels. More likely to be a relic or an icon. But I will say this: there is more than one way to fell a tree. Cutting off all the branches and leaves is as effective as severing its roots."

"Sit down, Francis."

Sunlight was pouring through the window, gleaming off the polished wooden surfaces. The paintings seemed very dark against the whitewashed walls. Walsingham looked at Cecil and saw the man's grave expression silhouetted by the window.

Cecil leaned on the table, pressing his fingers and thumbs on its surface. "The Catholic Treasure is a document. It is the marriage agreement between Lord Percy and the queen's mother, Anne Boleyn. If any traitors managed to seize it, they would have in their possession a notarial instrument that could be used to depose the queen on the grounds of illegitimacy."

"How do you know this? Is that what Clarenceux's plot..." Walsingham's trailed off as he saw the implications of what Cecil had just said. The queen's Secretary had been withholding information from him—information relating to a Catholic conspiracy that he, Walsingham, was supposed to be investigating.

"I am sorry, Francis. I should have told you earlier. Clarenceux knew the whereabouts of the document. I did not inform you. That was wrong and I apologize."

"Why?"

"Why did I not tell you? Well…" Cecil sighed. "I thought it best not discussed. Clarenceux would not have revealed its whereabouts—he is as stubborn as a mule. But he is also not the sort of person to use it himself. He is not a revolutionary by nature."

"But he has allowed it to pass to Widow Machyn."

"Or maybe she stole it from him."

Walsingham was still recovering from his shock. "How long have you known all this?" he asked, staring at the floorboards.

"About the document's existence? For years. That Clarenceux knew where it was: about six months. He told me—in strict confidence."

"So I am right. We cannot trust Clarenceux. He is one of them."

Cecil took a seat and moved it to face Walsingham. He spoke in a low voice. "It depends on whether he willingly colluded with the Knights or was betrayed."

"By Widow Machyn? Damn his eyes—he has probably sailed with her."

"Or is trying to find her in London. There are many reasons why he might be away from home. Some of them point to his innocence and others to his guilt. I hope he is innocent. But what I hope does not matter now. It is the conspiracy as a whole we must consider. By comparison, individual fates are trivialities."

36

Raw Carew shifted his position in the valley between the two roofs facing the quay of Southampton. He knelt, shielding his eyes from the sun. It was late morning and he was looking almost due south—straight into the glare. There was a ship approaching, just visible.

"Prouze has seen it," said Luke Treleaven. He was lying down and shuffled forward to peer over the edge of the roofs. He looked each way along the quay. "Who has the sharper eyes—Kahlu or Devenish?"

"Kahlu," replied Carew. "He is also the more cautious. Devenish will shout that he has seen it when he just thinks he has. Kahlu will wait and make sure."

"Then that is our ship." Luke shuffled back. "Kahlu is coming this way."

"Stay here. Watch Prouze. I'll be waiting inside the front door of the inn."

Carew went back toward the ladder. He climbed down to the gallery that linked the second-floor chambers and down the steps to the ground floor. Having passed through the hall he waited just inside the door, watching the movements of those outside. He saw Kahlu approaching and spoke to him as he entered. "What news?"

Kahlu pointed to the south, the direction of the ship. He jabbed his right middle finger against his left hand, palm up, indicating the middle mast, and then presented Carew with three fingers.

Carew moved to the door and peered out. The ship was a three-master, a fast-looking modern galleon. He checked the people nearby, then stepped out of the inn and walked across the quay to have a better look. Kahlu followed him and tapped him on the shoulder. He made the sign of a ship with his left hand and patted his heart with his right.

"True, my friend, that is indeed a boat to fall in love with. They've cut the forecastle down to make her faster through the water. Compact and maneuverable. Elegant."

Kahlu tapped him on the shoulder again and made a sign with his fingers meaning "money."

"I haven't forgotten." He looked around again at those on the quay. Then indulged himself once more in gazing at the boat. For these moments he could fantasize. She would not come to the quay and he had no vessel of his own with which to pursue and take her. In a short while he would be waiting for Prouze to off-load the treasure and soon after that the ship would be gone. But just for a few minutes he could dream of standing on the deck confident that nothing was faster. If he had a ship like that, no one would be able to catch him— no one except someone in an identical ship.

Carew and Kahlu went back to the inn to discuss their plans. Twenty minutes later, the crew was all at their agreed stations. Everything continued as usual around them. In the bright sunshine, the laborers hauled sacks and carts to the ships. The harbormaster made his tour of the vessels that afternoon and noticed nothing amiss. The heavy horses pulled on the largest wooden crane to off-load the heavy goods from a Mediterranean galley. Captains made agreements with merchants inside and outside of the taverns nearby. Sacks of cloth were stacked ready for loading onto two Portuguese vessels. And in and around the bustling scene men waited discreetly. Stars Johnson and old James Miller helped to carry sacks of oats from one pile on the quay to another. Hugh Dean was in a quiet corner near the end of the quay with all five of his pistols laid out in front of him, lovingly tending to them after their soaking in the wreck of the *Nightingale*. Every so often he cast a glance toward the ship with the three flags. John Devenish had cleaned his broad-bladed sword and hidden it in a sack; with this slung across his back, he was helping to off-load crates of chickens from a small boat onto a cart. Skinner Simpkins was just sitting on the quayside in plain view of everyone, whittling a stick. Luke was still at his post on the roof. Francis Bidder and Swift George Thompson were apparently in deep conversation at the southern end of the quay, both looking out to the vessel. The rest were waiting in the long hall at the back of the Two Swans and in the marketplace.

A skiff put out from the three-flagged ship. Carew and Kahlu joined Bidder and Thompson at the southern point and watched it. Five people were on board, two of them rowing. Carew waited until he was sure they were coming to the quay. "Kahlu, you stay here until they have landed, watch in case they change course and go toward the River Itchen. Swift, Francis, come with me."

He walked along the quay looking for Prouze and pretending to talk to Swift while Francis reported to them what was happening with the skiff. "She's about a hundred yards from the quay, coming straight toward where Skinner is sitting." Carew looked for Prouze, checking all the faces of those watching, searching them for subtle signs of recognition and communication. He looked up at the rooftop. Amy was pointing down at a group of men standing on the quay near Skinner. Two looked like yeomen in their rustic clothes, another looked like an unsuccessful merchant, dressed in garments that had once been smart. The fourth man was young. He had a tidy, short beard, a burgundy doublet, and was openly wearing a sword.

Carew glanced up at Amy. With a nod, she confirmed it was Prouze. "Swift," said Carew in a low voice, "give the signal to the men in the inn."

Prouze and his companions were standing directly behind Skinner, who was still whittling. Carew and his men were five or six yards away. More of his men casually gathered in groups of three and four nearby. As the seconds passed and the skiff came nearer, more of Carew's men gathered. There were thirty now. Prouze stopped speaking and walked closer to the quay.

Carew walked forward, nearer to the quay edge. He looked down into the approaching skiff. There was nothing there—no chests—just the people.

He walked away from the edge, shaking his head, then looked up at the place where Amy had been. She was not there. He caught the eyes of members of his crew silently looking to him for orders and gave a subtle signal with his right hand, palm down. *Wait.* He glanced back at Prouze. The boat had touched the dock now, and three of those aboard were disembarking. There was a woman in her early forties coming up the steps, with long dark hair, brown eyes, and a distinctive large mole on the side of her face. With her was a muscular man who greeted Prouze with a nod of his head, and a shorter man who was talking to him. Carew overheard the man say the words "from here on" and "return to London," but that was all. A moment later Prouze was leading the man and the woman along the quay. The third man said farewell to them and went back aboard the skiff. The oarsmen pushed off.

Carew turned and looked at his men. Their faces were full of questions. He could only shrug and nod toward the inn. Kahlu asked in hand signs whether the money was still on the ship.

"I do not know, my friend," replied Carew, drawing close. "Those people cannot be carrying it. My guess is that it will be unloaded later, after nightfall. They have come to make contact with Prouze first." He gestured for George Thompson to approach. "Follow them, Swift. Don't let them out of your sight. Take Skinner with you and keep me informed."

37

Clarenceux turned his head, unsure of whether he was awake or dreaming. He was lying spread-eagled on the floor, naked, apart from a blindfold. A long nail had been driven into the floorboards on either side of each wrist and then hammered to bend it over. The same had been done to his ankles. The air was unmoving and warm, like that of an attic.

He heard a woman's voice. It seemed to be coming at him from underwater, bubbling through his mind. He heard her say "Rebecca Machyn" and "betrayed us." Or did he imagine these things? Was she saying that Clarenceux had betrayed them or that Rebecca had? He did not understand.

He had the feeling that cold water was about to hit his face. He turned his head to avoid it but it was always on the point of hitting him. He shook his head, trying to rid himself of the feeling. As he did so, the whole house seemed to be bobbing on a deep ocean. His mouth tasted of bile. He was sweating. The blindfold itched.

He heard the woman's voice again. It was Mrs. Barker. She was not speaking to him but to someone else in the room. "Why did he come here?"

"To find Widow Machyn," said a man, who sounded like Emery.

"He knows we arranged for her to steal the document. He believes that she has betrayed him."

"That was not what Father Tucker believed, God rest his soul," said a second man. "Clarenceux knew that Widow Machyn had taken the document from him. He knew we were his enemies. Yet still he came. He came to kill us."

"No. Think about it from Widow Machyn's point of view," said the woman. "Suppose she did betray Clarenceux as well as us, and that he truly doesn't know where she is. Why did she betray both of us? If she did not want to use the document for a Catholic purpose—our cause—then what? She must have taken it to stop us, on behalf of the government. If so, she would have warned him. That is why Clarenceux came here—looking for more information on Cecil's behalf."

"We will soon see," said the second man.

Clarenceux felt the whip cut the skin of his inner thighs, first the left then the right. He bit his tongue. But he screamed at the first kick to his testicles, which followed soon afterward. His cry surged as the pain poured through him and the feeling echoed in his body.

"Maybe Widow Machyn told him what she was going to do," said the second man. "Maybe he gave the document to Cecil himself."

Clarenceux felt the two lashes again: left, right. He screamed even more at the second kick between his legs.

"Perhaps Lowe told him what we had planned," said Emery, "and he warned both him and Widow Machyn to flee. I do not doubt that he has come as a spy for Cecil."

Clarenceux felt the leather whip on each of his thighs. The next kick on his bruised testicles was excruciating.

"Where is she?"

Another two cuts with the whip and another kick. Clarenceux screamed again and this time his scream went on and on—as the pain resounded through his whole form. He started to talk, to tell the voices about going to see James Emery and Nicholas Hill.

"Why did you come here?" the woman's voice demanded.

Clarenceux heard his own voice, his words drifting apart—and then he heard his silence. High in the sky of darkness, high above the ocean of pain, a brown-winged moth was fluttering, rising up among the stars and the moon. He let himself fly with that moth, away from the pain and the questions. As he watched the moth fluttering in the moonlight, he knew that all he had to do to survive was to stay quiet. The silence of the moth was his blessing. The best way to keep quiet was to hide with the moth—and never to doubt that he could fly into the darkest reaches of the night and hide from every man and woman. In the bosom of the moth was a place of silence and refuge from all torture.

They would never find him here among the stars, so far away from his body.

38

Carew set his mazer down when he saw Skinner enter the inn. "Has she weighed anchor?" he asked.

Skinner shook his head—and grinned.

"Then the treasure is still aboard." Carew clenched his fist and thumped the table. "Hugh, prime all your pistols. We are going to take her. You will lead one skiff and board from starboard. I'll lead the portside attack. Ten men apiece."

"What are we after?" asked Dean. "The treasure or the ship?"

"The treasure *and* the ship, my friend. Can you imagine a sleeker, faster vessel in which to sail from Southampton? Who could possibly catch us in a vessel like that? In the *Nightingale* we were living on our wits, night and day. Aboard a beauty like that we could sail away with a smile and wave of a hat." He paused. "Why, in such a ship we could outsail everyone—bring gold from India, slaves from Africa, silver from the New World, spices from the Moluccas…"

Kahlu uttered some incomprehensible sounds.

"No slaves from Kahlu's tribe," said Carew, lifting his mazer. "Unless they are very pretty." He drained the mazer and rolled his shoulders, exercising his muscles. "The curfew bell is our signal. We'll board that boat, offer the crew terms, and send what treasure is needed back here. Pieter Gervys and his wife have looked after us well, and all the women here have treated us with kindness. What we can share, we will—and I hope it is plenty."

39

It was a gray midafternoon when Walsingham's men took up position in Little Trinity Lane. They had closed the road half an hour earlier, allowing pedestrians to leave the area but not return. The captain, a fierce Londoner by the name of Jack Walker, had personally reconnoitred the area. He was aware of the passages through the backyards of the adjacent properties. He had identified a small back door too. It looked to be an easy matter to isolate the house and make sure that all those within could not escape. He brought up a large cart to block the exit from the back door and left a musketeer there to guard it. Four other men armed with muskets were stationed in the backyards. The remaining nineteen were lined up and told to follow him in a line, silently.

Walsingham watched from a distance with John Richards and two guards. Both men were mounted. They said nothing as Captain Walker led the troop in a single file beneath the eaves of the houses, so they could not be seen from the windows of Mrs. Barker's house. When they were in position, Captain Walker knocked on the door.

Walsingham and Richards saw the door open and Walker's troops entering. There were shouts and a shot was fired. Then another. A man started screaming. Local residents who had no knowledge of what was happening came out to see what the matter was. Walsingham rode forward and ordered them to return inside their homes. Had he been on foot, his diminutive figure would have carried little authority, but looking down on them, dressed entirely in black and with an expensive lace ruff at this neck, no one questioned his commands.

Walker reappeared fifteen minutes later with his sword sheathed. He bowed briefly in salute to Walsingham. "We have a total of seventeen prisoners, including three men wounded, one gravely so and likely to die. An eighteenth individual resisted arrest and was shot dead. A nineteenth was already dead."

"Who are the dead men?"

"An old man and a priest. I don't know their names. The priest had been shot. His corpse was cold."

Walsingham accepted this news without a response. He turned to Richards. "I think the time has come for us to find who in that house sent the message to Lady Percy." He dismounted and took his horse by the bridle.

"There is one other thing, sir," said Walker. "In an attic room, there is a naked man nailed to the floor. He has clearly been tortured. There are cuts all over his thighs and lower abdomen, and blood on his hands where he has lost three fingernails recently—pulled off with a pair of pliers, it would appear."

Walsingham led his horse across to the house. "I don't suppose you know the name of this brave enemy of the Catholic cause?"

Walker followed him. "Yes, sir. He is Mr. Harley, the Clarenceux Herald."

Walsingham almost fell off his horse. "Clarenceux? Describe him for me—no, better still, take me straight to him."

Walker led Walsingham and Richards through the house and up

to the attic. The narrow stairs creaked with every step and it was dark: the attic itself was almost without light. There was a stench of sweat and fear. Clarenceux was pinned out, his naked body filthy and bruised. The blindfold had already been removed.

Walsingham peered over him, inspecting his face. "What are you here for? Is this punishment? Or are they trying to extract information from you?" He walked around Clarenceux, studying the marks on his body. Some showed signs of inventiveness. The interrogator had not been entirely inexperienced.

"Why are you here like this, Clarenceux? Answer me! Or this torture will not be over. In fact, you will begin to think it has not even started. What do these people want with you?"

"Mr. Walsingham, sir," said Richards from the doorway, "I think it would be better if you question this gentleman elsewhere."

"I did not ask you for your opinion," replied Walsingham. "But maybe taking him to my house would give him a chance to come to his senses. Find something with which to cover him up. Take four guards and make sure he doesn't escape—he has a history of it. Captain Walker, lead me to the other prisoners."

40

~

Raw Carew stood in the darkness on the deck of the *Davy*, looking up at the stars and listening to the wind in the rigging. A few minutes ago, he had cut Captain Gray's throat and pushed him over the side. It did not make him any happier but it did feel like justice, and that gave him a small measure of satisfaction. What lingered was the thought that there were too many men like Gray. They labeled him, Carew, a pirate and would feel justified in hanging him on sight. Yet they themselves abused and stole and committed all sorts of sin. Carew thought of Ursula's scarred face, cut by a man who claimed to be holy and to detest whoredom, and who thought that he would thereby save her. Society saw the stain of sin in itself and tried to remove it, but thereby only created more opportunities for corruption and sin. It was a festering thing, constantly turning on itself in vicious outrage. Out here, on the dark waves, men and women were always an inch from death. Everyone had to fight for themselves and to protect those they loved. It was simpler and more honest than the morality of those who lived on land.

Devenish came up on deck. "They are ready."

Carew called to Kahlu. They went over to the hatch and descended to the main deck. The crew of the *Davy* been lined up along one side, and Carew's men were on the other. The girl was still in the captain's cabin. Carew glanced in there; she had a pail of water and was washing the blood off the table. He turned to the men facing him.

"In case anyone here does not know who I am," he said, walking up and down, "my name is Carew. I am the bastard son of Sir George Carew and his mistress, Matilda, a wonderful woman with a heart of gold, worth ten of him. People call me Raw, though I was given the name Ralph. I grew up in Calais before the French took it, so now I am homeless. I have been at sea for more than half my life. Over the years I have tried to help people who, like me, have no home, no protector, and no money. I especially like to help those who have a price on their heads and who suffer from the self-righteous indignation of the justices. Anyone who tells you I am a pirate is a liar. I am an outlaw, certainly; I have been called the Robin Hood of the High Seas. But the only people who call me pirate are those who hope to profit from such calumnies."

He paused, looking from face to face. There were some who looked defiant, who might prove dangerous or might be good in a fight. There were some who looked eager. There were others who looked frightened.

"You have a choice. You can stay on this ship and serve under its elected captain. Or you can go ashore now. Before you make that choice, however, let me remind you that, if I am chosen to be captain again, then there are four rules aboard my ship. The first rule is that you follow orders. The second is: be honest with all your shipmates. The third is that you either throw your religion overboard or, if you can't lose it, keep it to yourself. The fourth is that you protect your fellow sailors and all the vulnerable women and children who come into your care. Many of you will find this code preferable to the one you are used to. Those of you who prefer the law of the land, you had better to return to it."

There were several firm assents, a few murmurs. Most of the men remained quiet. "Now is the moment of your choosing," continued Carew. "If you wish to return you may go—with my blessing. Go aloft and wait on deck. If you wish to stay aboard and follow my code, stay where you are."

At first, no one moved. Carew waited patiently. He had often seen this small drama played out. Suddenly and unexpectedly men who thought they knew one another well were asked to judge which side of the law really suited them best. Was the law that bound them to the manorial lords who owned their houses really so bad? And those who had responsibilities: would they leave them behind? If so, why? Would they see the chance to make themselves rich? Or were they running from an ugly or shrewish wife?

A bearded man stepped forward and walked boldly to the ladder. He did not glance backward. Two or three of the older men followed him, and then one or two younger ones. Then more went. Eventually there were only twelve men left. Carew surveyed them; they were mostly in their teens or twenties. They were looking at him and his men, not at one another.

"So, you want to stay." Carew looked along the line at each of the twelve faces, assessing them all. "Are you good enough? When I board a boat, I seek good men. Men who are good fighters, good sailors, and who are good in themselves. I do not want idle men, or men who think it is right to beat a woman as if she is a dog. So I ask you, would you be less inclined to serve me if I were to tell you that all your companions who have chosen to go on land, who are now aloft, will have their throats cut?"

Carew looked from face to face. Several seemed to have blanched. No one said anything.

"Well?" demanded Carew. Still no one spoke.

"If I was the sort of brutal thug who killed prisoners for no reason," he said, "you would now be thinking, 'Let me off this ship, I have made a terrible mistake.' I don't want that. But think about this also. Those men who have chosen to go ashore have just betrayed you. They have chosen not to help you when you and we are cast adrift on a wide ocean together. And you have betrayed them too, choosing to sail with an outlaw ship rather than your old companions. 'How did this happen?' you are asking yourself. But maybe you should be asking yourselves a different question. 'Where do the roots of betrayal lie?' In your own hearts, I tell you. No man is ever truly loyal—no woman is ever truly faithful. He must show his loyalty every day, not swear it, just as the faithful wife must show her loyalty every day. It doesn't matter if she shares your bed for fifty years; if at the end you find her in another man's clutches, she has betrayed you. And those men upstairs—after all the years you have sailed with them, they have chosen a different path from you, and you have chosen a different path from them. So before you choose to stay here, ask yourself whether you are a good man and can serve your captain and companions faithfully. Can you control the betrayal that is in your heart—for I *know* it is there. And if you cannot, you must leave, for no one else will have you. If you become one of us, you stay one of us until you die. You can never go home. Your former friends and neighbors will hang you."

He walked closer and looked into the face of one man in his twenties. "You, what is your name?"

"John Dunbar," replied the man.

"A Scottish name? Sounds as if your family has already jumped ship once. Are you sure you want to sail with me?"

"Yes, sir."

"Don't call me 'sir.' 'Captain' is fine." Carew looked the man up and down. He appeared strong. "What was your position aboard?"

"Gunner, sir...I mean, Captain."

Carew nodded. "Any other gunners among you?" Two other men lifted their arms.

"Good. You are especially welcome. The rest of you will be gunners too before long." He paused. "One last thing. Are any of you married? Because if you are, and you want to stay married, then you had better go ashore now. Sailing with us is the surest way of losing your wife."

"That's why most of us are here." Hugh Dean grinned.

None of the men admitted to being married.

Carew continued, "First, the money that belonged to the late captain of this ship is to be divided. We have a bill to pay ashore that amounts to more than twenty pounds. We also owe a fair sum to the landlord for his good will and trust, and his supply of women. I propose to send eighty pounds ashore: half for the landlord and half for two women who between them delivered us this boat, namely Amy and Ursula. When the messenger transporting that cash has returned safely, and when the rest of the crew are aboard, we will set sail for Dover—to take back the girl whom the late Captain Gray kidnapped. Half the remainder is to be shared among the crew. The last portion is ship's money. Those who are with me and wish me to continue as captain, say 'aye.'"

There was a roar of approval from Carew's men and one or two voices among the new recruits.

"Is that what you call a vote?" asked one of the new men, barely more than a boy. "Is there no one else to vote for?"

Carew's men laughed. Carew himself turned and looked at the lad. "When you have helped us take another ship, you too may have a say in who commands it. You yourself can stand for captain."

"Another ship? That will be ages…"

More laughter broke out among Carew's men. He waited until it had subsided. "Probably not as long as you think. Now, do you want to reconsider your decision? If not, prepare to set sail. With this southwesterly, we should make Dover tomorrow and London maybe the day after that. We don't want to be sitting here in the morning, when the authorities find out who has taken command."

41

Friday, May 12

Clarenceux awoke on a wooden floor and was relieved to find that he was no longer trapped. His body hurt where it had been beaten—bruised to the point that even to think about the pain was to feel it again. He gasped as he rolled over, feeling the stinging of whip marks and cuts on his legs as well as the agony of his inflamed testicles. He had been given a shirt, which seemed to be his own, and a pair of breeches, which were not. They were too small.

It was early in the day, not long after dawn. He blinked. The room was empty. There was an iron bar across the window and no doubt the door was locked. Nevertheless, he stood up and tried it. Not even to try would have been the worst failure of all.

He turned the handle. The door was indeed locked.

He sank down, trying to recall the events of the previous day. Some came easily to mind; others were lost. The order of events too was beyond him. Whatever intoxicating elixir his interrogators had used in the holy bread, it had left him unable to remember much of what had happened. One thing stuck clearly in his memory. The Knights did not know where Rebecca was. Nor the document. They thought he knew. In fact, they seemed to think he was concealing her, and working with Cecil to discover more about the plot.

He looked at the bloody mess on the ends of his fingers. Then he remembered: after what had felt like eternity, there had been a commotion downstairs. Shots had been fired and those in the attic had left. A short while had passed and then someone else had entered. With a strong London accent, he demanded to know Clarenceux's name. About five minutes after that Walsingham had spoken to him. He remembered the nails being levered away from his chafed wrists with a crowbar and a man throwing the breeches and shirt at him. He had been helped down the stairs and out into the night. A cart had been waiting. It took him to a house in sight of the Tower. Walsingham's house.

It had been a series of disasters from the beginning. And it was not over yet. Walsingham had been surprised to find him in Mrs. Barker's house—and even more surprised to find him nailed naked to the floor. Immediately that had raised questions in the man's weasel-like mind. Why were they torturing him? What did he know that they did not?

Clarenceux rose to his feet again, supporting himself with a hand on the wall. He ached, he was bruised, but no limbs were broken. He could walk, if he could bear the pain from his swollen testicles. He could run, if he had to. He gripped the door handle tight, then tightened his grip further. The pain rose and subsided in his fingers: if he had to hold a sword, he could. He was not finished yet.

He moved close to the window, reached past the iron bar, and pushed the shutter fully open. The chill clean air of early morning was welcome.

42

Carew liked to stand on deck with the wind ruffling his hair and the sound of the gulls in his ears. He liked the smell of the sea and the spray as the ship crashed into another wave and danced along the tides. He especially liked this ship, whose full sails pulled so well. She felt solid, compact, and durable—and she was maneuverable. Every detail had been carefully seen to, from the rigging to the oven in the hold. As for the guns, they were spectacular. There were only twelve of them, but as John Dunbar had pointed out, they were all of a standard caliber. Therefore the cannonballs all fitted perfectly and the charges were all a regular quantity. Dunbar and his two companions could easily teach Carew's men to fire them. In his old ship, when a cannon ran out of shot, it was useless. When its gunner was killed, leaving no one to calculate the correct charge, it was almost useless. Sometimes to fire another gun in the same direction required the whole ship be turned. These guns allowed the ship to fire in all directions until the last shot had gone and the last able man was dead.

Luke came down from the rigging. "Cold up there," he muttered.

"Bracing, not cold," said Carew, slapping him on the back. "Besides, you shouldn't say a word against the wind. High seas have saved us on many occasions. When the wind drops, we are simply waiting to be attacked."

"Why are we going to London?"

"To find a man called Clarenceux, who will tell us where Denisot is."

"I know that—you told us. But why? London is dangerous. They will recognize this ship."

Carew continued looking ahead. "Maybe, maybe not."

"Why are we going then?"

Carew looked into Luke's green eyes, gauging whether this was a sign of doubt in his command. He had been expecting it. "You know that feeling when you have an itch, and you want to scratch it, and you just can't quite reach it, and it infuriates you?"

"Yes," replied Luke.

"Well, this is nothing like that. This is more like you'd put a bullet in your own flesh rather than suffer the itch a second longer."

Luke wiped the sea fret from his face. "I still don't understand why."

Carew put a hand on his shoulder. "Just think of it in terms of completeness."

43

Late that morning, two guards took Clarenceux from his cell and led him, slowly, down to Walsingham's great chamber on the first floor. Clarenceux remembered the room: the last time Walsingham had brought him here, six months ago, he had had him beaten with an iron bar.

It was warm in the room; a small fire was on the hearth. Opposite was a wide, glazed window, facing south. Walsingham was seated on a large chair that made him look even smaller than he actually was. He was wearing the skull cap that covered his widow's peak, and his habitual black clothes. In front of him was a wide oak table. Piles of papers were neatly arranged at various places across it. A silver tray of sweetmeats was there also.

"When I was told that you were being tortured in Mrs. Barker's house," Walsingham began, "I was astonished. I wondered whether I had made a mistake. On the grounds that my enemy's enemies are my friends, I should have thanked Mrs. Barker and her companions, not arrested her. But of course, I had not made a mistake. She too is my enemy. In this line of work, one has no friends."

Clarenceux did not want to speak or even listen. He was tired. He wanted to sit down.

"Are you going to tell me why you betrayed her?"

Clarenceux remained silent.

Walsingham tapped the top of the table with his fingers. "Mr. Clarenceux, I know you well enough to expect you to be difficult. But let me be clear. What she started I will readily carry on. And judging from some of those marks, I can apply a more expert pressure to your body. You will talk. And this time Sir William Cecil will not save you."

Still Clarenceux said nothing. He was mindful of his bruises. He was hoping that his wife and daughters were safe. Walsingham knew Julius Fawcett's house, where they were staying, having grown up in Chislehurst. He had sent men to search it in the past.

"What did she want to know?"

Clarenceux closed his eyes.

Walsingham slammed his fist down. "For heaven's sake, man. Don't play dumb with me. It is about the Percy-Boleyn marriage agreement, is it not? Mrs. Barker wants to know where it is as much as we do."

Mention of the marriage agreement was like one more punch in the gut. "How do you know that?" Clarenceux blurted out. His throat was parched, his voice was a croak.

Walsingham almost smiled. "Sir William Cecil told me. He knew you had it."

Clarenceux shook his head, unable to believe that Cecil had revealed this information to anyone, let alone Walsingham. It implicated Cecil himself. Perhaps Cecil was planning to place all the blame on him, Clarenceux, and protest ignorance. Either way, it was not good. Cecil had chosen to betray him to Walsingham.

Clarenceux turned toward the wall, clenching his damaged left hand as he leaned against the painted plaster. His fingertips hurt; he used his anger to fight the pain.

"There was a letter," continued Walsingham. "It was addressed to Lady Percy, telling her that Widow Machyn had agreed to hand over the Catholic Treasure. You are not going to tell me that you do not know what the Catholic Treasure is, are you?"

Clarenceux clenched his left hand harder.

"So, why were they torturing you? Widow Machyn has betrayed them, it would appear. Either the two of you are working together or she has rushed off on her own, with that extremely dangerous piece of vellum. Clearly Mrs. Barker believes that the former is true. I am inclined to agree."

Clarenceux shook his head. "She betrayed me," he said hoarsely. "If she has betrayed Mrs. Barker and the Knights of the Round Table too, that has nothing to do with me."

"From the look of you, they spent some considerable time trying to get you to talk. I suspect you are lying."

"Heaven curse you, Walsingham!" rasped Clarenceux, turning around fully to face the man. "As God is my witness, she and I are not working together."

Walsingham got to his feet. "A moot point. God is not your witness. At least, I would not rely on Him to testify on your behalf."

Clarenceux put his head in his hands. His fingertips hurt even touching his forehead. He felt tears come to his eyes and struggled to prevent them. He bit his lip. "Christ help me," he muttered under his breath.

Walsingham walked toward the window, looking out briefly over the Tower moat toward the walls. "Betrayal—I see it every day. A critical moment in a man's life—maybe even signaling the end of that life. While for me, it is just another small mark in my notebook." He turned around to face Clarenceux. "But now I think about it, I might have made a slight error in your case. I presumed that, because you were still nailed to the floor of that house, you had not talked. That you had *not* told them where Widow Machyn has gone. But maybe you did." He paused, considering the situation. "I really cannot let you go now, can I? You have put in me in a very difficult position."

"I have put *you* in a difficult position?" Clarenceux was struggling to control himself, biting back the words. If he attacked Walsingham, he was lost.

"You or any of your friends might find that document as soon as I release—"

"God's wounds, Walsingham!" Clarenceux stepped forward, reached for the table and held on to it. "Lock the whole population up, why don't you? What kind of monster are you? You have no trust, you lack compassion. Are we just latitudes on a chart that you can cross off once you have sailed past us? The Lord knows I despise the people who tortured me, and I want to stop them; but I despise you more for suspecting me so much—so much—that you will not even tolerate the thought of me being loyal. Like them and like you, I want to know where that manuscript has gone. I do not know—but I do know this: if you want to stop whatever plot is in progress, you must find out who is keeping it and where they are, not punish and victimize your personal enemies."

"You are not my personal enemy. You are an enemy of the State."

"Wrong. On both accounts," said Clarenceux.

Walsingham frowned. "Personal enmity is the one privilege I cannot deny you. Why were you at that house? Did you go there voluntarily?"

"You know the answer. I went there to seek information, just like you."

"But you were the one who ended up nailed to the floor. If you went there to extract information from them, why was it not one of them who was nailed there?"

The question was absurd. "You might have noticed that I am not the sort of man to extract information from people by torturing them. I certainly would not think of torturing them in their own homes in front of—"

Walsingham waved his hand in the air as if he was not interested. "I have already spoken to those who were in the house last night. It seems that you went armed with two pistols, a sword, a dagger, and another knife in your boot."

"I needed to be prepared."

"For what?"

"For...for..." Clarenceux tried to remember. "I thought there would only be three or four of them there. I was planning to threaten to shoot Mrs. Barker, forcing the others to tell me where Rebecca Machyn had gone."

"Pah!"

"Then tell me, in God's name, what should I have done? What would you have done, if you had been me?"

Walsingham leaned over the table, looking Clarenceux in the eye. "You should have come to see me."

"Do you really think I trust you enough? After you struck me with a bar, almost crippling me, last time I was here? Or Sir William Cecil, after he charged me to keep that document and guard it with my life?"

The words hit Walsingham in the face. They hit him in the spine and the heart. Eventually he looked down, his head shaking slightly. "Did Sir William himself *ask* you to keep that document?"

"He did not tell you everything then."

"No, he did not," said Walsingham angrily.

"Let me see him," said Clarenceux, calmer now.

"No, I will go to Cecil House and see him."

"He has obviously betrayed you just as Rebecca Machyn betrayed me. Let us see him together."

Walsingham walked around the table. "I will go there now. We will have the truth out."

44

Walsingham rode to Cecil House in a foul temper, shouting at people to get out of his way as he struggled through the crowds in the city streets. The more he thought about the deception, the more furious he was. Had he not done everything that Cecil required of him? Had he not served him day and night, working to discover meanings, plots, and conspiracies? Had he not run terrible risks on behalf of the security of the realm—only for Cecil quietly to take all her majesty's praise and win her trust?

He arrived in the courtyard of Cecil House with a clatter of hooves. "Where is Sir William?" he yelled at a servant who ran out from the front door to attend to him.

"He is in attendance on the queen, Mr. Walsingham, at Richmond," shouted the servant.

"Hell's devils," cursed Walsingham. It was a nine-mile ride to Richmond. Turning his horse, he spurred westward and started to gallop along the Strand.

His anger did not abate with the journey. If anything, it grew worse. As he waited for the ferry at Putney, he rehearsed the grounds of his dissatisfaction with his patron. On the far side, he forced his horse again to gallop, kicking up mud and dust behind him. When a wagon on the road was in his way, he bellowed at the driver until he was allowed to pass. It took him over an hour to get to Richmond Palace—by which time his horse was covered in sweat and he himself was furious.

He could not gain access to Cecil. "Sir William says he will come to you as soon as he is dismissed from the queen's presence," explained a thin-lipped gentleman usher of the royal household. Walsingham was directed to wait on a stone bench at the end of a marble-columned corridor.

He could not sit still. He stood up, paced around, sat down. He stood up again and paced further. An hour passed before a door banged open and three courtiers strode out. Behind them was Sir William, a sheaf of papers under his arm. "I am sorry to have kept you, Francis," he said as he approached. His voice echoed in the corridor. "You know how it is with her majesty."

"I know exactly. You have told me often. It is one of the things you never fail to tell me."

"Is something the matter, Francis?"

"I have had my fill of your deceit, your covering up, your covert betrayals."

"That's enough," said Cecil in a warning tone. "Remember to whom you are speaking."

"I dislike you saying that to me too. I always remember to whom I am speaking. You do not seem to remember to whom *you* are listening."

"I said enough. What is the meaning of this?"

Walsingham took a deep breath. All the speeches he had prepared in his head disappeared. "I have dedicated my life to the pursuit of conspiracies and plots, as you bade me. And yet the most important document of all, one that demonstrates the queen's illegitimacy—"

"Keep your voice down, man!" Cecil tried to take Walsingham's arm and steer him down the corridor but Walsingham shook him off.

"Not only did you not tell me about it, you asked Clarenceux to guard it for you. Who is the plotter I am meant to be tracing? Who is it, if not you? You have acted in a deceitful manner. You have formed an alliance with that herald, a suspected traitor. How am I to separate the traitors from the loyal men when no one is being honest with me, not even you?"

"I see. You are right, of course. But this conversation should be conducted far away from here, as you well know. I am riding back to the city now. Let us discuss this on the way." He spoke louder. "Did you know that the Byzantine merchants in India are seeking English help in resisting the advances of the Portuguese—in spite of our ancient peace treaty with the Portuguese? In Constantinople itself, a Greek man has been tortured for declaring Christianity a finer religion than that of Mahomet."

Half an hour later, they were riding side by side, with Cecil's clerks and servants following at a distance.

"Why did you not tell me?" asked Walsingham.

"Clarenceux would never have given it up. I did the next best thing I could: I made him guard it with his life."

"That should now be forfeit."

"It would achieve nothing. If he has lost the document, then he is more useful alive than dead. He will try to find it."

"I found him last night in the attic of that house in Little Trinity Lane. He was pinned to the floor, badly bruised and cut."

Cecil drew in the reins to his horse. "They tortured him? What did he say?"

"I don't know. He claims to have told them nothing. But it seems

Widow Machyn betrayed him at their request and then she betrayed them too—at *his* urging. They say they do not know where the document is, nor where the woman is hiding. He claims the same ignorance of both matters."

"Everyone is betraying everyone else," said Cecil, looking across the meadows to the slow-flowing river.

"Not everyone," protested Walsingham. "I have served you many years and never withheld information from you. Yet you have lied to me. You have embarrassed me and compounded the betrayal of your deceit by concealing how you knew about that document."

Cecil started to ride on. "I did hope that, if my actions were revealed to you, you would understand."

"Understand? Sir William, I am very grateful to you for all you have done to advance me. But if I cannot trust you, her majesty's Secretary, I cannot trust anyone. I have given my life to your service, every waking hour; I will not be treated in such a manner."

"We are all puppets, Francis. We are all dependent on the higher authorities who pull the strings. The queen pulls my strings and I pull yours, and you pull those of your men, and they pull the strings of the ordinary men and women in the street…"

"And who pulls the queen's strings? Dudley?"

"No. God." Cecil looked ahead at a couple of low cottages by the side of the road. Two men were leading a cart along a lane to a large field. "You could say that you and I do too. The puppet, being strung to the puppeteer, controls him. The men and women in the street have a hold on your men, and your men have a hold on you, and you on me, and all of us on the queen…"

"And the queen on God? I do not think so." They rode on in silence.

"I am sorry I did not tell you," said Cecil after a short while. "It was most unwise of me. I should have realized that your spymaster's intuition would eventually determine that, as I knew that document existed and was in Clarenceux's possession, I had a role in him keeping it."

"I thank you for your apology. But I am still angry. This has wasted time. I should be interrogating Clarenceux, not hearing apologies from you. When Clarenceux says he went to Mrs. Barker's house willingly, to confront them, he is only half telling the truth. They lured him there. They know Widow Machyn is working with him. They know he knows where she is."

"I too want to know what Clarenceux has to say for himself. Will you bring him to Cecil House tomorrow afternoon?"

Walsingham looked at him suspiciously.

Cecil glanced back and understood his expression. "I promise I will keep him as securely as you would in your own house."

"If you are going to question him, I want to be present."

Cecil nodded. "Good. I would value your contribution. Let us set a time on it. Three of the clock. We will both have words with Mr. Clarenceux. We will both hear what he has to say for himself."

45

Clarenceux listened to the thin trickle of urine fall the two stories to the stone-lined vat in the basement. He adjusted his clothes, replaced the cushion over the opening, and prepared himself for what he would do next. He said a prayer, crossed himself, and left the closet.

The single guard accompanying him was waiting by the door on the far side of the chamber. He was a fair-haired youth of average height and, apart from the knife at his belt, he did not appear to be armed. Walsingham seemed to trust Clarenceux's wounds to restrain him. But this was the weakness in the plan.

"All done?" The fair-haired man smiled and gestured for him to go ahead.

Clarenceux could not bring himself to respond positively. He shuffled across the room slowly, reaching out for the doorframe, emphasizing his crippled state. But as he left the room, he lurched to the right, grabbing the latch and throwing the door back into place, almost shutting the guard on the inside. The guard was not so slow and managed to place his boot in the opening. "Hold fast!" he shouted. "Return to your room. You cannot get away…" He wrestled against the door, which Clarenceux was holding firmly. Both men struggled with it until Clarenceux let go and ran, as fast as his wounds would allow, toward the staircase. He did not take the stairs leading up to his chamber but those that led down to the front door. The guard was after him straightaway.

Clarenceux rushed down the stairs, hearing the younger man just behind him; he managed to reach the bottom first, without falling. "Stop! Stop him!" yelled the guard. Clarenceux saw a chair in the hallway and seized it, flinging it around desperately at his pursuer, catching him on the side of the head. But he did not knock the man to the ground. The act of turning had delayed him. There was no time for him to reach the door. A moment later, three other men had appeared in the hall from various rooms. Clarenceux was thrown against a wall. Holding him by the throat, they tied his hands and marched him back up the stairs to his cell on the second floor. They flung him on the floor and left him there, locking the door behind them.

46

Saturday, May 13

Carew had been awake most of the night. At dawn he was on deck with Stars Johnson, watching the depth of the heavens disappear behind the shallow light of the new day. They had made good progress, with the steady wind straight up the Channel. Now they were less than fifteen miles from Dover.

Carew had already examined almost every inch of the ship. When galleons were first launched, they were sometimes found to be unsteady, and the hull needed to be widened slightly through the insertion of wooden pegs between the ribs and the strakes of the vessel. The result was always a loss of speed and a little more seepage of water. But the *Davy* was a beauty; whoever had planned her had known his job perfectly and had made no error. She balanced in the water, turned easily, and had never needed modifications to her hull. He had been aloft too, and inspected the sails and rigging entirely, from the crow's nest to the stays. Whoever maintained her had been conscientious in his attention to detail, with no slack ropes nor any too taut or too frayed. It was a good sign that there were spare sails stacked in the orlop, but they would not be needed for a while yet as the existing sails were in good condition. It was reassuring; one storm could change everything. Whoever owned this ship was keen to make sure that his investment was safe. He had taken every precaution— all except that of the ship itself being taken by outlaws.

"What is the business with the girl?" Johnson asked. "Won't it delay us?"

Carew looked at the shore, with the deep-blue sky above it. "It's the moral of the thing, Stars. We take what we want. We kill men like that captain where we will. But if those are things we can justify, then we must stick by that code. And my code says we should protect women and children."

Johnson laughed. "You tell all the new ones to throw the religion overboard, but you've got more moral scruples than a priest."

Carew looked Johnson in the eye. "I should hope so. That's the point."

47

The bell in Cecil House rang four o'clock. Clarenceux had been standing for an hour in Sir William's study, his hands tied behind his back. He was dressed in spare clothes from Walsingham's house, worn-out items that the servants did not need. His shoes did not fit properly. He was tired, in pain, and exhausted, but still he refused the offer of a seat. He would stand until he collapsed.

"I don't understand," Cecil said to him. "You went to the house in order to interrogate Mrs. Barker and the Knights of the Round Table as to the location of the document. But they ended up interrogating you regarding that very same thing. Very well, Widow Machyn has betrayed you both. But you already knew that. Why did you go there?"

Clarenceux's mind was numb with tiredness. "Why did Walsingham go there? For the same reason, I imagine."

"I doubt it," replied Cecil.

"I wanted to find out where she went, where she took the document."

Cecil said nothing. He glanced at Walsingham. "I think we had better show him the message," he said. Walsingham watched as Cecil walked to the side of the room and reached into a wall cupboard, taking out a piece of paper. "We have been watching Mrs. Barker for quite another reason." He handed Clarenceux the transcript.

As Clarenceux read, Cecil added, "We ascertained that the bearer of that message, which was originally in code, was a servant in Mrs. Barker's house. So you see, the question is: how did *you* know Mrs. Barker was involved?"

Clarenceux read the words with grief. Rebecca Machyn had given her assent to a plan far larger than anything he could fight alone. According to this document, her brother had taken her by ship from London to Sandwich and then on to Scotland. She was beyond his reach now.

"Are you going to answer me?"

"I acted on a suspicion," he said. "I knew that Mrs. Barker had provided Rebecca Machyn with shelter in the past. I paid a visit to her house last Tuesday evening. Mrs. Barker told me the Knights of the Round Table had persuaded Rebecca to assist them in recovering the document. She suggested that I meet them."

"So you admit it," began Walsingham. Cecil silenced him with a gesture.

"Why was she so helpful at that time?" asked Cecil. "Why did she not take you and torture you then?"

Clarenceux shrugged. "I took her by surprise. Perhaps at that moment she did not know that Widow Machyn had betrayed her. Or perhaps it was bait—to make me return when the others were there."

Cecil turned to Walsingham. "Has Mrs. Barker said anything yet? Or any of her men?"

"She has said very little. My plan is to interrogate her further when we have extracted a confession from Clarenceux."

"Has she said as much to you as Clarenceux here has admitted she said to him?"

"No."

Cecil looked at Clarenceux. "Isn't that curious—that she should be so frank with you and then torture you?" He waited for an answer. None came. He continued, "What exactly did you intend to do with the document?"

"To look after it safely, as you bade me. I was acting out of loyalty to you."

"Highly commendable, do you not agree, Mr. Walsingham?"

"Not if he failed."

"Precisely. And because of that failure, Clarenceux, I cannot offer you my protection. Not now—at least, not outside this house. The best you can do is hope for a reprieve when this is all over. And retire quietly with your family to a provincial town."

"I cannot do that," said Clarenceux.

"I beg your pardon?"

"I cannot give this matter up," he replied. "Thousands will die, don't you see? I do not want there to be a Catholic insurrection. Every time there is a rebellion in the name of the old religion, the persecution grows worse. Property is confiscated. Houses are searched. Men and women are rounded up, imprisoned, tortured, flogged. Books are burnt, priests hanged, chapels desecrated. I cannot stop all this. I am on your side in wanting it not to happen, even though I do not share your religious outlook. The only way to bring an end to this reign of terror is for the rebellions to stop, so that Catholics are no longer a danger to the State. You have to help me find Rebecca Machyn!"

Cecil listened without gesture or expression. "You did not hear me correctly. To allow you to search for Widow Machyn in order to prevent a Catholic plot would be like allowing a wolf to guard the chickens lest a fox come and eat them. You are just as untrustworthy as she is."

"But thousands will die," Clarenceux pleaded.

Cecil nodded. "So you keep saying. And you are right. But it does not take a brilliant mind to come up with that prognostication. I am sorry. I will keep you here in this house until further notice. You will not be ill treated—I will make sure of it."

Walsingham stood up. "It would be more suitable if I were to guard him. You never know when he might try to escape. Last night he tried to run from my house while using a latrine—"

"Then it sounds as if your house is not secure," retorted Cecil, not looking at him. "This is a modern house. I have a first-floor room designed for accommodating distinguished guests of dubious loyalty. It has a closet attached. I can't guarantee that Mr. Clarenceux will be comfortable, but most certainly he will be safe."

48

Sunday, May 14

Clarenceux slept unexpectedly well. He had been taken straight from Cecil's study to a small room on the first floor at the back of the house. Like Walsingham's secure chamber, this had bars on the window. Once inside, they had untied his hands. There had been the last vestiges of the evening sun when he had arrived, but he had not bothered making use of the light to investigate his new surroundings. He had seen the bed—there was nothing else in the room apart from a pewter ewer and basin on the floor—and had stumbled across to it, laid down, and been asleep within seconds. He did not wake until the early hours, when he realized with a pang of guilt that he had not said a prayer for his wife and daughters.

It was thus at dawn, after his prayers, that he set about discovering the room. The door was secure and seemed to be fitted with more than one lock. The bars on the window were solid. Between them he could look out across Cecil's formal garden, with its intricately arranged beds of ornate shrubs and flowers in the early-morning light. Beyond were the graziers' fields north of the Strand, where the Convent Garden used to be before the Dissolution. There was a mist across the grass now. Above it, he could just see the top of Southampton House, to the east of the village of Holborn. Nearer, on the right-hand side of the garden, was Drury Lane; if he craned his head around to the right, he could see Drury House and Lincoln's Inn Fields. The wall between the garden and Drury Lane was quite high, but there was a door halfway along that seemed to lead out into the lane.

The house was still quiet. He wondered if he could use a part of the wooden bed frame to lever the door open, but it was as solidly constructed as the door. The wall too was plaster over stone—not a plaster and lath partition. He turned his attention to the door to the closet but here too the quality of the recent workmanship meant that there was no chance of him working loose the hinges or a section of the door itself.

There seemed no chance of breaking out of the room. The door was hopeless. The barred window was solid. There was no other aperture into the room—except the latrine in the closet.

Clarenceux remembered a chronicle he had read; it had described how the French had captured the great castle of Château Gaillard by making a man climb in through a latrine chute. He looked at this one. There was no hope of climbing through: the aperture in the wooden seat was too small. Even if he could get through, there was a risk he would fall into the cesspit two stories below. Gongfermors sometimes died of the fumes when cleaning out cesspits and were found dead in them. He might knock himself out and drown.

The chute was his only chance. He could not see the bottom, but the brick lining was visible. There had to be fingerholds. As his eyes adjusted, he became aware of a vague lightness at the foot. This being a relatively new house, there would be a barrel positioned below, in the hope of catching all that fell from above. Emptying barrels was easier and cheaper than clearing out cesspits.

The seat was a single piece of planed wood, about three feet wide, smoothed around the hole. It was built into the wall. As he looked closely at the edge, he saw the plaster overlap and wondered if it had only been plastered into place rather than mortared in with the bricks. He heaved on it, testing its looseness, but it held firm. He needed a sharp edge to gouge out some of the plaster. Going back into the room, he picked up the basin, and having emptied the water in it down the chute of the privy, he placed it against the wall, at an angle. The metal yielded easily to the force of his foot. The crease in the metal made a sharp strong edge and with this he set to prodding and breaking the plasterwork around the seat.

At first it was difficult—a lot of work went into removing barely a thumbnail of plaster—but as the gash grew bigger, it allowed more and more purchase for the metal point of the basin. After ten minutes, large lumps of plaster were coming away from the walls. He threw them down the chute: judging from the "plop," each piece seemed to fall into liquid several feet deep. After twenty minutes he had stripped all the plaster away from the walls along two sides of the seat and tried to lift the wood. It moved a little. Five minutes after that, he was able to pull it away from the wall altogether.

His bruises hurt, his fingertips were stinging, and he was panting—but he had done it. He was staring at a large square opening in the brickwork, about eighteen inches by twenty. He hesitated, mindful still of the gongfermors' fate. But, thinking of Château Gaillard, he knew that this was a lot easier than breaking into a castle by such a route—and facing a hostile army on the inside. He climbed into the chute, lowering himself at first and then using his feet and knees to jam his back against the stinking bricks.

As he went down, the smell became worse. He paid less heed to it, bothered more by the slipperiness than the stench and the slime. He descended slowly and prayerfully. He wanted to make the sign of the cross but he did not dare take his arms away from the walls. Down he went, whispering incantations to the Virgin, St. Peter, and the two saint-kings of England: Edward the Martyr and Edward the Confessor.

Slowly he descended into the rank darkness. Ten feet below the latrine seat, the brick was saturated with urine; it was both grainy and slippery at the same time. His legs hurt where he had suffered the lacerations on his thighs from the knives and whips. Down he went, another foot, and another. Eventually his foot lost touch with the chute, flailing in midair. He tried to look down, but the lack of space and the darkness prevented him from seeing anything. He moved his leg again—still there was nothing. He knew that if he fell now he would fall into several feet of decomposing excrement and urine. He waited and shifted his knees, so he could try with the other foot. He kicked with that one and heard a vague wooden thud. There was indeed a barrel. He inched down further and kicked again. It was a large barrel—larger than the chute—in order to catch everything that fell. But that meant the chute descended to a point just above the barrel.

Clarenceux lowered himself a little further and felt again with his foot. There was a space of about two feet between the top of the heavy barrel and the bottom of the chute. He would have to clamber through it. Gradually he maneuvered himself until his feet were on the rim of the barrel. He managed to put his hands on the slimy rim also, on all fours, retching at the overpowering vapors. He turned until he was able to slide off the barrel and through the gap into the basement.

He moved away from the barrel and chute as quickly as he could, stumbling across the floor. Now came the task of finding a way out.

A man like Cecil would not want such a large barrel and its noisome contents carried through the house, so there had to be a door somewhere—and the lock had to be on the inside, to avoid thieves and spies being able to gain entry. Clarenceux walked with arms outstretched across the cellar, looking for any signs of light around the edge of a door.

When he finally found the exit, he heard footsteps hurrying across the floor above. *Pray God, let them not find I have gone. Not yet. Not until I am out of this place.* He moved toward the day-lit outline of a large door—a double door, wide enough to move a large, full barrel. It was locked; a search with his hands revealed no bolts. The two doors were locked with a key—which was not in the lock. His heart thumping, cursing, Clarenceux felt around the edges desperately, hoping to find some way through. He tried lifting a door off its hinges, but each door was solid oak and fitted well within its frame. He felt around the tops: nothing. Then he felt around the bottom edges. One was bolted shut at the foot. He undid the bolt, allowing the two doors to move a little on their hinges. He held the ring handle that lifted the latch between them and pulled. More light shone through the crack between the two doors. He pulled again, even harder, so that he could see the silhouette of the lock between the doors. Again he pulled; this time he was able to slip his hand between the two doors and grab hold of its edge. Holding that and the handle, one last pull brought the lock's bolt out of its socket, and he staggered back into the cellar, blinded by the morning light.

He squinted. After a moment he saw a ramp to his right, leading up to the level of the garden. He went up it as quickly as he could, listening for shouts and warnings. Breathing deeply of the fresh air of the garden, he moved along to the corner of the house. Peering around it, he saw a tall wall that cut off the front from the back. Although there was an arch and a gate, this was clearly secured. Looking the other way, he spotted the small gate in the high garden wall that he had noticed from his window. The sun was beginning to rise, casting a long shadow from the wall over the dew-wet grass of the garden. He hastened toward the gate, hoping that no one in the house would notice him. To his great relief, the gate was secured by bolts: one at the top, one in the middle, and one at the bottom.

Undoing the bolts as quietly as he could, he stepped through into Drury Lane, pleased to feel the stones and grass under his feet and even happier to close the gate of Sir William's house behind him. Never before had he wanted to wash so much, so urgently. He started walking toward the graziers' fields to the north, to plunge his face in one of the dewponds there. And to hide. He would go home later, after Cecil's men had searched his house.

49

Apart from the dangerous currents at the mouth of the Thames, the *Davy* had had a remarkably fast passage to London. The southwesterly had stayed with them even after they sailed out of Dover, having left the girl with someone she knew. Although it meant that Carew had to tack heavily to sail up the Thames estuary, even he was surprised by the speed of their progress. By midday he was at Greenwich, almost in sight of the Tower of London, with the sun bright above them. There he dropped anchor. Even though his passage had been fast, news of the ship's loss would have traveled even faster. No doubt the owners of the vessel had already been informed.

He chose eight men to accompany him in one of the skiffs: Kahlu and Hugh Dean because he trusted them the most. Skinner Simpkins because of his rat-like cunning and his courage. Luke Treleaven because he was unquestioningly loyal. The four others he chose for their various skills. Francis Bidder had an extraordinary memory. Stars had an instinct for finding his way around and could sense which way was north. Swift George was the messenger. John Devenish was the carpenter.

Kahlu, Devenish, Skinner, and Treleaven took the oars and rowed the skiff along the south bank of the Thames to Southwark.

It was late morning and high tide, so they had no trouble negotiating the currents of the river beneath London Bridge. The water sparkled as they rowed, but their mood was solemn. They all knew the danger of being here. They moored at the steps not far from the bear-baiting theatre at Southwark, and Luke and Francis went ashore to ask for directions to Clarenceux's house.

The two men were away some time. Carew was silent and serious, checking every alley, every other boat that came near them. The crew spoke in low voices, waiting. Every so often they would catch a glimpse of one of their companions on the shore. But more than twenty minutes passed before they returned.

"Everyone has heard of him; no one knows where he lives," explained Luke.

"It took us ages to find someone who knew," added Bidder. He pointed across the river to the north bank. "That over there is Three Cranes Steps. If we go west, along past Queenhithe, Broken Wharf, Trig Lane, Boss Alley, Pole's Wharf…" As he named each of the stopping places and wharves, he moved his finger. "Past Baynards Castle, Puddle Wharf, there, that's the Fleet River and Bridewell beside it. North beyond that is the tower of St. Bride's Church. That's the parish. He lives on Fleet Street, the south side, just to the east of Hanging Sword Court. The man I spoke to suggested landing at Whitefriars and walking up from there."

"Good," said Carew. "When we land, Stars, you keep the boat ready. The rest come with me to find the herald. There's room in the skiff to bring him with us if he doesn't talk."

50

Clarenceux lay in the long grass at the edge of the field. A cloud drifted slowly across the face of the sun, plunging him into shadow. That was his life now. Things he could not control were coming between him and the light, the True Light, and he was left in shadow. Each shadow would pass after a time. But each shadow would have a successor.

He looked down at his shirt. He stank. He needed to get home and change. But he also needed a key. His house was locked and he had lost his clothes at Mrs. Barker's. He could wait here longer; but it was already midafternoon and it would be another six hours until dark.

Through the tall grasses he peered toward Drury Lane. His house was less than ten minutes' walk from here. But he dared not risk walking past Cecil House in broad daylight. He decided to walk up to Holborn and along to Holborn Bridge, and fetch the key he had hidden in the stable loft in the city.

An hour later, having fetched the key, he came to the bottom of Shoe Lane. After checking to make sure no one was watching the door of the house, he walked across Fleet Street and down the alley to his back door. He reached over the top to unbolt the gate into the yard, but to his surprise, it was already unlocked. *Cecil's men have already been here; they might still be inside*. He crept closer to the back door and inserted the key in the lock, but it would not turn. The lock had been broken.

Clarenceux backed away. There were sounds from within. He knew that, if he entered, he would be recaptured—all for the sake of clean clothes and a sword. *What is the alternative? If I can get across the river, I could walk to Chislehurst and seek refuge with Julius Fawcett. Or, if I go into London, there are friends who would shelter me, companions in the Skinners Company, or Tom Griffiths, the pelterer, or Robert Rokeby, the jeweler on London Bridge.* He turned around to leave the yard—and found himself looking down the barrel of a pistol.

Momentarily the metal of the wheel lock reflected the late afternoon sun into his eyes. A large man with a mop of thick black hair was looking at him. "Are you Clarenceux?" he demanded in a deep voice, his eyes seeming to smile.

"Who are you who asks?" replied Clarenceux. "Do you come from Cecil? Or Walsingham? Or Lady Percy?"

Hugh Dean jabbed the cocked pistol forward into Clarenceux's face. "Inside, now. Or you can answer the captain's questions with your brains spilling over your doorstep. Put your hands up."

Clarenceux turned slowly and put his hands up. He kicked the back door of his own house open and entered. Inside, it was cool and dark. He smelled the ale and wine casks in the buttery.

Two men were in the kitchen, helping themselves to food.

"Go on," ordered the tall man behind him. "Up the stairs." Clarenceux continued with his hands raised. He passed a man on the landing, who had brilliant green eyes. He entered the hall to see three more men—a fat bald man, a powerfully built Negro, and a shorter man with bright blue eyes and cropped fair hair. The smell of unwashed skin and the sea was on their clothes, noticeable even above the stench of his own latrine-smeared garments.

The shorter man walked toward him with a swagger, holding one of Clarenceux's silver-rimmed mazers. He lifted it to his mouth, watching him. As the man drank, Clarenceux noticed a heraldic design of yellow and black on an enameled ring.

"You are the herald Clarenceux?" said Carew.

"Why do you want to know?" asked Clarenceux, lowering his arms to his sides.

"Why? Because if I set about extracting some information from a man, I do prefer…"

Clarenceux suddenly felt his right arm grabbed from behind and his legs kicked from beneath him. He fell to the floor heavily, able only to break his fall with his left arm. The shock winded him. He struggled to regain his breath while Carew continued: "I do prefer to have the right man to begin with." He lifted the mazer to his lips again. "There are two ways to speak to me, Mr. Clarenceux. Humbly or with a gun. Since you lack any weapon—as far as I can see—I suggest you adopt the penitential position."

Clarenceux got to his knees slowly.

"Do you know who I am?" Carew asked him.

Clarenceux swallowed. "You are a member of the Carew family—originally of the manor of Mohun's Ottery in Devon."

Carew smiled. "Very good. You noticed my ring. So, again, I ask you: who am I then?"

Clarenceux looked up, aware that this was no agent of Cecil's or Walsingham. "The baseborn son of the late Sir George Carew," he muttered.

"Indeed. My name is Ralph Carew, but men call me Raw as a

result of an incident in my youth. I have come here to find out where Nicholas Denisot is. Tell me that and we will leave you now in peace."

"I have never knowingly met anyone called Nicholas Denisot."

"A bad start. Let us try again. Where is he? Under what name is he hiding?"

Clarenceux shook his head. "I cannot tell you, for I do not know. No amount of pressure will serve your cause because I do not know the answer."

A heavy blow from a large wooden stick to the side of his head sent him sprawling sideways across the floor. He passed out momentarily. When he opened his eyes, the room was swirling, and tiny lights were turning like flies in summer. He could hear a sound like metal vibrating on stone.

Carew walked over and put his foot on his neck. "I do not have time to play games, Mr. Clarenceux. I need that information. As soon as you give it to me, we will be gone. Otherwise we will take you with us. We will question you at sea and if you do not tell us, we will cut your throat and throw your body overboard, and come back to seek out the next person of your acquaintance for a similar treatment. Your wife, perhaps? Or maybe you have a brother or sister? Now, *talk*."

Clarenceux gasped and retched. Bitter bile filled his mouth, his stomach being empty. Carew pushed harder on his neck, causing him to choke, then took the weight off. "I am kind to my friends, ruthless to my enemies. Do you understand? Tell me where Denisot is now."

"What…makes you think that…I know?"

Carew heard footsteps and glanced through the door. He saw Skinner coming up the stairs. "He was followed," he said. "Two men in livery. Hugh Dean is holding them in the yard. Want them brought up?"

"Yes," said Carew, not taking his eyes off Clarenceux. "You ask me why I know. A woman told me. Or rather she told the captain of the ship I now command, before I cut his throat."

"What woman?"

"I cannot remember her name," said Carew, pushing down harder on Clarenceux's throat with his foot. Clarenceux beat at Carew's leg with his hand, and after a moment Carew reduced the pressure.

"Did she…have a mole…on the side of her face?"

Carew remembered seeing the woman brought from the *Davy* on the quay at Southampton. "Yes, now I think of it, she did."

Clarenceux retched again and coughed. "Where is she?"

Carew pressed down harder, forcing Clarenceux's throat against the floorboards. "*I* am asking the questions, herald. And I am asking where Denisot is. You know. She told Captain Gray that you know."

Clarenceux could not answer. He coughed and gagged. Carew lifted his foot slightly. "She lied," he gasped.

Carew's attention was drawn to the two men being led up the stairs. Hugh Dean walked behind them, a pistol in each hand. Both men had empty scabbards hanging from their belts.

Carew gestured for them to enter the room and stand in the corner. "Why were you following this man?"

The men looked at one another, uncertain as to who should speak. "He escaped from Cecil House this morning," said one warily. "Sir William Cecil ordered us to watch out for him. We saw him cross the road."

Carew looked down at Clarenceux. "Why was he locked up? Is he a felon? A traitor?"

"I don't know," replied one of the men.

"What are you?" Carew asked Clarenceux.

"Damn you, I am a herald! Not a felon, nor traitor, and I do not know where…" He paused. "Oh, for the love of man, let me up."

Carew removed his foot. "Speak truthfully now."

Clarenceux wiped his mouth on his sleeve, which still stank of rank urine. "I was attacked and tortured at the house of a Catholic gentlewoman in Little Trinity Lane. That house was raided by agents of Francis Walsingham, a Member of Parliament and an enforcer working under the auspices of Sir William Cecil, her majesty's Secretary. Yesterday I was taken to Cecil House where I was imprisoned again. I escaped by climbing down a latrine chute. That is why you see me in this stinking state."

There was a moment of silence. A few men started laughing. "You don't need to be clean where I am taking you," said Carew. "I want to know where Denisot is. If you do not tell me, the next clean linen on your back will be your shroud." He glanced at Cecil's guards. "Luke, tie those two up. We will leave them. As for this herald, we will question him on the ship. I don't want to stay here if the queen's men are spying on this house. Kahlu, John—you two bring him. Hugh, you cover our backs."

They took Clarenceux to the skiff at Whitefriars steps and downriver to the *Davy*. Once on board, Carew ordered John Devenish to put Clarenceux in the hold. Devenish grabbed the herald's arm and led him across the upper deck, stepping over the ropes and pulleys, directing him down through a trapdoor near the sterncastle. On the ladder, the smell of the living quarters rose to greet them. The humid darkness was most unpleasant, like that of a stagnant ditch in the height of summer, except that many urinals had spilled on the deck floor over the years, so that the smell immediately reminded Clarenceux of his escape from Cecil House. Four arched windows— two on either side—provided a little natural light. The beams were too low for him to stand up straight. He had had some experience of ships from his frequent crossings of the Channel, but most had been more orderly than the *Davy*. As he passed the main mast to another hatch, he saw belongings strewn around in an untidy fashion: pots, lanterns, blankets, clothes, knives, flagons, and other paraphernalia less easily identifiable in the gloom. A shirt lay draped across one of the cannon. A ceramic urinal lay on its sides where it had been knocked over.

Devenish directed him to go down. Below, on the orlop deck, Clarenceux could hardly see a thing. There were no windows, only two small hanging lanterns that between them gave off very little light. As his eyes adjusted, he saw barrels and crates down here, and baskets, chests, discarded clothes, and a few straw mattresses. There was a rack of muskets and about twenty large crates of cannonballs. As Devenish led him forward again to another hatch, he saw the piles of spare canvas and rope. Devenish lifted the hatch to the hold and held it open. He gestured for Clarenceux to descend. The opening of cold blackness looked ominous. There was no ladder. Devenish saw Clarenceux's hesitation, grabbed his shoulder, and pushed him down. He then closed the hatch and bolted it.

The hold was damp. It smelled of seawater. Every creak of the ship sounded loud in the darkness. Like the decks above, it was not quite high enough for Clarenceux to stand. The curved bottom of the boat was covered with a sort of wet gravel as ballast. He groped his way along to what he reckoned was the rear of the ship and came up against a brick wall. This was slightly warm; it housed the ovens in the inaccessible rear part of the hold. He sank down with his back against the brick, and felt the frustration and desperation welling up inside him.

The ship gently swayed from side to side and forward and back; this movement, made greater by the darkness and the lack of other sensation, soon gave rise to a nauseous feeling that overtook his self-pity. He could hear the faint sound of the water and shouts from the decks above, and the scurrying of rats nearby. Occasionally one brushed against his ankle or his sleeve and he would recoil, hating the things, kicking at them as filth and sin made animate.

He shivered, holding his legs beneath his chin for warmth. But after a moment, the movement of the ship made him feel ill, and he had to move. He retched. Nothing came up. He was famished, miserable, and tearful. The only way he could make sense of his situation was through God's will. The wheel of fortune that had lifted him up to a position of great happiness had turned, and he was now at the low point, because God wished to punish him for his pride. What other sins were there? He could think of none he had committed—none but his affectionate thoughts for Rebecca Machyn, the uncommitted sin in his heart. But how could his resistance to that temptation merit such a treatment as this? In what way had his sins deserved being repeatedly beaten and interrogated, starved and forced into the dank hold of a ship?

51

Monday, May 15

Clarenceux had bad dreams in the twelve hours he was in the hold. He dreamed that he was trapped below decks as the ship started sinking. Wet ballast was tumbling around him and he had no way of understanding which way was up, let alone the way out. There was only a sinking blackness, and he had no knowledge of how deep he was beneath the surface until the wall burst in and unseen water swallowed his drowned frame.

The first he knew of the new day was when he heard sounds on the floorboards of the orlop deck directly above his head. The bolt was shot and the hatch opened. Lantern light flooded in. A bearded face looked down at him. Clarenceux saw several rats scurrying away across the ballast as he got to his feet. His legs were cold, his befouled clothes sodden. He reached up and put his hand on the hatch opening; the bearded man grabbed his arm and pulled him up with as much care as if he were a sack of oats. "Up," he said, nodding at the ladder to the main deck. "Captain Carew wants to see you."

Clarenceux ached. He felt dizzy with hunger. But he could see light coming from the main deck and light seemed precious at that moment. It also meant clean air, and that was even more important. Only now he was out of the hold did he fully realize how oppressive it had been. He breathed deeply. Even the fetid air here on the orlop deck was better than down there.

It was daylight, about two hours after dawn. Clarenceux stepped gratefully and yet warily onto the deck. Gulls were calling above the ship and the coast was a mile away. The open sea. A number of men were in the rigging: all five square sails were full, the lateen sail also, and the ship was probably sailing at her maximum speed. He felt the wind in his hair. The brightness of the light almost burnt his eyes, a painful yet welcome glare. The sea air was purifying.

Carew was on top of the sterncastle with his hand on the whip-staff, shifting his attention between the direction in which he was steering the ship and the angle of the lateen sail above. He called out over the noise of the birds and the surf, "Are you going to tell me yet where Denisot is?"

"I do not know, as I told you."

Carew said nothing for a moment. Then he addressed the men around him. "Tie him up. We'll put him over the side and drag him around for an hour or so."

Clarenceux looked at the faces. "How can I get through to you? I have never even heard of this Denisot!"

"Maybe, maybe not. You'll be happier to talk after a good soaking, either way."

Luke Treleaven and James Miller—the bearded man who had brought Clarenceux up from the hold—then bound Clarenceux's hands and tied him to the end of a long rope. They directed him to the back of the sterncastle, more than thirty feet above the sea. Clarenceux looked at the water so far below in fear. They thought nothing of pushing him off. He fell, smacked against the water, went under, and came up gasping for air, finding it difficult to swim with his hands tied. Soon he was being pulled through the water by the fast-moving ship. The sunlight glistened in the crests of the white water as the waves went over his head. He had to catch his gulps of air when he could, hoping that when he was breathing the waves would not fill his mouth. Many times he took in a large gulp of salt water and had to swallow it, so that soon his empty stomach was full of salt water and he was retching at the same time as he was trying to inhale. Only after about a quarter of an hour did he realize that he would find it easier if he was on his back. Even then, one mouthful of air in ten was accompanied by a wave crashing over his face and mouth.

After what seemed like a very long hour, the ship started to turn. Several faces appeared above him, looking down over the wooden railing at the back of the sterncastle. Clarenceux spat out some water. Carew was not going anywhere but only sailing as fast as he could, drawing him through the water. The rope went tight and the men above started to haul him in, pulling him up by his hands. He could do nothing but allow them to hoist him up the outside of the vessel. They dragged him over the edge of the boat, bruising his ribs. He coughed and lay his head on the deck.

Carew walked over to him and pushed him with his foot on to his back. "Are you still alive?"

Clarenceux opened his eyes but said nothing.

"Do you want to go back in the water?"

Still he said nothing. He had withdrawn inside himself to the place of quiet, the refuge that he had discovered when he had been at Mrs. Barker's house. He offered no resistance to Skinner and Kahlu when they lifted him to his feet and dragged him to the ladder that led down from the top of the sterncastle to the upper deck, and from there down to the main deck, and through to the captain's cabin. There they made him sit on the same seat as Gray had sat on, facing the same table. They untied the ropes binding his hands and made him place both of them on the table, palms down.

Five minutes later, Carew came down. He saw Clarenceux sitting there, motionless. He looked at his dark hair matted with salt and seaweed and his bearded face. There were some small cuts and a gash above his eye where a piece of driftwood had struck him. Water still dripped from his clothes, a large puddle had appeared on the floor.

"Where is Denisot?" Carew demanded.

Clarenceux remained silent.

"The woman who said you would never forgive her, she had her transport paid for by Denisot. He paid one hundred and fifty pounds in gold. Why would he do that? I saw that woman; she did not look as if she was worth so much. It is my belief that you were the one who paid Denisot. You were the one who gave him his pseudonym."

Clarenceux moved his head a fraction. "What pseudonym?"

"Percy Roy."

From the depths of his numbness, Clarenceux stirred. He looked at Carew through eyes that felt puffy. "I don't know about Denisot but I can tell you who Percy Roy is."

"Go on then. Who is he?"

"Not 'he' but 'they,'" said Clarenceux, now staring at his hands. "Sir Percival, Sir Reynold, Sir Owain, and Sir Yvain. They are the four surviving Knights of the Round Table—a secret society founded to look after a document of great importance."

"And where do I find these knights?" scoffed Carew. "Camelot? Avalon? Lyonesse? Perhaps they are sleeping in—"

"London," said Clarenceux. "They were the ones who…" Then he remembered. They too would be prisoners now.

Carew gestured to Luke, who was by the door. Skinner was also there, and Kahlu too. Kahlu unfolded his arms.

"Whereabouts in London?"

"They were arrested. They are Catholic agents—they must have persuaded Rebecca Machyn to steal the document from me and then paid for her passage, after which she betrayed them."

Carew stood with one foot on the lid of the chest. "It is very convenient for you to say that all of the men to whom I need to speak are in prison. Too convenient. Start telling the truth or you will go back in the hold and I will put you in the sea after dark."

"Do your damnedest, Carew. Just do it," said Clarenceux impatiently. "You will not listen to what I say. You will not believe me, so do your damnedest."

Carew signaled to Kahlu. To Clarenceux he said, "I think my friend has something to say to you."

Clarenceux hardly stirred as Kahlu put a hand gently on his arm and leaned forward as if to say something. Clarenceux looked up and saw Kahlu's mouth was open. Inside, his teeth were black and rotten; several of them had disappeared altogether. But what astonished Clarenceux was the lack of a tongue. Here was just the stub at the back of his mouth and a deep scar across the bottom of his jaw. One side was also cut and scarred. Then the man shut his mouth and smiled.

Clarenceux heard the thud of the knife at the same instant as he felt the point pierce his hand. He screamed in an agony that surged and surged, redoubling its strength with every instant until it forced even more screams out of him. Instinctively he recoiled and tried to draw his hand away, and in so doing ripped the flesh more and screamed more, yelling from the pit of his sea water–filled stomach.

"You said it, Mr. Clarenceux. To do my damnedest. That was unwise. Deeply unwise."

Clarenceux wanted to answer back but the pain of the knife through his skin forced him only to scream. His breath came in shuddering gasps, and he shivered suddenly before the pain surged again and overwhelmed him, forcing him to scream again. He had been wrong to speak so loosely to the pirate captain. He had been wrong in everything. The moth-like angel that had sheltered him from pain at Mrs. Barker's had been stabbed. Its legs had curled and its wings were fluttering lifelessly in the breeze. There was no shelter now. No shelter anywhere. He glared through tear-filled eyes at Carew and knew what he had to do.

Gritting his teeth and snarling at his own pain, he seized the hilt of the dagger in his left hand and tried to withdraw it. It did not move. Skinner laughed, watching him. Clarenceux, with bared teeth, yelled and yelled, at him and at the knife. Skinner laughed more. Clarenceux screamed louder now, again and again. The knife did not move. But the sight of his blood seeping over his hand and over the table forced him to a pitch of fury that he had never known before. "God damn you all!" he shouted as he started to work the blade forward and backward through his own hand to loosen it, giving voice to his pain with every slight movement. "God damn you, God damn you!" he bawled as the blood spilled out of the wound. Suddenly the knife became loose in his left hand and finally, with a triumphant roar of victory made louder by the pain, he yanked the knife out of the wood and out of his hand, stood up, and held it in front of Skinner's eyes.

No one was laughing now. They could all see the fury burning in Clarenceux. He was armed and ready to kill. Luke and Skinner had already drawn the daggers at their belts and backed away. Kahlu had reached for his in a moment of apprehension and found it absent—his own blade was coming at that moment right toward him as Clarenceux clambered across the table, bellowing, "God damn you!" Then he lashed out, cutting Luke across the arm and only then, after he turned back, was Kahlu able to grab his right arm. He could not hold it; the strength of madness in Clarenceux had taken hold. He was in the grip of his fury, slashing at whatever came within reach.

"Hold fast!" yelled a deep voice from the doorway. A moment later there was an ear-shattering report of a pistol being fired. "Do not move. The next bullet is aimed at your heart."

But Clarenceux had gone beyond all such caution, beyond all but animal reasoning. He only wanted now to destroy, to give himself in a final act of destruction against his enemies. He threw the knife at Hugh Dean in the doorway, catching him in the arm, and hurled himself at Kahlu, punching him on the underside of the jaw with his left hand. Even though he was exhausted, even though he was in pain and bloody, the blow still had enough force to bang Kahlu's head backward against the cabin roof. It was not enough to do more than stun the big man. It did nothing to save Clarenceux from Skinner and Luke jumping on him, grabbing his sleeve and his collar, and smashing his head down on the blood-covered table, three times.

Everyone was gasping now—except Carew. "Have you finished?" he asked, looking at Clarenceux. He turned to Hugh Dean, whose shirt was red with blood, then looked back to Clarenceux. "Skinner, Luke, leave him be." The two men let go. Clarenceux did not move, remaining head down across the table.

"Do your damnedest, Carew," repeated Clarenceux, defiantly.

"You've made your point, herald. Luke, get this man something to eat and drink. Skinner, find him something to wash that wound with. Kahlu, sit down. Mr. Clarenceux, let's start talking."

Clarenceux looked at his hand. Blood was everywhere—smeared up his arm, across his fingers, dripping from the wound. There was a flap of skin hanging down.

"Sit down, Mr. Clarenceux." Carew moved the chair nearer. "I have never seen anyone else do that—draw out the knife. I have seen some try. It is difficult, I know."

"How would you know?" muttered Clarenceux, taking the chair and moving it away from the table before sitting down in it, feeling the pain throb through his whole arm, not just his hand. When he looked up, Carew had his right hand raised, showing him the palm. There was a red weal of a scar through the center.

"Who did it to you?"

"A man called James Parkinson, the captain of Southampton Castle and Calshot Fort."

"Did you kill him?"

"No. He is still there at Southampton, still controlling the ships that sail past Calshot."

Skinner appeared with a pail of cold water and a cloth. He placed it near Clarenceux and left the cabin. Clarenceux glanced at Carew and Kahlu, then reached down, took the cloth, soaked it, and started to wash his wound, flinching at every touch with the sting of the salt water.

Carew watched Clarenceux. "Men often tell lies but they rarely perform them—and never with passion. Men deceive with their words, not by their deeds. Not many men would risk their lives for the sake of a lie. In drawing out that dagger, you have made a persuasive case. What if Denisot, on behalf of these knights you mention, paid the late captain of this ship to take this man and this woman to Southampton and, in going along with them, she deceived you?"

Clarenceux stopped swabbing his hand and looked at Carew. "Did you just say Southampton?"

"I did."

"The Knights of the Round Table arranged that she should sail north," he said, "to Scotland. They intended her to change ships at Sandwich." He paused, feeling the pain in his hand, looking at the blood still seeping from the wound.

Carew stood up and opened the chest. He removed a fine cotton kerchief and brought it across the room, holding it out on one finger. Clarenceux took the cloth and pressed it against the wound, saying, "Your enemy, Denisot, must have deceived the Knights of the Round Table. Really he was acting in conjunction with Rebecca Machyn."

At that moment, Luke entered the cabin with a wooden trencher piled with two large pieces of cut cold beef, a piece of cheese, and half a loaf of bread. He set it down on the table with a flagon of wine.

Clarenceux looked at the food and drink. He reached forward with his good hand. "Was Denisot a Catholic?" he asked.

Carew spat on the floor of the cabin. "The worst kind. He worked for the old queen, when she was dying. Rather than see Calais pass to a Protestant queen, he betrayed the town to the French."

"Then if you want to find Denisot, you must help me find Rebecca Machyn." Clarenceux reached for the beef. Dry though it was, it made his mouth sing. It tasted so very rich, so sweet. He started to chew and turned to Carew. "She is the one who knows where Denisot is."

Carew lifted the flagon of wine from the table and took a draught, then handed it to Clarenceux. "Why not just let her go? It cannot be that important, this document."

"It is. With it she could start a war. An unnecessary war."

Carew shrugged. "Men fight. It is what we do. Sometimes we use swords, ships, and guns, and sometimes laws and money. I prefer ships and guns. More honest."

Clarenceux paused before drinking. "But do you understand what I am saying? If Rebecca Machyn and Denisot are working together, she is the way to find him."

"Then we will find her together. You know what she looks like, I know who escorted her from the dock. You can kill her or do what you want with her—but only after I have extracted the information I need."

Clarenceux looked again at his hand under the reddening cloth. It was still bleeding. It still hurt. He stuffed the remainder of the piece of beef in his mouth and reached again for the salt water and rough cloth. He gritted his teeth as he washed the wound again, looking at the fresh blood swelling out of it. "How is it I find myself abducted by the one person who can take me to her?"

"She led me to you, in a way," said Carew, breaking a piece from the loaf. He continued speaking as he chewed. "Your business about these Knights of the Round Table has nothing to do with me. I could not care less. All I want is Denisot."

"Why?"

Carew swallowed. "Revenge."

"For what?"

Carew held up a finger. "Now that is a long story, which I will tell you when…" He looked at the doorway where Hugh had returned, his arm in a bandage. "Mr. Clarenceux, may I present the quartermaster, my second-in-command, Hugh Dean. Hugh, I want you to forgive Mr. Clarenceux for drawing blood. He has suffered as much. A wound apiece, that's fair."

Clarenceux did not think it fair, but nor did he wish to argue. He accepted Hugh's hand with his left hand and shook it. Carew did not offer a hand. He seemed to assume that he was already for-given. Clarenceux tried to ignore him and returned to the business of staunching the blood.

"Come, Mr. Clarenceux," Carew said suddenly. "I want you to meet the crew."

52

Walsingham pushed the plate of sweetmeats across the table toward John Richards. They were in the writing chamber of his house near the Tower. Walsingham was seated. "What do you know about Raw Carew?"

Richards took a sweetmeat, standing before the table. He shrugged. "The same as most people, I suppose. He's a bastard by birth, the son of George Carew, who went down on the Mary Rose, and a Calais prostitute. He earned the name Raw when he was about fifteen, after he had a fight with another boy aboard the vessel on which they were sailing. The captain set the two of them ashore on a rock for a few days. Carew killed and ate his adversary. He turned to piracy after the fall of Calais. Over the last six years he has taken ship after ship and roamed between Africa and the New World. They say you can never catch him unawares—he is the Robin Hood of the High Seas to some people, a menace to others."

Walsingham held up his hand. "That is common knowledge—but do you know anything practical about him, such as where his home port is, or whether he has a wife?"

"With respect, Mr. Walsingham, I would suggest that that is the wrong way to think of such a man. He has seduced or raped a great many women, so the idea of him coming home to a wife is an unreal one. As for a home port, I suspect he takes shelter wherever he can."

Walsingham looked at Richards. "So you do not know anything about him either. It is astonishing. Everyone knows stories, stories, stories. No one knows anything of any real use about the man. He is indeed like Robin Hood: not just a hero and a villain, but a mystery too. If I did not have to concern myself with his actual deeds, I would wonder whether he really existed or was simply a product of the imagination of the poor. Can you tell me what he looks like?"

Richards shook his head. "I imagine him to have brown hair and a long beard, with a broad forehead, and to be taller than everyone else in his crew. Otherwise I have no idea. I cannot remember anyone ever describing him to me."

"Much as I thought." Walsingham stood up and started to walk around the room. He stopped at a window. "People invent an image of the man because they need to see him in their mind's eye when they tell stories about him. God forgive me for making a profane comparison but it is like people saying they know what Jesus looked like, even though none of us have seen Him. We talk about Him, artists paint Him, theologians expound on His acts—and over the years, we have drawn up a picture of Him that we adapt, trim, cut, and shade. So now we all dance happily around His image in our minds. That figure is instantly recognizable, for it fits our collective idea of the calm, strong-minded Son of God." He touched an inlaid box with his fingers. "We so happily deceive ourselves." He turned to face Richards. "We have done the same thing with Carew. A bearded giant of a man, hurling himself from the rigging of one ship onto that of the next, cutting the stays of a ship's mast while engaged in swordplay with Spaniards, Swedes, Frenchmen, or Englishmen, roaring a challenge to his crew to follow him. And yet I do not know anyone who has actually seen him. One thing I can tell you is that he is barely any taller than me."

"Is that a problem?"

"I have two reports that he was in London yesterday. One in a small boat at Southwark, the other in Fleet Street, in the house of the traitor Clarenceux. Two of Cecil's men stumbled in on them and witnessed Clarenceux being abducted; they heard Clarenceux address Carew by name. I also have a report that he seized a ship four days ago at Southampton. A very good ship—the *Davy*—owned by a consortium of men, headed by the ex-keeper of her majesty's ships. What was she doing in Southampton Water and not in the Port of London, where she was meant to be? If Carew has plucked Clarenceux out of the city, then heaven only knows where he will take him. We may have put the Knights of the Round Table into custody, but the *real* enemy—Clarenceux—is being held by pirates and I am at a loss to know what to do next."

"It is a very short time," said Richards. "Even if Carew had the wind behind him all the way, and sailed all through the night, it would have taken him three days to reach London—it's more than two hundred and twenty nautical miles. If he came all that way and went straight to find Clarenceux at his house in Fleet Street, he had prior knowledge of Clarenceux being there."

"It was no accidental meeting, that is clear."

"With due respect, Mr. Walsingham, you are not seeing my point. If Clarenceux were desperate for rescue, many Londoners who sympathize with his cause could have helped him. But the person who did must have alerted Carew before he took the ship from Southampton. Someone planned several days ago to take Clarenceux somewhere, probably Clarenceux himself, and he needs to be transported there by ship. Otherwise, why wait for Carew?"

Walsingham lifted a hand, trying to continue Richard's line of thinking. "You mean, you think Clarenceux and Carew are working together?"

"Not if Carew abducted him, as you said. But the message must have been received by Carew four days ago, on the eleventh. And it must have been sent from someone in London a day or two before that, at the least. And you yourself said Clarenceux knew Carew's name."

"Where is he going? Scotland, Spain, France? Clarenceux speaks the languages. He has the knowledge."

Richards started to draw an imaginary map on the table surface with his finger. "The seas might be very wide, but with clear sight-lines, a captain can patrol a thirty-mile-wide stretch of water with one ship. Admiral Lord Clinton can control the sea lanes north to Scotland by sailing just fifteen miles off the coast of East Anglia. Not many people will sail far out into the North Sea—certainly not more than thirty miles from land. As for Sir Peter Carew, he can patrol the Channel by placing two or three ships in the sixty-mile stretch between Cherbourg and the Isle of Wight."

"Sir Peter takes his messages from which port?"

"Portsmouth."

Walsingham nodded. "It's seventy miles to Portsmouth. A good messenger can do that in about fourteen hours, with a change of horses. It is now ten of the clock. He could be there tonight, and Sir Peter could receive a message as early as tomorrow. If the pirates are sailing to Spain, how long will it take them, with a fair wind?"

"Three weeks. Longer with a southwesterly."

"And Scotland?"

"They could be in Edinburgh in ten days."

Walsingham sat at his table. "I will write immediately. We will send urgent messages in Cecil's name to Admiral Clinton by way of Boston and Sir Peter Carew by way of Portsmouth."

"What will you order?"

Walsingham looked up in surprise. "To arrest Clarenceux, at all costs."

"And if the pirates fight back?"

"Well, all the more force will be required. I do not doubt Her Majesty would rather risk a few ships than her throne. If it meant us being rid of Raw Carew, so much the better."

53

Carew looked westward with his hand shielding his eyes from the late-afternoon sun. The breeze was full in his face, ruffling his hair. "Furl the sails and drop anchor," he said. They were on the sterncastle, three miles off the Kent coast. "We can't make headway against this." He glanced at Clarenceux and Kahlu. "Are you hungry?"

Clarenceux's ribs felt sore, his clothes were rough, the wound in his hand stung terribly. Other parts of his body that had been beaten were still tender.

"Yes."

Kahlu made a noise and gestured. He stood up and went down to the main deck.

"How did he lose his tongue?" Clarenceux asked.

Carew tied the whipstaff securely against the side of the sterncastle and sat down on an upturned keg. "Slavers. They cut out negroes' tongues for resisting branding and attempting to escape—women as well as men. They all fear that. But Kahlu was never going to stop trying to escape. They caught him once and cut out his tongue. That made him all the more determined. He escaped again. We were sailing in the *Santa Teresa* off the coast of Africa when he appeared in the water. When we pulled him out and spoke to him, he seemed not to understand us. I pointed to myself and said 'Carew.' He pointed to himself and tried to say the same thing. Skinner thought he was trying to say 'Kahlu' but unable to say the 'l' because he had lost his tongue, so we took that to be his name. Later we discovered that he thought that 'Carew' was our word for 'captain.' He was a chief of his tribe."

"Why doesn't he return to his own people?" asked Clarenceux.

"Because they would kill him. They will have another chief by now, one who can talk."

Carew looked down at the deck. He picked up a splinter of wood and started picking the grime out from beneath his fingernails. "That was four or five years ago now. He's a loyal man—the most loyal. A good fighter too. Always dependable. If I was going to sail around the world with just one other man, I would take him."

Clarenceux squinted in the sunlight and looked up at a small bird perched on the rope nearby. "What about the others? Have they all been with you long?"

"Some are new recruits. Alice has been with me for many years—I knew her before the fall."

"The fall?"

"Of Calais. She was a washerwoman's daughter in the house where…" His voice trailed off and he looked away for a moment, across the sea. "Old James Miller survived the wreck that claimed my father's life nineteen years ago. Most of the men aboard the *Mary Rose* that day drowned—either they were below deck or they were caught in the ship's antiboarding nets. Miller kept his head and cut his way out through the nets before the ship started to go down.

"John Devenish and Hugh Dean—they were on a boat that was captured by Spaniards. I found them working in the galley when I, in turn, took command. They were the sole survivors of their original ship. Francis Bidder ran away from Oxford because he did not want to obey his father and become a priest. I thought he was a spy, so I locked him in the hold and threw him in the sea—just like I did to you. He's educated and has a good memory, which makes up for his quietness. He will remember anything you tell him and can do difficult sums very quickly. Luke—he was recruited by Alice in Dartmouth. She heard him playing the fiddle and took him to bed. When she sailed, so did he."

Kahlu and James Miller came up to the sterncastle with a wooden bowl of meaty broth and some bread, one passing the bowl to the other at the top of the ladder. Skinner came along behind with a selection of wooden mugs, which were handed around. He filled a mug from the bowl and handed it to Clarenceux: lamb stewed with salt, onions and thickened with oats. Globules of fat were floating on the surface.

"What about you?" asked Clarenceux, watching the steam from his broth swirl away in the breeze. "You mentioned the fall of Calais. But what drove you to sea?"

Carew lifted the mug, sipped some of the hot stock, and wiped his mouth. He held up his hand, showing the enameled ring on his middle finger. It flashed in the sunlight. "This. It was the only thing I ever got from the Carew family. My father was captain of the Rysbank Tower at Calais twenty-five years ago. After his first wife died, he took a fancy to my mother, who was only about seventeen. She became pregnant with me. When she realized, fearing for her future, she asked him for some protection. He refused to acknowledge her child and told her not to presume to speak to him again. She stole this ring from him that day, determined that I should have some reminder of who my father was."

Clarenceux looked at it, the three black lions on a golden background. "I have seen a similar one."

"You met my father? Where?"

"I did meet him at the siege of Boulogne, but he must already have lost that ring by then. Your uncle, Sir Peter Carew, was wearing an identical one: Or, *three lions passant sable*. I tend to notice these things. I suppose there was a third ring as well. Your grandfather, Sir William Carew, had them made for his three sons. The one given to your other uncle, Sir Philip, I daresay is somewhere still in Malta."

"What is he doing there?"

"He was killed by the Turks."

Carew nodded. "What else do you know about my family?"

Clarenceux thought back to his study and the manuscripts that he had considered recently in preparing for his visitation of Devon. "Mostly heraldic things, not many stories. Coats of arms, seats, lands, estates, and titles. Your family motto is *J'espère bien*—which means 'I hope well' or 'I hope for good.' Your ancestors had extensive lands in Ireland. They used to yell the name as a war cry in battle, 'A Carew, a Carew.'"

Skinner spat a piece of gristle over the side of the sterncastle. "How is it you know more about his family than he does?"

"Because I am a herald. It is my business to know who is descended from whom, and which lines of which armigerous families have died out and how. If your ancestors had a coat of arms, then I would know about your family too."

Skinner looked at him. "My father had just seven acres. He also had seven children. I didn't go to sea to seek my fortune. I went looking for food."

"And look what fine fare a seafaring life has delivered," said Miller, lifting his mug. "As for a fortune, you've seven acres less than your father." He helped himself to some dregs from the bowl and looked at Clarenceux. "What about you then, herald? We're told you're looking for a woman who was on this boat. Are you in love with her?"

"He wants to kill her," said Skinner.

Miller grinned. "That sounds like love to me."

"She has taken something of mine. I want it back," said Clarenceux.

"Worth being nailed to a table for?" said Miller, looking at him over the top of his mug.

"It might stop a war. It may prevent the persecution of Catholics in England. People must learn to tolerate one another's religious beliefs."

None of the men said anything. Several shifted uneasily.

Carew broke the silence. "We have no talk of religion aboard this ship, Mr. Clarenceux. No talk of God or Jesus or the saints—no discussions of Catholics or Protestants. If you can't throw your religion over the side, keep it to yourself."

54

Tuesday, May 16

Clarenceux was woken by his need to urinate. He lay still, sensing the gentle swell of the sea. A thin light was creeping through the windows. The Spanish woman Juanita was walking between the bodies of sleeping men, steadying herself with a hand on the mast, trying not to wake anyone as she made her way back to the women's quarters.

Clarenceux threw off his blanket and went up the ladder. More men here were sleeping on deck, under the pink sky of dawn. Others were on watch. No one was speaking. There was a great tranquility. The sea was calm; apart from the lapping of the water against the hull, there was no noise. The ship did not creak as it had done the previous day.

Clarenceux went to the side of the boat and relieved himself. He watched the ripples of the waves across the wide expanse to the horizon, and saw the mainland in the distance. He looked up at the sterncastle and saw Carew standing there, silhouetted against the sky. He went up the ladder and joined him.

"Don't you ever sleep?"

"I'll sleep when I am old." Carew continued looking out to sea. "When Denisot gave the plans of Calais to the French, he betrayed England. He betrayed the Crown too; there can be doubt about that. So what was he doing in London?"

"I dare say we will have an answer to that question when we find Rebecca Machyn and her brother," replied Clarenceux. "The last time I saw her, she behaved strangely. She said she was going away and would probably never see me again. She and Robert Lowe must have planned with Denisot how they were going to escape from London."

"Two hundred pounds is a lot of money just to take two people to Southampton. And Denisot himself was not on the boat. He did not escape. That means he was not trying."

Clarenceux leaned on the gunwale. "How long do you think it will take us?"

"To get to Southampton? The wind has changed direction to a southeasterly, which is better. Four days maybe?"

Clarenceux gazed across the sea, watching the gulls swoop down and fly just above the waves. "Widow Machyn and her brother might be miles away from Southampton by then."

"We will go after them."

Clarenceux looked at Carew. "Why are you so desperate? This goes beyond revenge."

"Denisot did not just take away my hometown. He took away all the people who protected me, all the people I loved. He took away the women in the house where I grew up. He took away everything."

"You mean, when he betrayed the town."

"Then, and immediately after."

"Was it a house of ill repute, where you grew up?"

Carew smiled. "Ill repute? You mean 'was it a whorehouse'? Yes, it was. My mother turned to prostitution to keep us after her father died, the year after I was born. She was a good woman. All of them in the House of the Three Suns were good women. They had the biggest hearts, and they were always kind to me as a child. When my mother died, I was ten years old. The other women took on her role, trying to send me to school and paying for the weekly fee by taking in extra clients. It was my mother's desire that I should learn to read and write and not suffer the indignities of poverty. The others tried to continue what she started. I hated school and ran away to sea. Now, when I think back, I feel ashamed." He scanned the horizon, as if looking for something that might resemble hope. "For a long time it made me want to weep. Then it made me want to kill. Now when I feel I might cry, I do not shed tears. I shed blood—other men's blood."

He turned to face Clarenceux. Despite what he had just said, there were tears in his eyes. "It was because of religion. That is why no word of religion is to be spoken on my ship. No Bibles, no prayers. Never. Now you understand."

55

Clarenceux did not speak to Carew again for the rest of the day. He saw him bustling about the ship, giving orders, talking to everyone. Although just over one hundred feet in length, there were more than sixty people aboard, and as conversations over the day revealed, there should have been more. Clarenceux had never seen a ship so untidy, in which everyone was free to scatter their possessions. It was only later in the day that he realized why: these were not their possessions. The only things that seemed to be regarded as personally owned by the crew were weapons and musical instruments. It mattered to Hugh Dean that he had his pistols, and to Luke Treleaven that he had his fiddle. They were not the same men without them. Plates, mugs, mallets, spoons—all these things served the same function whoever owned them. The men and women aboard treated all such things as property in common.

The women aboard were "in common" too. No one referred to them as whores to their faces. Juanita was attractive but had a fiery temper and was as likely to stab a man as surrender to his advances. Charity was pretty and calmer than Juanita. She was more timid too and, as far as Clarenceux could see, more considerate. Occasionally he saw one of them in a corner with a man, or slinking off to the orlop deck hand in hand with someone. Alice seemed to be in charge of the women, and she presided over an area of the main deck reserved for their exclusive use. Apart from that, every other area was shared. The traditional distinction of ordinary sailors living before the mast and officers behind did not hold aboard Carew's ship. Everyone went everywhere. Thus no one gave much thought to keeping any area tidy. The captain's cabin was soon as untidy as the rest of the vessel. The surgeon's cabin was similarly despoiled. Alice took some ointments and salves from the surgeon's medical box; the rest were soon scattered underfoot. There being no surgeon aboard, no respect was paid to the tools of his trade. Technical instruments became general-purpose saws and knives.

Not long before midday, they hauled anchor and started once more to head into the wind, taking a course further out to sea. Clarenceux noticed various mariners about the ship carrying platters of food. He went down to the galley in the hold and was served by those tending the ovens. The ceramic bowl held a portion of salt beef and pea stew. He helped himself to an apple and some prunes that were in a basket and returned to the upper deck. The prunes were good, better than the stew, and Clarenceux was amused to see so many of the mariners ignore them. Most of them thought that only meat really counted as food fit for a man.

Nothing much happened that day. Clarenceux watched, talked to people, washed his wounds, helped carry food, picked up some of the broken ceramic things on the main deck, and observed Carew exercising command. Life aboard ship, he reflected, was more intense than on land. So many people were gathered doing so many different things in such close proximity. It was unlike a manor house where you might have just as many people doing just as many things but over a far larger area. At sea, lives overlapped. Sounds were different: always there were voices. Physical movement and feeling was different, because there was so much less space. People even looked at one another and things differently. Arguments broke out simply because there was nowhere else to go. Men rushed to settle disagreements between crew members—aware that trouble could easily spread or escalate into violence. Late that evening, John Dunbar, the gunner, exchanged harsh words with a Breton called Jean, who was supposed to be learning from him how to load and fire the cannon. Carew himself swiftly intervened and confiscated Jean's dagger, thereby saving both men: Dunbar from being stabbed and Jean from being hanged from the yard. Clarenceux was impressed. The chaotic state of the deck and the stench and mess everywhere made the ship seem as if she was running herself, or rather, that no one cared how she was run. Very clearly that was untrue: the captain and many of the crew did. But they were concerned only for the people, not the broken and cast-aside things strewn across the decks.

Clarenceux left the main deck shortly afterward. He went up to the forecastle and leaned out, looking over the sea. He heard Carew give the order to change tack, then shout as the lateen sail was swung across the sterncastle. He stayed where he was, his mind shifting between the events he had witnessed aboard and his experiences on land. He felt uncomfortable even thinking back to Mrs. Barker's house, remembering how he had gone there with guns to intimidate the Knights. He had been naive.

He thought of his family. He imagined Awdrey at Summerhill and his girls playing there in the hall. How were they managing without him? Awdrey was no doubt worried. He missed her conversation, telling him what she thought he should do. He missed the ordinariness of their lives together. He missed his daily routine: sitting down with his heraldic manuscripts and piecing together some ancient family's lineage and claims to coats of arms and titles. He missed knowing what his wife was doing while he was working. When he thought of her, and of his daughters' laughter, he felt again that sense of incompleteness that one has in an empty house.

He heard footsteps. Carew slapped him on the shoulder and leaned across the gunwale next to him, holding the dagger he had taken from Jean.

"These are extraordinary things. So often they are the cause of a problem and so often they are the only solution."

"You mean killing your enemy?"

Carew touched the sharp point. "No. That is normally the start of another problem. I was thinking: knives have probably saved more lives than taken them. Have you ever heard the story of Peter Serrano?"

"No, tell me."

"He was a Spaniard, so Pedro I guess was his real name. He was on board a boat on the other side of the world—beyond Cathay, in the Pacific Ocean—when his ship was caught in a storm and sank. Although he was wearing only a shirt and belt, he threw himself into the sea and swam for miles, finally coming across a small island, where he rested. The island had no trees, no shade, no grass, no streams—no fresh water. It was just two miles across and covered with hot sand. There he would have died had it not been for the knife he had tucked into his belt before he dived off the ship. At first he ate the seafood washed up on the shore, but without fresh water he knew he would soon die. So he swam out to sea where there were giant turtles and hauled them to the island. Once he got them ashore, he turned them upside down and killed them when he needed them. He roasted the flesh on the shells of other turtles in the heat of the sun and caught rainwater in their shells. For warmth he dried seaweed and other driftwood. There were no flints on the island. However, he eventually managed to make sparks by diving deep into the sea and finding a couple of stones that would make sparks when struck with his knife. So you see what I mean? Without his knife, he would have died. The thing that ends lives also saves lives."

"Did this man, Serrano, ever return?"

Carew looked at him. "I thought you were an intelligent man. Of course he survived—otherwise how would I know his story?" Carew looked back out to sea. "Seven years he was on that island. Three years he had to share it with another man, only having half an island."

"Surely the two of them had the whole island—they just had to share it?"

"No. They couldn't stand each other. They divided the island in half."

Clarenceux began to laugh. It seemed absurd. He looked at Carew and chuckled more. And then the laughter triggered something joyous in him and he laughed fully. Even Carew started sniggering, then he too laughed.

"Three years!" Clarenceux's eyes were watering. "The sheer absurdity of human suffering—it is never enough! We have got to make it worse for ourselves." He looked at his hand and held it up for Carew to see. And that too seemed funny. Carew showed him his hand, and their laughter doubled.

"But mine still hurts," said Clarenceux between bouts of mirth. "It still hurts like the Devil, you bastard!" Which only made them both laugh more.

When they had calmed down, Clarenceux said, "You are a strange man. Yesterday you stabbed me and here I am today laughing with you about it. If Walsingham had done that to me and was standing here beside me, I would throw him over the side—if it was the last thing I did. Why is it people allow you to get away with things? Why do people want you to like them?" Carew shook his head. "Not all people do. There are plenty who would hang me if they could." He turned to look across the upper deck. "They would hang my crew too—for just being aboard. Desperate men we all are. And the women. They will hang too, if we are caught. It was brave of those who came with me to London."

Clarenceux looked at the south coast of England, about seven miles away. "How much longer?"

"Depends if the wind holds. At this rate, I'd say another day and a half."

Carew made to go, but Clarenceux detained him. "Peter Serrano is really you, under another name, yes?"

"No," replied Carew. "He was a real Spaniard. I never met him—but I have been in a similar situation. I also refused to share my island."

56

Wednesday, May 17

Francis Walsingham dismounted at the front of Cecil House, passed the servant who bowed, and strode into the hall. There were red marks around his eyes.

"I am glad to see you, Francis," declared Cecil, beckoning him from the table on the dais where he was reading documents. There were several clerks around him, each holding sheaves of papers. Another clerk was sitting beside him, recording decisions in a large ledger.

"I thought you were going to wait on her majesty, at Richmond," snapped Walsingham.

"I was—and indeed I am. As you can see, I am still attending to some unfinished business." He rose and adjusted his formal robe. "We must talk in private."

He walked off the dais and through a wide doorway that led to a small parlor. Walsingham followed. "Close the door, please," said Cecil, standing with his back to the window.

"Sometimes you make me feel as if I am a schoolboy," Walsingham grumbled.

"Sometimes you leave me no choice," replied Cecil. "What do you mean by sending instructions in my name for Sir Peter Carew to fire on an English merchant ship? Are you out of your mind?"

"Richards told you? Is he now spying for you?"

"He is an intelligent young man, but even if he was a dullard he would have been able to see that it is not sensible to order one of her majesty's commissioned officers to fire on an English ship. Nor was it wise for you to issue such instructions in my name."

Walsingham shook his head. "There was no time to consult you. Besides, Raw Carew is in command of it, so it is no longer an English ship. It belongs to pirates—men of no nation." Walsingham looked away, exasperated that Cecil should intervene when he was making progress. "And most important of all, he has Clarenceux."

"You don't know that. You have simply heard a rumor and on the strength of that alone you have decided to blow a merchant ship out of the water."

"Your own men told me! They saw the two of them together at Clarenceux's house. Damn your eyes, Sir William—do you give me credit for nothing? Do you expect me to let him go? He will simply put his plan into action."

"Speak to me with civility, Mr. Walsingham, or you can say good-bye to both your freedom and your seat in Parliament." Cecil fixed him with a stern look. "I do not believe Clarenceux has the marriage agreement. I think he is chasing Rebecca Machyn, who has double-crossed him. I think he was telling us the truth."

"You cannot be sure."

"Neither can you. That is why I think it madness to sink a ship."

The two men confronted each other. Walsingham knew that he understood the situation better than Cecil. He could not understand Cecil's stance...not for some moments. Then a possible reason began to occur to him. He waited, thinking through the thought that had just entered his head. "Why did you only mention Sir Peter Carew? Why just him?"

"I am sorry?"

"Why not Lord Clinton as well?"

Cecil shrugged. "Well, of course, what I said applies equally to your message to Lord Clinton."

"No. You were only concerned with what I sent to Sir Peter Carew." He paused. "You *know* about this. You withheld news of this document's existence from me, and you did not tell me that you asked Clarenceux to look after it."

Cecil said nothing.

Walsingham continued, "You know—somehow—that Clarenceux has sailed south. Neither Richards nor I knew that. Carew came from Southampton but that does not mean he is taking Clarenceux back there. You have some other source. You know what is going on here."

"Listen, Francis. Yes, there is more going on here than I can reveal. But you must trust me, now more than ever."

"Damn you, Sir William! Damn you and damn your scheming! I did think that Widow Machyn was acting in accordance with Clarenceux, but now it seems that Clarenceux's partner in treason is you—none other than *you*, her majesty's own Secretary. I cannot believe your hypocrisy. You, of all people, who have urged me so many times to seek out and arrest conspirators—you are one yourself. You have lied to me repeatedly, about the marriage agreement, about Clarenceux seeking Widow Machyn, about—" He stopped suddenly. "Oh, by God's blood," he whispered. "You are not working with him. You are working with *her*."

Cecil walked to the door. He opened it and called across the hall to two guards. They approached and he spoke to them in a low voice. Then he turned back to face Walsingham.

"Francis, you saw that coded message. You yourself presented it to me. You saw what it said. Widow Machyn had agreed to help the Knights of the Round Table. I helped her disappear." He held Walsingham's gaze. "I knew she was under huge pressure to betray Clarenceux and so I decided to remove her from him and from the Knights of the Round Table. It was simply a precaution. It meant that the Knights of the Round Table and, as it turns out, their associate Mrs. Barker, were left without the document they so desperately seek. And Clarenceux was left without it too. That is why I know he is innocent."

Walsingham was furious. "He might be innocent, but you most clearly are not. You are a traitor! You did not destroy the document when you had the chance. You have arranged for it to be stolen and sent it by ship…God knows where. Where is it? Where has she gone? God's wounds—I should have you arrested. Indeed, I think I will, I am just that angry. I will speak to her majesty, and I will tell her that two traitors are being protected by Sir William Cecil—Clarenceux and Widow Machyn."

"Francis, that would not be helpful."

"But it would be true."

"Then you would be arresting me for the sake of my methods, not my intentions. And you would be protecting yourself, not the State."

"I…am…the…State!"

"No, you are not! Her majesty is the State. You are just a tiny part of her organization—one of the State's many instruments. A finger of the State, nothing more."

Walsingham's eyes narrowed. He held up his forefinger and turned it toward Cecil. "I have an itch. It is called treason. I will do the scratching."

Cecil shook his head. "Francis, you have to trust me. Believe me, I had to take matters into my own hands. I had to take the initiative. I did not think that events would turn out as they have and so I did not tell you. But you must trust me in this. What I have done is for all our safety—yours, mine, the queen's, everyone's. Even Rebecca Machyn's."

He stepped over to the door and signaled to the guards outside. "See to Mr. Walsingham's horse, please. He and I will be spending some hours together."

"This is betrayal," said Walsingham beneath his breath.

"No, Francis, sincerely, it is not. It is loyalty—to her majesty. If you expect me to show a greater loyalty to you, then you have misplaced your expectations. But I know that is not the case. I have simply surprised you. Rather than go to her majesty and accuse me of things that you do not understand, I suggest we call for wine and wafers and discuss this situation. I owe you the courtesy of a full explanation."

57

Carew and his men fought against the wind that day. While it came from the southeast their progress was fast, but toward midday it died down and they were almost becalmed. Then it shifted, and the next breeze came from the southwest, which made progress difficult. Carew ordered a change of tack every few minutes, so the ship beat its way into the headwind. He had little time for conversation with Clarenceux, who either stayed on deck, nursing his wounds, or paid attention to the gunners' lessons on how the cannon were to be fired.

"Unlike older ships, we have standard sizes of guns," Dunbar declared. "There are three sizes aboard: four demicannon, which fire thirty-two-pound shot; four sakers, which are five-and-a-quarter pounders; and four little falconets, which use a ball of just one pound. They all fire cast-iron cannonballs that fit exactly—we do not use stones to be chipped to an irregular shape and size. Each cannonball fits neatly into the cannon and the pressure as it explodes is even, lessening the chances of the cannon exploding in your face. That used to happen with the old culverins, especially if they were loaded with stone—but not anymore."

"What is the range?" asked Clarenceux.

"Of the demicannon? Half a mile or so. The sakers are almost as long in the barrel but fire a much smaller shot, so their effective range is three times that, depending on what you want to do. At a mile and a half you could tear down the sails of a ship—but you'd be damned lucky to hit anything at that distance. A blow from one of the demi-cannon at a hundred yards might well go through the main deck of the ship and out the other side. If you want to sink her, you need to drive the cannonball through the water and through the hull."

"And the falconets?"

"Best part of a mile. But that would be missing the purpose. Imagine the biggest handgun you could possibly fire by yourself. Very versatile."

The southwesterly wind brought with it a worsening of the weather. The men on deck fought with the lateen sail, swinging it across the sterncastle each time. The waves grew bigger so that by the early evening every change of tack resulted in the ship wallowing in a figure-of-eight pattern, from side to side and forward and back, so that Clarenceux felt quite sick. He went up on deck and leaned over the side of the ship, gazing at the heaving sea, unable to watch the young men scampering up the rigging. They climbed along a yard even though the ship was cavorting about like a large cork tossed on the water.

Clarenceux was still on deck at dusk, when the rain began to fall and a call came from the rigging. Snatched words of conversation soon alerted him that the shout from aloft had been serious. He saw Carew jump down from the sterncastle and start climbing a rope attached to the main mast, his strong arms lifting him so quickly that he barely touched the rope with his legs. A few seconds later, Carew was standing on the platform looking out to the southwest horizon. Then he climbed higher to the platform above, the crow's nest. Clarenceux turned away. The movement of the ship, wallowing in the waves, made the act of watching Carew at the masthead a sickening experience. He turned back to look at the seaweed-streaked blue-green water rising and falling before the ship.

Half an hour later, the swell had turned to black. It was still possible to see the masts and rigging stark against the sky, but not much else. He heard a sail flapping like a flag as they changed tack again. The calls of sea birds had long since ceased, leaving only the sound of the waves splashing against the hull as the ship rocked its way onward.

He heard someone approaching. "Lost your sea legs?" It was Hugh Dean.

"I thought I would have been used to it after a few days."

"This is choppy. It's been serene up until now. You want to see what it's like when the waves are higher than the ship. Out in the ocean, your heart fails, and your very bones turn to despair."

Clarenceux looked back across the deck. "Why are there so many men still up here in the rain? Why don't they go below?"

"Out there on the horizon, there are several ships. At least three, perhaps four. Large square-rigged vessels, like this one or bigger. They appear to be sailing together; it is a warning."

Clarenceux nodded. He was in darkness at sea. That in itself did not frighten him, but he had never before been aboard a ship in the darkness when it was under risk of attack. "Where is Carew?"

"Below on the main deck, talking to the gunners. He has ordered most of us to stay up on deck—in case those ships take advantage of the wind and come upon us in the darkness. You keep an eye out too. Yell if you see anyone coming aboard." Dean walked away.

Clarenceux closed his eyes as the ship rolled over another wave. If they were hostile and waited for the morning, they would be rested and the men aboard the *Davy* exhausted. If they attacked in the darkness…His mind recoiled from the thought. Three ships attacking in darkness was too much to contemplate. There would be no distinction. Carew and his men would be destroyed as pirates. But what was the alternative? To plunge over the side and swim in black sea toward the shore? He could not even see which way the shore lay.

With the rain coming down harder in the darkness, and the wind slapping the ropes against the mast, Clarenceux knelt down. He could not easily be seen against the forecastle. He would pray in silence.

58

Thursday, May 18

Clarenceux hardly slept. Throughout the night there were movements of men up and down from the deck and the sound of wind whistling through the open hatch and in the rigging. The ship was tumbling on the waves and his own mind followed its turbulent course, running through the possibilities of attack after attack. He tried to remain calm, telling himself that Carew was simply taking a precaution; but he still felt his heart beating fast. In the long hours of the short night, watching the candle flames sway behind the lanterns' glass, he asked himself searching questions. What if the ships attacked? Was he going to fight with Carew's pirates or against them? Was he going to seek refuge with the attackers or defend these men?

One question above all burnt in his mind: was he doing God's work or following the agency of the Devil? As he lay there, gazing at the flame, hearing the creaking of the boat, he sought the answer to that question. No answer came. Never before had he had reason to doubt, but now he was among renegades and killers—pirates by anyone's reckoning except their own. And the captain was a godless man.

He sat up, flexing his wounded right hand. He wanted to know how tightly he could grip a sword. The question had been lurking at the back of his mind for some time. Throwing off the blanket, he searched across the deck for a weapon. There were normally some to be found lying around. Not now. They had all been gathered up, betraying a readiness of which he had not been quite aware.

Was this a sign? That he should take no part in the fighting?

He went to the ladder and climbed aloft. It had stopped raining. The night sky was cloud filled and starless, and the cold wind hit his face. Even so he could make out the men on the wet deck, huddled in groups.

"Where's Captain Carew?" he said to a figure standing by the ladder to the sterncastle.

"Up here. Asleep. Best not to wake him."

"He sleeps? How can he?"

"Ask him—when he wakes up. We are sure that the ships have come closer."

Clarenceux shivered and looked at the eastern sky. It would soon be dawn. "Where can I find a blade? I need something to defend myself with if they come aboard."

"They are probably all taken," replied the man guarding the ladder to the sterncastle. "Besides, Captain Carew said you're not expected to fight. You're not one of us."

"What does he expect me to do?"

"Tend to the wounded, I suppose, or look out for boarders. That's what the women do."

"I am not one of the women."

"Lucky you," said the man grimly.

The wait for dawn was a long, cold one. Clarenceux sat with his back to the gunwale, wishing he was on land. He clasped his arms around him and considered going back down into the warmer heart of the ship and reclaiming his blanket, but he did not want to leave the fresh sea air. It was reassuring to him: it was a reminder of Creation and the company of God—the essence that meant to him that, although solitary, he was not alone. He watched others going about their business, and he listened in case anyone took news to Carew. Otherwise he shielded himself in his corner of holy reflection.

Carew. He was the one person to whom Clarenceux wanted to speak at that moment. Not that he had anything to say; he just wanted to know what the man was thinking. He trusted him; he did not understand why, but he did. Even though the man had caused a knife to be plunged through his hand, Clarenceux had confidence that Carew would see them through any and all adversity. He was like an irreligious miracle worker. *Does one have to believe in God to work miracles?* But how could he work this particular miracle? God would surely not favor a man who cared nothing for Him against the threat of the approaching ships, led by a pious captain.

He was startled out of his reverie by a shout from the masthead. A moment later, a figure leaped down from the sterncastle, not bothering to climb down the ladder, and started pulling himself into the rigging by his arms. Clarenceux struggled to his feet and went across to the other side of the boat. Four ships—not three—were dimly to be seen to the south and southwest, in a line, several miles away. He could not make out from this distance whether their sails were unfurled, but there was no doubt that they were the cause for alarm.

"Prime the guns, all others to the deck," shouted Carew from aloft, tugging at the ropes fastening one of the sails to the main yard.

People started running. Men emerged rapidly through the hatch from the deck below. Clarenceux looked again at the ships. For a moment he could not make out what was going on. The wind had changed direction, coming from the south, and the Davy was trapped between the vessels and the coast, five miles away. One of the ships already had its sails unfurled and full; two others were unfurling theirs. And there was the fourth ship on the horizon, further south-west, where they had first seen the fleet, ready to cut off their escape.

The air was filled with shouts of shipmen's jargon that Clarenceux did not understand. Kahlu leaped up the ladder onto the sterncastle and started untying the rope that fastened the lateen sail. Clarenceux was surprised to see it turn so that it was sending them toward the ship waiting for them to the southwest. He climbed up the ladder to the sterncastle himself and was about to speak to Kahlu when he saw the man look hurriedly to the east. He turned around—and understood. There had not been four ships, there had been five. During the night one galleon had sailed up the Channel and around to the east. It was now between three and four miles away and approaching fast. They were hemmed in, with ships coming at them from the east, south and southwest.

It was a hopeless situation—one in which any normal commander would have counseled surrender. But these men could not surrender, for they would simply be hanged. They had to fight to the death. In that instant, seeing the prow of the ship to the east bearing down on them, Clarenceux realized what he had to do. God's will was that he should fight, that he should survive. It was not a decision that he could have made in the silence of the night. It was not a question that could have been decided by looking at the silent doubt of a candle flame. It was an understanding that could only have been reached in sight of the cannon's mouth.

Carew was still aloft, shouting. The *Davy* was heading northwest, heaving up and down on the waves, trying to outrun the surprise ship from the east and at the same time avoid the three ships coming from the south. They were moving fast, with the wind fully behind them. Men bustled around him, but this, Clarenceux realized, was merely the calm before the killing started. Discreetly crossing himself, he shut his eyes and said a prayer.

A fizz in the air and the simultaneous boom of a cannon made him open his eyes. There was a splash in the sea not far away, to the west of the ship. He looked at the vessels to the south; these were still out of range. The galleon in the east, however, was less than a mile away. He saw a flash from its port side as a second gun fired. This too missed, splashing into the sea just short of the *Davy*. He heard Carew shouting and looked aloft, not understanding the jargon and wishing there was something he could do to help. He did not even have a weapon. He could not sail a ship—he did not know anything about managing sails. He heard the third report of a cannon and the fizzing sound in the air, then screams as two men fell from the foremast and part of the rigging snapped and recoiled.

He did know a little about guns.

Below in the dimness of the main deck, Dunbar, the master gunner, was measuring out charges of gunpowder into pots. Clarenceux said, "I've come to assist."

Dunbar continued measuring out the gunpowder. "You've been watching the demonstrations?"

"Yes."

"Ever fired anything bigger than your arm?"

"No."

"Main thing is to swab the barrel after every use. Put a charge of gunpowder down the barrel when it's still hot and fiery inside, and it'll ignite and blow the ramrod straight through your guts. The demicannon need six men to run them out, but you"—he looked Clarenceux up and down—"take that falconet." He turned and pointed. "Nick will show you what to do. Aim for the sails and the rigging—we need to slow them down."

Clarenceux went across to the gun that Nick Laver was heaving out beyond the gunport.

"Loaded?" asked Clarenceux, seeing Nick attach the ropes to stop the recoil.

"Aye, though I'm not sure about hitting anything. We wallow and rise too much."

Clarenceux bent down and forced down the rear of the gun, bringing back the wedge beneath the front of the barrel. Nick was right; the rolling of the ship from side to side made it difficult to aim. He looked along the four-foot barrel and searched around for the linstock. It was as yet unlit, lying alongside the cannon. He picked it up in his right hand, determined that the wound would not disable him, and turned to the lantern attached to the base of the foremast.

"Wait, I haven't primed the fuse yet," shouted Nick, clutching a flask of the fine gunpowder used for the firing. But at that moment there was an almighty burst of air and sound and the whole ship shook. Clarenceux was thrown against the base of the foremast. Splinters of oak lay all around, and there was a gash in the side of the boat where a heavy cannonball had struck. On the far side there was another hole where it had departed, splitting the strakes of the vessel and allowing a jagged brightness into the main deck. The ship in the east was almost on them. He knelt down and looked through the falconet's gunport. It was at forty-five degrees to their direction of sail, less than a hundred yards away.

There was shouting and more cannon fire. Men were running and stooping, yelling and cursing. Clarenceux looked around for where he had dropped the linstock and found it on the deck. The lantern was extinguished, its glass broken by the blast. There were flames flickering here and there, so his first reaction was to relight the lantern from the flames. His next thought was that the gunpowder was scattered. He shook his head, not thinking clearly. Two more loud booms came from the ships to the south.

A scream of pain rose from the far side of the deck. A man had been knocked out by the blast, had come to his senses, and felt the agony of the splinters of oak that had shredded his arm and the side of his face. There was a shout of warning nearby; a cannon fired and recoiled. Clarenceux looked at the wounded figure and saw it was the apprentice shipwright whom he had seen once or twice in the dark of the orlop deck with Alice. He turned to see where Nick had gone. The lad was on his back, lying over a crate, with half his head blown away, the brain exposed and a lifeless eye hanging by a nerve. Clarenceux crossed himself and turned away.

Dunbar was pouring gunpowder from the pots into linen pouches as steadily as he could, with the movement of the ship. Eight others were pushing out two of the long-barreled demicannon on the starboard side, and ten or eleven men were firing those on the port side. The man firing the other falconet on this deck was loading his gun with grapeshot and aiming high, to tear down the sails off the chasing ships.

Turning back to his own falconet, Clarenceux grabbed the flask of fine gunpowder from the next gunport and filled the priming hole. He refastened the flask and hung it on a hook above his own gunport and took up the linstock. The wounded man was still screaming on the far side of the ship; other men were yelling all around him. Clarenceux lit the linstock from that of another gunner nearby, and, having looked once more along the barrel, he stood to one side, waited till they were at the low point of the ship's wallowing, and applied the linstock to the priming hole.

The falconet burst with life, shooting back against the limit of the thick rope. Quickly Clarenceux looked through the gunport to see where the cannonball had gone. There was smoke all around the other ship; a moment or so later, he saw that the lateen sail had fallen. Whether it was his shot or that of another cannon he did not know, but the ability of the other ship to change direction was severely limited. Encouraged, Clarenceux shouted to Dunbar for another charge of gunpowder for the falconet and started the process of loading it again.

For the next hour and a half, Clarenceux lost himself in a frantic ritual of loading and firing this one small gun, putting a half-pound charge of gunpowder into the barrel, ramming it home with wadding, inserting the cannonball, and ramming that home with more wadding. Smoke filled the deck; shots that tore apart the oak sides of the hull sent splinters flying dangerously across the confined space. The smell of burning gunpowder filled the air. Shot by shot he mastered the technique of aiming and firing the weapon. A falconet might be a small gun, he realized, but as it was light enough for him to run out singlehandedly, he could take charge of the whole process and thus find his own rhythm. His third shot tore through the mainsail of the ship; his fifth smashed into the sterncastle. A two-inch piece of red-hot metal passing through did untold amounts of damage: that was obvious enough from those that hit the *Davy*. He fired fifteen shots, sweating and grimy with the effort, deafened from the explosions, wounded from the splinters and scorched from the burning of the hull.

With the swab in his hand, washing out the barrel of his falconet for the sixteenth time, he felt as if someone had suddenly placed their hands over his ears and tried to pull his head off. Thrown suddenly against the hull, he could see nothing. His head hurt, much more than his hand. A man was crying somewhere nearby, another howling. The ship was rolling from side to side even more than before. Clarenceux struggled to his feet and looked at where his gun had been. There was a gash in the side of the ship and the falconet was rammed into the wood. The wood had splintered outward, however. The cannonball had come through the ship from the other side and hit his falconet. He looked at the gaping hole in the opposite side of the ship. He turned back to his gun. It was now useless.

He walked through the smoke-filled deck, his head reeling, a singing noise between his ears. Only eight men were still firing—five attending to a demicannon on the starboard side and three firing one on the port. The body of Nick Laver had been blown from the position in which he had fallen and smashed like a doll against the mainmast. His cutlass, still tucked in his belt, had caught on the body of another man, who had also suffered from the massive splinters of smashed oak strakes. At the foot of the ladder was the naked upper body and head of a woman, Charity Pool. Clarenceux had been dimly aware of Charity and the other women going among them, trying to staunch the bleeding of the wounded. Her long hair had been burnt away and her skin scorched black. Her legs had gone entirely, torn off by a cannonball.

Clarenceux crossed himself, pushed the woman's remains to one side and went up the ladder. Everything was changed. The galleon that had surprised them, coming from the east, was still a hundred yards away but now it had only one of its three masts and no sails—partly due to his own work. The three ships that had been sailing at them from the south, however, were all close at hand. One had lost all but its topmost and lateen sails and was about three hundred yards to the south, but the other two were both within a hundred yards, and one of those had all three masts still intact—albeit with one sail ripped. The fifth vessel too had moved closer and now was about a mile away.

None of this surprised Clarenceux so much as the scene on the deck of the *Davy*. Bodies were lying everywhere, men groaning with broken limbs where they had fallen from the yards onto the deck. Some were screaming in agony. There were splashes of blood across the wood. Even those who were not wounded were lying down or crouched in corners as occasional gunshots hit the deck. One of the sakers stationed on the upper deck was surrounded by corpses; the other was still being manned by John Devenish, despite the blood across his shoulder and back. The mainmast had been split in two about ten feet above the upper deck and, restrained by the rigging, the top half had fallen down, hanging across the yard. The foremast was similarly broken, its jagged edges pointing into the blue sky. All the sails were down except one, and that was ragged.

The almost unscathed ship was moving fast toward the *Davy* on the port side, looking as though she was going to ram her. Musketeers were stationed on her deck, firing at anything that moved on the *Davy*, and men with bows were shooting arrows with incendiary pitch-covered heads at the ship. As these hit, the *Davy*'s crew rushed to throw them over the side. When they did so, the enemy opened fire with their muskets. Although their aim was wayward because of the pitching of the two ships, five or six guns being trained on the target made the task of clearing the deck a dangerous one.

Clarenceux ducked back down through the hatch and looked

across the wrecked main deck, wondering how to stop the fast-approaching ship. Through the smoke he could see men and boys scurrying around, carrying powder and shot and buckets of water for the swabs and to put out the fires. Only one of the demicannon was now in operation—the one on the starboard side. The other had been abandoned, with broken timber, blankets, eating vessels, and a mass of broken rubbish piled up behind it, preventing it from being drawn in to be reloaded. But the men firing the starboard gun were shooting at a ship that posed no immediate threat. Clarenceux needed to have these men fire the gun that was out of use. "The other gun!" he roared in his loudest, most commanding heraldic voice. He stepped down the ladder. "Take the other cannon. We are about to be rammed from the portside—fire the other cannon!"

One of the men grasped what Clarenceux was saying; the other four followed, bringing the linstock and gunpowder between them. Clarenceux helped them clear a path to pull in the gun. There was no time to swab it—and no need, as it had not been fired for some time. One man packed in the four-pound charge of gunpowder and the other lifted the cannonball and rammed it home. A fourth man saw to the priming and Clarenceux looked along the barrel, taking the linstock. "Run her out," he commanded, looking over at the fast-approaching ship. When the gun was ready, he still waited, picturing the nine or ten feet of ship below the waterline. It was a careful balance, between a shot that was too deep, which would barely damage the vessel, and one that was only just below the waterline. The ship heaved, the muzzle wavering between the waterline and the fore-castle. "Muzzle down," he yelled, watching the prow of the ship close in on them. Then "Stop!" he shouted, realizing that just below the waterline would be enough—the water pouring in would do the rest itself. He waited a moment, gauged the timing of the waves, and applied the linstock to the gunpowder.

He only just managed to dive out of the way in time. In concentrating on aiming the gun, he had forgotten about the recoil. In the second or so that it took the priming gunpowder to burn through, he remembered. The cannon shot back—more than two tons of bronze and iron-bound oak—restrained by the ropes with an impact as sudden as the initial deafening explosion.

Clarenceux got to his feet quickly and grabbed the swab from the neighboring gun as the other men hauled in the cannon. He glanced through the gun port as he cleaned the barrel, hearing the hiss of the water on the hot metal. There seemed to be no difference to the enemy ship. He gestured for the next charge to be inserted and picked up the linstock, as the thirty-two-pound cannonball was rammed home. Wiping the sweat from his face, he gave the order to run her out. Again he looked down the barrel, and aimed to hit the ship two feet below the waterline. Another deafening roar burst from the gun. Immediately Clarenceux picked up the swab and gave orders for the next shot to be prepared. When the smoke cleared and he could see the approaching ship, her prow was lower in the water. She was sinking.

Clarenceux ordered the men to continue firing the smaller guns and went back up through the smoke to the ladder. He crouched on the upper deck, shouting at Luke, who was loading a number of pistols arranged in a row in front of him. The body of Hugh Dean was nearby, his stomach a mass of blood and bone, ripped open by a cannonball. His mouth was open and his eyes too, still staring up through the smoke at the sky.

"Where's Carew?" shouted Clarenceux, moving over to Luke.

"He led a boarding party. He went in with Kahlu, Francis, Harry, and Skinner and used the ship's own cannon to blow a hole in the bottom of the hull. He's swimming his way back now, look."

Clarenceux glanced over the gunwale. The ship he had hit was going down prow-first, slowly. The second nearby ship was listing to port; its crew was in a panic. Some were jumping into the water; others, not knowing how badly holed she was, were trying to sail her toward land. Carew and Kahlu were swimming back to the *Davy* followed by the others. Clarenceux almost laughed at how lucky Carew had been to have chosen to sink the other one of the two nearby vessels. *The man has more lives than a cat.*

Clarenceux took stock of the situation. The ship to the east was without its sails, practically becalmed off the starboard side. As for the ship he had hit, the waves were over the deck now; only the masts and sterncastle were still visible. Men were swimming or clinging on to the rigging in the hope of a skiff coming along to save them. A number had already drowned, their bodies rising and falling lifelessly in the swell. The ship Carew had boarded was taking in water through its gun ports. But there were still two other vessels afloat.

The most distant one was now about half a mile to the southwest, as yet unscathed. The other ship, which had lost all but two of its sails, was still mobile and firing, about two hundred and fifty yards away to the south.

"We are just waiting for them," muttered Clarenceux to Luke, as Carew and Kahlu climbed up the outside of the ship and clambered over the gunwale. As he spoke, another cannonball from the ship to the east hit the main deck below. The impact shook the boat and knocked Kahlu off balance. He picked himself up as Carew approached.

"We're holding them," said Carew, "but only just. It would be better for us if we could sail."

A movement away to the east caught Clarenceux's eye. A skiff was setting out, full of men. "Here they come," he said, pointing.

"Go below, alert them," said Carew, turning to survey the rigging. For a moment Clarenceux considered telling him how few men were left alive below, but he thought better of it. Carew turned back to him, as if reading his thoughts. "Do what you can. Encourage them."

The ship rolled on a higher wave and a musket ball cracked into the sterncastle. Clarenceux ducked his head, scampered across to the ladder, and went down to the main deck. Men were still firing the gun on the port side and running around for more powder, more shot. Alice was nursing a man who had lost a leg and a lot of blood. She was mopping his brow—obviously she had given up on trying to save his life. Juanita was working fast, wrapping a tourniquet around the bleeding leg of a gunner, trying to staunch the rapid flow of blood. Stars Johnson had taken over from Dunbar in measuring out gunpowder. He looked up as Clarenceux jumped down the ladder.

"Where's Dunbar?" shouted Clarenceux.

"Down below, looking for more gunpowder."

Clarenceux looked down the timber-strewn deck. "Give me powder for that saker."

"This is all for the demicannon," replied Stars.

"For the love of God," yelled Clarenceux, "give me a charge anyway."

Stars passed a measure of gunpowder to Clarenceux who ran to the abandoned saker. A shot hit the outside of the hull and split the wood with an alarming crack. He looked and found a cache of shot for the gun and the priming flask lying on the deck. Pouring all the gunpowder into the barrel, he inserted the cannonball and wadding and primed the gun and, shouting for help, tried to run out the gun singlehanded. It hardly shifted. Juanita was suddenly beside him, grunting as she heaved on the carriage. Then another man joined them. "Fetch a linstock," Clarenceux shouted over the sound of muskets and shrieking from the upper deck. He knelt to look along the barrel.

The skiff was heavily laden, being rowed quickly toward him. He counted the men aboard: fourteen. *Is this the work of God? Or the Devil?* He closed his eyes.

"Here," shouted Junanita, thrusting the slow-burning linstock at him.

He took it and looked at her face, streaked with sweat, fierce. The determination showed in her eyes. She was fighting for her life—as much as Carew or anyone. *This is neither the work of God nor the Devil. This is war and I have chosen sides.*

Looking toward the skiff, which was now no more than sixty feet away, he lowered the gun, secured it, and applied the linstock. There was a moment while the priming sparked and burnt—and then the explosion. He watched the shot smash into the boat, splintering the rear of the skiff and sending the front of it and pieces of wood spinning up into the air. When they splashed down there were several men dead in the water, their heads bobbing on the reddened surface like fruit in a bowl. Only one of the survivors could swim and was fit enough to do so; he turned back to his own ship. The others screamed in panic as they thrashed about, drowning, clutching at the fragments of the boat.

Clarenceux clambered across to the other side of the main deck and looked out through a gunport. There were bodies, limbs, and pieces of timber around the *Davy*, bobbing about on the water: the flotsam of a battle. The ship to the south was closer, about one hundred and fifty yards. The fifth ship, still unscathed, was also only a few hundred yards away to the southwest.

Another cannon shot boomed out across the water. Clarenceux heard footsteps on the ladder and turned to see Carew stepping down.

"I didn't expect you to fight," Carew said.

"I'm fighting my own war. My cause is different from yours—but we're allies."

Carew nodded. "Good. Find yourself a blade. We are about to be boarded." He walked further down the main deck, inspecting the damage. "One ship might try to ram us against another, so we are attacked on both sides at once. If so, we will try to board whichever one has the most sails and, if we can take it, that will be our escape."

Clarenceux watched him go down to the orlop deck. Steam billowed up from the hatch. The *Davy* was sinking. One of the many blows she had suffered over the past two and a half hours of engagement had weakened the planking below the waterline.

Carew reappeared. "Galley's waist-deep in water." He glanced out of the gunport at the approaching vessels. "If they realize, they will just hold back until we go down. They had better attack soon."

Carew went over to Juanita, who had given up the struggle to save James Miller. She lay his head on the deck and closed his eyes. Clarenceux shook his head. He knew they had no chance of taking another ship; there were too few of them left. But that seemed not to concern Carew, who knelt down beside Juanita, placed his hand on James Miller's chest, then touched her face and kissed her.

Clarenceux steadied himself as another cannonball smashed into the *Davy*. He felt resigned; he was barely aware of what he was expected to do. He stumbled toward the hatch down to the orlop deck and descended the ladder. Steam was hot and wet in the air. There was light on one side where a cannonball had splintered two strakes of the hull. When the water reached that point, the ship would flood in a matter of moments. She would heel over and sink quickly.

He bowed his head, praying for salvation. He was past praying for anything in particular; he had no ideas left. All he could think of was to escape by trying to swim to shore. But that was miles away and he had never swum more than a few hundred yards. Also he would probably be shot in the water. Even if a bullet simply wounded him it might stop him from swimming so far. Carew would not reveal where Rebecca Machyn had gone either. All this would have been in vain. The best he could do was survive—and hope that the enemy commander would treat him as a herald and not as a pirate.

But he had fired on a boat full of men and killed them. He could not refuse to fight the boarding party now. He had committed himself.

Tears welled in his eyes at the thought of Awdrey and their daughters. He remembered little Mildred learning to climb the stairs. He prostrated himself, begging for mercy, for forgiveness. He prayed that his family might be safe and secure. He would have continued in that position, praying, had not another cannonball smashed through the hull just astern, sending splinters flying through the dimness, cutting his face and arms and leaving him gasping against a barrel. The shock and the pain brought him to his senses. He looked out through the newly made hole and saw the sea surging not far below. He crossed himself and went back up the ladder.

Clarenceux went between the corpses, looking for a blade. Remembering that Nick Laver had been wearing a cutlass, he searched for his corpse. He walked over and confronted the smashed head, the glistening brain, the loose eyeball. He saw the hilt of the weapon and drew it. As he did so, he noticed the other eyelid flickering.

Clarenceux hesitated. *How was it possible?* He bent down and listened to his breathing, seeing the eyelid flicker again. "Help me," whispered Laver. "End it now."

Clarenceux remembered the killing of the men in the skiff, how he had justified that to himself because it was war. Now Laver seemed like an apparition of one of them, making him confront at close quarters what he had done to those men at a distance. He was a living ghost, come from the sea, bloody and accusing. A ghost from the guns of warships.

I killed men who were not dying. Why is it difficult to kill a man who wants me to kill him?

Clarenceux suddenly jabbed forward with the dagger, aiming for Laver's heart. He hit the breast bone and had to twist the blade loose, causing Laver to scream a chilling greeting to death. He stabbed again and hit a rib, and Laver screamed again, lifting a trembling hand to the destroyed side of his head. Frantic, Clarenceux stabbed a third time and thrust the blade deep into the man's heart. The arm slowly fell, Laver froze into death. Clarenceux pulled the blade out, wide eyed with revulsion. He turned and ran up the ladder to the main deck in a blood-smeared daze, unable to think of anything but the need to stab his way clear of the ghosts plaguing his conscience. He bent down beside a corpse on the main deck, knowing that it was the body of John Devenish and that his Moorish blade was lying there. He picked it up, not even thinking about the musket bullets raining down from the two ships that were now only twenty or thirty yards from the *Davy*. He was barely even aware of the flames in the rigging. He ascended the ladder to the sterncastle as if they were the steps to heaven and looked down on the men sheltering there almost with disdain, as if their fear was contemptible.

"Get down," yelled Carew. "Get your head down!"

Clarenceux looked ahead, toward the approaching ship. He slowly counted the sails. They were intact: it had not yet entered the fight. He watched it close on them, yard by yard, and looked at Carew. "That is the one?" Then, without waiting for confirmation, he walked to the back of the sterncastle and prepared to hurl himself aboard. It was now just forty feet away, rolling on a higher wave. A man on the deck opposite was aiming a musket at him; he did not care. He raised his sword aloft and held the dagger at the ready. The shot cracked the air but only grazed his arm. Thirty feet. Another musketeer came forward, and another. Luke scurried across to kneel beside Clarenceux, laying out Hugh Dean's pistols on the deck. Carew came and stood beside him, staring at the men massed on the deck of the galleon. Luke took aim carefully and fired, striking one musketeer perfectly. The second shot missed. The third shot hit a man in the leg, the fourth hit a smartly dressed gentleman on the sterncastle in the arm. The fifth he did not shoot but held on to as he prepared to leap.

The ship came closer. They were all in a group now, anxious for it to be over, staring at the men on the other ship. Clarenceux stood alongside Carew, Kahlu, Francis Bidder, Harry Gurney, Skinner Simpkins, Swift George, Stars Johnson, Juanita, Alice, John Dunbar and about a dozen others. On the opposite ship there were scores of men, many armed with guns. Shots continued to crack the air, but the shouting had started. There was just twelve feet between the two vessels, then ten, nine, eight. Clarenceux gripped the Moorish blade. Six feet, five—he leaped, eyes white-wide as he slashed at the mariner ready to greet him with a sword.

It was a desperate fight. Clarenceux overpowered and killed the first man he fought, then charged down the deck, slicing with the wide-bladed sword and stabbing with the cutlass in his other hand. One man he slashed across the face; another lost his entire leg to a heavy blow. Another man suffered from the cutlass that Clarenceux jabbed upward, cutting his throat. As he fought his way into the men on the deck he saw Carew climbing the rigging while fighting two men, the pirate swung down and kicked one in the head as he stabbed the other. Luke saved his bullet for one man whom he singled out. He ran toward him, discharged the gun in his face, and then drew his sword. Juanita proved terrifying, the rage in her spilling out in a wide-eyed scream and a savage cutting and thrusting. But the desperation of the *Davy*'s crew could not hold back the tide of men they faced. Clarenceux saw Kahlu cut down, surrounded by four men. The silent hero fell to his knees on the deck and was immediately subjected to a frenzy of stabbings, leaving his body a bloody mess. They decapitated him and threw his head into the sea. Clarenceux himself was caught by surprise by a quicker swordsman and cut across the back of the wrist. Startled, he was knocked down from behind a moment later by the butt of a musket. Very soon only Carew and Skinner were still fighting. They had seized the masthead and were sheltering on the wooden platform, protected by it from the muskets fired from below. They beat off the attacks of those climbing the rigging, sending them tumbling into the sea.

Clarenceux was disarmed, his hands were tied behind his back and he was dragged across the deck to the foremast, where he joined the other survivors, lying facedown. Of all those who had leaped, eight were dead, including Kahlu, Gurney, and Swift George. Juanita had tried to drown herself by jumping into the sea rather than surrender; the men had immediately gone after her in a skiff, dragging her out of the water. They started tearing her clothes off before they had even returned to the ship. Clarenceux was one of nine in a row at the foot of the foremast, alongside Francis and Luke. He reflected on the morality of the victors: in a battle against a foreign enemy, there would have been mutual respect. As this was a matter of policing, the vanquished were condemned criminals—regardless of how well they had fought. The victors believed they had a right to make use of a woman who had sided with those in the wrong.

After a quarter of an hour, the gentleman whom Luke had wounded in the arm came among them, lifting each man's head. When he came to Luke he recognized him; those green eyes were unmistakable. Holding his head up off the deck by his thick black hair, he spat in his face. Then he smashed his head down onto the planking three or four times. He stood up and kicked him hard, causing Luke to cry out. Finally he drew a pistol with his left hand. Luke, with his head to one side, pleaded through a bloodied mouth to show mercy. "I was only doing what anyone would have done, what you too would have done," he shouted, laying with his cheek against the deck.

"I follow my own orders," snarled the gentleman. He slowly wound the wheel-lock key with his teeth.

"The fight is over, let him live," said Clarenceux. "It will only do your soul harm to kill him."

The gentleman kicked Clarenceux in the stomach. "Shut that mouth of yours, if you don't also want a bullet." He stepped on the back of Luke's neck and then aimed his gun at the back of Luke's head, holding the barrel just a few inches above the skull. Clarenceux saw Luke open his eyes; the next moment there was an ear-shattering report and Luke's skull was like a smashed pot, its red contents spilled across the deck. The gentleman wiped his bloodied boot on Luke's body and walked away.

59

It was early evening. Clarenceux was still lying on the deck. They had thrown Luke's corpse over the side about an hour earlier but the smeared bloodstains were still there. He touched his lips with his tongue; they were dry and caked in salt. He was thirsty, hungry, cold, and tired. His killing of the men in the skiff in cold blood now seemed a thing of the distant past. So too did charging across the deck in a paroxysm of rage, killing and maiming. Only Luke's death was still vivid. How had it come to this? Why had he ended up on a stolen ship with godless pirates fighting the forces of her majesty?

A boot kicked him. "Your turn."

Clarenceux looked up. A red-bearded figure was looking down on him. "The boatswain will speak to you. What's your name and parish?"

"I am William Harley from the parish of St. Brides, London. I am Clarenceux King of Arms, an officer in her majesty's—"

"*You're* Harley? Good. To the captain, then."

Clarenceux was surprised. "How does he know I am here?"

"Get up."

Clarenceux struggled to his feet. He looked out to sea; the *Davy* had sunk, shipping its sad cargo of corpses to the seabed. The two other ships remaining above water were close at hand. Men were aloft, fitting new sails.

He was taken across the deck to the sterncastle. Here a door led directly from the upper deck into the captain's cabin. It was paneled and had glazed windows on the port, stern, and starboard sides, allowing in plenty of light. There was a bed beneath one of the windows and a chest beneath the other. A table in the center, fixed to the floor, was set with a basket of bread, a pewter plate of meat, a silver mug, and a wooden wine flask. Beside it stood a large, broad-shouldered gentleman, aged about fifty, with a very long double-forked black beard and black hair. Both beard and hair were streaked with gray, adding to the man's air of distinction. There was a flash of mischief across his dark eyes too, giving a sense that this was a man of daring and charm. He was dressed in an old-fashioned leather jerkin slashed repeatedly to reveal the white shirt beneath, with no ruff but a sword on his plain leather belt. His black cap sported a white feather. Clarenceux's eyes were drawn to the ring: Or, *three lions passant sable*.

"We have met before, haven't we, Mr. Harley?" said Sir Peter Carew in a deep Devonian accent.

"Nineteen years ago," said Clarenceux. But as he said the words, he reflected that he knew the man much better than past acquaintance. Sir Peter was famous. He was a fearsome soldier and a fearless naval commander, and one of the most respected of all English seafarers because of his mixture of courtliness and courage. He had traveled to see the Ottoman Emperor in Constantinople and visited Buda when it was under siege—just so he could see what an oriental army looked like. He was a staunch Protestant who had led the suppression of the Catholic rebels in Devon and Cornwall in 1549. He had served as an MP, largely due to the influence of his patron, Lord Russell. He had been knighted by the old king. But most of all, he had done more than anyone else to clear the seas of pirates—at least, those pirates whom he had not befriended in the course of his duties. He also was perpetually in debt; he owed a small fortune to the Crown.

"It was at Boulogne, was it not?" said Sir Peter.

"Indeed. I was with the duke of Suffolk's men. I am a herald now—Clarenceux King of Arms."

"I realize." Sir Peter's eyes moved over Clarenceux's scorched and scarred figure. "But you have not entirely given up the sword for the pen, I see?"

Clarenceux said nothing.

"Leave us, Gardiner," said Sir Peter. The man by the door bowed and left the cabin.

When the door was latched, Sir Peter walked over to it and pushed the bolt across. He paused and then said, "You owe me an explanation—at the very least." He returned to the table and took the top off the wine flask and poured a draught into the mug. He resealed the flask.

"Is it not straightforward? You attacked the *Davy* because she had been taken by your nephew, Raw Carew…"

Sir Peter held up a hand. "Stop right there. The man who calls himself Ralph Carew may have been the fruit of my late brother's loins, but that was simply recreational. Not procreational. Don't presume that I recognize him as a member of my family." He looked Clarenceux in the eye. "If I see a reflection of my own youth in his exploits, then that is a private source of amusement. Publicly, you understand, he is nothing but a common thief and a pirate."

Clarenceux remembered Sir Peter had come very close to being a renegade in the past. He had been expelled from various schools and had ended up serving at the court of the French king and in the service of the Marquis of Saluzzo, an ideal education for a courtier. But character aside, he had just sustained terrible losses at the hands of his illegitimate nephew. *Why is he not angry? Why is he not seeking explanations?*

Sir Peter took a draught of his wine. "I received a letter from Francis Walsingham two days ago telling me to intercept the *Davy* and to take you prisoner. He instructed me to sink the ship rather than let you get away."

Clarenceux looked around the room, his brain struck with the surprise. *How had Walsingham known?* "I thought you were patrolling against pirates and that I just was unlucky," he replied.

"Think again. Ralph of Calais is a dangerous adversary—he has both imagination and courage. If he had chosen a different path in life, I would be glad to acknowledge him. But I held back in this ship during this morning's encounter for good reason. I was not certain that four ships would be enough to capture you while he was in command of the *Davy*. So I count this a great success. I only lost two vessels and my men either killed or captured the whole misbegotten crew sailing with Ralph—and that will include the rare bird himself, when he comes down from his perch. On top of that, I succeeded in my main mission."

Sir Peter picked up a stool and placed it near the table. Just as he did so, a larger wave tipped the ship slightly further than usual and he had to steady his wine mug. The flask fell off the table. He picked it up and sat down, facing Clarenceux. "I know Walsingham from Parliament. He is a devious man—I knew the letter came from him, even though he sent it in Sir William Cecil's name, because there was no seal. Cecil, as the queen's Secretary, would have applied the queen's seal. So I am intrigued that Walsingham did not explain the meaning or purpose of this mission. Men who are physically weak, as he is, are always wary of how military men see them, so they tend to explain everything at tedious length. But he did not. That makes me curious. It makes me hopeful that you will tell me."

"It is a long story."

"Then sit down and start telling it. It will while away the time until Ralph of Calais considers his position. Be careful you leave nothing out."

Clarenceux sat down. He placed his left hand on the table and explained about the Percy-Boleyn marriage agreement and how Sir William Cecil had entrusted it to his keeping. He spoke of Rebecca Machyn and how she had taken it on the instructions of the Catholic Knights of the Round Table and then betrayed them. He spoke about how Nicholas Denisot had paid for her to go to Southampton in the *Davy*, and how he, Clarenceux, was even now trying to track her down. He mentioned his being tortured in the house of Mrs. Barker, knowing that the indication of his opposition to a Catholic cause would appeal to Sir Peter; and he told him about the scar in his right hand, where Kahlu had cut him three days earlier.

"Show me," demanded Sir Peter. Clarenceux placed his right hand on the table. Sir Peter looked at it and grunted. "What happened to that man, Kahlu?"

"Your men killed him on the deck of this ship."

"You have been avenged then," said Sir Peter.

"I am not looking for vengeance. If I were, I would spend all my time fighting old battles."

"A wise man. What are you looking for?"

"The woman who betrayed me."

"Not so wise after all." Sir Peter scratched his bearded chin. "I still do not see why Walsingham is so desperate to capture you."

"Hatred. Distrust. I don't know—you would have to ask him yourself. But this much I do know: if that document stays in the hands of Catholic leaders, there will be a war. Walsingham believes that my purpose is to ensure it reaches them. In truth, I am trying to reclaim it and stop that war. You know from your own experience how damaging a Catholic conspiracy can be."

Sir Peter did not like to be reminded of the fact. His suppression of the rebellion in 1549 had led to a massacre so that his name was a byword for horror in his native county.

"There are reasons not to trust you," he said. "You escaped from Cecil House—very much to Sir William's embarrassment, I imagine."

"I had no choice."

"And you consorted with pirates."

Clarenceux looked into Sir Peter's eyes. "Again, I had no choice."

"And, finally, you yourself are a Catholic."

Clarenceux hesitated. "In that too I have no choice."

Sir Peter rose to his feet. "You cannot pass all your faults on to God, Mr. Clarenceux. You cannot blame Him for your sins, for your misdeeds, saying you have no choice. You cannot blame those who locked you up for the fact you escaped. You cannot blame the man who orders you to commit a wrong; you can always rebel. That is why Protestantism—to protest—is the only way."

Clarenceux watched as Sir Peter walked to the window, looking out to sea. "You too could protest," he said to the man's back.

"What do you mean?" asked Sir Peter.

"You could rebel. You do not have to take me to Walsingham.

You could set me ashore in Southampton—and tell Walsingham I was still on the *Davy* when she sank. You know what is at stake."

Sir Peter shook his head. "I do not need to disobey orders. I have lost too much even to entertain the idea. You are going to come with me and face Sir William Cecil. If you are as well intentioned and as innocent as you claim, he will let you go."

At that moment Clarenceux heard the loud report of a musket shot. Suddenly there were many shouts of alarm from outside. There was a second musket shot.

Sir Peter reluctantly turned away from Clarenceux and unbolted the door just as there came a loud knocking. "What?"

"One of the pirates has jumped. He climbed to the top of the mast and jumped into the sea."

"Stay here," Sir Peter said to Clarenceux, shutting the cabin door behind him.

Clarenceux clenched his fist in frustration. He could see no way out of this situation. He would be taken back to London. No one would stand up for him now. He felt so tired—too tired even to shed tears. He heard the shouts and stood up to look out of the window on the landward side of the ship. It was a good six miles to the shore. He had no doubt that it was Carew who had jumped; but even so, he had not resurfaced. The sea was rough and there was no sign of anyone swimming. Even if Carew could swim the six miles, doing so against the currents would have been nigh on impossible, especially in heavy seas. He had made a final, desperate bid for freedom—and that desperation would be his end. It was a reflection of the man's spirit. No one could destroy him—only he could destroy himself.

Clarenceux crossed himself and said a short prayer for the pirate, lest his atheistic soul spend eternity in damnation. He forgave him for kidnapping him. He looked at the wound in his hand and forgave him that too. He forgave him for leading him into the disaster he now faced. He forgave him everything.

The seas rolled, green and gray-blue. A seagull swooped low, fighting against the breeze, before turning and flying northward. In the distance, pieces of broken timber from the *Davy* and the other sunken ships bobbed about on the water. No one was bothering to rescue the dead bodies from the sea. They were just floating, to be glimpsed for a moment at the swell of a wave, then to disappear.

He turned from the sea where Carew had plunged and looked east, from the rear of the galleon. There was no debris. Maybe battles would be fought there one day and for a brief hour or two it would be a blood-soaked, timber-littered place of fear and sorrow. When the guns fell quiet, it would gradually clear itself and return to being just another stretch of water, rolling for eternity.

Running his hand across the window he moved around and looked toward the south. Here an even wider stretch of water, unbounded by land, presented itself. He knew the Channel here was sixty miles wide. Apart from a ship on the horizon, there was nothing to see at all but the waves. Sky and sea: a simplicity that reminded him again of the Creation story. And on that sea there was nothing: no birds, no flotsam, nothing. Just that one tiny, distant ship.

As he looked across the great swell of the sea, however, he noticed a head. A wave rose and the head rose and fell with it. He looked harder and saw it again.

Raw Carew was swimming—toward France.

60

Clarenceux was placed in the hold with the other captured men. Skinner had given himself up shortly after Carew had leaped from the masthead. He had been soundly beaten, so that his face was bloody and one eye swollen; and then he had been whipped, so that his back was cut and sore. Eventually he had passed out. After lying on deck for a short while, he had been woken and dragged down into the ship and dropped into the hold, joining the others. All eight of them were hungry and thirsty, having had nothing to eat or drink since the previous day. All were despondent—and certainly no happier for knowing that the captain of the ship was the indomitable Sir Peter Carew.

Clarenceux lay against the side of the ship, feeling it rolling. Everything had gone wrong. It even seemed that Raw Carew had abandoned them to their fate. The man's instinct, Clarenceux decided, was self-preservation. That allowed him only a limited scope for saving his companions. Besides, what could he do now? He had no ship, most of his men were dead, and the few who were not were prisoners aboard a ship captained by Sir Peter. The only stroke of luck that they had had was that Sir Peter had not hanged them immediately. He was inclined to take them to London to be hanged on the dock. He wanted an audience.

The bilge water had long since soaked Clarenceux's feet. But his extreme tiredness meant that every so often he would drowse. When he did, he dreamed of being in a battle and lying on the ground, tied up, waiting for the victorious enemy to put a bullet in his brain. He also dreamed of being at the top of the mast of an extremely tall ship, hundreds of feet above the deck, swaying from side to side in a huge storm, trying to time his jump so that he missed hitting the boat. Lightning was striking around him. Then, at the moment of jumping, he would wake himself with a jolt, leaving his dream-self forever falling into the turbulent sea.

"I wonder where is Raw now," muttered Johnson. "And the others."

"Being eaten by fish," replied Francis. "We are all that's left— except Alice and Juanita."

"You don't think Raw got away?"

"How high is the main mast? He must have fallen seventy feet. He didn't come up again."

"He did," Clarenceux said in a parched voice. "I saw him. He started swimming toward France."

Francis laughed. "France is nearly sixty miles away." Then he realized the truth of his words and stopped.

There was silence.

"He's abandoned us then," said John Dunbar.

"What else could he do?" replied Francis. "He can't rescue us all, not singlehanded."

There was a groan.

"Skinner? Are you awake?"

"He timed it—the jump," said Skinner.

"What was his plan?" asked Johnson.

"Just to jump. A musket ball had gone through…through his leg," said Skinner. He coughed and choked, and vomited. "The shot had smashed the bone and he was in a lot of pain. He reckoned he had to go then, before he grew more tired."

Clarenceux was amazed. "He jumped seventy feet with a broken leg? And swam away?"

"You saw him."

There was a long silence as the men appreciated the courage and determination and the probable futility of the act. After a while Johnson said, "He'll be back. He's probably already planning how to rescue us."

"Clarenceux, have you spoken to the captain?" asked Francis.

"Yes. Why?"

"Is he going to let you go?"

"No."

"Why not? You told him you're not one of us?" said Johnson.

Clarenceux did not want to admit that he himself was the reason the *Davy* had been attacked. "I took part in the fighting too."

"You could tell him about his family history," said Skinner, who was now trying to sit up. "I bet he has…more than seven acres."

"He's penniless. He owes the Crown more than two thousand pounds. Last year he sold Mohuns Ottery, the estate in Devon that his family had owned for two hundred years."

"He should join us then," said Francis.

Clarenceux gave a mock laugh. "There's not much distance between him and piracy. He knows that… That's why he's so wary. We all know it takes a pirate to catch a pirate, so the only way he can stay on the right side of the law is to keep hauling in you lot."

"He must have done something wrong in the past," said Francis.

"He was attainted for treason along with Thomas Wyatt in the last reign. For some reason, though, only Wyatt was executed. Sir Peter was given a reprieve."

A long silence followed. Clarenceux shifted his position, trying to make himself more comfortable. The scratch on his arm stung with the salt encrusted on the wound. His injured hand also hurt. He tried to remember the hours at Mrs. Barker's house. That had been a hell of a different sort, a drugged hell. He shifted again in the stinking darkness. This could not be attributed to a drug. There was no doubting its reality.

"No money, a pirate at heart, and capable of treason. He sounds like a man who would be open to a bribe," said Francis.

"It would need to be a very big bribe," answered Clarenceux. "Two thousand pounds would disappear straight away. I do not have that sort of money."

"Raw does," said Johnson. "He keeps it buried in a secret location on an island."

"That's a lie," replied Bidder. "He's always without money."

"He told me," Johnson insisted. "He buried a lot of treasure from the old days. On an island."

"And you believed him? He's a storyteller but you are an even better dreamer."

"Ireland," muttered Clarenceux aloud.

"Island or Ireland?" asked Francis.

"Ireland—the barony of Idrone. The lands in Meath and Cork too." Clarenceux sat up, trying to recall his heraldic notes on Devon and his conversation earlier in the year with John Hooker about the family of Carew of Mohun's Ottery. Tiredness made images and ideas tumble through his mind—a cascade of knights and horses, blazons, caparisons, breastplates, surcoats, castles, women in ermine-trimmed tunics, parchments, documents…But there was something in there, something Hooker had said about Carew and Idrone.

"Why do you say 'Ireland' particularly?" asked Johnson.

"Some treasures are made not of gold or silver," replied Clarenceux, now remembering clearly. "Some are made of the skin of a dead sheep. Vellum can be more valuable than gold."

He leaned forward to the piles of cold, wet stones that served as the ship's ballast, found a rock that was large enough, and stood up. Then he started hammering on the boards above his head. After about ten minutes someone on the orlop deck heard and shouted through, "What do you want?"

"This is William Harley, Clarenceux King of Arms. Tell Sir Peter Carew I wish to speak to him urgently."

61

Friday, May 19

Sir Peter Carew gestured to the stool and Clarenceux sat. Sir Peter himself continued to stand, the early-morning light through the eastern windows of the cabin silhouetting his robust figure. His poise was like that one might see in a portrait—chest out, proud.

"I am a man of instinct, Mr. Clarenceux, and my instinct tells me that you are no fool, no charlatan, and no friend of the government. Most of the Catholics I have met have not deserved a moment of my time, but you—you seem to be, how should I put it? Sharper. More realistic. Yes, there will be bloodshed. But you cannot expect that I will release you on such speculation. I have orders from Cecil to return you to London."

"Walsingham. You know that letter came from Walsingham."

"But the orders were in Sir William's name. And if Sir William has reasons to want you back in London, then make no mistake—I will do my duty. Your admission that you escaped from his house only confirms the need for that duty to be performed."

Clarenceux remained calm. "So you will stop me in my quest to find this document."

"Don't I have to? Especially as that Calais pirate bastard bane of my existence has escaped—and I will lay a pile of gold on the fact he has not drowned—he has Carew blood in him. And so, if I were to lose you too, I would have nothing to show for sinking the *Davy*. You ask too much."

"A pile of gold, you say?" Clarenceux paused, tapping his fingers on the table, thinking. "You will wager a pile of gold?"

Sir Peter cleared his throat. "It is a metaphorical pile."

"Would you be prepared to bet a real pile?"

"On his not drowning?"

"No. On the *Davy* having got away."

Sir Peter laughed, a deep fruity sound. "I have little doubt that the *Davy* sank. I saw her go down with my own eyes. So did hundreds of others. So did you. Why, if you wish to bet that she is still floating, then I will take your money now."

Clarenceux took a deep breath. "I know that she sank—but Mr. Walsingham doesn't. He need not know that this engagement ever took place. Or that Raw Carew escaped. Remember, whatever you say, Walsingham will suspect you of complicity in his escape. But the important thing from your point of view is that I am not betting with my money; I am betting with yours."

Sir Peter frowned. "Mine? What do you mean?"

"You could sail your fleet out further into the Channel for a few days. Only those aboard your ships know that you found the *Davy* and sank her. Only those aboard this ship know that Raw Carew escaped. If you set me and the remainder of his men ashore quietly in Southampton, no one is going to know that it was your doing— except your own men. And they will not inform Walsingham…"

Sir Peter held up a hand. "Why do you say you are betting with my money? That is what I want to know."

"Have you ever heard of the barony of Idrone, in the west of County Carlow, in Ireland?"

"Perhaps. What of it?"

"It is rightly your inheritance. So too are various estates in Meath and County Cork, bringing a total annual income of more than four thousand pounds. It belonged to your ancestors and, after the death of your brother without a legitimate child, is rightfully yours—and could be yours again. All it takes is for you to prove your claim in a court of law."

Sir Peter looked Clarenceux in the eye. "Go on."

"Your family lost those estates in the reign of Richard the Second. They were taken by force, by the Kavanaghs. Now the English government supports their descendants in enjoyment of that possession, illegally. I know where the documents are that can prove your claim."

Sir Peter shifted uneasily on his stool. He stood up and walked to the window at the rear of the cabin. "And in return for the information about how I might prove my claim to this land and title, you want me to release you all and pretend the Davy is somewhere out at sea, still afloat, and still commanded by that…by my illegitimate nephew."

"Yes. Obviously you will need to find a lawyer. But it will be a straightforward case. You need to see two men, one who has the documents that prove your family's entitlement to that land, and another who can prove your unbroken line of descent from the grantee."

"You are merely offering me what is mine by right."

"No. I am offering you the means to remedy a great wrong—to you and your family."

"Damn you, Clarenceux! I suspected that you would be trouble the moment I received that writ. I should hang you now, you and all your fellow scoundrels, but you first—for consorting with pirates, for attempted bribery, for evading arrest, for sinking one of her majesty's ship, and for being just too clever for anyone's good."

"Then you will be much the poorer."

Sir Peter walked to the other side of the cabin. "I cannot agree with your offer. I cannot. It goes against everything I stand for."

"When I said four thousand a year, I was not exaggerating. It is at least that much. It could be much more."

"Damn you," said Sir Peter, walking across the cabin again. "No, I sank the *Davy*. That is a fact and I will not deny it. People will have seen the ship go down from the shore. And there are prisoners—they will hang. I have done my duty, and my men have paid with their lives. I will send you to Sir William."

"Is that your final decision?"

"God's wounds, yes!" Sir Peter glared at him. "I care for my name—and that is worth more than four thousand a year!"

Clarenceux responded with silence. He let Sir Peter think about what he had just said. Then he rose to his feet, looked at the other man, walked across to the door, and undid the bolt.

"Your freedom. Yours alone," said Sir Peter behind him.

Clarenceux stopped. "And the others?"

"They will hang. I will not lie about the *Davy*. I will have to admit that the pirate captain who claims my family name escaped. But I will show Sir William and Walsingham that I did my duty. I will take the prisoners to London and hang them at London Dock. I need them to show that I did not come away empty-handed."

"The women too," said Clarenceux, turning and looking at Sir Peter. "Your men have foully abused them. They have acted in a most ungodly manner, worse than the pirates."

Sir Peter raised his hands and let them fall, despondently. The proud portrait-like figure was now round shouldered. He rapped his knuckles on the table and looked up. "What is this? I receive orders to capture a man aboard a boat, and to sink it if necessary. I sink the boat, capture the man and the pirate captain, and rid the world of most of his crew. And what happens? The captain escapes, I am asked to deny the ship ever sank, the captured man walks free, and my men are accused of acting in a vile manner. How in God's name am I supposed to accept this? And who are you to preach at me in this way? Are you telling me you did not take up arms? Do you expect me to believe you did not fight and kill my men?"

The words hit home. The memory of the skiff supplanted all other thoughts in Clarenceux's mind.

Thou shalt not kill.

He was guilty. Sir Peter was right, and nothing could remove that stain from his soul. No absolution would be enough. He tried to think of other things. He thought of Luke being shot in the head and how he himself had killed Nick Laver. He thought of Charity's burnt torso. He thought of Skinner lying in the hold, and Stars Johnson, Francis Bidder, John Dunbar, and the others. All of them were waiting in the darkness, expecting Raw Carew to rescue them, not knowing that they were going to be taken to London and hanged. Clarenceux had seen the bodies of pirates on the dockside gallows himself. They left them there to rot—until their decomposing necks gave way. Or they fastened them just below the high-water mark, so that the water washed over them and made them stink more. Showing them putrefying was a way of showing others the stench of their sins.

"The women too," Clarenceux repeated. "They deserve better. They only followed their men."

"I am not as soft as you. I have made my inquiries. I hear that the

Spanish whore who jumped in the sea would as soon cut your throat as kiss you. And the other woman, Alice—she is not a follower of men as women should be. Made of iron, she is. But you may have your whores. Now, you need to fulfill your side of the bargain. And I want it all in writing."

Clarenceux nodded. "First, you take the three of us to Southampton. When we are ashore, I will give you letters of introduction to the men you need to see, with details of what you need to prove your case."

"What if these men refuse to help me?"

"They will help you, Sir Peter. I know that for certain. One of the men in question is an antiquary and a friend from Devon. He knows you; I have no doubt he will assist."

"And the other?"

"The other man is me."

62

It was late evening when Clarenceux, Juanita, and Alice walked along the quay at Southampton. Four men had rowed them and Sir Peter Carew into the harbor from where his ship had moored in Southampton Water, and all of them had gone to the harbormaster's house for Clarenceux to draw up the letter of introduction and instructions for John Hooker, antiquary and Recorder of Exeter. In addition, he supplied the indenture by which he asserted that Sir Peter Carew was a direct descendant of Sir William Carew and his wife Avice, daughter and sole heiress of the lord of Idrone, who had inherited the estate in the time of King John, as well as a signed letter in which Clarenceux declared his wholehearted faith in the veracity of the descent and listed the various pedigrees he had consulted to confirm the same.

When all was done and agreed, Sir Peter shook Clarenceux's hand and promised to come to London for the pedigrees when the time arose; and to disembowel the herald personally if it emerged that he had lied in so delicate a matter or revealed any part of these dealings to another person. With this threat ringing in his ears, Clarenceux watched the four oarsmen take Sir Peter back toward his ship.

No one spoke as the three of them walked toward the Two Swans.

Juanita and Alice did not need to be told that a deal had been agreed between Clarenceux and Sir Peter Carew. As far as they could see, Clarenceux had not saved them so much as betrayed the others. It went without saying that he had no obligation toward any of the pirates, but equally it went without saying that a man who had fought alongside them should not have abandoned them to the justice of the gallows. Clarenceux, having agreed not to tell a soul about the deal made with Sir Peter, could say nothing on the matter.

He followed the women into the front hall of the Two Swans. There were about twenty men inside, sitting at tables drinking and talking. His first impression was that it was a respectable wine tavern, even though he knew that it was much more than that. Alice told him to wait by the door while she made inquiries. Juanita left him with a brief word of farewell shortly after. Clarenceux sat on a bench and closed his eyes, listening to the sounds of all the conversations, inhaling the welcome and familiar odors of a good tavern: the herbs scattered in the rushes, the smell of dogs, the stale scent of spilled wine, and the savory lingering aroma of roasted pork. For a moment he almost relaxed, letting go of a tension that had twisted his mind and bound him physically since that terrible moment on the morning of Rogation Sunday, when he had found that the marriage agreement had been stolen. Almost—but not quite. He was in a strange place surrounded by people he did not know and without any money. The authorities had issued instructions for his arrest or death—and he had not yet found the document or Rebecca Machyn.

Alice returned, her large figure coming toward him in a slow gait as if there was no reason in the world to hurry. She nudged him along the bench, so she could sit down beside him. "Amy is not here. Pieter, the landlord, says he will provide us with a meal. Where's Juanita?"

"I do not know. She just said good-bye and walked off."

"Ungrateful cow. Probably hightailed her way to sleep with the nearest merchant heading back to Castile."

"Can you blame her?"

"We're the lucky ones. Think of the men still in the hold of that ship."

"There was nothing I could do. I tried."

"It is not right for us to be sitting here and them being taken off to their deaths. I never really liked Skinner, and Stars was a bit delicate, but Francis was a good man. The best of them are dead."

She fell quiet. Then she said under her breath, "Raw is upstairs."

"Here? He made it back?" Clarenceux was astonished. "He made it back here faster than we did."

"I don't suppose he was keen to stay too long in the water."

A young woman with a scar on her face walked between the tables toward them. "Alice," she said.

Alice looked up. "Ursula," she breathed, struggling to her feet. She embraced the woman and held her a long time. Clarenceux reflected that he had seen almost no sign of emotion from Alice since he had met her, and only now was it seeping through, like a flood just beginning to break through the cracks in a dam.

"So many," said the bond woman, tears on her cheek.

Alice said nothing. She simply held on to Ursula. Eventually they broke away. Alice turned to Clarenceux who had remained seated. "Come on," she said. "Let us go and see the Robin Hood of the High Seas."

Clarenceux followed Ursula and Alice up to the attic chamber. There was a large bed and very little else. A baby boy, aged about twelve months old and dressed only in a shirt, was sitting in the corner of the room, playing with some wooden blocks. Raw Carew was lying on the bed, sweating, with his legs naked, attended by a red-haired young woman with a pair of tongs. There was blood all over his right thigh.

"It's not coming," she said, concentrating on the gash and dabbing at the fresh blood.

Carew shook his head. "It hurts—I can't believe it." He started laughing. "It's funny, it hurts so much." He turned to Alice and held out a hand toward her. "I'm glad to see you," he said, squeezing her hand tightly.

Clarenceux looked at the mess of Carew's leg. The musket ball had not broken the thigh bone—Skinner had been wrong on that point.

"How did you escape?" Carew asked, looking at Alice, still holding her hand.

"He hasn't actually said so, but I think Mr. Clarenceux here did me and Juanita a good turn," she replied.

"Just you and Juanita?" Carew looked at Clarenceux. "Not the others?"

"There was nothing I could do," Clarenceux said quietly. "Your uncle intends to take them to London."

"And hang them there, on the pirates' dock at Wapping, no doubt." Carew suddenly winced and then cried out, panting through gritted teeth. He started whooping and then laughing again. "They call me the bastard but he deserves the title far more." He gasped at the pain from the operation. "You should have saved them too."

"Hold on; this is going to hurt," said the woman, gritting her teeth as she sponged the blood away and delved deeper with the tongs.

"It damn well hurts already!" shouted Carew, laughing more with his eyes closed, pulling himself up by his stomach muscles. He bent his forefinger and bit it to try to control the pain. "Damn Peter

Carew! Damn the lot of them." Another howl of laughter escaped his finger biting.

Amy pulled the tongs out of the wound, clutching the musket ball. It was large—three quarters of an inch in diameter. "There's your friend."

"Friend?" exclaimed Carew, lying back, breathless. "I think not."

Clarenceux felt he was not wanted. He was disappointed to see Carew in this position, making jokes even though he had so recently lost so many men. Saying that *he*, Clarenceux, should have rescued the other prisoners. He turned and went downstairs, found the landlord, and asked for some food. Provided with a bowl of ham and pea broth and a large hunk of dark bread, he took himself off to an empty bench and sat there eating in silence.

After a while his indignation began to subside and he began to take more of an interest in the tavern. This was where Rebecca had been seen; perhaps she was still in the vicinity? He looked among the men in their shirts, jerkins, and doublets; they all looked like mariners or ship owners. She could have sailed on from here to anywhere in the world. Perhaps that was why Denisot had sent her here, so she could be taken on to France.

Just then, Alice appeared. "He wants to talk to you," she said.

"What sort of mood is he in?"

She gave a little laugh. "He'll claim he walked here on water, if he thinks that will impress you. But we love him nonetheless."

"He shows so little…regret."

Alice shrugged. "He cannot afford to be regretful. Not when he's seen so much and lost so much. You have to regard people as liable to leave you—whether through betrayal or through death. He is not as thoughtless as you think."

Clarenceux stood. "I'll go up and see him."

"Where did you disappear to?" Carew asked as Clarenceux entered. Amy had finished bandaging his thigh and was leaving the room with a bucket of bloody water.

"I went to have some food. And to think about those still aboard that boat."

Amy stepped past Clarenceux and closed the door behind her. The two men were alone.

"Who is still aboard?"

"Stars Johnson. Francis Bidder. Skinner. A few others."

Carew closed his eyes. "Harry? Luke? Swift?"

"Dead. Kahlu too."

"Kahlu will show up yet. There's no one who can get the better of him."

Clarenceux shook his head solemnly. "I saw him cut down, with my own eyes. I saw him killed."

"So have many men, Mr. Clarenceux."

Clarenceux walked across the room to the window. He looked out, bending his head to avoid the angle of the roof. The quay was as busy as ever.

Carew shifted on the bed. "Come, are you not glad to be alive? We cheated them. We cheated death. Does that not give you a thrill?"

Clarenceux turned. "A thrill? We did not cheat anyone, least of all Death. Death picked off whom he wanted, laughing all the way. We offered to send Death men by the whole boatload—and Death gladly accepted. You are a godless man and I despise that in you. Whatever has taken the place of God in your heart is cold and evil. Every single one of those corpses now rotting in the sea has more good in it, even now, than you!"

Carew raised himself onto one elbow. "Every man who fought for us knew he was risking death. The women too. None were pressed men aboard my ship. Not one."

Clarenceux looked Carew in the eye. "There you lie."

"Who?"

"Me."

Carew raised a finger, pointing at Clarenceux. "We had an agreement. I would bring you here to Southampton and help you find that damned woman and you would tell me where Denisot is. I have fulfilled my part of the bargain. You have not."

"You did not bring me to Southampton. Your natural father's brother did—and not out of kindness, I might add. He had orders to take me to London—and to sink the *Davy* rather than let me go."

Carew took a moment to comprehend what Clarenceux had just said. He swung his legs around and sat on the bed, biting his lip with the pain. "You mean, Sir Peter Carew sank the *Davy* because of you? Not because of me?"

"I am sorry if it injures your pride but yes, that is the fact."

"All those men died just because you wanted to find that woman?"

"Oh, for pity's sake."

Carew suddenly became solemn. "No, no, Mr. Clarenceux. You misunderstand me. You may think me godless—and I am, thankfully—but we are allies, as you once said. Your enemy is my enemy. Whoever wanted to arrest you killed my men."

"We came here to find Rebecca Machyn. Now we are here, will you still help me? Avenge those deaths?"

Carew stood. Clarenceux heard him and turned to watch him. Blood started to run through the dressing and down his leg.

"Amy!" Carew shouted. "*Amy!*" She came quickly, almost in a panic. She looked at his wound, but Carew was not calling her because of the blood. "That woman who came on the *Davy*—Swift George told me that she and the man with her got into a small boat that day with John Prouze. Where did Prouze take her?"

She was astonished to see him on his feet. "Have a mercy, Raw, what are you standing up for?"

"Just tell me. Where did he take her?"

"I don't know. The fort, I suppose."

"Which fort?"

"Calshot. Prouze serves Captain Parkinson at Calshot."

Clarenceux was curious. "What did he say to you?"

Amy gently pushed Carew back onto the bed and grabbed a towel to wipe the blood away. "He said the Catholic Treasure was going to arrive that day. But it was late. That is why he stayed with me that night."

"This man, Prouze, knew in advance?" asked Clarenceux. "Not *after* she arrived? And he used the words 'Catholic Treasure'?"

"Does that make a difference?" asked Carew.

Clarenceux turned to him. "Of course it makes a difference. The Catholic Treasure is the document that was stolen from me. If he was expecting her to bring it, then he had been forewarned by someone else."

"The treasure is your document?" asked Carew, forlorn. "Hell's breath, I thought it would be gold."

Clarenceux started pacing across the room. "If Nicholas Denisot not only paid for her to come to Southampton, he probably arranged for her to be received here too. It was either him or someone who was privy to the same information as him. Either way, Denisot hijacked the Knights' plot. 'Percy Roy' he called himself—just as they did in their letter. He was pretending to be them."

"There was a man with her when she came too," said Amy, wiping the blood off the floor. "A tough-looking man."

"Robert Lowe," said Clarenceux. "Her brother. He was mentioned in the secret message that Cecil showed me. No doubt it was through him that Denisot learned about the Knights' plot. He and Denisot spirited Rebecca Machyn away from London and brought her here, far from Scotland and the reach of the Knights." He looked at Carew and then at Amy. "But why would they have sent a message to John Prouze?"

Amy stopped wiping. "They didn't. It was sent to Captain Parkinson."

"Parkinson is corrupt," added Carew, "but he is loyal; he would not lift a finger against the queen. He knows he only controls this port because he is trusted in Westminster—but he would hide anyone in that fort at the end of the spit, if you paid him well enough. If Denisot could afford to pay two hundred pounds for the woman and her brother to come here, then it sounds to me as if money was freely available."

Clarenceux scratched his beard. "But why? Why bring her here?"

Carew picked up a pair of breeches from the floor and started to put them on. "Because from here the document could be taken anywhere in the world."

"Then how do we set about finding it?"

"We go to Calshot Fort," replied Carew, struggling to get his right leg into his breeches. He grimaced as he tried to bend it.

"Raw, don't be stupid," gasped Amy as the dressing partly came away and more blood flowed down his leg.

"Shut up, woman—kind though you are," replied Carew. "It's just a deep cut. It's not going to slow me down, still less is it going to stop me getting dressed. Or taking this gentleman to see Captain Parkinson."

63

Clarenceux lay under a blanket on the rushes on the floor of the hall. He slept for short periods, drowsing more than sleeping, as he had been accustomed to since finding himself on board a ship. When he heard footsteps coming down the stairs in the darkness, not having a knife, he felt vulnerable. Tensing his muscles, he listened to the movements as whoever it was felt their way around.

"Mr. Clarenceux?" whispered a woman's voice.

"Who is it?"

"Ursula." He heard her moving in his direction. She felt where he lay and knelt down beside him.

"Mr. Carew has asked me to offer you a bed for the night," she whispered. "He wishes to assure you it is more comfortable than the hall floor."

"A bed?" Clarenceux sensed her crouching down close to him. "Is that all?"

"A bed and anything else you might want. He has a great deal of respect for you."

"How much is he paying you?"

"Sir, he is good to us. The last time he was here he gave me and my sister twenty pounds each, so we could help her little boy get well and look after each other. That was after he had left—he did not ask for anything in exchange. I am not expecting you to do anything you do not wish to do, and nor is he. I am simply offering some small kindness, which is a mark of his respect for you and mine for him."

Clarenceux raised himself onto one elbow. He clasped her shoulder. "You humble me. I was too quick to judge. Carew confuses me—callous one minute, kind the next. Confrontational then respectful. He seems to act selfishly while quietly being generous. Most men are the opposite: they pretend to be more generous than they really are. He shows me my faults. I am too proud."

She touched his face, running her finger over his cheek and down over his beard. "Come up to my bed. There you can be as proud as you want. Or as humble as you want. It is up to you. I will not think the worse of you either way."

64

Saturday, May 20

Next morning Clarenceux was able to bathe at the Two Swans and eat another meal. Once Pieter and Marie Gervys realized that their guest was not only a friend of Raw Carew but a gentleman and the bearer of a royal commission, they went out of their way to help him. They even provided him with a clean set of clothes, which, if they were not of the finest quality, nevertheless gave the impression that he was far from being a pauper. Gervys lent him his own cloak. Ursula trimmed his hair and beard. As she reminded him, there was no point going to see Captain Parkinson and expecting him to part with valuable information if he looked like a shipwrecked sailor. She kissed him and pressed into his hand a small dagger. "For luck," she said. "In case it turns out to be bad."

Amy had arranged for them to borrow a sloop. Carew shook off her assistance, determined to walk to the quay as normally as possible, even though the wound caused him to flinch. He admired the sloop: the fore-and-aft rigged sails were new and the rudder freshly greased, and without waiting to be helped he climbed down into the boat. Clarenceux followed.

It was a bright but blustery morning, with clouds scudding across the blue sky. Carew took charge of the sailing, forbidding Clarenceux to touch a single rope. The herald was happy to watch the man in his most natural state: judging the wind and the currents, looking out for the patterns in the water. It was like watching a man have a silent conversation with the elements. At one point he wondered whether Carew in old age would be like those who find it easier to move on water than on land. He had heard of such instances: kings and dukes who wanted only to travel by water in their advanced years, even sedan chairs being too much for them. But then he put the thought out of his mind. Raw Carew was not a man destined to grow old.

"How did you escape from Sir Peter Carew's ship?" Clarenceux asked, when they were about a mile from Southampton.

Carew loosened the sheet and let the twisted hemp run through his fingers, still concentrating on the wind. "I jumped when the mast was leaning over at its greatest angle. Everyone would have expected me to swim to shore. So I swam underwater and hid beneath the sterncastle. No one could see me there—not from the gunwales, not even from the top of the sterncastle itself, because that projects out beyond the hull. When I had got my breath back, I swam as far as I could underwater, surfaced, and swam again. Not many people could hit a man's head in a heaving sea like that, so when I was five hundred yards out I started to swim around the ship in a wide arc and came ashore near where we are heading to—Calshot."

Clarenceux was impressed. "But that must have been more than six miles—did you not worry about your leg?"

Carew continued to look at the horizon. "I reckoned that if I was going to bleed to death, no one would ever have found me. I would have passed into legend, into stories. Otherwise—well, I did not have anything else to do. So I just swam."

Clarenceux felt humbled again. "It was God's will—you know that. It might not have been a miracle, but it was the will of God that you survived."

Carew shook his head. "You're aboard my ship, Mr. Clarenceux. No religion. Otherwise you'll be the one doing the swimming."

"One day I will talk to you about God. One day when we are not on a ship."

"You'll be wasting your time. All that stuff about saints, holy bones and holy water, spirits and souls—you know it's all just ghost droppings."

"What?"

"Ghost droppings. The excrement of phantasms."

Clarenceux was sickened by the blasphemy. He looked down the water toward the keep of Calshot Fort, four miles further on.

"Look," Carew told him. "I have sailed further than most people, further than God too it would appear, because I have been to places in Africa where the people have not heard of God. They have their own gods. And you will tell me that their gods are not real—and they would say the same about yours. In the end, all we can do is make up our own minds. I see no sign of God, I hear no word of God, I feel no hand of God—not your god nor any others. I do not smell the odor of divine sanctity, and if I did I would not trust it."

"Just because you do not see something does not mean it isn't there."

Carew untied a sheet and hauled it in tighter. "And what, exactly, is that supposed to mean?"

Clarenceux looked across the water, wondering whether some divine vision would appear to help him make this God-denying man understand. None appeared. "The other morning I was looking out from my window and could not see my wife but I knew she was there, over the hills to the south. God is like that. Or like a night that the waking man does not see. God brings blessings and we do not see them but that does not mean they do not happen. It is like the sightedness of a blind man—"

"Let us ask God to steer this boat. We will end up where the current takes us, not at Calshot."

"The sightedness of a blind man," repeated Clarenceux. "Imagine you are in a room in a house, looking at something, like a plate or a book. As the light fades in the evening you see less and less—until you can see nothing at all. Then what do you see?"

Carew did not even look at him.

"What do you see?" insisted Clarenceux. "You see nothing. It is not that there is nothing there. Our inability to see God is like that darkness." Carew stood up, adjusting the sheet he had just fastened. "You are not listening to me," Clarenceux sighed.

Carew tied a knot. "Ghost droppings. You've got more important things to be worrying about."

"What could possibly be more important than a man's salvation?"

"His survival."

Clarenceux looked away.

The wind caught the sail at the wrong angle and it started flapping. Carew made a small adjustment to calm it. "I don't think you've properly thought this through," he said. "You are going to go in there empty-handed. You have nothing to offer Parkinson, except your head."

"You're not accompanying me?"

"No. I pick my fights carefully."

Clarenceux felt the breeze chill on his face. "It is something I have to do. Regardless of the danger."

"I know that. But if the Catholic plotters did send word of Widow Machyn's arrival to Calshot then it stands to reason: Captain Parkinson is no friend of yours. He may have stolen the document from her on arrival, killed her, and then taken her body out to sea. He is the sort of man who would do that. Calshot is a good place to get rid of corpses."

Clarenceux looked up at the clouds, which were darker now. There was a colder edge in the air, as if it might start to rain at any moment.

"My friend," Carew said after a few minutes, "we might not agree on religion. Nor on the pleasures of loving. But you have to agree with me on this: you need an offer. And you need some form of escape."

"You sound like my mother."

"Your mother wouldn't deliver you to your executioner."

Half a mile short of Calshot, Carew steered the sloop toward the western side of Southampton Water, aiming for a secluded bit of beach. There was an inlet here, and a couple of sturdy posts used by shipbuilders. The woodland stretched along to the spit of shingle that led out to the fort. "Best to alight here," he said.

"Why not nearer?" asked Clarenceux, gesturing to the fort. There were two boats tied to a wooden jetty there, and another two pulled up on the shingle bank nearby.

"Look on the roof: there's someone on guard. Parkinson would recognize me." Carew fastened a sheet around one of the shipbuilders' posts. He held the sloop steady and gestured for Clarenceux to disembark. "I'll be watching out. Come to this point and wave when you have spoken to Parkinson. But remember, you are on your own. I don't have the men to rescue you if you fail to reappear."

Clarenceux stepped over the side of the boat and down into the shallow water. He nodded at Carew but said nothing as he reached the dry shingle above the seaweed.

"Don't trust him," called Carew as he pushed against the post, sending the sloop back into the water. "Don't believe his promises."

Clarenceux began to make his way along the stones toward the outcrop fortress at the mouth of the estuary.

65

Calshot Fort was a modern building. It had been designed to house guns to guard the approach to Southampton Water during an invasion scare about twenty-five years earlier. There had been several such forts along the south coast, finely built of stone. Each one was set low, making it difficult to attack with cannon. This one had a circular central tower of three stories on an octagonal plinth and a circular perimeter wall with embrasures for guns. It had been built on the end of the spit that projected out into Southampton Water, in order to look out in all directions and to fire across the maximum area of open sea, guarding the long approach to the port and town. Being relatively small, it did not look formidable so much as bleak. But that bleakness was striking even from a distance. On the desolate shingle, with the waves crashing below its walls and the wind howling over its forty-foot battlements, it was like an island, the last outpost of Christendom.

The spit on which the fort was built was about half a mile long and narrow, no more than thirty yards wide. Clarenceux paused on the edge of the wood. From this point on he would be exposed, with no shelter at all. Apart from two cottages, situated about eighty yards from the fort, the spit was home to nothing but a few tussocks of grass. The low wooden jetty he had seen from the estuary was about twenty yards from the cottages. He looked up at the dark gray clouds; it felt as if it should have started raining already. The waves pounded on the shore to his right. Beyond them, across the other side of a wide channel, he could see the hills of the Isle of Wight. On his left there was the long expanse of Southampton Water, leading up to the town in the distance. The waves here lapped gently at the shingle. Between these two sections of water, the spit stretched away to the fort.

Clarenceux started to walk. A track had been made across the shingle where earth had been packed down. He noted a man on the battlements at the top of the central tower, a black figure against the sky. On one side of the tower he could see the muzzle of a cannon protruding, looking out to sea. On the opposite side, in the outer wall, was a gatehouse, a small two-story structure built of the same light-gray stone. Two long oak beams protruded from it at first-floor level; these were the supports for the drawbridge.

Clarenceux felt the spatter of a large wave and drew Gervys's cloak close around him. The drawbridge was down, as to be expected in peacetime, but the gate itself was shut. The cottages near the fort were small and old. Seashore plants had started to grow in the thatch on the nearside cottage, which looked abandoned. There were two linen shirts or smocks hanging on a line near the other. The shutters downstairs were closed.

He approached the fort, bent down, and picked up a rock from the path. Then he walked across the drawbridge, the hard stone of the gatehouse looming above him. Without hesitation he knocked hard on the studded oak gate. A voice came ten seconds later. "Who calls?"

"William Harley, Clarenceux King of Arms. To see Captain Parkinson."

Clarenceux waited. He looked to his left, back up the estuary. Carew's boat was no longer to be seen—it had become one of the dozen or so indistinguishable vessels in Southampton Water. Minutes passed. Eventually he heard footsteps, and the snap of two bolts. The gate opened; a man of about thirty appeared. He was clean shaven and had a fleshy face, blue eyes, and light brown hair. His voice was quite soft but his words were clipped, and his tone not at all friendly. "This way."

Clarenceux stepped forward beneath the teeth of the portcullis. "Are you John Prouze?"

"My name is Christopher Serres. Prouze is upstairs. I thought you wanted to see Parkinson?"

"The person I most want to find is Rebecca Machyn."

"Then you need to speak to Captain Parkinson." Still not making eye contact, the man gestured with his right arm for Clarenceux to stand aside while he shut the gate. He locked it and drew across the drawbar, sealing them off from the outside world. Without another word he led the way out through the gatehouse and across the narrow yard, opening a small door in the central tower. Clarenceux followed him inside.

The wind whistled through the windows and apertures of the building, the notes rising and falling. By the light of a small window he could see Serres ascending the steps. He followed him, his left hand on the stone. He could hear men's voices from upstairs; two of them laughed. There was a doorway on his right, apparently leading down. *That will be the magazine*, he thought as he went past. The steps turned again and opened into a large guard room on the first floor. It was spacious but not very light. All but three of the low windows were shuttered, there being no glass. Several mattresses and blankets lay on the floor. A pewter flagon lay on its side just inside the doorway. Three men were playing cards at a table by a fireplace on the right-hand side of the room. Their conversation ceased as they heard footsteps. When Clarenceux glanced in, two looked back at him silently. Another deliberately did not turn but instead tended to the fire. None of them spoke.

"Up," commanded Serres.

Clarenceux continued to climb the stone steps. On the second floor the doorway opened to reveal several rooms partitioned off behind a screen. He could see a fire glowing in a hearth in a wall on the far side. Directly opposite was a cannon aiming out to sea, the shutters of its embrasure open. A second gun was in an aperture to the right, beside a partitioned area. There was an earthenware jug on the table and three mazers.

"Keep going."

Clarenceux turned and went up the final flight of stone steps. He could see daylight at the top. It seemed bright after the semidarkness of the first- and second-floor rooms, where most of the shutters had been closed. He blinked as he walked out on to the windswept roof.

"He's here!" shouted Serres.

Clarenceux looked across the roof. There were five cannon, one facing toward Southampton Water, one to the mouth of the estuary, and the other three pointing out to sea. A tall man dressed in black stood by one of the sea-facing guns. He did not turn around. Serres went back to the door to the staircase and stood guard.

Clarenceux walked part of the way across the roof, his hair pulled by the wind. "Captain Parkinson?" he called. Still the figure did not turn.

Clarenceux had no doubt that the captain had heard him. He looked at the back of his head and studied the brown curls, the thick neck. The man exuded power.

"What finally brought you here?" Captain Parkinson spoke quietly. The wind coming from the southeast carried every syllable.

Clarenceux had been expecting an ordinary soldier stuck in a boring routine, with all the frustrations and opportunities for personal advancement that a remote command offered. Someone corrupt enough to accept the Catholics' silver. But this man who still had his back to him was no ordinary soldier. He was very clearly his own man. There was a reason that he had been singled out as the guardian of Rebecca Machyn. Far from being alienated by this position, captain of a windswept fort, Parkinson seemed at home, staring out to sea—as if the waves too were part of his command.

Clarenceux understood now why Carew was not here. He was afraid of Captain Parkinson.

And then the captain turned around.

Clarenceux felt the horror creep over him as if it was a chill air touching his skin. There was authority in that brow, a handsome structure to the face marked by the sneer of cold command. But the skin was scarred—three quarters of his face was covered with the marks where smallpox pustules had scabbed and discolored the skin. In that instant, Clarenceux saw the tragedy and the monstrosity of Parkinson's life. With scars like that, men would see that he had been blighted by God, struck with a disease that killed thousands. But Parkinson had survived—he had triumphed even over the deadly ailment.

"I asked you a question," Parkinson repeated. "What brought you here?"

Clarenceux was totally disarmed. He could not think; he was incapable of being evasive. All he could say was the one thing he wanted to know. "Rebecca Machyn," he said. "You have heard of her, of the

Catholic Treasure. Your man John Prouze escorted her from the boat in which she arrived a few days ago. We need to know where he took her and her brother, Robert Lowe. The other man we need to track down is the one who paid for and arranged their passage—Nicholas Denisot, a traitor to her majesty and the State."

"You say 'we.' That is you and who else?"

Clarenceux knew he could not lie. He could not say "Cecil." He saw matters too clearly to be anything other than honest. Cecil had shown him the letter with the words "Catholic Treasure." Cecil had been the one who had known that the document was in Clarenceux's keeping. Cecil had known about Rebecca. Cecil's name had been on the instructions to sink Carew's ship. All the royal dispatches to Captain Parkinson would have passed by Sir William Cecil.

"You and who else?" Parkinson repeated.

Clarenceux swallowed. "Until coming here I did believe, in all good faith, that I was acting on behalf of Sir William Cecil."

Parkinson walked slowly toward Clarenceux. His movements were elegant, cat-like; his attention intense. "Now what do you believe?"

Clarenceux looked out to the sea as if something might come to his aid. "In God Almighty," he whispered.

"You have blundered, herald. Like the dumb animal that stands patiently in line while the beasts ahead of it are slaughtered. You insult me with your presence. You insult Sir William too. Did you think you could fob me off with some idle conversation about coats of arms and deeds of valorous men? He wrote to tell me that you might try. He told me that you were clever, that I was to be wary of you. What manner of traitor walks up to a loyal castellan and asks for—"

"I am no traitor," interrupted Clarenceux, recovering some of his self-confidence. "I am an officer of her majesty, Queen Elizabeth. I am Clarenceux King of Arms."

"I have nothing to say to you. You are under arrest, in the name of her majesty. You will not leave this building. I will write to Sir William inquiring as to your fate."

Clarenceux turned suddenly, wondering if he had time to flee, but Serres was standing immediately behind him. Serres searched him from the ground up—he soon found the dagger that Ursula had given him, strapped beneath Clarenceux's shirt. When he had finished, he nodded to Captain Parkinson.

"Tell me what happened to her," asked Clarenceux. "Is she alive or dead?"

"Go downstairs."

Serres turned and walked to the door, holding Clarenceux's knife and dagger. He held it open, waiting. Clarenceux heard Parkinson following. He started to move. As he neared the edge, he looked over the parapet toward the gatehouse; it was a leap of eleven or twelve feet. The parapet of the gatehouse was nearly ten feet lower than the tower, so it might be possible. But he quailed at such a risk. If he missed, there was a thirty-foot drop. Onto the flagstones.

"Move," ordered Parkinson.

Clarenceux realized the captain had guessed his thoughts. He went down the stairs to the second floor. The guard showed him in, directing him to the table. Captain Parkinson followed, picking up the mazers and jug and setting them on the floor. "Sit down." Clarenceux sat on the bench and placed his hands on the table. "Are you going to stab me in the hand?"

Parkinson glanced at Clarenceux's wound. "That depends." He gestured for Serres to close the door. "Sir William Cecil wanted that woman to disappear completely. He did not want anyone to find her, least of all you. I want to know what brought you here. Who told you?"

Clarenceux looked down. He was being forced to betray someone. No, he was being *asked* to; he did not need to say a word. If he spoke the truth, he would incriminate Carew and endanger the women at the Two Swans. If he did not speak, he would no doubt suffer himself.

Parkinson walked behind him, his footsteps sounding on the stone. "Tell me. I am not known for my patience." The wind was howling a low note through the window where the cannon pointed out to sea. The fire in the cubicle behind him crackled.

"Damn you!" shouted Parkinson, slamming his palms simultaneously on the table. "Speak—or I will begin by slicing off your ears."

Clarenceux closed his eyes and remembered the attic in Mrs. Barker's house. He remembered the moth. He remembered the image of the moth curled and dead when Kahlu struck his hand with the knife.

"This is your last chance."

"Carew," said Clarenceux, looking up at Parkinson. "Raw Carew." He held up his hand, showing the palm to Parkinson. "You can believe this, since you did the same to him. Rebecca Machyn gave my name to the captain of the boat she traveled on. The captain gave it to Carew. Carew came looking for me in London."

"Are you telling me you are here because of him? What did he want with you?"

Clarenceux breathed deeply. "He thought that I could lead him to Nicholas Denisot. He offered to take me to Rebecca Machyn if I would lead him to Denisot."

"And did you?"

Clarenceux looked down at the table, trying to keep calm. He had discovered the limits of Parkinson's knowledge. "No."

"Why not?"

"Because the agreement was that he should lead me to Widow Machyn first. Only when I had seen her and discovered why she had betrayed me—only then was I going to lead him to Denisot."

Parkinson bent down and lifted the jug, swirling around the liquid. He raised it to his lips and drank, looking at Clarenceux. "Do you want some? It's not good," he said, offering the jug.

Clarenceux hesitated, then decided it was a sign of peace. He took it, drank a mouthful of the old wine, and handed it back.

"Where is Denisot now?" Parkinson demanded.

Clarenceux was about to answer that he did not know. But at that instant he realized that that was not true. *If Denisot paid for Rebecca to be taken to Southampton, and if Cecil had sent the instructions ahead to Captain Parkinson, then Denisot was taking orders from Cecil.*

"In London," he said. "He works for Sir William."

Immediately he said the name, Clarenceux regretted it. He watched Parkinson take another draught of wine, set the flagon back on the floor, and walk toward the sea-facing cannon.

"You were going to barter information concerning one of Sir William's men in order to find Widow Machyn?"

"What makes you think I was going to tell Carew?"

Parkinson turned and studied him. "You aren't the double-crossing type. Also, Carew would cut you to ribbons rather than let you make a fool of him. Were you with him in the skirmish with Sir Peter Carew?"

Clarenceux said nothing.

"And Sir Peter let you go?"

"He interrogated me and found that I was on board Carew's ship unwillingly."

Parkinson bent down and picked up the wine jug. He took a step nearer Clarenceux, who held up a hand as if to say he was not in need of more wine. But then Clarenceux saw the momentum of his arm as Parkinson swung the earthenware jug as hard as he could against his head. It smashed against his temple, sending him sprawling on the floor, reeling, spattered in wine. "Don't you lie! Don't you dare lie!" shouted Parkinson. "You told me you had made a deal with Carew—so don't tell me that you were on board that ship unwillingly. And if you misled Sir Peter in that way to save your skin, you deserve worse than whatever fate Sir William has in mind for you."

Clarenceux tried to get up. He was dizzy, unable even to support his weight on his arms. He fell back to the stone, gasping. The smell of the wine and the dizziness together made his stomach lurch and heave. He vomited where he lay on the stone.

Parkinson curled his lip in disgust and stepped over him. As he left the room he said to Serres, "Take this deceiving, lying, vomiting rat down to the magazine. Clear up the floor when you have done it. And bring me some paper—I am going to write to Sir William."

66

~

It was dusk. On the roof of the tower Paul Coad felt the rain begin to fall. He raised his cloak above his head to ward off the worst of it, but a moment later it began to pelt down. He ducked into the doorway and descended the stairs. The smell of vomit rose to greet him—still lingering even though it had been mopped up several hours ago. He cursed. It should have been John Prouze's turn to be on the roof this evening, not his. Prouze had been sent off by the captain with an urgent message for Sir William Cecil, telling him that Clarenceux had arrived and was now locked in the magazine.

Coad listened to the rain and heard its force weakening. Not wanting to be shouted at by the captain, he made his way back up the stairs to shelter just inside the doorway.

A mile away to the west, Raw Carew dragged the sloop out of the water, putting the weight on his good leg. He took the rope and grappling iron he had brought with him and sat down with a tablecloth he had taken from the inn. He glanced toward the fort in the fading light and cursed as he saw the rain come down. Sheltering beneath a tree, he started to bind the cloth around the grappling iron, ripping off thin strips and tying them on tightly. As he worked, he kept a regular check on the battlements; the guard was no longer to be seen. That was good news for him approaching the fort but bad news for when he was inside. According to Amy, there were seven gunners stationed there, plus the captain. He had seen one man leave; unless there were any occasional visitors, seven were left, including Parkinson. The grappling iron was ready. He tossed it onto a rock a few times; it did not clang. He slung the rope over his shoulder and started to limp through the wood.

Ten minutes later he was sitting in the undergrowth at the edge of the spit, his wounded leg stretched out. He was watching the clouds to the west. From long experience he knew the light from the west would reflect off the water, even though there was no sunset. The waves would be silvered with the brightness of the sky. To someone at the fort, the spit itself would appear like a dark shadow between the two surfaces of light. He waited for another cloud to pass, so more light would reflect off the water. Crouching down on the lower inland side, so his silhouette would not show against the sea, he began to crawl the long distance toward the solid hulk of the fort, moving on his arms and knees, using his weak leg as best he could.

Captain Parkinson was in the guard room on the first floor with most of his men. Some were seated like the captain; others were sitting on the floor. There were bowls around them. They were playing cards by the light of a tallow candle. All the shutters were closed except one.

William Knight flung down the Queen of Clubs. A small cheer went up from the others. His amiable red-bearded face broke into a broad grin.

"You've been hiding that up your sleeve," declared Lewis Fletcher, a pale, thin young man. He threw down his cards and dropped two pennies into the pot in the middle of the floor.

"Should have played dice," declared Bill Turner, doing likewise. He was the oldest member of the garrison, in his fifties and gray haired.

"No, not dice," said Parkinson, tossing down his cards. "Cards at least have some skill, even if it is little more than memorizing a few numbers. Dice is nothing but luck."

"But luck is the will of the Lord," said Christopher Serres.

"And so is the luck of the cards," replied Knight, lifting up his cards for Serres to see.

"For that, you can take all these bowls to Widow Reid's," said Parkinson.

"Tomorrow," pleaded Knight, passing his cards to Serres.

"Now," insisted Parkinson. "On your way back up, bring some more wine. And tell Kimpton he should bar the gatehouse when you come back through."

In the darkness of the magazine Clarenceux heard Serres and Knight go down the stairs. He heard one of them drop a bowl and curse and place the rest of his load on the floor. He listened to the conversation as they left the tower and went out across the yard, and noted the phrases "Paul on the roof" and "Widow Reid the washer-woman" and "Captain says bar the gate when we're back." As they passed out of hearing he caught the end of a sentence: "he sent John in the rain with a letter for Cecil."

Clarenceux sank down against the wall of his cell. He was disappointed with himself. Carew had been right; he had not thought deeply enough about Parkinson. No one knew where he was and the message to Cecil had already been dispatched. The stench of sulfurous gunpowder in the magazine was nauseating. The taste in his mouth was worse. He was hungry, not having eaten since that morning. And the only person who knew his whereabouts was Carew—a man who had recently turned his back on several men who had risked their lives for him. Perhaps worst of all, he now knew that Cecil was the architect behind all this—that Cecil was the one who had arranged for Rebecca's escape from London by ship. Cecil had been playing games with him all along.

What now, William? What now? At least he could be sure they would not bother him tonight. It must be dark by now and they could not enter here with a burning light for fear of sparks or dropping the candle. That meant he had the night to think.

He understood now why Rebecca had been so anxious that last time he had seen her. She had already had discussions with Mrs. Barker and the Knights and they had persuaded her to steal the document for them. They had planned her journey away from London. Only someone else had got to her first: Cecil himself. Using Denisot to contact the captain of the *Davy* and Parkinson to arrange Rebecca's reception in Southampton, he had effected a smooth escape for her. All Cecil had to do was to arrange for someone to collect the document from her, wherever she might be. It was a brilliant coup. It meant Cecil got the document and left the Knights and Mrs. Barker thinking Rebecca had betrayed them. And it left him, Clarenceux, thinking the same thing.

Yes, thought Clarenceux, Cecil had almost pulled it off. But he could not afford to risk the herald telling anyone else what had happened. That messenger who had gone off to Cecil—he would certainly return with a death warrant. It would be an unwritten one. They were the most deadly kind.

67

Carew pressed his face to the shingle, tasting the saltwater as the waves lapped around his face.

He was hiding behind an upturned rowing boat. His left leg and sword were in the waves and his right one was stinging as if the Devil's claws were fastened in it, but he dared not move. It was not quite dark enough. Two men were talking to a woman in front of the cottage only twenty feet ahead of him. If he stood up now, they would probably hear him on the noisy shingle. They would certainly see him.

He listened intently. He heard the waves beside his ear and the rain falling around him. The men at the door to the cottage spoke about a butcher in Southampton and the amount of gristle that one of them had had in a meal. He heard that a man called Paul was on the roof in John's place because John was "taking an urgent message to the queen's Secretary." That told him enough. Clarenceux had been detained but Parkinson was not bold enough simply to kill him without authority. The herald was a lucky man.

A little later, he heard the woman close the door to the cottage and watched the men return to the fort. He was alone in the near-darkness, with only the waves and the rain for company. Just as he wanted.

Creeping forward to the drawbridge, he knelt at the foot and tested the strength of the ropes that connected it to the beams above. An instant later he was climbing one of them. Swinging his wounded leg over the edge of the beam, he bit his lip to control the pain in his thigh. But he was up. He shifted along to the gatehouse wall and took the rope from his shoulder. Looking up, he carefully swung the muffled grappling iron; it landed beyond the crenellations on top of the gatehouse. Even if the man on the tower roof had heard that dampened noise he would be unlikely to see anything. Nevertheless Carew waited, listening. After a minute he climbed; twenty seconds later he was on the roof of the gatehouse, crouched down inside the darkened battlements.

He took the rope and coiled it again, deciding his next move. He had thought initially that he would use the grappling iron to get on to the roof of the tower, but even a muffled grappling iron would be bound to alert the guard. Swinging hard across the gully would mean a loud landing against the tower wall and a hasty climb, with the certainty of an unfriendly greeting at the top. A better plan was required.

He climbed over the battlements of the gatehouse and, holding on to the parapet, lowered himself down as far as he could. He let himself drop the last two feet onto the top of the perimeter wall, then moved to a point directly above one of the embrasures, through which the cannon fired, and climbed down onto one of the cannon, which he could just make out in the darkness. From there he slipped soundlessly onto the courtyard flagstones. Flat against the wall, he moved in a clockwise direction, crossing the gatehouse passage, until he was facing the door to the tower. He moved closer, listened, heard nothing, and tried the door. The two men he had seen earlier had left it unlocked.

Inside it was completely dark. But he had been here before, when he had had his last run-in with Captain Parkinson, and knew that there were a few steps and then the passage turned forty-five degrees to the left. The door to the magazine was on the right, and that was where Parkinson would have put Clarenceux. It was where he himself had spent three tedious nights a few years ago. There were no other places in the small fort where a prisoner could be secured.

Carew looked up the stairs. No light, not even the flicker of a candle. The gunners must have closed the door to the guard room at the top of the stairs.

Inside, Clarenceux had found a sack and had emptied it of its contents to have something softer than the stone to sit on, but even when he had doubled it over, the hemp gave him little comfort. He shifted again, thinking of Awdrey at Summerhill, talking to Julius. If truth be known, they were probably boring each other. She did not share Julius's antiquarian interests and he had scant concern for anything that was not connected with the chivalric past, theology, or the management and improvement of farming land. He imagined her tucking their daughters into bed by the light of a candle and sighing with relief that Julius would have gone off to his study with a pint of sack and a pile of papers. She would be worrying about where he was, never thinking of this darkness, this smell of sulfur, or the corruption in the government that she so trusted. She would not have believed the duplicity of Sir William Cecil, nor the double standards of his wife Mildred. *Lady Cecil's offer of an ambassadorial post must have been part of Sir William's plot to get us out of London. Lady Cecil must have known.*

Suddenly he heard a soft knocking in the darkness: three short taps on a piece of wood. *Was that a rat? Or a noise from upstairs?* "Who's there?" he said quietly, testing the silence.

Three more quiet knocks. That was all.

Clarenceux's heart leaped. "Carew?"

One knock.

Clarenceux scrambled to his feet and felt his way to the steps that led up to the door. He pressed his mouth to the jamb. "Can you get me out?"

There was a pause. He heard the sound of Carew kneeling down beside the door. Then a whisper: "There is no key, but I will do my best."

Clarenceux was so surprised that he hardly cared that the man had no means of freeing him. Someone knew where he was. He sat on the steps and said a prayer for Carew. Even though the man was a godless creature, he had shown faith—in him, Clarenceux.

"What is your plan?" he whispered again. But there was no answer. Time started to flow slowly through the darkness, as if it had been frozen and was now melting.

The six men in the guard room played cards, argued, and drank late into the night. Only once were they alerted to something unusual; two of them noticed a distant clatter of metal on stone. William Knight went over to the window nearest the noise, opened the wooden shutter, and examined the embrasure; there was nothing to see. The guttering candlelight only showed the blank space and the flagstones of the embrasure—a wide space in the thick wall designed to allow the cannon the widest possible range and elevation. Had he crawled into the embrasure itself and looked up, he would have seen the cause of the disturbance, for Carew was hanging by his hands from the edge of the second-floor embrasure, pulling himself up. But Knight did no such thing. He closed the shutters and rejoined the card game.

"Lock the door to the tower," said Parkinson, who was more alert to the possible dangers than the rest of his men.

Carew pulled himself up slowly into the darkness of the embrasure on the second floor. He found the edges of the shutters and tried to open them. There was a fastening in place, stopping them from banging in a high wind. Pulling out a knife, he ran it up the central crack between them and lifted the catch. Hearing nothing but the wind and the waves, and laughter from the men on the floor below, he opened the shutters and crept in. He closed them behind him and made his way across the chamber toward the stairs, where the single flame of a wall-mounted candle was burning.

Paul Coad was huddled in the most sheltered corner of the roof, as Carew knew he would be. Over the wind Coad heard a voice call him from the direction of the door. "Paul? Captain says you've done your shift. You can go in. William will take over."

Coad did not recognize the voice. Nor could he see anyone in the darkness. The clouds concealed the half-moon that had risen earlier. Nevertheless the message was welcome and he rose to his feet and made his way to the dark silhouette of the door. He reached out with his left hand and turned inside. Carew was waiting with a knife. Coad opened his mouth but never spoke. A hand clamped over his face and the blade slipped through the skin and muscle of his neck. He struggled and kicked for barely a second before all the life force drained out of him with a spurt of blood that splattered against the wall of the staircase. Then he slumped, a dead weight in Carew's arms.

Carew hauled the corpse back onto the roof and dragged it across to the point where Coad had been sitting earlier, in the concealed lee of the battlements. With the body stowed in the darkness, he fastened the grappling iron over the battlements and let himself down the outside of the wall to the first floor. He tucked himself into one of the embrasures, to wait and listen to the conversations within.

Half an hour passed. He cursed the cold of the wind but knew it was his safety. None of the men within would open the shutter and allow a gale to blow through the warm room. He heard bets placed and coins dropped into the pot. He heard one man accuse another of cheating and the shouts of Captain Parkinson bringing them to order. He heard John Prouze's name and the comment that he had probably got no further on his journey than the Two Swans, where he had a sweetheart. "He had better be halfway to London by now," said Parkinson in a serious voice. "No time for common women."

"You should have let him have a go at that one he brought here," replied Lewis Fletcher. "If you had, he wouldn't be so desperate for Amy."

"Where is she now, that dark-haired one with a mole?" asked William Knight. "She was good."

"She was good because she was scared," added Serres. "When they're scared they really want to please you—they'll do anything."

"She was supposed to be protected, not molested," Parkinson snapped. "She was sent here by Sir William Cecil. If I had been here it would not have happened. And I seem to recall saying that the condition for forgiving the incident was forgetting it—and that means not mentioning it."

"Where did you send her?" asked Turner.

"Somewhere she is safe from you," replied Parkinson, "so you will be safe from Cecil."

"I bet she's at Southampton Castle," said Serres, looking at Parkinson. "I bet you sent her to your own chamber."

"No, she's not at Southampton," answered Turner. "She's at Netley."

The drunk men laughed. But then Knight added, "No. Kimpton took her to Portchester where she's a nurse—servicing mutilated soldiers."

The four gunners burst out laughing.

"No, in truth, she is," said Knight, himself laughing.

Parkinson was not drunk. Carew heard the laughter stop. Suddenly there was a great clatter of objects as he kicked the cups and mazers aside and struck out at those nearest to him. "You laugh!" he shouted. "You laugh at the orders you fail to follow. You drink and laugh at your own stupidity. I know it is tedious here and I turn a blind eye to your indiscretions, but you shame me. You have no loyalty. You have no values. You are weak, all of you!"

There was a long pause. Carew imagined Parkinson glaring at the men and he smiled to himself. "Knight, you fetch Kimpton. Serres, you summon Coad. I want to speak to all of you."

"Sir, have a mercy, it's late," ventured Fletcher.

"I swear, by these hands, that if you so much as utter another syllable before morning, I will strangle you and dump your body in the Channel."

Carew crept away from the shutter, back to the rope. Suddenly this was not going the way he had hoped. His plan had been to wait until the men were asleep and then challenge Parkinson, alone. Now there were just seconds to spare before the body on the roof would be discovered. There was no time now to think or plan.

He grabbed the rope and swung out, pulling himself up as fast as he could, despite his wounded leg. He was too late. As he hauled himself over the parapet between the crenellations he heard Serres call for Coad and saw the black figure of the man beside the doorway. "Who's there?" Serres shouted. "Paul? Paul! Damn it—speak, man." As Carew drew near, with a dagger drawn, Serres sensed him and backed away. Carew went after him, limping. Serres started running. Carew lunged and caught his sleeve near the staircase. He raised his knife, meaning to cut his throat but Serres threw himself sideways, into the stairway. He missed his footing and fell with a shout. He tumbled halfway down to the point outside the room on the second floor, where there was an angle of the staircase.

One moment Carew was looking at Serres's prostrate body halfway down the stairs, in the light of the wall-mounted candle. The next he saw Captain Parkinson, sword in hand, come up the stairs and step over the injured man. Parkinson glanced up—and they looked into each other's eyes. There was one moment of recognition in the small golden light, one moment of them both understanding the depth of their mutual hatred. Then, like a huge bull preparing to charge at a small man, Parkinson started to climb toward Carew.

Carew drew his own sword and waited.

It was a mistake. As Parkinson came closer, his body blocked out the light. All Carew could see was a silhouette against the candlelight. When Parkinson made his first lunge, for Carew's stomach, the latter only managed to deflect the blow by watching his attacker's shoulders; he could not see the blade. He tried to dislodge Parkinson's sword with a flick of his own, desperate to end the fight before the other man realized his advantage. But Parkinson gripped his weapon too firmly. Carew's sword darted up, to cut the captain around the face or neck; Parkinson saw the move, parried the attack, and started thrusting at Carew's legs and body, all the time drawing closer, a rising shadow. Carew had to step back. He drew his dagger with his left hand and held it ready, more out of desperation than a feeling of opportunity. Again he had to parry a thrust as Parkinson's sword swept up to his throat.

Serres began to cry out from where he lay on the staircase. "Christ Holy, Lord God, I cannot move my legs, sweet mother of God, I cannot move my legs!" Over and over again he called out. Parkinson came up another step, ignoring the man's cries.

Carew felt his mouth dry. The staircase was too narrow—there was no room to move. Nor could he see the man's eyes—he could not read Parkinson's face or predict his thrusts. It was like fighting smoke. He parried another thrust and tried to come forward again, jabbing at the left side of Parkinson's face with his sword. He almost reached Parkinson's neck but Parkinson reacted in time, smashing Carew's blade against the wall. Immediately Carew drew it back across his line of vision and jabbed the other side. Parkinson dodged the cut, tried to grab Carew's sword hand with his left hand, and lunged with his own blade at Carew's abdomen. Carew did not see the thrust coming. He felt Parkinson's blade pierce his skin, sinking deep into the flesh above his left hip. When it was suddenly withdrawn it felt as though his guts were slithering out through a hole of pain.

Carew's face creased but he dared not look down at the wound. He fended off another downward slashing cut, and another, as Parkinson tried to finish him there. Suddenly, with a chilling clarity, he realized he might very well die here on these stairs. It was not the pain so much as the new feeling; the thought of his entrails slipping, his nerves sparklingly cold. How disappointing it would be, to die here! How mundane. All his life he had believed he was indestructible. Now, through a simple mistake, everything was undone. Everything he had ever learned was going to be unlearnt, unknowable, unknown.

Gasping, he looked at Parkinson. The captain took another step up and paused for a moment, looking at him. Carew sensed the man was smiling.

The pain, the thought of dying in Calshot Fort and his adversary's smile were all too much for Carew. Fury seized his mind, hatred took hold of his body, and his spirit lifted him. Suddenly everything was so simple. He only had one enemy—one enemy in the whole world. The rest of his life could be spent killing him. He took a step down toward the captain and whisked the tip of his sword across his gaze, drawing it back and just touching the man on the head for an instant before withdrawing it to parry the man's next thrust. All the things he had hoped for and fought for—they were all gone now. All there was, was this dark staircase and this murderous black shape.

Taking another step forward, he remembered the war cry that Clarenceux had told him was what his ancestors used to shriek in Ireland. It was his birthright, no matter that he was a bastard. If ever there was a time to use it, it was now. "A *Carew*! A *Carew*!" he yelled, his face twisted with anger and the desire to kill. He advanced three more steps. Parkinson lifted his sword and hacked at him hard, once, twice—but the third time he saw Carew's blade suddenly coming straight into his face. He stepped back and prepared to lunge at the oncoming pirate, but he was not prepared for the ferocity of the attack.

Carew cut furiously, bellowing "A *Carew*! A *Carew*!" over and over again. He could see better now—he could see the shape of his enemy's face. And he cut harder and faster.

Serres screamed again on the stairs. Men started shouting on the floor below. Parkinson shouted back. "Damn you! Knight, Fletcher, Turner! Come—*now*!" He redoubled his efforts and put his foot on the step above, stabbing at Carew's bleeding thigh, but Carew twisted his sword before his eyes and unexpectedly cut sideways, catching the captain above his left eye, then cut down, slicing open two inches of the man's left cheek. Blood flowed straight into Parkinson's eye and down the side of his face, forcing him to retreat several steps while he wiped it away. He felt the wide cut of the wound. Down came Carew's sword again, forcing him to lift his sword and look through the red cloud of blood. "Knight, Fletcher—fetch weapons!" he roared again. "Come up here and fight!" He wiped his eye and tried to come forward, the side of his cheek hanging loose. "Curse your soul, Carew. This is where this ends."

The blades clanged together as Carew's steel met Parkinson's. A second time he met Parkinson's cut, and a third. Then he made an attack of his own, catching Parkinson's shoulder and slicing his tunic open, cutting his skin. With blood in his eyes, the captain had to give up yet another step and stumbled on the hysterical Serres, who cried out again. Surprised to find flesh beneath his feet, he retreated two more steps.

At that moment, a movement behind Carew caught Parkinson's attention. Carew saw the captain shift his gaze. The guards had not come to Parkinson's aid because they had found Carew's rope.

Carew did not turn around. Seizing the one opportunity open to him, he swung his sword into the candle on the wall, extinguishing it while he dived into the dark of the second-floor room. He then stretched out with his hand and made his way to the right as men shouted in the darkness and Serres yelled and Parkinson tried to give orders. Serres suddenly fell silent, his wind pipe cut.

Carew touched a wooden partition and tried to crouch behind it. The wound in his abdomen was painful; his clothes were already stiffening with the blood caked on them. He felt his way toward the embrasure nearest to where his rope was hanging and stumbled. For an instant there was a flicker of golden light in the doorway.

"Give me that torch," shouted Parkinson. "Go and fetch the others, and more lights. Kimpton, you follow me."

Carew sheathed his sword, put his dagger between his teeth, and pushed himself toward the shutters. He felt the catch, pulled them open, and climbed out into the embrasure.

When Parkinson entered the second floor with the flaming torch held aloft, he looked around the central area, and then within each partitioned chamber. The shutters to the embrasures where the two cannon were positioned were open as usual, but so was a third set of shutters. He went to them and looked out. There was no one there. Curious, he placed the torch on the stonework and climbed through the opening. Being considerably larger than Carew, it took him longer. Once out, he took the torch and held it out beyond the wall. He looked down but could see nothing—the torchlight did not extend so far. He looked both ways around the wall; there was only a limp rope. If Carew had left the second floor, he had made his escape very quickly.

Suddenly, Parkinson heard a scuffling behind him. He turned— just in time to see the shutters close.

"Damn you!" he cursed, kicking hard at them. They did not open. "Kimpton!" he roared. "Open the shutters!" He called in vain. Kimpton was lying in a pool of blood. Carew had swung around and climbed into another embrasure, and had re-entered the second floor in dark- ness. He had seen Kimpton's silhouette against the door, grabbed him, cupped his hand over his mouth, cut his throat, and let him fall. He now had his shoulder against the shutters, blocking Parkinson from re-entering. He jammed his dagger into the catch, holding the shutters fast. "Open these shutters, you dog!" shouted Parkinson. Then he fell silent, realizing that Carew was on the other side.

Carew waited, gasping, touching his abdomen, and feeling the wetness of the blood. He tried to quiet his breathing. He wanted to listen. When Parkinson tried to descend by the rope, he would cut it. Parkinson would fall onto the jagged edges of the stonework below. But as Carew listened, he heard more footsteps on the stairs and saw more flickering lights. The remaining gunners were coming in search of him. He limped across the room and opened another set of shutters and climbed into the embrasure there, and lowered himself from the edge by his arms until he was hanging from his fingers. The pointed top of the embrasure of the first floor was now level with his shoulders. Fighting the pain in his abdomen and leg, he began to swing his lower body to and fro—and when he had enough momentum, he let go, falling into the first-floor embrasure. Picking himself up, he turned and lowered himself again, dropping onto the octagonal plinth on which the tower was built. He pressed himself to the stone in the darkness and shuffled around to where his rope hung down, directly below the embrasure where Parkinson was shouting.

Inside, Parkinson's men were afraid and confused.

"Captain Parkinson," called William Knight from the staircase, a torch in one hand and a sword in the other. "Captain, are you there?" He darted across the doorway and held the torch aloft. Peeping around the jamb he could see nothing in the room. He glanced at Bill Turner, also holding a torch and a sword, and entered tentatively. He heard a kick against the shutters and moved to see who was there. He saw the dagger fastening the catch. "Bill, come here. Cover me." As soon as Turner was near, Knight set down his sword and pulled out the dagger, undid the catch and opened the shutter.

"Kill him," snarled Parkinson as he climbed back through. "Find Carew and kill him. I want him dead within five minutes." Holding his torch, he strode to the doorway and stepped over Serres's corpse. He looked up the stairs and down. "Bring me Carew's head."

"Where is he?" asked Turner. "Tell us and we will find him."

"I wounded him. Look for the blood," shouted Parkinson.

Knight looked at the captain's ruined face; he wanted to point out that he too was bleeding heavily. There was also blood on the roof, blood on the stairs, and pools of blood around Coad, Kimpton, and Serres—but he said nothing. When Parkinson was this angry, there was no saying what he might do.

Outside, Carew flicked the rope and dislodged the grappling iron. It fell with a heavy muffled clang in the yard. He hid in the shadows until he was certain there was no one there. Then he began to wind the rope.

"Where's Fletcher? Where's Coad?" demanded Parkinson, standing beside Serres's dead body in the doorway to the second-floor room.

"Coad is dead—on the roof," replied Knight. "Carew cut his throat."

"And Fletcher went to warn Widow Reid," said Turner. "He hasn't come back."

"Bloody coward!" shouted Parkinson. "I'll lock him up for a month." He looked at Knight and Turner, both holding torches. There was a moment of complete silence, in which only the wind whistling through the shutters could be heard. "What are you waiting for?"

Knight started to look around the room, in each of the partitioned areas.

"You, go and fetch the rope he's been using," said Parkinson to Turner. "It's hanging from the roof."

Turner stared at Parkinson in frightened astonishment. He put a hand to his wrinkled forehead. "There are only the three of us left. What if he is…"

Parkinson struggled to control his anger. "Lean out of that embrasure near you," he hissed, "and cut the rope you find there. That will stop him escaping. When you have done that, we will go up on the roof together. And if he is not there, that means he is not in the upper part of this tower."

Turner did as he was told. He placed his torch down carefully and climbed through the window with some awkwardness. He felt around to the left, then to the right. He checked both sides again. There was a long pause. After a minute, he started to crawl back into the room. "There's no rope there, Captain Parkinson."

As Turner and Knight looked at Parkinson's grim face in the torchlight, they heard a distant, knocking sound. The sound of wood on metal.

"What's that?" said Knight, looking at Parkinson. "The prisoner?"

Parkinson waited, listening further. "Go down and find out."

Knight hesitated. "By myself?"

"Yes, by your God-abandoned self. Why am I surrounded by cowards?"

Knight left the room and started to creep downstairs.

Turner picked up his torch. "Sir, there is no rope outside. At least none I can feel."

Parkinson looked at the door. "Knight!" he shouted. The red-bearded man had not gone far and soon reappeared in the doorway. "From here on, we stick together. We will search this tower inside and out, starting from the top. All three of us. I will lead. Knight, you watch our backs. Turner, you follow in the middle."

The three men started to climb the staircase, all clutching torches in one hand and swords in the other. Parkinson took each step very slowly as he neared the top, listening for any sound of the pirate. With a couple of steps still to go, he stopped and silently gestured for Turner to take his torch, allowing him to go on ahead unseen. He drew near to the top step and pressed his back against the wall, holding his sword ready for a quick thrust. His left arm he held up as protection. But no blow came. He eased himself into the doorway and then through. The next moment he moved swiftly away from the door and swept his sword along the top of the roof over the staircase. No one. "Come up," he commanded, trying to look around the roof in the darkness. Turner emerged with the torch and then Knight, each looking apprehensive. Parkinson took his torch again and saw the body of Coad lying against the wall. He examined the crenellations all the way around; there was no sign of the rope. "It must have been a hook," he said "He must have shaken it loose after he went down."

"Does that mean he has gone?" asked Turner.

Parkinson held up a hand. He could hear the sound of knocking on wood again. Except that now there were two knocking sounds: one louder than the other. One was coming from within the fort, the other from the beach.

"What is he doing?" asked Turner.

The three men stood there with their torches, listening to the sounds. In the magazine Clarenceux had found the remains of a broken barrel and was smashing at the lock with one of the staves. On the far side of Widow Reid's cottage, Carew was smashing the bottoms of the boats moored there.

Eventually, Parkinson realized what was happening. "He's scuttling the boats."

"Why?" asked Knight.

"To cut us off—or perhaps to draw us out of the fort."

"Why would he want to do that?" asked Turner.

The torchlight was bright against Parkinson's bloody face as he listened and thought. "He expects us to send for help from Southampton Castle. Without the boats we cannot. At least, not safely. If we send a man alone by land, Carew will ambush and kill him. And then the next man."

"This is going to go on all night." Turner sounded ready to give in.

"The three of us could take him by land," said Knight.

Parkinson said nothing to either of them.

"In the name of sweet Jesus Christ," murmured Turner. "This is a one-man siege."

"At least we know now where he is," said Knight.

Still Parkinson said nothing.

The knocks coming from the spit were slow now. About ten sec-onds passed between each heavy thud on the wood. Those in the basement were much lighter and more frantic, made with a smaller piece of wood.

"What do you think, Captain?" said Knight.

"Clarenceux cannot break out. As for Carew—he has lost a lot of blood. He is tired so he wants us to go out there."

Turner shut his eyes and, still holding his torch and sword, turned and discreetly made the sign of the cross.

"Do we…shall we all go together?" asked Knight.

Parkinson looked macabre in the torchlight, with the thick flap of skin hanging from his pockmarked cheek and blood all over his face. "If he was dying, he wouldn't be trying to scuttle the boats. Knight, you will guard the gate. Turner, you will go to him with a torch and start talking—ask him what he wants, anything. Use your experience—negotiate a truce. You distract him and I will creep close in the darkness. He's got nowhere to hide."

Parkinson ducked and made his way down the stairs, followed by Turner and Knight. He stepped over Serres's body and continued down to the door leading to the magazine. He paused, listening to the knocking sound from within. He felt the key on his belt and jingled it. The knocking stopped.

"Carew?" Clarenceux said from within.

"Carew's mortally wounded. Stop knocking—or we'll come in there and silence you ourselves," replied Parkinson.

Clarenceux said nothing.

Parkinson strode out of the tower and through to the gatehouse passage. There he gestured to Turner to go ahead. Turner reluctantly went out onto the drawbridge. Parkinson and Knight followed him. "You wait here," Parkinson said to Knight in a low voice. He handed him his torch. "Turner, you go ahead. I will follow."

Turner started to walk out into the night. Parkinson waited fifteen seconds and set off into the darkness, keeping low, veering to one side. He watched Turner make his way slowly toward where the boats were pulled up. Despite being fifty feet away, he could still hear Turner's footsteps over the waves; the cascading shingle made a lot of noise. He tried to time his own feet to coincide with Turner's.

It was only a hundred yards across to the jetty. Between them there were the two cottages. Parkinson waited until Turner was near the buildings and then, stooping, he hurried across to take cover behind them, creeping around the back wall to watch as the man approached the boats. He saw the torchlight and Turner's face in the glow. Two upturned boats lay on the shore; another was half sunk in the water beside the jetty.

Carew was not there.

Turner stopped and turned. He stood on the jetty, listening to the crashing of the waves. In the shadows, Parkinson realized he had not heard the knocking sound since Turner had left the fort.

After a couple of minutes more, Parkinson stepped forward from his cover by the cottages, near enough so Turner could hear him but not so near he was illuminated in the torchlight. "There are only three boats here. There were four. He's on the water. Can you see him?"

Turner lifted his torch high and looked around, across the dark water, chilled by the wind, and the thought of Carew out on the sea somewhere, watching them. "No, I cannot see anything except waves."

"Look again, carefully. He cannot be far."

A yell came from behind them, back at the fort. Swords clashed.

Parkinson swore, drew his own blade, and started to run. His feet crunched on the shingle. Knight had dropped his torch on the drawbridge; by its light, Parkinson saw Carew lunge forward and stab him, then whip back his blade and slash him across the face before stabbing him a second time, sending him falling from the drawbridge into the moat with a splash. Carew looked toward Parkinson and the sounds of footsteps on the shingle. Calmly he reached up with his sword and cut the ropes for lifting the drawbridge, so Parkinson could not climb up onto the projecting beams. Then he went inside the castle, shutting the gate behind him and pulling the drawbar across.

Parkinson ran on to the drawbridge. "Open this door. I am the queen's Keeper. I have the right to enter freely." He stood fuming, as the clouds parted and the half-moon shone briefly on the scene. Turner also arrived and his torch cast Parkinson's shadow on the gate.

Suddenly there was a rattle of chains above them as the portcullis came down. Parkinson only just stepped back in time to avoid being skewered on its teeth.

"Damn you!" he hissed.

Carew watched them from the upper window of the gatehouse, clutching his wound. He was having difficulty moving now. He had rowed as fast as he could from the jetty at the moment he had seen the torches in the gatehouse, and the effort had caused his wound to bleed more. Running as fast as his leg would allow him across the shingle had made him dizzy for a moment before he attacked the guard on the drawbridge, and he had felt dizzy again after forcing himself up the gatehouse stairs. He watched now in the sincere hope that Parkinson and Turner would abandon the fort. He saw their torches move across the beach. A few minutes later they found the small boat, as he had intended; Turner even waded out and hauled it up onto the shingle. But neither man got in. They spent a long time simply talking, too far away for him to hear what they had to say. Eventually Turner passed the torch to Parkinson and got into the boat by himself. Parkinson stomped off over the shingle to the cottages. Turner vanished into the night.

Carew leaned back in the darkness. He felt weak and sick. He did not want to get up, but he knew he had to. He still had not seen any keys, although he had no doubt where they were—hanging from Parkinson's belt. He rose to his knees and then, holding the wall, struggled to his feet and went down the stairs to the gatehouse passageway. He listened. He felt cold. *John Prouze was sent away with a message. Parkinson is in or near the cottages and one man has just left in the boat. That's three. One dead man in the moat, four; another on the roof, five. One dead man on the stairs, six; another on the second floor, seven. One man more—one man would make it eight. The fugitive— where did he go?*

Carew stopped in the darkness, gasping with the pain. He felt his way across the yard to the tower, but with a hand against the wall he stopped. He could not do this. He felt his wound. His clothes were wet with yet more blood; he was slowly bleeding to death. Kneeling down, Carew rested his head against the flagstones. He could hear the sea in the distance, beyond the walls of the fort. *The sea. The one thing that has never deserted me; it has always helped me. I have been listening to it most of my life.* It seemed that it was a good way to die, listening to the waves. But that thought was followed by another, like waves of thought rolling in, breaking on the shore of his mind. There was no good way to die, not for Raw Carew. Death was the end of everything—and he had not finished what he intended to do.

Struggling to his feet, he took a deep breath then continued to cross the yard.

Captain Parkinson closed the door to Widow Reid's cottage and walked back across the shingles to the fort. He had a large coil of rope over one arm made up from several shorter pieces. Widow Reid herself had been shocked at his appearance and had bandaged his face. She watched him in silence as he knotted the ropes together in the glow of her rushlight.

The clouds broke again for an instant, illuminating the fort with silver light. Then they drifted over the half-moon. Parkinson stood looking up at the gatehouse shadow, estimating the height. He tied a noose in the rope and threw it toward the crenellations. It fell back heavily onto the drawbridge. He felt for the noose and got ready to throw again. If it took all night, he would do it.

Carew placed his hand on the tower wall and started to climb the steps to the magazine.

He felt in the darkness for the edge of the doorframe, ran his fingers over the lock, and steadied himself. He swung the grappling iron against the door jamb, trying to lodge it between the door and the frame. He missed, the blunt iron point only denting the wood. He tried again.

"Carew?" called Clarenceux. "Is that you?"

"Hold on, herald," gasped Carew. "We're not safe yet. Is there anything in there you can use to open this door?"

"Do you think I haven't been trying?"

Carew clenched his teeth, trying to forget the agony in his abdomen. "You owe me a favor as big as the one you offered my uncle. I hope you realize that."

Outside in the half-moonlight, Parkinson felt the rope catch on one of the gatehouse crenellations. He pulled it; it held firm. Placing a foot against the portcullis, he began to climb. In a few seconds he would be on the beam that supported the drawbridge mechanism. After that he had to haul himself up about fifteen feet to the window overlooking the gate. If he could just get in there, he would be in the fort—and able to stalk Carew just as Carew had stalked him earlier.

Carew swung the grappling iron at the oak. Again he missed the mark. And a third time. He put the iron down, drew his eating knife, and jammed it into the gap between the door and its frame. Picking up the grappling iron again, he knocked the knife further into place, widening the gap. Placing the tip of one of the hooks of the grappling iron into the gap, he started to lever the door and the frame apart, forcing harder and harder on the frame. The grappling iron came out of the nook; the knife fell. Patiently Carew reinserted the knife and then the hook, and started to lever the two apart again.

Parkinson pulled himself up higher, standing on the royal coat of arms above the gate. He put his right hand forward again and looked up; he was nearly at the window. Hauling himself up another couple of feet was not easy but he did it, placing his foot on the shuttered window. He kicked at the shutter; the catch held good. Holding the rope with one arm and steadying himself with both legs outstretched, he drew his sword and pushed it through the gap. The catch was hard to lift; it took him a couple of minutes, during which time he had to re-sheath his sword and change hands on the rope. But eventually he inserted the sword point in the right place, pulled the shutters open, and clambered through into the darkness of the gatehouse chamber.

In the main tower, at the magazine, Carew was still pulling on the grappling iron. He had splintered the edge of the doorframe and broken the blade of his knife. He could feel the tension in the timber—but the door was solid. Still he heaved, even though he felt faint. Another effort was rewarded with a crack; the oak frame broke at the top and the piece of timber into which the bolt of the lock shot partly came away, hanging by a pair of nails. He moved the grappling iron in the darkness and pulled the frame apart, allowing the door to open.

As he pulled out the last piece of timber, he heard a noise in the darkness behind him and froze. He knew the captain could not see him, for the passage was in total darkness, but Parkinson could hear him. He stood still, waiting for the man to approach. His hand moved slowly to the hilt of his sword, hearing the captain place his foot on the first of the five steps between Carew and the door. At the same time, beside him, he heard the door to the cell swinging open. With his eyes long-accustomed to the darkness, Clarenceux saw the vague outline of Parkinson in the passageway. Carew leaned over and took his sleeve, pulling him down, directing him to the ground, where the grappling iron was lying. He felt Clarenceux rise again to his feet and, slowly, he drew his sword. It rasped agonizingly as he took it from its sheath.

Parkinson took another step toward them, his sword at the ready. Clarenceux saw the blade. Hours spent wondering in the darkness what his fate might be had torn at his wits. He had felt frustrated, fearful, and humiliated. Now he could hold himself back no more. Seeing Parkinson advancing, he raised the three-pronged curved iron and, with a sudden shout that made both men jump, he stepped forward and brought it down hard. Parkinson sensed the movement and drew back; the grappling iron glanced off the side of his head and struck his elbow. Clarenceux launched himself forward again, seizing Parkinson's sword hand with his left hand and raising the iron hook to hit him again. A second blow caught Parkinson's head, dislodging his sword hand and drawing back the blade through Clarenceux's grasp, cutting his thumb and finger. The sharp pain spurred Clarenceux on to an even more frenzied attack, swinging the hook down and bludgeoning Parkinson with a blunt edge on his temple. The force sent Parkinson reeling. He stepped backward, sweeping his sword behind him as he tried to regain his balance. But Clarenceux was already upon him, swinging the hook, gasping and snarling like a maddened beast. Carew tried to move forward with his sword but there was no room in the passage for him. Again Clarenceux wielded the grappling iron, smashing it against Parkinson's sword hand, but Parkinson was not done yet. He lashed out with the blade, yelling at Clarenceux, "Traitor! Murderer!" and swiped his sword across Clarenceux's face, drawing blood. Snarling, Clarenceux hefted the grappling iron and went for him. Parkinson stabbed in the darkness, missed Clarenceux, struck the wall with the point, and was disempowered for an instant. It was enough. He never saw the grappling iron coming toward his brow. When it connected he fell backward, stumbling and falling. Frantic to save himself, he scrambled away, allowing Clarenceux to throw his shoulder at the tower door and shut it, pulling across the drawbar.

It took some moments for Clarenceux to get his breath back. He could hear Carew also breathing heavily in the darkness. "How badly wounded are you?"

"It's not important—it's manageable," Carew gasped. "Listen, I overheard one of the men say that the woman you are after—she is at Portchester Castle. There is a hospital there, where she is nursing. She was mistreated here by the garrison. Captain Parkinson sent her away."

"There's some good in the man then."

Carew inhaled through his teeth, feeling the pain. "It wasn't his will. He feared what Sir William Cecil would say, if he found out."

"We know too whom your enemy Denisot is working for. It must have been Cecil who gave him instructions to pay the captain of the *Davy*."

"I know. I realized that when you didn't reappear."

"Is that why you came looking for me?"

"More or less. As you once said, we're fighting our own wars—but we're allies." Carew coughed and spat. "If you can get to Cecil and confront him with what he has done, maybe you can save Skinner, Stars, Francis, and the others."

"They're a long way ahead. Sir Peter Carew left on the eighteenth; he will get to London in the next day or so."

"Not with an easterly wind, he won't. If you ride hard, change horses, you could do it."

"I need to see Rebecca first. To find out what happened to the document. Cecil will not listen to me unless I do."

Carew spat again, tasting blood. "Portchester is our next stop then."

"Do you think you can get there?"

"No—but trying to is—better than staying here. I left the boat in some undergrowth near where I set you ashore."

Clarenceux put his hand on the door. "We have to go out there."

"Maybe." Carew bent down and started gathering in the rope attached to his grappling iron.

Clarenceux thought. There was no way off the roof. He had ruled out jumping across the gatehouse in daylight; to do so in darkness would be madness. He felt blood trickling down from his forehead, where Parkinson's sword had grazed him. He wiped it away. "We have to go out of this door—we don't have a choice."

"We've always got a choice," muttered Carew. "There are always other options. Like in chess. Do you play chess, Mr. Clarenceux?"

"Of course."

"Situations are like chess. There's always a good move there somewhere. It's just you can't always see it."

"What do you suggest?"

"He could be outside that door, waiting for us. He could have climbed onto the plinth and pulled himself up into one of the embrasures and entered the tower by...by a first-floor window." Carew paused, breathing with difficulty. "He might be creeping down the stairs at this moment. Or he might have reckoned we have to leave by the gatehouse, so we need to raise the portcullis...and he might be waiting for us there."

"There are two of us. He cannot attack both of us at once."

"He will—if we are in the same place. This is Captain Parkinson we are talking about. I think it is best if we go our separate ways."

"What?"

"I'm going on ahead of you. Parkinson cannot get into this building through this door or through the basement." He breathed in sharply, with a hiss, struggling with the pain. "He can only climb up...and enter through the first floor, so that is the way I am going out. If he is there, I will fight him, and from the noise you will know where he is. Then you can safely get out through this door to the gatehouse. You'll need to go through the first-floor window as the portcullis is down. But if you hear nothing, then you will know it is safe to follow me."

"Where are you going?"

"The sea. Out of the embrasure, I am going to drop down into the yard and cross to the outer wall. Then I am going to climb through one of the embrasures there and lower myself into the moat. It's close to the sea—he cannot follow me there. I still have strength in my arms; I can still swim."

Both men listened for sounds of Parkinson in the darkness.

"You take the sword," said Clarenceux eventually. "You'd better go."

Carew lifted the rope and grappling iron. Clarenceux heard it scrape on the floor. "I can't swim with this rope," he said. "I'll leave it hanging from the outer wall."

Clarenceux heard the silence now. Not the silence of them not speaking but the greater silence that surrounded the fort and consumed them entirely—containing all that they were not saying. They were going to face a killer in the darkness. He himself was going to do so unarmed. And Carew, this man who was a hero to many but, as Clarenceux now realized, was like a lost boy wherever he was in the world—was going out to throw his wounded body into the sea.

"Clarenceux," whispered Carew, gritting his teeth. "Promise me you'll save the others."

"I will try."

"Don't let any of them die at Wapping." Carew exhaled slowly with the pain. "You always seem to do what you set out to, even if you make some damned-fool mistakes along the way. I trust you." He spat again, and breathed heavily with the pain. "What is my family's motto?"

"*J'espère bien*. I hope for good."

"Does your family have a motto?" asked Carew.

"No. But I am thinking of adopting one. 'In all our struggles, the last word is hope.'"

Carew reached out and put his hand on Clarenceux's shoulder. "You have 'hope' too, like the Carews. We may be different sorts of men, and we may believe different things and be on different sides of the law, but in that one thing—hope—we are brothers. And that is the most important thing." He paused. "Say good-bye to Amy and Ursula for me, and Alice."

Clarenceux felt Carew's hand move from his shoulder, then he heard him start up the stairs, dragging his feet. His progress seemed very slow. If Parkinson found him, he would not be able to run. Nor could he easily defend himself. He would not be able to do anything, in fact, but warn Clarenceux with his death.

It seemed that Carew was climbing the stairs for a very long time. In the darkness each step seemed to take a minute as he dragged his failing body toward its final destination, the sea. Clarenceux felt as if he should be helping him, but that would have defeated the whole plan. He could only wait and listen. Eventually the sound diminished so that there was hardly any noise at all. He could just hear Carew walking unsteadily across the first floor, stumbling against something in the middle of the room. Then there was silence.

Minutes passed. Clarenceux started to wonder when he should move. *What if Carew has been killed noiselessly? Parkinson will come looking for me.* He could hear nothing of Carew now, only the vaguest whistling of the wind through the tower. Had he heard that before? Or did it mean there was now a set of shutters open where before they had been closed? All he knew was that Carew had not shouted or clashed swords with Parkinson. That meant Parkinson was probably waiting outside this door, or in the gatehouse.

Clarenceux counted slowly until he reached one hundred and then started to move in the direction of the stairs. He touched the cold stone of the wall, balancing himself. Without a sword he felt vulnerable. He went up another step, placing his leather sole gently on the stone and increasing the weight, so his footfall was silent. Another step, still touching the wall, listening as he moved. Three minutes later he reached the turn in the stairs and went to take the last step into the first-floor room.

It was colder here. The fire had gone out, the window on the far side of the room was just visible, the darkness of the sky being the tiniest shade lighter than that of the room. Clarenceux paused. *Carew must have left the window open.* He stepped forward with more confidence.

Beside the window, Captain Parkinson waited.

Parkinson had heard Carew drop down from the tower and had watched the outline of the man as he limped into the sea. He knew it was Carew; Clarenceux was taller. He had let Carew go—Clarenceux was the important one. Parkinson had climbed into the tower the same way that Carew had climbed out. If Clarenceux followed, he would walk straight into him.

Clarenceux could hear the wind in the casement and the waves beyond the outer wall. As Parkinson held his sword ready, unable to see his prey but listening to him, Clarenceux took another step closer. He hesitated, barely five feet away in the darkness.

That hesitation was seconds long. Teetering on the very edge of stabbing him, Parkinson shifted his weight. His shoe made a tiny scraping noise on the stone floor. It was enough. Clarenceux realized he was not alone.

Suddenly, Parkinson lunged—and missed. Clarenceux heard the man move and heard the swish of the sword moving through the air as Parkinson sought him.

"Where are you?" Parkinson shouted, stepping toward Clarenceux and slashing with the sword. It caught Clarenceux's right arm, cut the cloth and the skin. Parkinson advanced, cutting again, catching Clarenceux—this time on the shoulder. He followed it up with an attempted thrust into his body. Clarenceux threw himself back across the room, toward the doorway, desperately feeling for the opening. Knowing the layout of the room better, Parkinson reached the doorway first, blocking Clarenceux's way. Frantic now, Clarenceux tried to push past him, getting in too close for Parkinson to use his sword. Parkinson grabbed Clarenceux around the neck and tried to stab him, but the herald seized his wrist, preventing him. Parkinson then attempted to wrestle him to the ground. Clarenceux elbowed him painfully in the gut, but still Parkinson did not let go. Reaching for the man's face, Clarenceux felt the bandage and tore it away as Parkinson yelled and tried again to throw him to the ground. Both men fell heavily on the stone floor and Parkinson's arm gave way. Clarenceux rolled quickly to one side, knowing the captain's sword arm was now free. He heard the blade strike stone and grabbed at the hilt; finding Parkinson's wrists, he tried to shake the sword from his grasp but the man was too strong.

Clarenceux knew he had only an instant to get away. Scrambling to his feet, he heard the clang of Parkinson's sword on the stone behind him as he pushed himself up the stairs, hoping to get up to the next room. Each man climbed as fast as he could, Parkinson falling a few feet behind as he struck out with the sword. Clarenceux stumbled on the body of Christopher Serres, allowing Parkinson to close on him; he felt a sharp cut as Parkinson's sword struck the back of his thigh. However, he forced himself on and up in the darkness—and then realized that he had trapped himself. There was no escape from the roof—none except leaping down from there to the gatehouse.

Clarenceux rushed out of the stairway. Making the sign of the cross on his heart, he stepped up onto the parapet beside the entrance and readied himself to jump. He recalled the twelve-foot gap down to the top of the gatehouse, and his heart failed him. He could not make the jump.

Stepping down from the parapet, he ran to hide beside one of the cannon. Parkinson did not immediately follow. Instead he waited at the top of the stairs, fumbling with something on his belt, before walking out slowly across the roof. He found the dead body that lay in the lee of the battlements and nudged it with his foot, holding his sword ready. He moved between the guns, tapping with his sword in the crevices and shadows.

Clarenceux looked up; the clouds were thinning, the silver half-moon was about to appear. The light would reveal him. He had to reach the stairs.

He felt a few pieces of gravel beneath his knees and threw them across to his left. Parkinson heard the noise and turned in that direction. The clouds began to part.

Parkinson was just a few feet to one side of his path but Clarenceux could wait no longer. Rising to his feet, he sprang forward, running straight across the roof. Wrong footed, Parkinson tried to sweep his sword around but was too slow. Clarenceux reached the stairs and found out that the door there was now closed. To his horror, it was also locked.

Parkinson could see Clarenceux clearly in the half-moonlight. He walked slowly toward him, raising his sword. Clarenceux tugged at the door again but his struggles were useless. Parkinson was ten feet away, eight, six. With a glance to his right, the herald once again saw the jump that he had not dared to make, its stomach-churning drop. But this time he could see the edge of the gatehouse wall in the moonlight. He made a decision, stepped onto the parapet, and hurled himself with all the force he could muster across the dark space.

It seemed he was a long time in the air, falling. Time crystallized. Each instant seemed to last for several seconds, and in each of those seconds, he felt the air rushing past him and heard the sounds of the night. Yet he did not have the time to think—only to feel. He did not even have the presence of mind to lift his legs or prepare to land. When he crashed heavily on the lead of the gatehouse roof, all the instants compressed themselves suddenly once more. His right knee hurt, his left shin, the ribs on his left side, his left shoulder, and his still-bleeding left hand, which had instinctively been protecting his head. He lay still, aware that he was not breathing. Then the desire for air came upon him overwhelmingly. Yet he could not breathe. He was suffocating, it seemed, unable to open his lungs. He reached out and steadied himself on all fours, finally drawing a sweet full breath. In that position, gasping still, he felt the various pains in his body begin to prioritize themselves, his left hand and ribs most of all. He could feel the wind on his face and hear the sound of the waves... and then the scrape of a drawbar being pulled across down below. Parkinson was coming after him.

Clarenceux struggled to his feet, holding on to the gatehouse battlements, and stepped along the edge of the roof, looking for a way down. The light of the moon revealed only a trapdoor—but he saw Parkinson's curl of rope around the stonework, hanging down above the gate. He limped over to it and tried its strength.

Inside the gatehouse, Parkinson was running up the stairs to the first-floor chamber. He reached the door as Clarenceux let himself down between the battlements, clutching the rope. Clarenceux's left hand hurt as if the Devil's claws were in it; his pierced right one was not much better, but he gritted his teeth and held on. Down he went, hand over hand, cursing and feeling a trickle of blood over his left wrist. He heard Parkinson's feet running across the floor of the guard chamber. He kicked away from the wall and tried to descend faster, but the panic made him lose his grip and he started to fall. He tried to slow himself but the rope tore through his hands. The agony was too much; he let go and crashed the last ten feet to the drawbridge.

Looking up, he could see Parkinson reaching for the rope. He struggled to his feet and limped as fast as he could away from the fort. Moonlight shimmered off the sea on both sides. He heard Parkinson land on the drawbridge and start running. The man was closing on him. As Clarenceux passed the cottages, Parkinson was just ten or twelve paces behind him. Veering off the path, he made for the jetty, where Carew had broken the boats, and ran into the sea, stumbling on the wet shingle through the shallows, until he was waist deep in the water. Then he started to swim. His ribs hurt with the effort but he pushed himself on, not stopping, fearing Parkinson's sword. He did not slow down nor turn until he had swum about eighty yards; then he pulled a few more strokes, listened, and looked back.

In the moonlight he could see the dark figure of Captain Parkinson still standing on the shore.

69

Sunday, May 21

Clarenceux swam across to the west bank of Southampton Water, finding his way by the shapes of the hills against the night sky. He hoped to find the place where Carew had left him the day before. He crawled out of the water, shaking with cold, and sat looking at the dark estuary, listening to the gentle waves. There was no sign of the boat; he was too tired to go looking for it. All he could do was listen to the waves and shiver. In that state he remained for about an hour before he moved to a clump of trees, lay down beneath some bushes, and rested. Later he slept.

The moment he awoke he was in a panic. It was daylight. Parkinson would be looking for him. Apart from the waves and the breeze in the trees above him, there was no sound. He cursed himself for not finding the boat before dawn. He had to get to Portchester discreetly and as quickly as possible.

It took him half an hour to find Carew's boat. There were no oars, which presented him with a problem as he had very little experience of sailing. Also, the tide was halfway out. But having hauled it down to the water, he attempted to use the rear sail. After a few minutes he managed to catch enough wind to move in more or less the right direction. In combination with the rudder he sailed eastward, aided by the wind coming up the Channel.

He reckoned the time was about seven o'clock. There were already some larger ships coming into Southampton Water and others departing. Several large waves smacked against the side of the boat, splashing him and chilling him again. With every moment of the crossing, he prayed that he would reach the far side of the estuary before Parkinson's men saw him.

An hour later he landed. With the tide completely out, he drew the vessel up onto the shingle beach and started to walk inland. He knew from itineraries he had consulted during his travels as a herald that Portchester was a little way to the east, in the middle of Portsmouth harbor. Every step that took him further away from Southampton Water seemed a blessing; every step took him nearer to Portchester, to Rebecca and to the answer to where the document had gone.

The land here was relatively flat, but many trees and bushes blocked his view. He found a lane and started to follow it. A couple of farmhands leading a bull confirmed that he was heading the right way. "Go on here until you come to the Fareham Road," said one of them, "then turn left. The bridge at Fareham is what you need. It's about an hour on foot. And the best part of an hour after that to the castle."

Clarenceux thanked them and started walking briskly along the lane. What was he going to say to Rebecca? Up until now he had thought it would be easy. There would be a confrontation and he would demand that she return the document she had stolen from him. As he walked through the trees overlooking the estuary, he knew things were not that simple. Carew had said Parkinson's men had abused her. It was not the first time it had happened. Many men saw widows as outside the usual order of things. Such women had no father or husband to guard them, no protector to claim that family honor had been impugned. If such women were attacked away from home, they had very few defenses. He felt for her—but that was not why things had changed. He now understood that she had not stolen the document willingly: the Knights had made her do it. She had been trapped by Sir William Cecil, who had sent word ahead to Captain Parkinson to send a man to receive her. She had not just been maltreated at Calshot; at every step of the way she had been manipulated—by the Knights and by Cecil too. No doubt Cecil had made her give up the document. There could be no confrontation. The best he could hope for was to find out who had taken it from her.

He stopped beneath some beech trees and began to reflect. He himself had told Parkinson that he had come to find Rebecca Machyn. Parkinson knew Rebecca was at Portchester—Carew had heard him say so. Parkinson knew where he was going.

He started to run. *What if Parkinson has sent men on ahead? He is captain of Southampton as well as Calshot—does he have command of Portchester too? No, that is presumably the person in charge of the hospital, in the absence of whichever nobleman has the income for the official title of constable of the castle. Who is that? Sir Henry Radcliffe, brother of the earl of Sussex. But he is in Ireland. His deputy is not in a position to resist Parkinson.*

Clarenceux came to the Fareham Road, panting, his chest bursting with pain, especially around his bruised ribs, desperate to stop. But he did not let himself; the farmhands had said it would be an hour to the bridge and an hour beyond that. He turned left, around some trees. *If Parkinson sent men at dawn, they would be there by now. If so, there is no point in running. But maybe Parkinson has not been so quick; he does not know that I know where Rebecca is.*

He looked for a turning westward, to the harbor. Soon he found one, leading past a couple of old farmhouses. At the second farmhouse a dog barked and ran at him, attempting halfheartedly to bite at his heels. He did not slow down but went straight on, east. He would not go all the way to Fareham Bridge; he would swim the river.

He reached the trees above the beach on the edge of Portsmouth harbor and stepped down to the water. He could see the castle on his left, on the promontory jutting out into the harbor, about three miles away. Within those massive Roman walls was the medieval castle, which he had visited once, with its tall square keep and royal palace. In the outer bailey was the priory church and the buildings now used as a hospital. Three miles to the southeast he could see the narrow mouth of the estuary, where Portsmouth and its naval dockyard were situated. He could just see the church and houses along the foreshore, in between the ships scattered about the huge natural harbor.

Taking a deep breath, Clarenceux started running along the fishermen's path at the top of the beach, which wove between the trees and bushes. He could see the mouth of the river now, and the trees on the far side. Ahead was a long overgrown inlet, its banks muddy with the low tide. He did not hesitate but splashed through, swimming for a few strokes when the water came up to his chest, and then running on. He was heading for a point he could see directly ahead. There was a small wooden jetty there, with a rowing boat. For a moment he thought it meant an easy crossing. Then he saw that, once again, there were no oars. He walked to the end of the jetty and jumped into the shallow water and started to wade toward the deeper flow. Low tide meant that the river was only four hundred yards wide. Portchester Castle was within three miles.

70

Rebecca Machyn watched Mr. Wheatsheafen, the surgeon, as he drew the specially sharpened small knife from his set of tools. He was a kindly man, a little too portly to be able to move around the confined space with ease. She knelt by the wounded sailor's bed and set the bowl beneath his elbow, pulling away a loose piece of straw that was poking through the old mattress. The patient's shirtsleeve had already been rolled up and pinned so it would not be made dirty by the bleeding. His inner arm was punctuated with the scars of earlier cuts. He was about twenty years of age and bearded. His head was in a bandage.

"You've been bled a good few times before, William," said Mr. Wheatsheafen.

"Those were precautionary," the sailor replied, blinking. His eyes were bloodshot. "My father used to say that to be bled once a moon was the best way to be sure of a long life."

Wheatsheafen smiled. "Yes, well, we're not living in the dark ages now. I don't believe in bleeding unless it's necessary. Are you ready, Nurse Machyn?"

Rebecca nodded. William tensed his muscles and looked at the roof beams. His toes squirmed as the surgeon carefully felt for the basilic vein and pressed deeply, cutting through the skin. Blood seeped rapidly into the cut and then began to flow steadily into the bowl Rebecca held.

"How was his urine this morning?" asked Wheatsheafen as he watched the blood. He dabbed a finger in the bowl, raised it to his lips, and tasted it.

"Still cloudy and brown, but not as brown as yesterday," Rebecca replied.

"And the smell?"

Rebecca hesitated. "I'm sorry, Mr. Wheatsheafen. I do not know how to describe it. I've kept the flask, as you suggested. I will get it for you after this."

"Good. Yes, I will have a sniff. Now, just a minute more and then this sacrificial lamb will have shed quite enough blood to improve his health." He looked at the patient. "Get those humors back in balance, eh, William? Calm those turbulent brown waters of yours." Wheatsheafen lowered his voice and bent closer to Rebecca's ear. "Have you looked at that dressing on Brownjohn's leg this morning?"

Rebecca did not look away from the bleeding. "I know it is unhealthy to move a dressing unnecessarily. So I left it as it was."

Wheatsheafen nodded. "I agree. And I understand. I would not want to move it either. But you know what we are likely to see?"

"I fear so, Mr. Wheatsheafen."

"You're a good woman, Nurse Machyn."

"Indeed she is," said William, looking at her as she staunched the flow and wound the bandage around his arm. "There is something about a pair of brown eyes that makes being bled much sweeter."

"Quite," replied Wheatsheafen. "The medicine of beauty is a

wonderful thing. I hope you can stay here, Nurse Machyn. Or may we call you Rebecca?"

"You may call me Rebecca, if you wish," she said, getting to her feet. "As for staying…I have no pressing commitments elsewhere. If you need me here for another week or another month, then let us see. I never meant to come here but, now I have employment, I feel more at home than I have done since my husband died."

"There you go, William," said Wheatsheafen. "Your prayers are answered. You are bound to be cured of that blessed head wound of yours, with both Rebecca's loving care and my surgical knife." Then to Rebecca he said, "Come, we must attend to Brownjohn."

Rebecca followed Mr. Wheatsheafen along the hall, past the hearth and five other beds to where a young man of seventeen lay. He was lying on his side, shivering with fever; his chin covered in stubble, his dark hair a mess, his brow covered in sweat.

Mr. Wheatsheafen gestured to Rebecca to remove the bandage that covered his right leg. "How are you feeling, John?" he asked.

John did not stir or look up. "Chilled as a reptile, hot as a fire. More in pain than the dead. More dead than in pain."

Rebecca started cutting the bandage with a pair of scissors. The smell of the necrotic flesh was nauseating: Wheatsheafen watched her out of a corner of one eye. She gagged with the smell but continued cutting. Slowly the bandage came away to reveal a horrifying sight. The flesh of the young man's lower leg had rotted away on the outer side, leaving a greenish-yellow mess around the bone. Lower, the blackness of gangrene had consumed the foot. The two smaller toes were shriveled and blackened, and looked like those of a long-buried corpse; the larger ones simply were not there. Flesh, bones, tissue—everything had rotted away, leaving a suppurating indent of green slime in that part of the blackened foot.

Rebecca closed her eyes, struggling with the smell and the urge to be sick.

"I've seen worse," said Wheatsheafen brightly, looking hard at the area of the lost toes and the rotten leg. "But that is too far gone to use either leeches or maggots. It seems to me best, John, if we take you through to the fire in the clerks' hall. You'd like some mutton, wouldn't you? And some chicken broth. Rebecca, would you go and fetch Robert and Christopher from the castle, to help carry John? And fetch two quarts of sack from the store for our young friend, to ease his pain."

He gave her a knowing look. She understood. They were going to have to cut off the young man's leg, and it would take three of them to hold him down after they had got him drunk and tied him to the chair. Few men could stay calm while a surgeon sawed through the bone. Still holding her breath and looking white as a sheet, she stood up and walked down the center of the hall past the beds, to the door, and out into the bright light.

There was a girl waiting there, about ten years of age, with long brown hair and a slightly grubby mulberry dress. Rebecca recognized her as one of the villagers' daughters. "Are you Widow Machyn?" the girl inquired.

Rebecca was still feeling ill. She did not want to speak. She took a deep breath and looked at the girl. "I am. Why do you need to know?"

"There's a man come to see you," she said nervously. "He said to tell you, if you be still at liberty, please to meet with him immediately."

Rebecca glanced across the rutted mud and grassy tufts of the outer bailey to the gatehouse. No one was rushing toward them; there seemed no immediate danger. Why say "if you be at liberty"? She began to walk toward the castle in the corner of the bailey. "Did he tell you his name?"

"Clarion…Clarying—something like that." The girl was walking beside her.

Rebecca stopped. "Clarenceux?"

"Yes, that's the name," the girl said, pleased with herself. Then she saw the look on Rebecca's face. "Have I said something wrong?"

For what seemed a long time, Rebecca did not move or say anything. Then she asked, "No, no…What color hair does this man have? Is he bearded? What is he wearing?"

The girl looked back toward the gatehouse, as if she wanted to run away.

"His hair is curled, black, and he has a beard the same color. He is a very tall man, and very dirty and wet, from the river."

"Oh my God." Rebecca looked back at the long barracks building that served as the hospital hall, where she had just been. She could not leave now, whatever the problem. She knelt down beside the girl, holding her hand. "This is important. Take Mr. Clarenceux to Widow Baker's house, as quickly as you can. If Widow Baker is there, tell her that I need to speak to Mr. Clarenceux and that she should look after him until I am free of my duties here. If she is not there, tell Mr. Clarenceux to conceal himself in the yard. I will come as soon as I can. Go now, quickly."

Rebecca was distracted throughout the operation on young Brownjohn. He had not reacted well to the news that he would lose his leg. Mr. Wheatsheafen had explained how the gangrene would kill him if the leg was not taken off. "It is a very simple choice," he told him. "You can either live with one leg or die with two."

What followed was a half-hour of trauma. They forced Brownjohn to drink too much wine, tying his body and leg to the seat and his gangrenous foot to a small trestle. They applied a tourniquet, gagging

him, and then tying him tighter. Then there had been the waiting—
the awful waiting—while the knives and saws were revealed and
arranged. Mr. Wheatsheafen had made a deep incision, to slice
through the good flesh, well above the knee. Blood had flowed.
Brownjohn had bucked and struggled in his bonds while the two men
held him with ropes and Rebecca pressed her face to his, trying to
comfort him in the only way she knew. Then, when Wheatsheafen
finally had sliced through the flesh, exposing the muscle, sinew, veins
and fat, he picked up the saw. This terrified the young man even
more than the slicing through his flesh. The men from the castle
were hard pressed to hold him still and the sound of the blade grating
through the bone was terrible; but they were strong and experienced.
Rebecca put her hands over John's eyes and kissed him, trying to
soothe him while the sawing was in progress. When it was done, and
the severed limb was lying in a bucket, she dressed the wound as Mr.
Wheatsheafen directed, although her hands were trembling. Later,
when Brownjohn was more at peace and drowsy, and the gag had
been removed, she cleaned the sweat and grime from his brow.

She turned away from Brownjohn and looked at Mr. Wheatsheafen,
who was washing his hands in a bucket of water. She waited until he
had finished, then washed her own hands. As she did so, and he dried
his on a towel, she said to him, "I have to go now."

"Was it the cutting? There are other patients to see to; attending
to them will help you forget this."

"No, it's not me. It's not the cutting. I have to see someone
urgently, at Widow Baker's."

Wheatsheafen said nothing at first. "Come back as soon as you
can, Rebecca. You know how much you are needed here." He handed
her the towel. "I appreciate your work. Most good women only want

to look after their own kin, or attend to babies and children. Few and far are the kind souls who really care for others."

Rebecca put down the towel and turned toward the door. Opening it, she stopped and drew back. Striding toward the long hospital hall from the outer gatehouse were two men. One of them was Captain Parkinson.

"Rebecca, is everything all right?" asked Wheatsheafen.

"Those men," she said. She turned to him and spoke urgently. "I need to get back to the village, Mr. Wheatsheafen. I need your help. Please. Those men out there are looking for me."

"You have a past that is not yet past. I thought you were too good to be true."

"No, believe me—I am going to come back here. I mean to stay and help with the hospital. But the man who is waiting for me—it is complicated. I need to talk to him. I cannot begin to tell you how serious this is. I must hide…"

"There is a path around the walls," said Wheatsheafen, "from the Watergate."

"I'll show her the way," said Robert. "There's a door that leads out of the back of this building; the path will take us to the churchyard. From there it is easy to reach the gate."

"Thank you. Quickly, I must go now," she said.

"When will you be back?" asked Wheatsheafen.

"Later today, I hope."

"Good luck. I look forward to your return. Your past is mysterious—I am intrigued."

71

Rebecca was nervous as she followed Robert through the churchyard. She knew that at any moment she could be called back by Parkinson. What then? Robert was from the castle garrison, a royal soldier; he could not disobey Captain Parkinson. But no one did call her. They passed the far side of the church and approached the gate facing the water. No one stopped them as they went out that way and walked between the old walls and the beach, eventually finding the path that led into the village.

Widow Baker lived in a cottage on a bend in the lane leading back to Fareham. She also assisted in the naval hospital in the castle, where Rebecca had been helping for the last week. Hers was the only house outside the walls Rebecca had visited; it was more in hope than in confidence that she had directed Clarenceux there. Hence she felt doubly nervous as she approached. She bade Robert to return to the castle when she was within sight of the cottage.

It was not a pretty building. The thatch needed attention and there was a shirt hanging from an open upstairs window. The door was locked, which suggested Widow Baker was out. Rebecca knocked with her knuckles; there was no answer. She walked around the side of the house across the dusty yard, toward a hen house and a partly collapsed, ivy-covered cart house at the rear.

Clarenceux saw her approaching and stepped out slightly from where he was hiding, behind the cart house. He looked awful. His hair and beard were filthy, his shoulder covered in blood, his forehead cut, his clothes torn, and his legs covered in mud. He was clutching his side, where his ribs were causing him pain. His clothes were all wet and he was shivering. His hands were covered in dried blood. Everything about him was changed from the proud herald she had known in London. Only the intense dark eyes were the same.

He said nothing. He looked at her dowdy clothes, her blood-flecked smock and gown, her coif and plain leather shoes. She had always had an air of tragic beauty about her, a terrible sadness that made the expression in her brown eyes seem all the more moving; but now that sadness seemed also to speak about other people's suffering.

"You are wet," she said at last.

He swallowed and felt the tears well up in his eyes. "I had to swim the river. I was lucky—Carew killed all Parkinson's men and destroyed his boats at Calshot, so he had to—"

"Carew? Who is he?"

Clarenceux was about to explain but suddenly the recent past did not seem important. Looking into her eyes he saw the same affection, the same loveliness he had always seen in her. He longed to hold her but he knew he looked and smelled disgusting. And under it all there was the knowledge that she had betrayed him.

"I need to know what happened—about the document," he said hoarsely. "I need to know why you agreed to take it."

Rebecca looked away. "I wish there was somewhere we could go to talk."

"Tell me here. Now, right now." There was more force in his voice than he intended.

She looked back at him. "Very well. My life has been hell ever since last December. First my husband died. You remember that? They tortured him to death. Then there was that sheer panic as you and I struggled to stay alive. And then, when all was well again for me, they started to use me…"

"Who?"

"The Knights of the Round Table and Mrs. Barker. By God's love, was I mistaken about her. I was so grateful for her care and attention when Henry died, but all the time she was just trying to get close to me, to get the document from me. After I told her you had it, she changed. She became more insistent. She would send a man for me and entertain me with rich food and give me money, and always she would slip in questions about you and your family. She wanted to know whether we had met, whether we had been intimate, whether I had seen the document in your house. She asked where you kept your books, how often you entertained friends and guests, and how often you went down to the country. When I stopped going to see her, in March, she sent two men to demand I come to her. When I refused, they hauled me there. You can guess the rest."

"No, no, I can't. Tell me."

Rebecca sighed and spoke with her eyes closed. "Mrs. Barker and the three men who were always there demanded that I steal the document from you. At first they asked kindly, then they tried to bribe me. They offered me two hundred pounds for it, then two hundred and fifty, then three hundred…"

"Why did you not tell me?"

"Because they said if I told you, they would have to resort to a different strategy. They were going to take your wife and daughters and threaten to drown them in front of you unless you gave them what they wanted. And no doubt they would have used me similarly. They knew I loved you and that you were fond of me. They *knew* that."

The words she had just spoken, so long whispered in Clarenceux's mind, words of love, touched his heart.

Rebecca raised her hands in desperation. "What could I do? Eventually I had to give them something, so I said I would help. They told me they had a plan. On a certain day, my brother was to help me break into your house—blacksmiths are good at these things. The other Knights were to come with us too, and some of their helpers, to distract you or to overpower you and anyone else who might be in the house. The next morning, Robert and I would be taken by ship to the north. We were to be lodged at a place that had been arranged, and then we were to go on into Scotland by road, when it was safe, to meet the Queen of Scots and give her the document in person. The day set for the theft was a Saturday, in the afternoon. But that morning my brother came to me and told me to go with him immediately, and to bring nothing but the clothes I was standing up in. He led me to the docks, where we boarded a boat, the *Davy*, which took us to Southampton."

Clarenceux was dumbfounded. "You did not steal the document?"

Rebecca looked at him, puzzled. "It was taken? I did not know."

"I thought that you would be able to tell me who had taken it from you."

"Surely it was Mrs. Barker and the Knights?"

"No. They interrogated me, wanting to know where it had gone and where you…" He raised his hands slowly. "O, Lord Almighty—it was

Cecil." Clarenceux struck his forehead. "Cecil gave the instructions for you to be brought to Calshot. He preempted the theft by removing you and took the document himself. Such duplicity…What happened to your brother?"

"He abandoned me. A man called Prouze was sent to collect us from the port. There was a delay. When we arrived at Calshot, Captain Parkinson was not there. After one day of waiting, my brother said he was only supposed to accompany me as far as the fort…" She stopped and put her hand to her mouth, nauseated by the memory. "They were just flirtatious at first, and I played along. Then one evening they got drunk." She swallowed, choking back her memory. "How could he leave me there? How could anyone regard their kin so coldly and be so selfish?" Then she wiped her eyes and said wearily, "Now, you must tell me: why have you come here?"

"When I set out to find you, it was because I believed you had stolen the document on behalf of Mrs. Barker. Then I thought you had stolen it in league with Nicholas Denisot. Now I realize that Cecil used you to mislead both me and the Knights. This journey…" Clarenceux shut his eyes, thinking back. He remembered being tied to the rope and dragged from the *Davy*, Kahlu plunging the knife through his hand, firing the cannon at the boatload of boarders, attacking Sir Peter Carew's ship, being locked in the magazine at Calshot Fort, and fighting Parkinson in the darkness before making that jump onto the gatehouse roof. "This journey, which has been the worst experience of my life, has all been in vain—except for one thing. I have seen you again, and you are alive."

"That is nothing; it is unimportant."

A tear ran down his cheeks into his beard. Then another. "No, it is not unimportant. For if you had just disappeared, I would never have been happy. I would never have forgotten you, but always would have worried about you, not knowing what had happened."

Rebecca looked at his clothes. "You need to wash and dress in something else before you go anywhere. And those wounds need attention."

"I have no clothes—these are borrowed. I am a hundred miles from home, sodden, covered in mud, without a penny, let alone enough to sustain me. If the wound in my shoulder goes bad and kills me, it will probably be the best thing that has happened since…" He wiped his face on his sleeve. "I've reached the end, Rebecca. I can't think or act anymore."

"William, this is not like you," she said, dismayed. "You are always so strong, so purposeful. I have never before heard you admit defeat. True, you have made yourself a powerful enemy in Sir William Cecil—I always thought you should not have trusted him as much as you did—but you are still standing. You are still alive. So am I. Where are Awdrey and your daughters? Are they safe?"

Clarenceux shrugged. "I do not know. They went down to Julius's house. Since then I have heard nothing."

"You have lost no one. You have some cuts, that is all. Some dents to your pride. I myself have been treated shamefully and unkindly. I have been made to feel like a whore—worse, for a whore is at least paid. A whore can at least say no. I have been stripped of my dignity, my home—everything. Yet I am not beaten. I have not 'reached the end,' as you put it. In fact, I have found something in this last week that is good and true. I have found that I can be useful to some people, and valued. After months of doubt and shame, I have at last found a place where I can make a kind gesture and it is appreciated. And I can do an unpleasant task and be respected for it, not scorned or insulted for lowering myself. I have rediscovered what it is to be a woman in a world ruled by men. I can help and heal and caress and encourage—and all these things touch men's and women's hearts equally. I may only have been here a few days, and I might have had to go through hell to get here, but I have glimpsed the path I will take from now on."

Clarenceux listened. Tears of shame came to his eyes. Tears of shame for the way he had presumed he knew her and what she wanted. Tears of shame because he had thought of her only in terms of his own desire for her womanliness, even though he could never offer her more than friendship. If he had thought of her in any other way, it was that she had betrayed him. He had never properly understood the trauma of the months since her husband had died. Now he was glad for her. Mingled among those tears of shame and regret were tears of another kind. Not of joy but of satisfaction, the sort that is not a momentary ecstasy but the result of completeness and harmony.

Rebecca stepped forward and wiped his face with the sleeve of her dress. He took her hand and pressed it to his bearded cheek. "I am sorry for the pain I caused you," he said. "I am sorry for suspecting you betrayed me. I am sorry that in trying to protect me you have suffered. I am glad for you now, that you have found your path. I am glad." He kissed her hand.

Rebecca looked at the wound in his right hand and the blood caked on his doublet. She reached down for his left hand and looked at that, inspecting the fresh cuts, the missing fingernails. "When Parkinson has gone, I will take you to the hospital and—"

Clarenceux withdrew his hand. "Parkinson is here? He will be looking for you too."

"Only because of you. Sir William Cecil ordered him to keep me safely. I will not be in danger when you have gone."

At that moment, Rebecca turned; an old woman with a clean

white headscarf was walking slowly along the side of the house into the yard, her expression apprehensive. When she saw them, she relaxed and walked toward them. "Oh, Rebecca, Mr. Wheatsheafen told me you had come to meet someone at my cottage, and that I should leave off the washing of sheets and make sure all is well."

Rebecca nodded. "Thank you, Margaret. This is Mr. William Harley, Clarenceux King of Arms." She turned to him. "Although his appearance is somewhat less refined than usual, he is a good man and has come a long way to see me on a matter of importance. I hope you do not mind us using the yard of your cottage for our conversation."

"Of course I do not mind, Rebecca. Can I offer you and Mr. Harley some refreshment? Would Mr. Harley like to wash?"

Clarenceux nodded. "Some hot water would be most welcome," he replied.

72

Captain Parkinson glared across the table at the lieutenant of Portchester Castle. "You assured me that you would keep a close watch on her. As Sir Henry Radcliffe's representative, you should know better than to break your word or shirk your duties. Where is she now?"

The lieutenant was a man of about forty, his hair flecked with gray. He rose from his seat. "Captain, I have two things to say in reply. First, I am no man's jailer—nor any woman's either. You entrusted this woman to my safekeeping and I gave her work in the hospital. She was there this morning, and as far as I can see, she is still under my protection."

"You let her go. You let her escape."

The lieutenant continued, "The second thing I have to say is that, if you wish to speak to her, I suggest you wait until she returns. As Mr. Wheatsheafen has told you, she will not be gone long. He has every confidence she will be back."

"She has gone to meet the man who killed four of my men at Calshot."

"Really? You told me that that was the pirate, Raw Carew. This man, Clarenceux, seems to have killed no one."

"Damn it, the two men were together—Clarenceux and Carew—

last night. I stabbed Carew and he threw himself into the sea. Clarenceux was coming here to see the widow. So if she has suddenly disappeared off to meet someone, I have no doubt who it is."

"Then why do you not simply follow Mr. Wheatsheafen's advice and ride after them? Portsmouth is not far. You are wasting time talking to me. If you really do believe she is going back to London, go after her."

Parkinson smashed his fist down on the table and shouted his reply. "Because I do not believe that fat surgeon."

"Captain Parkinson, if you do not believe Mr. Wheatsheafen or anyone else under my authority, that is your problem. You have given me no reason to believe that my men are deceiving you, still less that they are deceiving *me*—and in any case, it is not against the law to tell a lie. Nor to conceal a truth. What is against the law is to accuse my men or Mr. Wheatsheafen of dishonesty. That is defamation of character and is punishable in the church courts—as you would know, if you ever went to church. Now I must ask you to return to your post—at Calshot or Southampton. I have nothing more to say on the matter."

Parkinson searched for some response. Nothing came to mind.

The lieutenant placed his hands on the table. "While you are here, I will offer you a word of advice. Sir Henry is aware of the way you manage things at Southampton. He has so far withheld from writing to Sir William Cecil on the matter, but your continued willfulness and extortion of the local population will not serve your reputation any favors."

Parkinson marched from the room without another word.

73

Widow Baker wrung out Clarenceux's shirt over the tub in which he was bathing as Rebecca washed around the cut in his arm and the stab wound near his shoulder. She carried the wet shirt across to the other side of the room. "I won't put this one near the fire, or it will smell of smoke. I have a trick for drying shirts, my dear. A flat stone. Once the stone is hot, it dries the shirt quite quickly and flattens the creases too."

Rebecca turned back to Clarenceux and spoke in a quiet voice. "Where will you go? Are there no heraldic gentlemen in these parts you could call on?"

"None that I know personally. I have never undertaken a visitation of Hampshire. I have passed through here a few times over the years, when sailing abroad or traveling to the West Country. But that is all. Besides, I have to go back to London. To see Cecil."

He flinched as she washed the cut on his forehead. "I'm sorry," she said, dabbing at the blood.

"No matter," he replied. "First, I am going to Southampton. I have to pass on the news about Raw Carew to the women he left behind there, in the Two Swans."

"Did you say you are going to Southampton?" asked Widow Baker, returning across the room. "You should catch the carter, Roger. He's my son-in-law. He'll take you."

"There's your carriage," said Rebecca. "Who are these women at the Two Swans?"

"Prostitutes."

"Really? That is not like you."

Clarenceux went a little red. "They are sisters called Amy and Ursula and a woman called Alice. All were friends of Raw Carew's. I promised I would pass on his farewell message to them. Alice he had known for years. Amy was his sweetheart. Although so was Ursula, I gather. His personal life seems to have been a little confused. They both held him in a special regard."

"Lucky man."

Clarenceux thought about this. He was at first inclined to agree; but then he thought of the long days and nights at sea, the poor food, the fear, the alienation, and the not being accepted anywhere. Then he thought of the man limping off into the sea, still bleeding from his guts. "No. Everything he had, he had to fight for. And the women weren't his, as such, like wives. In fact, he had to share them with any man who paid—and many men did. Including John Prouze, the man who took you to Calshot."

"Ah—*that* Amy. Now I remember. The men at the fort mentioned her. They suggested I be taken to the Two Swans 'for safekeeping, like Amy.' Is she pretty?"

"Yes. But probably not for long. Her sister Ursula has a large scar across her face. Sooner or later it will happen to Amy too."

"Sooner or later it happens to all of us. It doesn't always show though."

Clarenceux looked at her. "You are not the only one who feels it, you know. I carry scars too—some because of you, some because of what you have suffered, and some because of what my wife has suffered on account of me."

"Scars that can be concealed are easily overlooked."

Clarenceux stayed only an hour and a half longer at Widow Baker's house. While he was still in the bath, Rebecca shaved off his beard to make him less noticeable in the streets. Afterward he waited in a towel while both women worked on drying his clothes with hot stones. While he dressed, Widow Baker heated some pottage that she had cooked the previous evening, adding a small portion of mutton that she had put by for her Sunday dinner, and shared it with them. Then she led Clarenceux and Rebecca through the back paths to the carter's house, avoiding the lanes as far as possible. The carter agreed to take Clarenceux into town and lent him a hat and cloak for the journey. In the yard, standing beside the cart, Clarenceux gave his thanks to the old lady and then turned to Rebecca.

"I don't know how to say good-bye to you," he said.

"You don't have to. Maybe when people part for the last time it is better that they do not say anything."

"Especially if they love each other."

"Yes, especially," she said. A tear ran down the side of her face.

"My dear, you shouldn't be letting him go, if he feels so tenderly about you," the Widow Baker said kindly. "It's a marked rare thing in a man. And he doesn't look so bad when he's cleaned up."

"Thank you for your kind words, Margaret," said Clarenceux, wiping away his own tears. "Look after her. I find it very hard to leave her. She once told me it was best for both of us if we never met again. And now I know it, in my mind." He stepped forward, put his arms around Rebecca, and kissed her on the lips. "Not good-bye but thank you," he said as their lips parted.

"Be brave, be careful," she replied in a whisper.

He climbed onto the cart and turned, waving once. He could not smile; it hurt too much. Instead he faced forward, along the lane. He did not look back again. He wanted to preserve the thought that he could turn around and look at her just once more for as long as he could, even after the cart had passed out of sight of the village.

74

Clarenceux was in a melancholy state when he arrived in Southampton. He walked through the alleys to the Two Swans trying not to think of Rebecca. He tried to think of Carew instead, and of what he was going to say to Sir William Cecil, but his thoughts inevitably swung back to her. There was a pain in his chest at the thought that he would never see her again.

When he walked into the Two Swans there was the familiar smell of old wine and woodsmoke in the air. Four men were discussing their business at one table, two merchants were sitting at another. Clarenceux recognized no one except Marie Gervys, serving a plate of cold beef and bread to the merchants. At first she didn't recognize him but looked at his clothes, realizing they had belonged to her husband.

"It's William Harley, the Clarenceux herald."

"Ah." Marie gestured to his face. "The beard."

"Yes, I cut it off. Tell me, is either Amy or Ursula here? I have news for them."

Marie beckoned Clarenceux closer. "Amy has gone with a man who owns a skiff she borrowed. Really she is looking for Carew, though. Ursula has paying company."

For a moment the incongruity of Ursula's position hit Clarenceux. No doubt she had to be all smiles and soft and loving, despite the fear of what might have happened at Calshot. "Where is Alice?"

"In the hall at the back. Go through the door over there," she said, pointing.

Clarenceux thanked her and went over to the door.

Alice was kneeling beside a large tub of hot water, singing a tune as she washed sheets. Steam rose into the air. She hauled out a length of material and started rubbing it on the scrubbing board. Clarenceux could smell the potash of the soap. He watched her for a few moments, her upper arms wobbling as she scrubbed, her ample breasts bouncing with the movement of her body. There was a child near her, Amy's son, dressed in a linen smock, playing in the dirt of the floor with a stick.

Clarenceux coughed. Alice turned around.

"Oh, it's you, Mr. Clarenceux," she said amiably. Then she stopped and let the sheet slip into the water. "Where is he?"

Clarenceux walked closer and crouched down beside her. "I have to say, it does not look good. He asked me to say good-bye to you, and to Ursula and Amy."

"What happened?" She remained kneeling, her hands now on the edge of the tub.

"He came to my rescue at Calshot. He freed me from the room where I was held and then helped me escape. But he was badly wounded. He is probably still out at sea, or at best lying wounded on a beach somewhere."

Clarenceux stood up and walked across the hall to where there were two small benches side by side. The child laughed, playing with his stick, smiling up at Alice. Clarenceux picked both benches up and carried them back to the tub. He placed one down for Alice and sat on the other himself. He began to tell her everything, from the moment that Carew had set him down on the beach away from the jetty. He told her about his meeting with Parkinson and about being imprisoned. He talked about listening to Carew as, one by one, he picked off the soldiers, and about their desperate bid for freedom.

"So," said Alice grimly. "The Robin Hood of the High Seas is floating out there on the waves somewhere. Possibly forever more."

The child threw his stick out of reach and started crawling toward it.

"I presume that's Amy's son? Is he better now?"

"He's Amy's. Raw's too—or so Amy says. That's why he's called Ralph."

"Raw's? But…he never said anything about a son."

Alice shrugged. "If Raw had acknowledged all the children he'd fathered, he'd soon forget which ones he'd acknowledged and which weren't his. As he saw it, he'd never really know if this boy was his or not, unless he grew up to look like him. He loved all children dearly—he went out of his way to help a girl we found aboard the *Davy*—but he would never take responsibility for one of his own. He thought looking after children was a woman's job. He thought quite a lot of things were women's work. It's what comes of him being brought up in a whorehouse."

Clarenceux felt guilty, having left Carew out at sea, not having gone to search for him—having practically abandoned him.

Alice sighed. "I feel very sad. When all is said and done, he was my oldest friend and the man who did more to help me than any other man I ever met in my life. He gave me shelter, he gave me purpose and friends, he gave me money, and he protected me. I know he killed people, stole, blackmailed, murdered, seduced—I know all that. But he loved, cherished, protected, helped, and gave hope too. When we sailed with him, we knew who we were and that we were in the hands of a good commander. I am going to miss him terribly."

"I am sorry," said Clarenceux. "But he did think of the three of you when he knew he was facing death. And who knows? He may still be alive, on a beach somewhere, recovering his strength. Maybe in a few days he will walk through the door of this inn."

Alice dried her hands on a towel at her side and stood up, steadying her large frame on the edge of the tub. "You don't believe that, Mr. Clarenceux, and you saw him last. Your coming here has been a brave thing. If I thought for one moment you had betrayed him, I would have torn you to pieces with my bare hands. But you would not have come here to tell me of his loss unless you felt that you had to. I know it is your conscience that moves you."

Clarenceux leaned forward, his elbows on his knees, his hands together. "In that case, if you trust me, I need your help. Raw made me promise something else too. To help the other prisoners—Skinner, Francis, Stars, and the other men that Sir Peter Carew is taking to London. Sir Peter sailed three days ago; maybe they are already there. Maybe Sir Peter is sailing up the Thames with one man hanging dead from each of the yards of his ship—I don't know. But yesterday, as we sailed to Calshot, Carew said the wind would be holding him up. If I can borrow a horse strong and swift enough, I could get to see Sir William Cecil and ask him to pardon the men."

"Why would Sir William Cecil agree to pardon our friends—even though they be your friends and you a gentleman? He thinks they are pirates."

"Because I will go to him and tell him that I know what he has done. I will tell him what he is guilty of. I will show him that his immortal soul is in danger."

Alice looked down at him. Putting two fingers under his chin she lifted his face, making him rise to his feet. "You are going to have to do better than that. Sir William Cecil is a man of power. You understand power, don't you? It is a sort of religion. It demands total obedience. It requires men to make the ultimate sacrifice. It makes a man think differently about his soul—and gives him the authority to kill. I doubt Sir William Cecil will take kindly to your request."

"But we have to do something!" Clarenceux exclaimed.

"Indeed, we do. I will find you a horse, and you will set off as soon as you can. But damn it, Clarenceux, when you go to see Cecil, make sure you have something stronger on him than telling him to his face what he has done. He already knows that—and if he feels guilty about it, the easiest way to stop you reminding him is to add one more name to the list of those to be hanged."

"You will find me a horse?"

"You are talking to Alice Prudhomme," she said, pinching his jowl between her thumb and forefinger. "And I can make anything happen. If I wanted you to do something, believe me, sooner or later you would do it."

Clarenceux tried to smile.

She looked at him and suddenly laughed. "You don't like subtlety, do you, Mr. Clarenceux? You're afraid of it. Think it smacks too much of deceit. Take some advice from a woman, if you can. When you go to see Cecil, be subtle. Not deceitful—*subtle*."

Clarenceux nodded. "If Carew comes back here, I want to know. If he does, will you send me word?"

"You know that he does not write any more than I do. It was his mother's greatest wish that he should learn, and also of the women who looked after him after she died, but, you know…"

"You knew him back then, didn't you?"

"What—in Calais? Of course. I've known him all my life. I worked in the same whorehouse. Too fat to do the fucking, they said; I got to do the laundry."

"Why was he so keen to destroy Denisot? I mean, he told me it was because Denisot betrayed Calais, but there was more to his hatred than that. He also said it was because of religion—but Carew did not really care about anyone's religion."

Alice heard Ralph splashing his stick in her tub of soapy water. A moment later she saw him trying to tip himself forward into the tub. She went and picked him up, kissed him, and set him down further away from the water. She then came back to Clarenceux.

"He hated religion, hated it because of what happened in Calais. Denisot was a fervent believer in the old religion, a Catholic among Catholics. No doubt that was why Mary appointed him to survey the walls and defenses of the town. He did so, in great detail. But while he was making his survey, something happened. It was in the whorehouse—not that I saw it. I was washing sheets at the time. Denisot had an argument with a Huguenot gentleman customer who denied the primacy of the pope and a number of other things that provoked Denisot. There was a fight. The women, who knew and liked the Protestant gentleman, threw Denisot out in a state of partial undress. He left angrily, accusing them of favoring Protestants. A few days later he had handed a copy of his survey of the town to the duke of Guise, by which the duke learned all the weak points of the town. The town fell easily as a result. What should have been a measure to preserve Calais ended up with the town falling to the French. The young men had to leave—and so did most of the women. Raw and I lost all our friends, our protectors, and our home. Raw also lost all the women who had looked after him after his mother had died and who had tried to help him with his lessons. Denisot led the French troops to the whorehouse and told them to set it alight. The house was old and made of wood. The walls were covered with painted cloths and every bench and bed had cushions on it. The place went up so fast it almost exploded. Only two women escaped. Raw returned to see it on fire. In his dreams, he said, he still heard their screams; they were like the waves of a sea on which his life floated. And when he felt like crying he did not shed tears but the blood of his enemies."

"I remember him saying that about tears." Clarenceux turned to the boy, once more splashing his stick in the water. "I see now. I could not have turned the other cheek either, even though Christ would have wanted me to."

"We are all human, Mr. Clarenceux. Whatever the Bible says about forgiveness."

Clarenceux put his arm around her shoulder: "Find me a horse, Alice Prudhomme—the fastest one you can."

75

Wednesday, May 24

Francis Walsingham watched as Sir William Cecil sat down at the table in his study and signed a paper, which he thrust into the hand of the nearest clerk. "See to it that he receives it today. Is there anything else pressing, may I ask?" Neither of the clerks accompanying him said a word. Cecil clapped his hands once and rubbed them together. "Good. If you will all now leave me in peace, I would like to attend to some business of my own."

He watched them leave, then picked up the sealed letter that had been delivered to him twenty minutes earlier. "There it is," he said, tossing it across the table. Walsingham walked over, picked it up, and inspected it. One side was marked: *Sir William Cecil, her majesty's Secretary.* On the other side it bore Clarenceux's seal, in red wax.

"He is back in London then," said Walsingham.

"That's not the point. Read it."

Walsingham picked up the paper, unfolded it, and began to read.

Right worshipful friend and kinsman, I respectfully recommend myself to you and to the majesty to whom you and I both owe allegiance. I will not *deceive you; I have been much vexed and threatened lately by the manner in which I have been treated by certain men who deem themselves loyal servants of the Crown. First, a <u>document</u> was stolen from my house which, apart from its intrinsic historical value, cast the legitimacy of her majesty the queen in a new light. Second, <u>unless</u> that document has now been presented to her majesty, I can only suppose that the perpetrator is harboring it for treasonable—as opposed to historical—purposes. Third, <u>despite</u> being a herald and a member of her majesty's household, I was detained without trial contrary to the terms of Magna Carta by two royal servants, namely yourself and Mr. Walsingham. Fourth, <u>letters</u> were issued in your name to Sir Peter Carew to destroy a royal ship on which I was known to be sailing, the Davy, in order to inhibit my investigation of the theft of the said historical document. Fifth, <u>every</u> crew member of that vessel who was not killed was incarcerated by Sir Peter Carew—even though each had undertaken to help me in my quest for the document. Sixth, <u>you</u> know well that the widow of Henry Machyn of London, merchant tailor, was detained recently, contrary to the terms of Magna Carta without trial at Calshot Fort in the county of Southampton, which lies under the command of a royal officer, Captain Parkinson, who received his orders to detain the woman directly from you. As Widow Machyn had undertaken to steal the document in question, there will be a public infamy that her detention is a consequence of your desire to obtain the document for your own ends and, unless it has been presented to her majesty, this calls into question the integrity of your loyalty to the Crown.*

In the hope that I can yet ascertain the further truths connected with this matter, and identify the true protagonists, and thereby clear your name of the terrible slander that will pertain to it should these six facts become more widely known and notorious, I desire that you come to my

house at precisely four of the clock this twenty-fourth day of May. Come
alone, and you will be met kindly, in friendship and reconciliation.

Your obedient and willing servant,
Clarenceux

"Arrest him," said Walsingham, replacing the paper on the table. "Hang him. Wash your hands of him. You know where to find him."

Cecil rose to his feet. "Yes, well, Francis, you will forgive me if I do not follow your advice. I will go alone."

Walsingham frowned. "I am sorry, I do not understand."

Cecil picked up the letter. "Do you believe a man of Clarenceux's intelligence is simply going to allow himself to be arrested—after both you and I have failed to keep him under lock and key? Do you think he trusts me? Can't you see the message in this letter?"

"It's too vague to be a real threat." Walsingham shrugged. "If you do not do as he asks, what will he do? Come and find you?"

"Damn you, he will send this same letter to Robert Dudley."

"He wouldn't dare."

"Francis, open your eyes! He has spelled Dudley's name out in this letter." Cecil picked it up and held it out, shaking it, in front of Walsingham. He stabbed the page with his forefinger. "Look, there— where those words are underlined. Why did he do that? See that word, which is underlined, beginning with 'd'? Then the next one that is underlined, beginning with a 'u.' And so on. Do you think it is an accident that he has named both Dudley and the people who can testify to the truth of his story?"

"We will go together. Take guards—surround the house. He will not be able to get away."

Cecil carefully put his hands flat on the table. "Clarenceux is not the danger. It is the information he carries that is dangerous—and he knows it. If I arrest him, it will confirm the truth of all this. I do not doubt that a copy of this letter will go to Dudley straight away. Clarenceux won't be the one who sends it."

"So what do we do?"

"I will go, as he requests, alone. He will be watching me—but so will you. Have just three or four men around his house, in sight of one another. If he tries to abduct me, or hold me to ransom, you will move in with my own guard, who will stand outside, and half a dozen other men-at-arms whom you will conceal nearby. Go and requisition an appropriate house now."

76

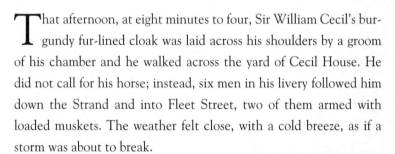

That afternoon, at eight minutes to four, Sir William Cecil's burgundy fur-lined cloak was laid across his shoulders by a groom of his chamber and he walked across the yard of Cecil House. He did not call for his horse; instead, six men in his livery followed him down the Strand and into Fleet Street, two of them armed with loaded muskets. The weather felt close, with a cold breeze, as if a storm was about to break.

Cecil carried no sword but listened to the jangling belt-harnesses of the men behind him. Approaching Clarenceux's house, he glanced at the front. The shutters on the ground floor were closed, as always. Those on the first floor were open, however. So too were those on the second floor. He turned to the men behind him. "Three of you, go to the back of the house and guard the rear exit. No one goes in or comes out except those men under the command of Mr. Walsingham. The other three, stay here. The same applies to this entrance."

Cecil knocked hard on the door with his gloved hand. He waited. No answer came. He knocked again and noticed the door move a little. When it became apparent that no one was answering, he tried turning the handle. It was unlocked. He pushed it open and went inside.

The mustiness of an empty house greeted him. "Mr. Harley?

William?" There was a slight echo along the dark passageway beside the staircase. Dust had fallen on the stairs but it had recently been disturbed in the center. He began to climb, the wooden boards creaking beneath his feet. "William?" he called again from the landing, looking through the door into the hall.

He went in. Everything seemed to be in its place, from the elm table by the window to the carpets covering the two chests at the opposite end of the room. The four pictures on the white plaster looked at him accusingly from their gilt frames.

"William?"

Cecil began to look around the hall. Only when he came close to the elm table did he realize that it was not in its usual place. It had been drawn forward, nearer to the middle of the room. On it was a book: the Old Testament in Latin. There was a piece of paper tucked inside. He opened the volume. The piece of paper marked the pages of the Book of Job, chapter seven. Verses 11 and 12 were underlined: *quampropter et ego non parcam ori meo loquar in tribulatione spiritus mei confabulabor cum amaritudine animae meae. Numquid mare sum ego aut cetus quia circumdedisti me carcere?* Cecil knew these lines: "Therefore I will not stop my mouth; I will speak in the anguish of my spirit; I will complain in the bitterness of my soul. Am I a sea or a whale that you surround me in prison?"

He picked up the paper. It was sealed with Clarenceux's seal. He knew he would see his own name written on the front even before his eyes actually recognized the words. He broke open the seal and read Clarenceux's message.

Right worshipful friend and kinsman, if you do genuinely desire that we be reconciled, and that all threats between us be as words in the wind, go to

London Bridge and find the jeweler who goes by the name of Robert Rokeby this same afternoon, before six of the clock. His shop is near the center of the bridge. Follow his instructions and you will find me. Come alone, and you will be met kindly, in friendship.

Cecil abruptly turned and walked out of the hall, running down the stairs to the front door. "Call the others," he snapped to the guards. "We are going to London Bridge."

Cecil did not speak all the way. Walking fast, with the guards following him, he pushed past merchants and tradesmen without a thought, thinking of how he was going to deal with Clarenceux. Turning down alleys, he did not care for the state of his shoes as he splashed through the mud. He strode past the wardens on London Bridge, to a point about one third of the way across. There were several jewelers' shops here. "Find Rokeby," Cecil said to the guards with him. "His shop is somewhere near the middle."

Cecil hated being the subject of attention from the passersby. Those who knew who he was simply gawped at him standing in the middle of the street in public. Those who did not wondered who he was. Cecil felt their eyes pry into him and wished one of his men would find the shop quickly. He looked up at the houses overlooking the bridge; there were even two female servants looking out of an upstairs window at him. He turned around and pretended not to notice. There was a rumble of thunder in the distance. It would start to rain soon.

"Sir William," said one of the guards, "Rokeby's shop is that one, with the shutters closed."

Cecil walked to the door. It was oak, old, and ill fitting, but locked securely. An external padlock fitting was not in use. "Damn it, search the place. If Clarenceux is in there, bring him out."

Two guards stepped up to the door. One knocked hard with a knife hilt. There was a pause, which irritated Cecil even more. These houses on the bridge were small—fourteen feet in total length—so even if Rokeby had been upstairs, he should have been there promptly. Cecil gestured to the guard who had spoken to him. "Call his name."

"Rokeby!" the guard called.

The door opened.

"Are you Robert Rokeby?" demanded Cecil, stepping forward.

Rokeby was a short, gray-eyed man of about sixty, clean shaven, with a narrow face and almost bald head. "I am. And you must be Sir William Cecil. Godspeed to you, Sir William."

"Where is Clarenceux?"

"You will have to come in if you want to—"

"By God's blood, man, tell me. I have lost my patience and you will lose your life if I have to play any more games. Tell me, here and now!"

The man was terrified. "I cannot, Sir William. Mr. Clarenceux told me I had to show you."

"Then damn well show me. Show all of us."

Rokeby pushed his door as far open as it would go and Cecil gestured for his men to follow him in. "No, no, you cannot all come in," spluttered the jeweler. "If I am to show you, I must lift the trapdoor."

Cecil was standing in a tiny shop, barely six feet deep by seven feet wide, made smaller by the cupboards fastened against the walls and the workbench. There was only room for four men to stand in there, besides Rokeby. The jeweler himself was standing in a narrow doorway that led to a back room. "What trapdoor?" Cecil asked.

"This one. It is the way Mr. Clarenceux told me to tell you to go."

Cecil stepped forward. Set in the middle of the floor of the back room was a trapdoor, about two feet square. Rokeby opened it and Cecil looked down. About thirty feet below was the base of one of the pillars of the bridge, with a large flat cutwater—called a starling—visible above the waterline. The water churned around the stone of the starling. He looked hard at Rokeby. "Is this a joke?"

Rokeby gestured upward. Above the trapdoor hung a rope ladder. He reached up and pulled on a cord and the rope ladder unfurled itself, tumbling through the trapdoor and trailing into the water below. "It is my escape way, in case of fire. Mr. Clarenceux asked me to show it to you. He said he doesn't want anyone to follow you."

Cecil looked behind him at the men in the doorway. He said nothing. He looked again at the river below, its brown water twisting around the starlings. The starlings themselves were platforms of rubble shaped like sharp-nosed boats. They projected out either side of the bridge and caught small branches drifting downstream. Cecil now understood why Clarenceux had been so specific about the times; at high tide this platform would be completely covered. As it was, the tide was coming in, and boats were able to sail upstream and downstream. At low tide, this point would become almost impossible for vessels traveling in either direction. The arrangements had been sophisticated. He could no longer hide behind his men. From now on, he would have to go on alone or not go on at all.

"What happens down there?"

"A man will meet you. He has room in his boat only for one, or so Mr. Clarenceux said. If you step into that boat alone and go with him, Mr. Clarenceux will come to you. That is all he told me and all I can tell you."

Cecil looked from the trapdoor to Rokeby. "You are going to be in trouble, for helping a criminal. You know that." He turned to his men. "Go to the banks, find boats, commandeer them, and follow me. Remain discreet—don't make Clarenceux aware of your presence unless you see a struggle."

Rokeby watched as the queen's Secretary leaned forward and tested the strength of the rope ladder. Hesitant at first, Cecil suddenly stepped onto it and swung, his feet striking the side of the trapdoor. Then he began to climb down toward the water.

He looked up at the beams of the houses, cantilevered seven feet out over the edge of the bridge. He had seen them from the river before but never from this angle, this close. A bird flew out from the shadows. As he took another step, and another, the rope ladder swayed, but soon he was down on the stones of the starling. He looked downstream, then upstream. No one seemed to be coming for him. He saw the rope ladder move, pulled up—presumably by Rokeby. "Leave it," he commanded. Rokeby did as he was told. Cecil stood on the starling and waited for a boat to approach.

"Sir William," said a voice behind him. "This side."

Cecil cautiously turned. A stout man in his fifties with a hat and an unkempt gray beard was there. He nodded for Cecil to come the other side of the great pillar supporting the bridge that arose from the center of the starling. Cecil walked across the uneven surface toward the man. When he came within a pace, he stopped. The man smelled of a tanyard.

"Who are you?" asked Cecil.

The man said nothing. He stepped forward, so he was within an arm's length of Cecil. "I am directed to check you for weapons, Sir William."

Sir William shook his head. "How dare you?" But after waiting a moment, he slowly opened his cloak and let the man—a pelterer who had recently unloaded a cartload of skins—feel his doublet for a pistol or knife.

"This way." The pelterer led Cecil around the other side of the pillar to a wherry moored against the side of the starling. Cecil got in. The pelterer arranged the oars, pushed off, and started to row upstream. Cecil checked the boats along the banks; he caught a glimpse of two of his men running along the quay, trying to find a suitable craft in which to follow him. The others he could not see anywhere.

"Where are you taking me?"

"Up the river. Mr. Clarenceux will meet us when he is sure it is safe."

Cecil sat in the boat, apprehensive. He looked behind; no one was approaching—none of his men nor Clarenceux. He looked along the quays on both the south and north banks. There were men loading and unloading barges on the north; and smaller ferries, skiffs, and light boats all across the river, but no sign of Clarenceux. He looked at the timber-framed houses on the south side and the extraordinary mix of buildings on the north: quays, stone turrets and towers, staircases, jetties, half-timbered houses, platforms, and cranes. There were timber supports holding firm the banks of the river. Other timbers propped up the quays where boats were moored. But still no sign of Clarenceux.

Clarenceux, in fact, was just getting into a boat, a larger one with a black canopy that covered the rear half. It was manned by a young fellow called John Gotobed, whose uncle was the clerk of the Skinners' Company. They were concealed around a corner of the dock that had been built up just south of the Strand, not far from Cecil House.

"There's the boat," Clarenceux said, seeing Tom Griffiths, the pelterer, rowing upstream.

"The watchers have signaled," replied Gotobed, looking along the quay to where a man was holding his hand aloft steadily. The man on the opposite bank was similarly signaling. "There is no one following them."

"Let's go," said Clarenceux, sitting back beneath the canopy. Gotobed pushed off from the side of the quay and started to row to a point upstream where he would meet Griffiths and Cecil.

Cecil saw the larger, half-covered boat approaching. He felt annoyed, defeated by Clarenceux's stratagem. He consoled himself; when this was over, he would still be the queen's Secretary and he could manage the eventual outcome of this episode much more to his liking. This was just something he had to do first.

Gotobed's boat came alongside Griffiths's. Cecil caught Clarenceux's eye. "I suppose you want me to come across and join you."

"We have important things to discuss, Sir William. And we need to discuss them now."

Clarenceux and Gotobed did their best to steady the two boats while Cecil climbed over, but even so it was an ungainly operation for the queen's Secretary. He was not as physically active as he had been in his youth. But he managed it and took a place on the covered bench to Clarenceux's left. Griffiths also crossed and tethered his boat on a long rope to the rowlocks of Gotobed's, so that it drifted along behind. Then the two oarsmen took their places and started to row the canopied boat back downstream.

Cecil noticed the change of direction and the purposefulness of their stroke. "Where are we going now?" he asked.

It began to rain. Clarenceux watched the droplets scatter themselves across the gray water. "Wapping," he replied.

"Are you taking me to watch one of your pirate friends be hanged?"

Clarenceux looked at Cecil. "I know it was you. It took me a lot of time and pain to find out. You lied to me over and over again.

You saw that letter to Lady Percy and you took action. Or, to put it another way, you panicked. You faked Rebecca Machyn's theft of the document, and you sent her to Captain Parkinson."

Cecil looked away. "It was for the best."

"How can you say such a thing? How can you? Do you have any idea how many men have died as a result of you playing this game? Hundreds. Hundreds of men and women have died. Many others are wounded. You had a clever idea of how to fool me into thinking that a woman had stolen that document, thereby saving it from falling into the hands of Mrs. Barker. But what was the result?" Clarenceux held up his right hand, with the scar where Kahlu put his knife through it. "That is just one small result. The man who did that is now dead. So is the captain and almost all of the crew of the ship on which it happened. So are many of the crew members of the ships sent to blow us out of the water."

"It was for the best," repeated Cecil. "It was for the security of the State. I would do it again—and then ten times more."

"It was a mistake," replied Clarenceux. "When I make a mistake, only I suffer, and those who depend on me. It is forgivable. But when you make a mistake, hundreds die. It is unforgiveable. Powerful men cannot afford to make mistakes."

"Listen to me. I meant well. I had to stop a rebellion—"

"You meant well? Ah, that makes everything fine. Those men did not really die—because you meant well. This wound never happened, and the young woman I saw blown in half aboard the *Davy* did not die in vain, because you meant well. Sir William, damn your meaning well, if this is what it does—and to hell with your good intentions. If hundreds die and many suffer, it does not really matter whether you meant well or not, does it? You failed us."

"Clarenceux, a friendly warning: don't make this worse for yourself."

"Worse? How do you think this possibly could be any worse?"

"By insulting me. By threatening to send information to Dudley. By demeaning me—by dragging me into this miserable boat."

Clarenceux shook his head. "I told you to come alone. You paid no attention. I watched you. Six men followed you to my house. More were already stationed around it. You demean me by thinking that I am so stupid I will allow you to arrest me. And then you insult me by thinking I will not notice your soldiers. If I seem threatening to you, perhaps you ought to ask yourself what you are afraid of. Of me? Of me telling the truth? Or of the truth itself?"

It was raining hard now, as they approached London Bridge again. Clarenceux looked across the water. Few boats were in use; most had taken shelter. One or two were still on the water, including one setting out from just this side of London Bridge. Clarenceux pointed to it. "You see what I mean? Row faster, Tom, John; there are men approaching from the north bank."

A flash of lightning lit the sky for a moment. Thunder rolled across ten seconds later. The rain came down harder. Griffiths and Gotobed continued rowing. "Keep going," Clarenceux shouted. "There is a bonus for both of you because of the inclement weather."

Clarenceux turned back to Cecil. "It is the lies that disturb me most. You discovered the threat from the Catholics and you chose to deceive me. You never gave me the benefit of the doubt. You could have asked me for the document and that would—"

"You would never have given it to me," snapped Cecil. "Besides, how was I to know you were not complicit? You favor the old religion. The Machyn woman was complicit, so why not you?"

"She was only playing for time," said Clarenceux. "She was scared. For herself. For me and my family too."

"Where is Awdrey?" asked Cecil.

"Safe. Where is Nicholas Denisot?"

"Why do you ask?"

"Someone I know wants to meet him."

Cecil looked at the rain hitting the gray water of the river. "He is in Ireland. I sent him there so no one could connect Captain Gray and the *Davy* with me." He put his hand to his face and rubbed his forehead. "I cannot apologize for taking measures. You understand that."

"You could have taken measures that would safeguard more people, that would have at least protected me and my family, and Rebecca Machyn. I expect you to apologize for risking so many lives." They were passing London Pool, the main docks just east of the Tower.

"How much do you want?" asked Cecil. "Every man has his price. You have reason to feel aggrieved. Tell me how much you want in compensation."

"Sir William, you know me better than to ask such a thing. Every man may have his price, but a man's beliefs are beyond purchase. If something I had done had hurt so many people, I would feel it a sin. A black stain on my soul. In your shoes, I would feel that what I had done was enough to damn me to hell. It would not matter what I had hoped to do or what my intentions had been. I would want to atone for my sin—not with money but with something more meaningful. If I have a price, it is your soul."

"Have I been tricked aboard this boat just to hear a sermon? Or do you have something more practical in mind?"

"There are some men at Wapping due to be hanged as pirates. They were taken there by Sir Peter Carew—they arrived yesterday. One of them is already dead; I arrived too late to save him. But I want you to see him nevertheless. I want you to pardon him and his companions."

"You have lost your mind."

"No. I arrived yesterday morning, as the men were being led out. I had forged a letter from you, staying their execution until they could receive a trial. I said you would come along today in person to grant them a pardon. You are going to do that."

"I do not have the authority to grant a pardon. It has to be done under the royal seal. You know that. I do not have the seal with me."

"No. But I do."

"What?"

Clarenceux reached inside his doublet and pulled out a large leather pouch six inches in diameter. He opened the drawstrings and pulled out the gilt bronze die that was the royal privy seal. "I watched you leave Cecil House. While you were at my house, I was in yours."

"Is there no end to this? How did you get in?"

"Through the garden."

"I will not do it. I cannot free men just because you think I have committed a sin."

"And yet you can still send them to their deaths? Your morality astounds me, Sir William."

They neared Wapping. Clarenceux looked behind; Cecil's men were still following, but they were a long way back. They had chosen a boat with only two oars.

Three minutes later they landed. There was another rumble of thunder as Cecil and Clarenceux disembarked. John and Tom dragged the boat a little way up the shingle bank and Cecil followed Clarenceux to the line of gallows in the heavy rain. Six men were dangling from ropes, dead. The stench here was nauseating, that of moldering gray death—old death, not a fresh kill. As the river rose it soaked their lower parts, so that fish ate the flesh of the dead men for several hours a day. Eventually their maggot-infested corpses fragmented into the river.

"Look at him," said Clarenceux, approaching the second man in the row. The corpse was still intact. Cecil retched, retched again, and then was sick with the smell. "Damn you, look at him!" Clarenceux shouted, his hair and clothes soaked. "His name was John Dunbar. He was a Scot, a master gunner, captured at sea and forced to serve on the *Davy*. He was on board when you sent the ship to Southampton. All he did was follow the orders of his English captain—orders that you gave to that captain by way of Nicholas Denisot." Water ran through Cecil's clothes, cold. It poured from Clarenceux's grief-stricken face. "When the ship changed hands again—when Carew took over—Dunbar was given one chance to flee. He stayed aboard with the men he knew rather than be cast ashore in England. He was no pirate. He simply was shoveled from one ship to another. Thus he had to defend himself when Sir Peter Carew attacked the *Davy*. Many more men like him died in the waters of the Solent. You did not see that—I did. I watched them die. Women too. I blew a hole with a cannon in a boat carrying men who were coming to kill me. You cannot know what it was like. You are just the chess player; we are the pawns in your game, unable to retreat."

Clarenceux looked at the river. The boat with Cecil's men was coming into the bank. One jumped out and held the prow of the vessel as the others disembarked. Thunder rolled overhead again, almost immediately after a flash of lightning.

"Tell them to go back to Cecil House," said Clarenceux. "If I am not alive and at liberty to prevent it happening, copies of that letter you received, each with a copy of the text of the Percy-Boleyn marriage agreement, will be sent to Robert Dudley, Lord Winchester, and Robert Throckmorton. Your career will be over—and perhaps your life too. It will be of small comfort to you that you acted as you did and told so many lies, for the sake of steadying the ship of State."

Cecil waited in the rain as two of his men seized Griffiths and Gotobed. The other four rushed toward Clarenceux. When the first two were about to seize him, Cecil raised his hand. "Leave him be. He is a friend and a kinsman. We are both supporters of her majesty the queen. Let his oarsmen go too."

The men to whom he addressed his remarks were flummoxed. "Sir William, are these truly your orders?" asked one.

"They are," he said. "Wait for us. Find some shelter from this rain, all of you." Then turning to Clarenceux, he added, "Show me your pirates."

When they had found the jailers, Clarenceux and Cecil were led to the makeshift prison where Skinner, Bidder, and the others were being held. It was made of wood, huge oak bars, sunk into the ground. The men inside were up to their knees in watery mud. One man was dead, lying face down in the brown water. No one spoke inside. The smell of feces was as strong as that of decomposing bodies drifting over from the riverside.

Cecil took one look at the limbs hanging on to the beams of the cage and asked, "How many of them do you want?"

"All those who were aboard the *Davy*," Clarenceux replied.

"You, open the door," Cecil commanded one of the jailers, as the thunder crashed again. "Bring them out one by one."

"For Christ's sake, let them all go," muttered Clarenceux.

"I will pretend I did not hear that," replied Cecil, as the first man was led out of the waterlogged pit. He had suffered a huge cut on the side of his face. His shirt was almost torn entirely from his shoulders; what remained was a filthy rag. His breeches were covered in mud and excrement. "Was this man on the *Davy*?"

"He was," replied Clarenceux. "Stars Johnson is his name."

If Clarenceux found the sight of Johnson traumatic, the following men were even more disturbing. Francis Bidder's arm had been broken, and the bones had ruptured the skin. The wound had begun to rot, and blood poisoning seemed to have taken hold. He was unable to stand, barely alive. "Mr. Clarenceux, are you saving us or turning us over to the Devil?" shouted one man. "Will you join us at the water's edge?" yelled another. "You fired the cannon too," cried a third voice. Clarenceux said nothing. Even worse were the screams of those who had not been aboard the *Davy*, whom the jailers thrust back into the cage.

When the last of the *Davy*'s eleven surviving crew members had been removed from the pit, they were led—carried in Bidder's case—to a dry room in a house a hundred yards further inland. Sir William Cecil stood before them and addressed them. "As her majesty's Secretary," he began, "I am going to draw up a pardon for you all, in line with the demands of this man, your erstwhile companion, Mr. William Harley, Clarenceux King of Arms. Your crimes committed to date are forgiven, your punishments outstanding revoked. I will deliver the collective pardon, sealed with her majesty's privy seal, to Mr. Clarenceux."

A murmur of appreciation gave way to voices of relief and even surprised happiness. "With all thanks to you, Mr. Clarenceux," said one man. Skinner made the effort of bowing low. Stars Johnson fell to his knees, in tears.

Cecil cleared his throat. "Lest there be any doubt, this pardon does not extend to any crew members of the *Davy* who are not here, nor to any crimes you commit in the future. In view of this, I will need a list of your names."

One by one Clarenceux gave the names, which Cecil wrote on some paper provided by the jailers' clerk. Cecil looked down the list when it was complete. "I do not want them to re-enter the city. If there is trouble, I will hold you responsible." He looked Clarenceux in the eye. "Is that all?"

Clarenceux shook his head. "That is all with these men, Sir William, but not for you and me. Not by a long way. I want to believe I can trust you again. I want you to trust me. And I don't believe that that will be possible until we are entirely honest with each other. Even now, we are evading each other. You still have the document at the heart of all this. The root of all this betrayal lies in your distrust of me."

"Come outside, Mr. Clarenceux," said Cecil.

The two men left the building. Immediately, despite the pouring rain, Cecil rounded on Clarenceux. "Listen to me," he began, but at that moment there was a flash of lightning and the thunder crashed and rolled, silencing him for several seconds. "I will never forgive you. Never. This humiliation is…unsupportable."

"By God's wounds, Sir William. What crime have I committed that was not in self-defense and an attempt to right wrongs? What have I done? I kept the document as you ordered me to. I guarded it with my life. It went missing and *you* led me to believe that Rebecca Machyn had stolen it. You even told the ship's captain that Rebecca was being sent to Southampton by Percy Roy—knowing full well that I would equate those initials with the Knights of the Round Table: Sir Percival, Sir Reynold, Sir Owain and Sir Yvain. You deliberately misled me. Nevertheless, I did all I could to recover that document in good faith. I risked death. I went to Mrs. Barker's house and I was tortured. I was taken by Walsingham and locked up. You too imprisoned me. Almost immediately after escaping, I was captured by a pirate who believed I could lead him to the traitor Denisot, whom I now discover is in your pay. I was stabbed in the hand, dragged behind a ship on a rope, and forced to fight for my life against Sir Peter Carew. I ended up at Calshot being imprisoned by Captain Parkinson and had to fight for my freedom. In all that, what have I done that deserves your condemnation? Nothing! You on the other hand, were making me look after a document that was your insurance in case a Catholic queen should come again. If there had been an invasion, and if it had gone the way of the Queen of Scots—you would have called for that document. Publishing it would have been your glory and the final nail in the hopes of our present queen. She would have gone the way of her cousin Lady Jane Gray to the block. You may keep the document now if you feel you must, but it is not with my blessing. I have suffered too much."

Cecil shook his head. "I do not have it."

"What?" Clarenceux did not believe Cecil and simply stared at him. But he saw no evasiveness. The man was telling the truth.

"If…you didn't take it, who did?"

"Your wife."

The word hit him. He felt suddenly weak. He wanted to sit down. "I don't believe you."

"I am going to say this just once," said Cecil, his face soaked with rain, "and then I am going to walk away. You and I will not see each other nor speak to each other. You will send your letter to no one and I will take no action against you. You will say nothing against me nor I against you. This matter ends here."

Cecil took a deep breath. "I knew Lady Percy would never let matters rest, so I had Walsingham put a watch on her house. That coded message from Mrs. Barker, who is Lady Percy's sister living under cover in London, was brought to me on the fifth day of May. I recognized the code as a cipher instantly and I stayed up late that night, after Walsingham had left me, working out its true meaning. I deciphered it that same night—long before Walsingham. It told me that Rebecca Machyn was acting with the Knights of the Round Table and was going to deliver the Percy-Boleyn marriage agreement to them. I believed that that meant you were also in accord with her decision. I could hardly ask you to your face. The message also told me that she would be taken by ship with her brother two days later to Scotland.

"I had very little time to act. I knew your wife was coming to my house to see my wife and so I confronted Awdrey with what I knew. She declared that you would never betray me, that you would never give the document to Widow Machyn, even though she knew how fond you were of her. From this I established that she knew about it. That did not surprise me; a wife often knows more of her husband's secrets than he realizes. I explained to her my fear that you would give it to Rebecca Machyn because of your love for that woman. I asked her to give me the document to prevent that happening. Still she refused to do so. She would not betray you, she said. Desperate, I made a deal with her that afternoon—the day we discussed you being ambassador to the Low Countries. I would arrange for Rebecca Machyn to disappear at the same time as Awdrey took the document and hid it. That way, the Knights would not get it, and you would believe that Widow Machyn had betrayed you, so Awdrey could be sure you would forget her. The pair of you would then leave the country and go to the Netherlands. As it was, you were just too suspicious and too attached to that document and to Widow Machyn for the plan to work. But the truth is that I meant it for the best—and so did Awdrey. She did what she did because she loves you. And she never wanted anyone to come between you—not Rebecca Machyn, not me, not even a document that could dethrone the queen."

Clarenceux said nothing.

"Now, if you please, I will have the queen's seal."

With a shaking hand, Clarenceux reached into his doublet and pulled out the bag. He handed it to Cecil without a word. He stood still as Cecil walked back to the river. His eyes were unfocused as the man embarked on the covered boat, to return to the city. Nor did he acknowledge Griffiths when the man came to him, standing still and sodden, asking him if he wanted to be taken home. He started to walk to the river, water running down from his hair.

The storm moved away. Tom Griffiths rowed him back to St. Bride's parish in the small boat. But the rain continued to run down his face long after the clouds had passed.

Epilogue

~

It was a difficult reconciliation. It took place in Chislehurst parish church on a bright afternoon on the last day of May. Clarenceux watched Julius walk with Awdrey across the common to the church and stop short, allowing her to come to him alone, as Clarenceux had specified in his letter. Without a word they had then gone inside, knelt and prayed together, and left, almost without a word passing between them.

The argument took place in the churchyard. It was an argument that had to happen—not for one side to win or the other to lose, but so both of them had a chance to say to each other what they felt, as firmly as they needed. Awdrey accused Clarenceux of being too close to Rebecca, and he had to confess his feelings were strong. But, he protested, he had never betrayed her, his wife. She maintained the same. "Nor did I ever betray you," she said. "Sir William Cecil asked me to steal the marriage agreement from you and I refused him. I refused because I am your wife and I will always be loyal to you."

"How did you know where it was?"

"There are two small holes in the door to your study. Through those holes I saw you often checking that *chitarra*. Once, when you were out, I put my fingers inside it and felt a document hidden there. But I never told Sir William. I never betrayed you."

"You might not have betrayed me, but you misplaced your trust," answered Clarenceux. "That is a betrayal of another kind."

"And you misplaced your affections," she responded. "That too feels like a betrayal."

"That was not my fault. I can't control my feelings…"

"And do you think I can control my trust any more than you can control your emotions?"

Clarenceux had no answer to that. Or, rather, he knew that the easiest answer was a false one. The truth was that they had somehow lost touch with each other. What bound them together completely encompassed them—so much so that they did not normally even think of their union. In being so much a couple they each had forgotten the other person. They had forgotten each other's vulnerability. In their separate selves, they had grown apart: Clarenceux to dwell on the affection outside his married life, Awdrey on the stifled ambition in her husband—the man on whom she depended for food, warmth, money, status, and everything.

"I met a man," he began. "A man who said he did not believe in God—who said there *was* no god. He was a pirate. He cut me and killed others, seduced women, stole, and thought nothing of these things. And I believed he was a godless man—a man without conscience. And yet this man risked his life for me. He saved my life, and in so doing lost his own." Clarenceux sighed heavily, thinking back to the moment when Carew left him in Calshot. "If a godless man can do a godly thing, is there not room in the world for every sort of good? Certainly there is no good in Catholic and Protestants fighting one another. If Jesus were to return now, I do not believe He would be Catholic or Protestant."

Awdrey noticed the deep scar in his hand. "It is a pity that you had to go so far to realize that," she said. She looked at his forehead and at his shoulder. "It is a pity you had to suffer for all the lessons you have learned. And it is a pity that you had to lose your beard. I liked you more with it."

"We have these passions, don't we, Awdrey? We feel things and we act. I am sorry if I have offended you. I am sorry if you lost trust in me."

She took his right hand and looked at the scar. "I too am sorry. I apologize for putting my trust in Sir William and not in you. It would be better to go to the Devil with you than live in Heaven alone. Without you it could not be Heavenly."

Clarenceux raised an eyebrow. "That is a very secular thing for you to say, Mistress Harley."

She gave a smile. "We are just human, whatever it says in the Bible."

Clarenceux smiled back at her. "I heard those very words not long ago from a washerwoman in a house of ill repute in Southampton."

"Then it must be true. What were you doing there, may I ask?"

"I've got a lot to tell you, my love."

Almost three weeks later, Clarenceux was sitting in his hall checking his cook's account when his servant Thomas announced a visitor.

"Show him in," said Clarenceux, not looking up.

"Sir, I think you might want to receive him at your door. It is Sir William Cecil."

Clarenceux leaped to his feet. "He said he did not want to see me again."

"He must want to see you, sir, for he has come in person."

Clarenceux went downstairs and greeted Sir William at the front door of the house. Sir William stood there very formally, with his hand on a small staff. He asked to come in and speak to Clarenceux privately. The herald showed him up to the hall and closed all the doors.

"I have come for two reasons," Sir William began. "The first is that I have been thinking a great deal about our last conversation, at Wapping. I said things then that perhaps—no, definitely—were better left unspoken and, better still, unthought. I said them because I was angry and anxious. And I was guilty. I did come between you and your wife like an interloper in the dark. I did try to steer her trust away from you, and you were quite right in the boat to ask me if it preyed on my conscience. I maintain that my answer was right: for the safety of the State, I would do it all again, and send all those people to their deaths—but personally I was in the wrong. I should *not* have doubted your loyalty, nor should I have come between you and your wife."

Clarenceux did not know what to say. Cecil's morality had long ago left him perplexed. But there was no denying that the man was here, in person, and apologizing to him in his own home. He had no wish to be Cecil's enemy. He bowed his head. "Sir William, your apology is most warmly received and heartily accepted. If in my speech I did offend you, in my accusations, I apologize in return."

Cecil seemed happy. "You have made things well again with your wife?"

Clarenceux nodded. "We are administering loving medicine to each other."

"Good." Cecil put his hand inside his mantle and felt for something in a pocket of his doublet. "This other thing may be of interest to you. Either way I am obliged to ask you to respond. I have heard from Southampton by way of Captain James Parkinson's man, John Prouze, whom I believe you know. Yes?"

"I know his name."

"Apparently Carew's body was washed ashore several days after he went missing. It had been badly eaten by sea creatures and had to be identified by the ring on his finger. Prouze said that you would be able to confirm it was his."

Cecil held out the ring of the Carew family. Clarenceux took it. He nodded when he saw the familiar arms. "There were only three of these made. One was given to Sir Philip Carew, who was killed in Malta. One was given to Sir Peter Carew, who still wears it on his finger. The third was given to the eldest son, Sir George Carew, and taken from him by his mistress when he abandoned her, so she could give it to her son by him." Clarenceux remembered seeing it for the first time, in this very room—just after he had escaped from Cecil House. He closed his eyes and recalled once more—as he had so many times—the last conversation in the tower at Calshot, and those final requests. He was glad now he had delivered them. Silently, in his mind, he said a prayer for the pirate.

"So it is definitely his?"

"He would never have let it go—he would rather have died. It was the only thing that bound him to his true identity. If it was found on a corpse near Calshot Fort, there is no doubt that the corpse was his."

Cecil nodded and took the ring back. "It is certainly not Sir Peter's," he said. "He saw me yesterday. He is going to set sail for Ireland shortly."

Clarenceux felt sad. A part of him had hoped that Carew would have survived. "Could I have the ring?" he asked. "Raw Carew left a son who would benefit from knowing which ancient heraldic line sired him. With this, one day, I will be able to tell him of his more illustrious ancestors."

"Raw Carew had a son? Was he married?"

"No. The child is a bastard. But he will learn who his father was either way. Maybe giving him this heirloom will make him mindful of his more noble heritage."

Cecil thought about this. "I suppose I have no further use for it." He handed it to Clarenceux. "Now, I thank you for listening to me. I bid you good day, Mr. Clarenceux. Perhaps, having gone through this together, we will be closer friends in future?"

"I hope so, Sir William."

Only after Cecil had gone did Clarenceux properly think about Raw Carew. A life had been lived and lost—but how rich a life it had been. He cast his mind back over the men aboard the ship, and the life experience of men like Hugh Dean with his black hair and grin, and Kahlu coming from Africa and making his way through life without speech but so much knowing. He thought too of the women that Carew had loved and those whose lives he had touched—Alice, Ursula and Amy, even Juanita. No doubt there were many others, unknown to him. Most of all, he remembered that moment in Calshot Fort when he realized that Carew had come back for him. A godless man had indeed done a blessed thing.

He looked at Carew's ring and its three black lions. Old Sir William Carew must have thought three rings for his three sons would bind them forever. He could never have known that membership of that confraternity would pass to the son of a Calais maid and from him to the son of a Southampton whore. He felt the weight of the ring; it was floating on the deep ocean of the human spirit, passing from hand to hand as if those hands were waves.

And then he noticed something. There were nine words carved in tiny letters around the inside. He took it closer to the window and examined it carefully. As he read the words, the most powerful emotion rose in him and overwhelmed him. Tears flooded to his eyes. He started to smile and weep at the same time as a great joy broke open and flowered in his heart. Someone had put this ring on the corpse, someone who wanted to deceive Cecil and at the same time let Clarenceux know the truth. The name of Raw Carew did not just live on in legend—the name was dead and the man himself lived on. For there, inside the ring, Clarenceux could clearly read the words that he had spoken to Carew at Calshot.

In all our struggles, the last word is hope.

Author's Note

This is a work of fiction—pure fiction. I use that term over and above the usual publisher's disclaimer at the front of a novel because I want to stress that this story is entirely a modern invention. I often come across historical novels described as "accurate," including my own *Sacred Treason*, the prequel to this book. This is an area of huge misunderstanding. Very simply, if a historical text is truly "accurate" in relation to the past, then it is a work of history. No work of historical fiction is historically "accurate" because any verisimilitude it possesses relates to something going on in the novelist's mind, not the past. The workings of the mind may well include the absorption of historical evidence; and in my case it is certainly based on what I have learned about Elizabethan daily life from many years of being interested in the period, but that does not mean the story relates to real events. Where the names of historical characters are mentioned, they are merely emblematic, signifiers of character. My Sir William Cecil is a signifier for a powerful loyal conspirator prepared to stoop to underhand methods. The real Sir William Cecil never said or did any of the deeds mentioned in this book, with a couple of minor exceptions that are incidental to the plot.

Having said that, certain historical facts have inspired this story.

As readers of *Sacred Treason* will be aware, there really was a company of men called the Knights of the Round Table, and one of its members was Henry Machyn, a merchant tailor who died in 1563, leaving a chronicle or diary (which is now in the British Library). His first wife bore him a son, John, who survived him and whose second wife (in reality called Dorothy, not Rebecca) bore him three children who died in infancy. They did live in the parish of Little Trinity, London. Similarly, elements of Clarenceux's domestic situation are drawn from historical evidence. His real name was William Harvey, not Harley, and he was Clarenceux King of Arms from 1557 until his death in 1567. One picture of him is known, from a manuscript illumination of an initial. He lived in the parish of St. Bride's and his wife was indeed called Awdrey, and their daughters were Annie and Mildred.

Certain other characters are based on real historical personages. Francis Walsingham, for example, is so famous that he needs no introduction. Mildred, Lady Cecil (wife of Sir William), was pregnant in May 1564 as described in this book, and she was godmother to William Harvey's younger daughter. Sir Peter Carew and his brothers George and Philip were also real people. Sir Peter was commissioned in 1564 to sweep the Channel clear of pirates, and later he spent years trying to claim the barony of Idrone in Ireland. George Carew was captain of the Rysbank Tower after the death of his first wife; he died on the *Mary Rose* as described in this book. The third Carew brother, Philip, did die on Malta. The family crest is accurately described, as is the motto. The story of Pedro Serrano is taken from Edward Leslie's remarkable book *Desperate Journeys, Abandoned Souls* (Macmillan, 1988), and I'd like to thank my friend Andy Gardner for bringing this to my attention and lending me a copy.

The point at which a historical personage took this story in a new direction was when I did a little research into James Parkinson, who was captain of Calshot and constable of Southampton Castle for many years in the late sixteenth century. For a long time I was undecided whether to locate the Two Swans in Portsmouth or Southampton. I eventually opted for Southampton because of the situation of Calshot and the fact that Captain Parkinson did indeed run a local extortion business in Southampton Water, exploiting his official position as the queen's officer in charge of the defense of the two forts. The description of Calshot is based on a close examination of the building (my thanks go to the very patient gentleman on duty that day, who kept the fort open for me long after everyone else had left) and the early eighteenth-century engraving of it by Samuel and Nathaniel Buck. Those who see the fort in its modern state and think of attempting the leap mentioned at the end of this book should, of course, not even dream of doing anything so foolhardy; but I should point out that it was an even bigger distance in the sixteenth century, as the gatehouse was enlarged considerably in about 1780. Just in case anyone feels that this precision means that this part of the book might be "accurate," let me dispel such thoughts by saying that, in the absence of any known picture of Parkinson, I based his appearance on the marble bust of the Roman Emperor Caracalla in the museum at Naples, which I spent an hour or so looking at in the summer of 2010. If you are trying to think through a dramatic scene involving a despot, and find yourself looking into the marble eyes of the very embodiment of cruel authority, it is difficult not to be affected by what you see.

Since childhood I have tried to understand what it was like to live in past ages. I am therefore sensitive to the fact that attitudes toward the "old religion" were changing very rapidly in Elizabeth's reign, as was the rhetoric about recusants, and it would be very difficult to "get it right" because at any time there was a wide spectrum of opinion. The worst of the anti-Catholic legislation did not materialize until after the pope "deposed" Elizabeth in 1570, and the worst persecutions were not passed until after the coming of the first Jesuit priests in 1580. With reference to Raw Carew's atheism (which would have been unthinkable fifty years earlier), this accusation was leveled at several Elizabethans, albeit more frequently later in the reign; and so I have felt justified introducing this element as a foil to Clarenceux's religiosity. As for the document that lies at the heart of this story, I would refer readers to the historical note at the back of *Sacred Treason*, where the possibilities of such a document having existed, and its implications, are explained. Needless to say, no such document exists today and probably nothing resembling it was ever made. Again, it is merely a signifier for a series of circumstances, in this case the much-discussed possible illegitimacy of Queen Elizabeth I.

As for Raw Carew, let's just say that I met him once, in a pub.

—(Ian) James Forrester (Mortimer)

About the Author

J ames Forrester is the pen name (the middle names) of the historian Dr. Ian Mortimer. Fellow of the Royal Historical Society and winner of its Alexander Prize for his work on social history, he is the author of four highly acclaimed medieval biographies and the *Sunday Times* bestseller *The Time Traveler's Guide to Medieval England* and *The Time Traveler's Guide to Elizabethan England*. He lives with his wife and three children on the edge of Dartmoor.

Sacred Treason

James Forrester

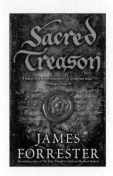

Your God. Your country. Your kin. Who do you betray?

1563: Anyone could be a suspect; any Catholic could be accused of plotting against the throne. Clarenceux keeps his head down and his religion quiet. But when a friend desperately pleads with Clarenceux to hide a manuscript for him, he is drawn into a web of treachery and conspiracy he may never untangle. Is there no refuge if your faith is your enemy?

Bestselling author Dr. Ian Mortimer, writing as James Forrester, has crafted a chilling, brilliant story that re-imagines how the explosive mix of faith and fear can tear a country apart. *Sacred Treason* tells a thrilling story of murder, betrayal, and loyalty—and the power of the written word.

Praise for Sacred Treason:

"I liked this novel intensely. A gripping read." —*Philippa Gregory*

"Vivid and dramatic." —*The Guardian*

"Arresting." —*Daily Telegraph*

"An Elizabethan romp featuring a conspiracy, a secret manuscript, and whispers about Anne Boleyn." —*Sunday Times*

For more James Forrester books, visit:

www.sourcebooks.com